A
Swiftly
Tilting
Planet

A
Swiftly
Tilting
Planet

MADELEINE
L'ENGLE

SQUARE
FISH

FARRAR, STRAUS AND GIROUX

SQUARE
FISH

An imprint of Macmillan Publishing Group, LLC

Library of Congress Cataloging-in-Publication Data
L'Engle, Madeleine.
A swiftly tilting planet.
p. cm.
Summary: The youngest of the Murry children must travel
through time and space in a battle against an evil dictator
who would destroy the entire universe.
ISBN 978-0-312-36856-2
[1. Science fiction.]   I. Title.
PZ7.L5385 Sw 1978
[Fic]   78-09648

Originally published in the United States by Farrar, Straus and Giroux

mackids.com

Book design by Jennifer Browne

Square Fish logo designed by Filomena Tuosto
First Square Fish Edition: May 2007

ISBN 978-1-250-18915-8 (special sales edition)

1   3   5   7   9   10   8   6   4   2

AR: 5.2 / F&P: V / LEXILE: 850L

For Hal Vursell

Contents

ONE

In this
fateful hour

The big kitchen of the Murrys' house was bright and warm, curtains drawn against the dark outside, against the rain driving past the house from the northeast. Meg Murry O'Keefe had made an arrangement of chrysanthemums for the dining table, and the yellow, bronze, and pale-gold blossoms seemed to add light to the room. A delectable smell of roasting turkey came from the oven, and her mother stood by the stove, stirring the giblet gravy.

It was good to be home for Thanksgiving, she thought, to be with the reunited family, catching up on what each one had been doing. The twins, Sandy and Dennys, home from law and medical schools, were eager to hear about Calvin, her husband, and the conference he was attending in London, where he was—perhaps at this very minute—giving a paper on the immunological system of chordates.

"It's a tremendous honor for him, isn't it, Sis?" Sandy asked.

"Enormous."

"And how about you, Mrs. O'Keefe?" Dennys smiled at her. "Still seems strange to call you Mrs. O'Keefe."

"Strange to me, too." Meg looked over at the rocker by the fireplace, where her mother-in-law was sitting, staring into the flames; she was the one who was Mrs. O'Keefe to Meg. "I'm fine," she replied to Sandy. "Absolutely fine."

Dennys, already very much the doctor, had taken his stethoscope, of which he was enormously proud, and put it against Meg's burgeoning belly, beaming with pleasure as he heard the strong heartbeat of the baby within. "You are fine, indeed."

She returned the smile, then looked across the room to her youngest brother, Charles Wallace, and to their father, who were deep in concentration, bent over the model they were building of a tesseract: the square squared, and squared again: a construction of the dimension of time. It was a beautiful and complicated creation of steel wires and ball bearings and Lucite, parts of it revolving, parts swinging like pendulums.

Charles Wallace was small for his fifteen years; a stranger might have guessed him to be no more than twelve; but the expression in his light blue eyes as he watched his father alter one small rod on the model was mature and highly intelligent. He had been silent all day, she thought. He seldom talked much, but his silence on this Thanksgiving day, as the approaching storm moaned around the house and clapped the shingles on the roof, was different from his usual lack of chatter.

Meg's mother-in-law was also silent, but that was not surprising. What was surprising was that she had agreed to come to them for Thanksgiving dinner. Mrs. O'Keefe must have been no more than a few years older than Mrs. Murry, but she looked like an old woman. She had lost most of her teeth, and her hair was yellowish and unkempt, and looked as if it had been cut with a blunt knife. Her habitual expression was one of resentment. Life had not been kind to her, and she was angry with the world, especially with the Murrys. They had not expected her to accept the invitation, particularly with Calvin in London. None of Calvin's family responded to the Murrys' friendly overtures. Calvin was, as he had explained to Meg at their first meeting, a biological sport, totally different from the rest of his family, and when he received his M.D./Ph.D. they took that as a sign that he had joined the ranks of the enemy. And Mrs. O'Keefe shared the attitude of many of the villagers that Mrs. Murry's two earned Ph.D.s, and her experiments in the stone lab which adjoined the kitchen, did not constitute proper work. Because she had achieved considerable recognition, her puttering was tolerated, but it was not work, in the sense that keeping a clean house was work, or having a nine-to-five job in a factory or office was work.

—How could that woman have produced my husband? Meg wondered for the hundredth time, and imaged Calvin's alert expression and open smile.—Mother says there's more to her than meets the eye, but I haven't seen it yet. All I know is that she doesn't like me, or any of the family. I don't know why she came for dinner. I wish she hadn't.

The twins had automatically taken over their old job of setting the table. Sandy paused, a handful of forks in his hand, to grin at their mother. "Thanksgiving dinner is practically the only meal Mother cooks in the kitchen—"

"—instead of out in the lab on her Bunsen burner," Dennys concluded.

Sandy patted her shoulder affectionately. "Not that we're criticizing, Mother."

"After all, those Bunsen-burner stews did lead directly to the Nobel Prize. We're really very proud of you, Mother, although you and Father give us a heck of a lot to live up to."

"Keeps our standards high." Sandy took a pile of plates from the kitchen dresser, counted them, and set them in front of the big platter which would hold the turkey.

—Home, Meg thought comfortably, and regarded her parents and brothers with affectionate gratitude. They had put up with her all through her prickly adolescence, and she still did not feel very grown up. It seemed only a few months ago that she had had braces on her teeth, crooked spectacles that constantly slipped down her nose, unruly mouse-brown hair, and a wistful certainty that she would never grow up to be a beautiful and self-confident woman like her mother. Her inner vision of herself was still more the adolescent Meg than the attractive young woman she had become. The braces were gone, the spectacles replaced by contact lenses, and though her chestnut hair might not quite rival her mother's rich auburn, it was thick and lustrous and became her perfectly, pulled softly back from her face into a knot at the nape of her slender neck. When she looked at herself objectively in the mirror she knew that she was lovely, but she was not yet accustomed to the fact. It was hard to believe that her mother had once gone through the same transition.

She wondered if Charles Wallace would change physically as much as she had. All his outward development had been slow. Their parents thought he might make a sudden spurt in growth.

She missed Charles Wallace more than she missed the twins or her parents. The eldest and the youngest in the family, their rapport had always been deep, and Charles Wallace had an intuitive sense of Meg's needs which could not be accounted for logically; if something in

Meg's world was wrong, he knew, and was there to be with her, to help her if only by assuring her of his love and trust. She felt a deep sense of comfort in being with him for this Thanksgiving weekend, in being home. Her parents' house was still home, because she and Calvin spent many weekends there, and their apartment near Calvin's hospital was a small, furnished one, with a large sign saying NO PETS, and an aura that indicated that children would not be welcomed, either. They hoped to be able to look for a place of their own soon. Meanwhile, she was home for Thanksgiving, and it was good to see the gathered family and to be surrounded by their love, which helped ease her loneliness at being separated from Calvin for the first time since their marriage.

"I miss Fortinbras," she said suddenly.

Her mother turned from the stove. "Yes. The house feels empty without a dog. But Fort died of honorable old age."

"Aren't you going to get another dog?"

"Eventually. The right one hasn't turned up yet."

"Couldn't you go look for a dog?"

Mr. Murry looked up from the tesseract. "Our dogs usually come to us. If one doesn't, in good time, then we'll do something about it."

"Meg," her mother suggested, "how about making the hard sauce for the plum pudding?"

"Oh—of course." She opened the refrigerator and got out half a pound of butter.

The phone rang.

"I'll get it." Dropping the butter into a small mixing bowl en route, she went to the telephone. "Father, it's for you. I think it's the White House."

Mr. Murry went quickly to the phone. "Mr. President, hello!" He was smiling, and Meg watched as the smile was wiped from his face and replaced with an expression of—what? Nothingness, she thought.

The twins stopped talking. Mrs. Murry stood, her wooden spoon resting against the lip of the saucepan. Mrs. O'Keefe continued to stare morosely into the fire. Charles Wallace appeared to be concentrating on the tesseract.

—Father is just listening, Meg thought.—The president is doing the talking.

She gave an involuntary shudder. One minute the room had been noisy with eager conversation, and suddenly they were all silent, their movements arrested. She listened, intently, while her father continued to hold the phone to his ear. His face looked grim, all the laughter lines deepening to sternness. Rain lashed against the windows.—It ought to snow at this time of year, Meg thought.—There's something wrong with the weather. There's something wrong.

Mr. Murry continued to listen silently, and his silence spread across the room. Sandy had been opening the oven door to baste the turkey and snitch a spoonful of stuffing, and he stood still, partly bent over, looking at his father. Mrs. Murry turned slightly from the stove and brushed one hand across her hair, which was beginning to be touched with silver at the temples. Meg had opened the drawer for the beater, which she held tightly.

It was not unusual for Mr. Murry to receive a call from the president. Over the years he had been consulted by the White House on matters of physics and space travel; other conversations had been serious, many disturbing, but this, Meg felt, was different, was causing the warm room to feel colder, look less bright.

"Yes, Mr. President, I understand," Mr. Murry said at last. "Thank you for calling." He put the receiver down slowly, as though it were heavy.

Dennys, his hands still full of silver for the table, asked, "What did he say?"

Their father shook his head. He did not speak.

Sandy closed the oven door. "Father?"

Meg cried, "Father, we know something's happened. You have to tell us—please."

His voice was cold and distant. "War."

Meg put her hand protectively over her belly. "Do you mean nuclear war?"

The family seemed to draw together, and Mrs. Murry

reached out a hand to include Calvin's mother. But Mrs. O'Keefe closed her eyes and excluded herself.

"Is it Mad Dog Branzillo?" asked Meg.

"Yes. The president feels that this time Branzillo is going to carry out his threat, and then we'll have no choice but to use our antiballistic missiles."

"How would a country that small get a missile?" Sandy asked.

"Vespugia is no smaller than Israel, and Branzillo has powerful friends."

"He really can carry out this threat?"

Mr. Murry assented.

"Is there a red alert?" Sandy asked.

"Yes. The president says we have twenty-four hours in which to try to avert tragedy, but I have never heard him sound so hopeless. And he does not give up easily."

The blood drained from Meg's face. "That means the end of everything, the end of the world." She looked toward Charles Wallace, but he appeared almost as withdrawn as Mrs. O'Keefe. Charles Wallace, who was always there for her, was not there now. And Calvin was an ocean away. With a feeling of terror she turned back to her father.

He did not deny her words.

The old woman by the fireplace opened her eyes and twisted her thin lips scornfully. "What's all this? Why would the president of the United States call here? You playing some kind of joke on me?" The fear in her eyes belied her words.

"It's no joke, Mrs. O'Keefe," Mrs. Murry explained. "For a number of years the White House has been in the habit of consulting my husband."

"I didn't know he"—Mrs. O'Keefe darted a dark glance at Mr. Murry—"was a politician."

"He's not. He's a physicist. But the president needs scientific information and needs it from someone he can trust, someone who has no pet projects to fund or political positions to support. My husband has become especially close to the new president." She stirred the gravy, then stretched her hands out to her husband in supplication. "But why? Why? When we all know that no one can win a nuclear war."

Charles Wallace turned from the tesseract. "El Rabioso. That's his nickname. Mad Dog Branzillo."

"El Rabioso seems singularly appropriate for a man who overthrew the democratic government with a wild and bloody coup d'état. He is mad, indeed, and there is no reason in him."

"One madman in Vespugia," Dennys said bitterly, "can push a button and it will destroy civilization, and everything Mother and Father have worked for will go up in a mushroom cloud. Why couldn't the president make him see reason?"

Sandy fed a fresh log onto the fire, as though taking hope from the warmth and light.

Dennys continued, "If Branzillo does this, sends missiles, it could destroy the entire human race—"

Sandy scowled ferociously. "—which might not be so bad—"

"—and even if a few people survive in sparsely inhabited mountains and deserts, there'd be so much fallout all over the planet that their children would be mutants. Why couldn't the president make him see? Nobody wants war at that price."

"It's not for lack of trying," Mr. Murry said, "but El Rabioso deserves his nickname. If he has to fall, he'd just as soon take the human race with him."

"So they send missiles from Vespugia, and we return ours to them, and all for what?" Sandy's voice cracked with anger.

"El Rabioso sees this as an act of punishment, of just retribution. The Western world has used up more than our share of the world's energy, the world's resources, and we must be punished," Mr. Murry said. "We are responsible for the acutely serious oil and coal shortage, the defoliation of trees, the grave damage to the atmosphere, and he is going to make us pay."

"We stand accused," Sandy said, "but if he makes us pay, Vespugia will pay just as high a price."

Mrs. O'Keefe stretched her wrinkled hands out to the flames. "At Tara in this fateful hour . . ." she mumbled.

Meg looked at her mother-in-law questioningly, but the old woman turned away. Meg said to the room at large, "I know it's selfish, but I wish Calvin weren't in London giving that paper. I wish I'd gone with him."

"I know, love," Mrs. Murry replied, "but Dr. Louise thought you should stay here."

"I wish I could at least phone him . . ."

Charles Wallace moved out of his withdrawn silence to say, "It hasn't happened yet, nuclear war. No missiles have been sent. As long as it hasn't happened, there's a chance that it may not happen."

A faint flicker of hope moved across Meg's face.— Would it be better, she wondered,—if we were like the rest of the world and didn't know the horrible possibility of our lives being snuffed out before another sun rises? How do we prepare?

". . . in this fateful hour," the old woman mumbled again, but turned her head away when the Murrys looked at her.

Charles Wallace spoke calmly to the whole family, but looked at Meg. "It's Thanksgiving, and except for Calvin, we're all together, and Calvin's mother is with us, and that's important, and we all know where Calvin's heart is; it's right here."

"England doesn't observe Thanksgiving," Sandy remarked.

"But we do." His father's voice was resolute. "Finish setting the table, please. Dennys, will you fill the glasses?"

While Mr. Murry carved, and Mrs. Murry thickened the gravy, Meg finished beating the hard sauce, and the twins and Charles Wallace carried bowls of rice, stuffing, vegetables, cranberry sauce, to the table. Mrs. O'Keefe did not move to help. She looked at her work-worn hands, then dropped them into her lap. "At Tara in this fateful hour . . ."

This time nobody heard her.

Sandy, trying to joke, said, "Remember the time Mother tried to make oatmeal cookies over the Bunsen burner, in a frying pan?"

"They were edible," Dennys said.

"Almost anything is, to your appetite."

"Which, despite everything, is enormous."

"And it's time to go to the table," Mrs. Murry said.

When they were in their places she automatically held out her hands, and then the family, with Mrs. O'Keefe between Mr. Murry and Meg, was linked around the table.

Charles Wallace suggested, "Let's sing *Dona nobis pacem*. It's what we're all praying for."

"Sandy'd better start then," Meg said. "He's got the

best voice. And then Dennys and Mother, and then Father and you and I."

They raised their voices in the old round, singing over and over, *Give us peace, give us peace, give us peace.*

Meg's voice trembled, but she managed to sing through to the end.

There was silence as the plates were served, silence instead of the usual happy noise of conversation.

"Strange," Mr. Murry said, "that the ultimate threat should come from a South American dictator in an almost unknown little country. White meat for you, Meg?"

"Dark, too, please. Isn't it ironic that all this should be happening on Thanksgiving?"

Mrs. Murry said, "I remember my mother telling me about one spring, many years ago now, when relations between the United States and the Soviet Union were so tense that all the experts predicted nuclear war before the summer was over. They weren't alarmists or pessimists; it was a considered, sober judgment. And Mother said that she walked along the lane wondering if the pussy willows would ever bud again. After that, she waited each spring for the pussy willows, remembering, and never took their budding for granted again."

Her husband nodded. "There was a reprieve then. There may be again."

"But is it likely?" Sandy's brown eyes were sober.

"It wasn't likely then. The pussy willows, nevertheless,

have budded for a good many springs." He passed cranberry sauce to Mrs. O'Keefe.

"In this fateful hour," she mumbled, and waved the sauce away.

He bent toward her. "What was that?"

"At Tara in this fateful hour," she said irritably. "Can't remember. Important. Don't you know it?"

"I'm afraid not. What is it?"

"Rune. Rune. Patrick's rune. Need it now."

Calvin's mother had always been taciturn. At home she had communicated largely in grunts. Her children, with the exception of Calvin, had been slow to speak, because they seldom heard a complete sentence until they went to school. "My grandmother from Ireland." Mrs. O'Keefe pointed at Charles Wallace and knocked over her glass.

Dennys fetched paper towels and mopped up the spilled liquid. "I suppose, cosmically speaking, it doesn't make much difference whether or not our second-rate little planet blows itself up."

"Dennys!" Meg cried, then turned to her mother. "Excuse me for using this as an example, but Den, remember when Mother isolated farandolae within a mitochondrion?"

He interrupted, "Of course I remember. That's what she got the Nobel Prize for."

Mrs. Murry held up her hand. "Let Meg speak."

"Okay then: farandolae are so minuscule and insignificant it doesn't seem they could possibly have any importance, and yet they live in a symbiotic relationship with mitochondria—"

"Okay, gotcha. And mitochondria provide us with our energy, so if anything affects our farandolae, that can affect our mitochondria—"

"And," Meg concluded, "if that happens, we could die from energy loss, as you well know."

"Go on," Sandy said.

"So if we blow up our planet it would certainly have some small effect on our solar system, and that could affect our galaxy, and that could . . ."

"The old chain-reaction theory?" Sandy asked.

"More than that. Interdependence. Not just one thing leading to another in a straight line, but everything and everyone everywhere interreacting."

Dennys threw out the wet paper towels, put a clean napkin over the soiled tablecloth, and refilled Mrs. O'Keefe's glass. Despite storm windows, the drawn curtains stirred and a draft moved across the room. Heavy drops of rain spattered down the chimney, making the fire hiss. "I still think," he said, "that you're overestimating the importance of this planet. We've made a mess of things. Maybe it's best we get blown up."

"Dennys, you're a doctor," Meg reprimanded.

"Not yet," Sandy said.

"But he's going to be! He's supposed to care about and guard life."

"Sorry, Sis," Dennys said swiftly.

"It's just his way of whistling in the dark." Sandy helped himself to rice and gravy, then raised his glass to his sister. "Might as well go out on a full stomach."

"I mean it and I don't mean it," Dennys said. "I do think we've got our priorities wrong, we human beings. We've forgotten what's worth saving and what's not, or we wouldn't be in this mess."

"Mean, don't mean," Mrs. O'Keefe grunted. "Never understand what you people are going on about. Even you." And again she pointed at Charles Wallace, though this time she did not overturn her glass.

Sandy glanced across the table at his baby brother, who looked pale and small. "Charles, you've eaten hardly anything, and you're not talking."

Charles Wallace replied, looking not at Sandy but at his sister, "I'm listening."

She pricked up her ears. "To what?"

He shook his head so slightly that only she saw; and stopped questioning.

"At Tara in this fateful hour I place all Heaven with its power!" Mrs. O'Keefe pointed at Charles and knocked over her glass again.

This time nobody moved to mop up.

"My grandma from Ireland. She taught me. Set great store on it. I place all Heaven with its power . . ." Her words dribbled off.

Mrs. O'Keefe's children called her Mom. From everybody except Calvin it sounded like an insult. Meg found it difficult to call her mother-in-law anything, but now she pushed her chair away from the table and knelt by the old woman. "Mom," she said gently, "what did your grandmother teach you?"

"Set great store on it to ward off the dark."

"But what?"

"*. . . All Heaven with its power,*"

Mrs. O'Keefe said in a singsong way,

> "*And the sun with its brightness,*
> *And the snow with its whiteness,*
> *And the fire with all the strength it hath—*"

At that moment it seemed as though a bucketful of water had been dumped down the chimney onto the fire. The flames flickered wildly, and gusts of smoke blew into the room.

"The fire with all the strength it hath," Charles Wallace repeated firmly.

The applewood logs sizzled but the flames gathered strength and began to burn brightly again.

Mrs. O'Keefe put a gnarled hand on Meg's shoulder and pressed down heavily as though it helped her to remember.

> *"And the—the lightning with its rapid wrath,*
> *And the winds with their swiftness along their path—"*

The wind gave a tremendous gust, and the house shook under the impact, but stood steady.

Mrs. O'Keefe pressed until Meg could barely stand the weight.

> *"And the sea with its deepness,*
> *And the rocks with their steepness,*
> *And the earth with its starkness—"*

Using Meg's shoulder as a lever, she pushed herself up and stood facing the bright flames in the fireplace.

> *"All these I place*
> *By God's almighty help and grace*
> *Between myself and the powers of darkness."*

Her voice rose triumphantly. "That'll teach Mad Dog Bran-what's-his name."

The twins looked at each other as though embarrassed. Mr. Murry carved some more turkey. Mrs. Murry's face was serene and uncommunicative. Charles Wallace looked thoughtfully at Mrs. O'Keefe. Meg rose from her knees and returned to her chair, escaping the unbelievably heavy pressure of her mother-in-law's hand. She was sure that her shoulder was going to hold black and blue finger marks.

As Meg moved away, Mrs. O'Keefe seemed to crumple. She collapsed into her chair. "Set high store on that, my grandma did. Haven't thought of it in years. Tried not to think. So why'd it come to me tonight?" She gasped, as though exhausted.

"It's something like *Patrick's Breastplate*," Sandy said. "We sang that in glee club in college. It was one of my favorites. Marvelous harmonies."

"Not a song," Mrs. O'Keefe contradicted. "A rune. Patrick's rune. To hold up against danger. In this fateful hour I place all Heaven with its power—"

Without warning, the lights went out. A gust of wind dashed across the table, blowing out the candles. The humming of the refrigerator ceased. There was no purring from the furnace in the cellar. A cold dampness clutched the room, filling their nostrils with a stench of decay. The flames in the fireplace dwindled.

"Say it, Mom!" Charles Wallace called. "Say it all!"

Mrs. O'Keefe's voice was weak. "I forget—"

The lightning outside was so brilliant that light penetrated the closed curtains. A tremendous crash of thunder followed immediately.

"I'll say it with you." Charles Wallace's voice was urgent. "But you'll have to help me. Come on. In this fateful hour I place all Heaven with its power . . ."

Lightning and thunder were almost simultaneous. Then they heard a gigantic crackling noise.

"One of the trees has been struck," Mr. Murry said.

"All Heaven with its power," Charles Wallace repeated.

The old woman's voice took up the words. "And the sun with its brightness . . ."

Dennys struck a match and lit the candles. At first the flames flickered and guttered wildly, but then steadied and burned straight and bright.

> *"And the snow with its whiteness,*
> *And the fire with all the strength it hath*
> *And the lightning with its rapid wrath . . ."*

Meg waited for the lightning to flash again, for the house itself to be struck. Instead, the power came back on as abruptly as it had gone off. The furnace began to hum. The room was filled with light and warmth.

"... *And the sea with its deepness,*
And the rocks with their steepness,
And the earth with its starkness,
All these I place
By God's almighty help and grace
Between myself and the powers of darkness."

Charles Wallace lifted the curtains away from one corner of the window. "The rain's turned to snow. The ground's all white and beautiful."

"All right—" Sandy looked around the room. "What's this all about? I know something's happened, but what?"

For a moment no one spoke. Then Meg said, "Maybe there's hope."

Sandy waved her words away. "Really, Meg, be reasonable."

"Why? We don't live in a reasonable world. Nuclear war is not reasonable. Reason hasn't got us anywhere."

"But you can't throw it out. Branzillo is mad and there's no reason in him."

Dennys said, "Okay, Sandy, I agree with you. But what happened?"

Meg glanced at Charles Wallace, but he had his withdrawn, listening look.

Sandy replied, "Much as we'd like it to, a freak of weather here in the northeastern United States isn't going to have anything to do with whether or not a South American madman pushes that button to start the war that very likely will be the war to end wars."

The baby moved within Meg, a strong affirmation of life. "Father, is the president going to call again?"

"He said he would when—when there's any news. One way or other."

"Within twenty-four hours?"

"Yes. I would not want to be in his position at the moment."

"Or in ours," Dennys said. "It strikes me the whole world is in it together."

Charles Wallace continued to look out the window. "The snow's stopping. The wind has shifted to the northwest. The clouds are moving. I see a star." He let the curtain drop.

Mrs. O'Keefe jerked her chin toward him. "You. Chuck. I come because of you."

"Why, Mom?" he asked gently.

"You know."

He shook his head.

"Stop him, Chuck. Stop Mad Dog Bran . . . Stop him." She looked old and small and Meg wondered how she could have pressed down so heavily on her shoulder. And twice Mrs. O'Keefe had called Charles Wallace Chuck. Nobody ever called him Chuck. Occasionally plain Charles, but never Charlie or Chuck.

Mrs. Murry asked, "Mrs. O'Keefe, would you like some tea? or coffee?"

Mrs. O'Keefe cackled without mirth. "That's right. Don't hear. Think I'm crackers. Not such a fool as all that. Chuck knows." She nodded toward Charles Wallace. "Woke up this morning, and wasn't going to come. Then something told me I was to come, like it or not, and didn't know why till I saw you with them big ancient eyes and the rune started to come back to me, and I knowed once more Chuck's no idiot. Haven't thought of the rune since my grandma and Chuck, till now. You've got it, Chuck. Use it." Her breath ran out. It was the longest speech they had ever heard her give. Panting, she finished. "I want to go home." And, as no one spoke: "Someone take me home."

"But, Mrs. O'Keefe," Dennys wheedled, "we haven't had salad, and it's got lots of avocado and tomato in it, and then there's flaming plum pudding."

"Flame yourself. I done what I come for. Someone take me home."

"Very well, Mrs. O'Keefe." Mr. Murry rose. "Den or Sandy, will you drive Mrs. O'Keefe home?"

"I will," Dennys said. "I'll get your coat, ma'am."

When the car had driven off, Sandy said, "One could almost take her seriously."

The Murry parents exchanged glances, and Mrs. Murry replied, "I do."

"Oh, come on, Mother, all that rune stuff, and Charles Wallace stopping Mad Dog Branzillo singlehanded?"

"Not necessarily that. But I take Mrs. O'Keefe seriously."

Meg looked anxiously at Charles Wallace, spoke to her mother. "You've always said there was more to her than meets the eye. I guess we've just seen some of that more."

"I rather think we have," her father said.

"All right, then, what was it all about? It was all—all unnatural."

"What's natural?" Charles Wallace asked.

Sandy raised his eyebrows. "Okay, little brother, what do you make of it, then? How do you plan to stop Branzillo?"

"I don't know," Charles Wallace replied seriously. "I'll use the rune."

"Do you remember it?" Meg asked.

"I remember it."

"Did you hear her call you Chuck?"

"I heard."

"But nobody ever calls you Chuck. Where did she get it?"

"I'm not sure. Out of the past, maybe."

The phone rang, and they all jumped. Mr. Murry hurried to the phone table, then drew back an instant before picking up the receiver.

But it was not the president. It was Calvin, calling from London. He spoke briefly to everybody, was sorry to miss his mother and Dennys; but he was delighted that his mother had come; his paper had gone extremely well; the conference was interesting. At the last he asked to speak to Meg again, and said only, "I love you," and hung up.

"I always fall apart on overseas calls," she said, "so I don't think he noticed anything. There isn't any point telling him when he can't do anything about it, and it would just make it awful for him . . ." She turned away as Dennys came in, blowing on his fingers.

"Calvin called from London." She swallowed her tears. "He sends you his best."

"Sorry to have missed him. How about some salad, now, and then that plum pudding?"

—Why are we trying to act normal? Meg wondered, but did not speak her thought aloud.

But Charles Wallace replied, "It's sort of like the string holding the package together, Meg. We'd all fall apart otherwise."

Her father said, "You know, my dears, the world has been abnormal for so long that we've forgotten what it's like to live in a peaceful and reasonable climate. If there is to be any peace or reason, we have to create it in our own hearts and homes."

"Even at a time like this?" Meg asked. The call from

Calvin, the sound of her husband's voice, had nearly broken her control.

"Especially at a time like this," her mother said gently. "We don't know what the next twenty-four hours are going to bring, and if it should be what we fear, then the peace and quiet within us will come to our aid."

"Will it?" Meg's voice faltered again.

"Remember," Mr. Murry said, "your mother and I take Mrs. O'Keefe seriously."

"Father," Sandy chided, "you're a pure scientist. You can't take that old woman seriously."

"I take the response of the elements to her rune seriously."

"Coincidence," Dennys said without much assurance.

"My training in physics has taught me that there is no such thing as coincidence."

"Charles Wallace still hasn't said anything." Meg looked to her small brother.

Dennys asked, "What about it, Charles?"

He shook his head slowly. He looked bewildered. "I don't know. I think I'm supposed to do something, but I don't know what. But if I'm meant to do something, I'll be told."

"By some little men from outer space?" Sandy asked.

"Something in me will tell me. I don't think any of us wants more salad. Let's turn out the lights and let Father flame the pudding."

"I'm not sure I want the lights out," Meg said. "Maybe there isn't going to be any more electricity, ever. Let's enjoy it while we have it."

"I'd rather enjoy the light of the plum pudding," Charles Wallace said.

Mrs. Murry took the pudding from the double boiler where it had been steaming, and turned it out onto a plate. Dennys took a sprig of holly and stuck it on the top. Mr. Murry got a bottle of brandy and poured it liberally over the pudding. As he lit the match, Charles Wallace turned out the lights and Sandy blew out the candles. The brandy burned with a brilliant blue flame; it seemed brighter than Meg remembered from other Thanksgivings. It had always been their traditional holiday dessert because, as Mrs. Murry remarked, you can't make pie crust over a Bunsen burner, and her attempts at mince or pumpkin pie had not been successes.

Mr. Murry tilted the dish so that all the brandy would burn. The flames continued, bright and clear and blue, a blue that held in it the warmth of a summer sky rather than the chill of winter.

"And the fire with all the strength it hath," Charles Wallace said softly.

"But what kind of strength?" Meg asked. She looked at the logs crackling merrily in the fireplace. "It can keep you warm, but if it gets out of hand it can burn your house down. It can destroy forests. It can burn whole cities."

"Strength can always be used to destroy as well as create," Charles Wallace said. "This fire is to help and heal."

"I hope," Meg said. "Oh, I hope."

TWO

All Heaven
with its power

Meg sat propped up on pillows in the old brass bed in the attic and tried to read, because thinking hurt too much, was not even thinking but projection into a fearful future. And Calvin was not beside her, to share, to strengthen . . . She let the book drop; it was one of her old volumes of fairy tales. She looked around the room, seeking comfort in familiar things. Her hair was down for the night and fell softly about her shoulders. She glanced at herself in the old, ripply mirror over the chest of drawers and despite her anxiety was pleased at the reflection. She looked like a child again, but a far lovelier child than she actually had been.

Her ears pricked up as she heard a soft, velvety tread, and a stripy kitten minced across the wide floorboards, sprang up onto the bed, and began grooming itself while purring loudly. There was always at least one kitten around, it seemed. She missed the old black dog. What would Fortinbras have made of the events of the evening? She would have been happier if the old dog had been in his usual forbidden place at the foot of the bed, because he had an unusual degree of sensitivity, even for a dog, to anything which could help or harm his human family.

Meg felt cold and pulled her battered quilt about her shoulders. She remembered Mrs. O'Keefe calling on all Heaven with its power, and thought shudderingly that she would settle for one large, loving dog. Heaven had shown considerable power that evening, and it was too wild and beyond control for comfort.

And Charles Wallace. She wanted her brother. Mrs. O'Keefe had called on Charles to stop Branzillo: he'd need all the powers Heaven could give him.

He had said good night to Meg in a brusque and preoccupied way, and then given her one quick blue glance which had made her keep the light on and the book open. Sleep, in any event, was far away, lost somewhere in that time which had been shattered by the president's phone call.

The kitten rose high on its legs, made three complete turns, and dropped, heavily for such a little creature, into the curve of her body. The purr slowly faded out and it slept. Meg wondered if she would ever again sleep in that secure way, relinquishing consciousness without fear of what might happen during the night. Her eyes felt dry with fatigue but she did not want to close them and shut out the reassurance of the student lamp with its double yellow globes, the sagging bookshelves she had made with boards and bricks, the blue print curtains at the window; the hem of the curtains had been sagging for longer than she cared to remember and she had been meaning to sew it up since well before her marriage.— Tomorrow, she thought,—if there is a tomorrow.

When she heard footsteps on the attic stairs she stiffened, then relaxed. They had all got in the habit of automatically skipping the seventh step, which not only creaked when stepped on, but often made a sound like a shot. She and Charles Wallace had learned to put one foot on the extreme left of the step so that it let out only a long, slow sigh; when either one of them did this, it was a signal for a conference.

She listened to his progress across the attic, heard the rocking of the old wooden horse as he gave it his usual affectionate slap on the rump, followed by the whing of a dart going into the cork board: all the little signals they had built up over the years.

He pushed through the long strands of patterned rice which curtained the doorway, stood at the foot of the bed, and rested his chin on the high brass rail of the footboard. He looked at her without smiling, then climbed over the footboard as he used to do when he was a little boy, and sat cross-legged on the foot of the bed. "She really does expect me to do something."

Meg nodded.

"For once I'm feeling more in sympathy with the twins than with Mother and Father. The twins think the whole thing is unreasonable and impossible."

"Well—remember, Mother always said there's more to her than meets the eye."

"What about the rune?"

Meg sighed. "She gave it to you."

"What am I supposed to do with it?"

"Stop Branzillo. And I guess I'm feeling like the twins, too. It just doesn't make sense."

"Have you ever really talked with her? Do you know her at all?"

"No. I don't think anyone does. Calvin thinks she stopped herself from being hurt long, long ago by not letting herself love anybody or anything."

"What's her maiden name?" Charles Wallace asked abruptly.

Meg frowned. "I don't remember. Why?"

"I'm not sure. I feel completely in the dark. But she said her grandmother gave her the rune . . . Do you know her first name?"

Meg closed her eyes, thinking. "Branwen. That's it. And she gave me a pair of linen sheets for a wedding present. They were filthy. I had to wash them half a dozen times, and then they turned out to be beautiful. They must have been from her hope chest, and they had embroidered initials, bMz."

"Z and M for what?"

"I don't remember . . ."

"Think, Meg. Let me try to kythe it."

Again she closed her eyes and tried to relax. It was as though too much conscious intensity of thinking made her brain rigid and closed, and if she breathed slowly and deeply it opened up, and memories and thoughts were freed to come to her consciousness where she could share them with Charles Wallace.

"The M—" she said slowly. "I think it's Maddox."

"Maddox. It's trying to tell me something, Maddox, but I'm not sure what. Meg, I want you to tell me everything about her you possibly can."

"I don't know much."

"Meg—" The pupils of his eyes enlarged so that the iris was only a pale blue ring. "Somehow or other she's got something to do with Branzillo."

"That's—that's—"

"—absurd. That's what the twins would say. And it is. But she came tonight of all nights, when she's never been willing to come before. And you heard her say that she didn't want to come but she felt impelled to. And then she began to remember a rune she hadn't thought of since she was a child, and she told me to use it to stop Branzillo."

"And she said we thought she was crackers."

"But she isn't. Mother and Father know that. And nobody can accuse them of being dimwitted daydreamers. What does the Z stand for?"

Again Meg shook her head. "I don't know. I don't even remember if I asked, though I think I must have."

"Branwen Maddox. Branwen Z. Maddox." He rubbed his fingers over his forehead. "Maddox. There's a clue there."

The kitten yawned and went *brrtt* as though they were disturbing it. Meg reached out and gently knuckled its hard little head and then scratched the soft fur under the chin until it started to purr again and slowly closed its eyes.

"Maddox—it's in a song, or a ballad, about two brothers fighting, like *Childe Harold* maybe. Or maybe a narrative poem—" He buried his head in his hands. "Why can't I remember!" he demanded in frustration.

"Is it that important?"

"Yes! I don't know why, but it is. Maddox—fighting his brother and angering the gods . . ."

"But, Charles—what does some old story have to do with anything?"

"It's a clue. But I can't get enough . . . Is it very cold out?"

Meg looked surprised. "I don't think so. Why?"

Charles Wallace gazed out the window. "The snow hasn't melted, but there isn't much wind. And I need to listen."

"The best listening place is the star-watching rock."

He nodded thoughtfully. The large, flattish glacial rock left over from the time when oceans of ice had pushed across the land, and which the family called the star-watching rock because it gave them a complete and un-obstructed view of the sky, was indeed a good place to listen. When they lay on it to watch the stars they looked straight across the valleys to the hills. Behind the rock was a small woods. There was no sight of civilization, and little sound. Occasionally they heard the roar of a truck far away on the highway, or a plane tracking across the sky. But mostly it was quiet enough so that all they heard was the natural music of the seasons. Sometimes in the spring Meg thought she could hear the grass grow. In the autumn the tree toads sang back and forth as though they couldn't bear to let the joys of summer pass. In the winter when the temperature dropped swiftly she was sometimes startled by the sound of ice freezing with a sharp cracking noise like a rifle retort. This Thanksgiving night—if nothing more unusual or horrible happened—would be quiet. It was too late in the year for tree toads and locusts and crickets. They might hear a few tired leaves sighing wearily from their branches, or the swoosh of the tall grasses parting as a small nocturnal animal made its way through the night.

Charles Wallace said, "Good idea. I'll go."

"I'll go with you."

"No. Stay here."

"But—"

"You know Dr. Louise was afraid you were going to get pneumonia last week when you had that bad chest cold. You mustn't risk getting cold again, for the baby's sake."

"All right, Charles, but, oh—"

"Meg," he said gently. "Something's blocking me, and I need to get unblocked. I have to be alone. But I'll need you to kythe with me."

She looked troubled. "I'm out of practice—" Kything was being able to be with someone else, no matter how far away they might be, was talking in a language that was deeper than words. Charles Wallace was born with this gift; slowly she became able to read the thoughts he sent her, to know what he wanted her to know. Kything went far beyond ordinary ESP, and while it came to Charles Wallace as naturally as breathing, for Meg it took intense concentration. Charles Wallace and Calvin were the only two people with whom she was able to give and receive this language that went far beyond words.

Charles Wallace assured her. "It's like swimming, or riding a bike. Once you learn, you never forget."

"I know—but I want to go with you." She tried to hold back the thought,—To protect you.

"Meg." His voice was urgent. "I'm going to need you, but I'm going to need you *here*, to kythe with me, all the way."

"All the way where?"

His face was white and strained. "I don't know yet. I have a feeling it will be a long way, and yet what has to be done has to be done quickly."

"Why you?"

"It may not be me. We're not certain. But it has to be somebody."

—If it's not somebody, Meg thought,—then the world, at least the world as we know it, is likely to come to an end.

She reached out and gave her little brother a hug and a kiss. "Peace go with you."

She turned out the light and lay down to wait until she heard him in her mind. The kitten stretched and yawned and slept, and its very indifference was a comfort. Then the sharp sound of a dog barking made her sit up.

The barking continued, sharp and demanding, very much like Fortinbras when he was asking for attention. She turned on the light. The barking stopped. Silence. Why had it stopped?

She got out of bed and hurriedly slipped into a robe and slippers and went downstairs, forgetting the seventh step, which groaned loudly. In the kitchen she saw her parents and Charles Wallace all stroking a large, nondescript dog.

Mrs. Murry looked with no surprise at Meg. "I think our dog has found us."

Mr. Murry pulled gently at the dog's upright ear; the other drooped. "She's a 'yaller dog' in looks, but she appears to be gentle and intelligent."

"No collar or anything," Charles Wallace said. "She's hungry, but not overly thin."

"Will you fix her some food, Meg?" Mrs. Murry asked. "There's still some in the pantry left over from Fortinbras."

As Meg stirred up a bowl of food she thought,—We're all acting as though this dog is going to be with us for a long time.

It wasn't the coming of the dog that was strange, or their casual acceptance of it. Fortinbras had come to them in the same way, simply appearing at the door, an overgrown puppy. It was the very ordinariness of it which made tears prickle briefly against her lashes.

"What are we going to call her?" Mrs. Murry asked.

Charles Wallace spoke calmly. "Her name is Ananda."

Meg looked at him, but he only smiled slightly. She put the food down and the dog ate hungrily, but tidily.

"Ananda," Mrs. Murry said thoughtfully. "That rings some kind of bell."

"It's Sanskrit," Charles Wallace said.

Meg asked, "Does it mean anything?"

"That joy in existence without which the universe will fall apart and collapse."

"That's a mighty big name for one dog to carry," Mrs. Murry said.

"She's a large dog, and it's her name," Charles Wallace responded.

When Ananda had finished eating, licking Fortinbras's old bowl till it was clean, she went over to Meg, tail wagging, and held up one paw. Meg took it; the pads felt roughly leathery and cool. "You're beautiful, Ananda."

"She's hardly that," Mr. Murry said, smiling, "but she certainly knows how to make herself at home."

The kettle began to sing. "I'm making tea against the cold." Mrs. Murry turned off the burner and filled the waiting pot. "Then we'd better go to bed. It's very late."

"Mother," Meg asked, "do you know what Mrs. O'Keefe's first name is? Is it Branwen?"

"I think so, though I doubt if I'll ever feel free to call her that." She placed a steaming cup in front of Meg.

"You remember the sheets she gave us?"

"Yes, superb old linen sheets."

"With initials. A large M in the middle, with a smaller b and z on either side. Do you know what the Z stands for?"

"Zoe or Zillah or something unusual like that. Why?"

Meg answered with another question. "Does the name Branwen mean anything? It's sort of odd."

"It's a common enough Irish name. I think the first Branwen was a queen in Ireland, though she came from England. Perhaps she was a Pict, I'm not sure."

"When?" Charles Wallace asked.

"I don't know exactly. Long ago."

"More than two thousand years?"

"Maybe three thousand. Why?"

Charles Wallace poured milk into his tea and studied the cloudy liquid. "It just might be important. After all, it's Mom O'Keefe's name."

"She was born right here in the village, wasn't she?" Meg asked.

Her father replied, "There've been Maddoxes here as far back as anybody remembers. She's the last of the name, but they were an important family in the eighteenth and nineteenth centuries. They've known hard times since then."

"What happened?" Charles Wallace pursued.

Mr. Murry shook his head. "I keep thinking that one of these years your mother or I'll have time to do research into the early years of the village. Our roots are here, too, buried somewhere in the past. I inherited this house from a great-aunt I hardly knew, just at the time we were making up our minds to leave the pressures of the city and continue our research in peace and quiet—and getting the house swung the balance."

"As for time for other interests"—Mrs. Murry sounded rueful—"we don't have any more time than we did in the city. But at least here the pressure to work is our own, and not imposed on us."

"This Branwen—" Charles Wallace persisted, "was she an important queen?"

Mrs. Murry raised her fine brows. "Why this sudden and intense interest?"

"Branwen Maddox O'Keefe was extraordinarily interesting this evening."

Mrs. Murry sipped her tea. "I haven't thought about the mythologies of the British Isles since you all grew too old for reading aloud at bedtime. I suspect Branwen must have been important or I wouldn't remember her at all. Sorry not to be able to tell you more. I've been thinking more about cellular biology than mythology these last few years."

Charles Wallace finished his tea and put the cup in the sink. "All right if I go for a walk?"

"I'd rather not," his father said. "It's late."

"Please, Father, I need to listen." He sounded and looked very young.

"Can't you listen here?"

"Too many distractions, too many people's thoughts in the way . . ."

"Can't it wait?"

Charles Wallace looked at his father without answering.

Mr. Murry sighed. "None of us takes Mrs. O'Keefe and all that happened this evening lightly, but you've always tended to take too much on yourself."

The boy's voice strained. "This time I'm not taking it on myself. Mrs. O'Keefe put it on me."

His father looked at him gravely, then nodded. "Where are you going?"

"Not far. Just to the star-watching rock."

Mr. Murry rinsed his teacup, rinsed it, and rinsed it again. "You're still a child."

"I'm fifteen. And there's nothing to hurt me between home and the star-watching rock."

"All right. Don't stay long."

"No longer than necessary."

"Take Ananda with you."

"I need to be alone. Please, Father."

Mr. Murry took off his glasses, looked at his son through them at a distance, put them on again. "All right, Charles."

Meg looked at her mother and guessed that she was holding back from telling her youngest child not to forget to put on boots and a warm jacket.

Charles Wallace smiled toward their mother. "I'll wear the blue anorak Calvin brought me from Norway." He turned the last of his smile to his sister, then went into the pantry, shutting the kitchen door firmly behind him.

"Time for the rest of us to go to bed," Mrs. Murry said. "You particularly, Meg. You don't want to catch more cold."

"I'll take Ananda with me."

Her father objected. "We don't even know if she's housebroken."

"She ate like a well-trained dog."

"It's up to you, then."

Meg did not know why she felt such relief at the coming of the big yellow dog. After all, Ananda could not be her dog. When Calvin returned from London they would go back to their rented apartment, where pets were not allowed, and Ananda would remain with the Murrys. But that was all right; Ananda, she felt, was needed.

The dog followed Meg upstairs as though she'd been with the Murrys all her life, trotted through the cluttered attic and into Meg's room. The kitten was asleep on the bed, and the big dog sniffed the small puff of fur, tail wagging in an ecstasy of friendliness. Her tail was large and long, with a smattering of golden feathers, which might possibly indicate some kind of setter or Labrador blood in her genetic pattern, the kind of tail which could create as much havoc in a china shop as a bull. The kitten opened its eyes, gave a small, disinterested hiss, and went back to sleep. With one leap, Ananda landed on the bed, thumping heavily and happily with her mighty tail. The kitten rose and stalked to the pillow.

As she had so often said to Fortinbras, Meg announced, "Sleeping on the bed isn't allowed." Ananda's amber eyes looked at her imploringly and she whined softly. "Well— only up here. Never downstairs. If you want to be part of this household you'll have to understand that."

Ananda thumped; light from the student lamp glinted against her eyes, turning them to gold. Her coat shone with a healthy glow.

"Make way for me." Meg climbed back into bed. "Now, Ananda"—she was taking comfort in reverting to her child's habit of talking out loud to the family animals—"what we're going to do is listen, very intently, for Charles Wallace. You have to help me kythe, or you'll have to get off the bed." She rubbed her hand over Ananda's coat, which smelled of ferns and moss and autumn berries, and felt a warm and gentle tingling, which vibrated through her hand and up her arm. Into her mind's eye came a clear image of Charles Wallace walking across what had once been the twins' vegetable garden, but which was now a small grove of young Christmas trees, a project they could care for during vacations. Their magnificent vegetable garden had been plowed under when they went to college. Meg missed it, but she knew that both her parents were much too busy to tend to more than a small patch of lettuce and tomatoes.

Charles Wallace continued to walk along the familiar route.

Hand resting on Ananda, the tingling warmth flowing back and forth between them, Meg followed her brother's steps. When he reached the open space where the star-watching rock was, Ananda's breathing quickened; Meg could feel the rise and fall of the big dog's rib cage under her hand.

There was no moon, but starlight touched the winter grasses with silver. The woods behind the rock were a dark shadow. Charles Wallace looked across the valley, across the dark ridge of pines, to the shadows of the hills beyond. Then he threw back his head and called,

> "In this fateful hour
> I call on all Heaven with its power!"

The brilliance of the stars increased. Charles Wallace continued to gaze upward. He focused on one star which throbbed with peculiar intensity. A beam of light as strong as a ladder but clear as water flowed between the star and Charles Wallace, and it was impossible to tell whether the light came from the piercing silver-blue of the star or the light blue eyes of the boy. The beam became stronger and firmer and then all the light resolved itself in a flash of radiance beside the boy. Slowly the radiance took on form, until it had enfleshed itself into the body of a great white beast with flowing mane and tail. From its forehead sprang a silver horn which contained the residue of the light. It was a creature of utter and absolute perfection.

The boy put his hand against the great white flanks, which heaved as though the creature had been racing. He could feel the warm blood coursing through the veins as the light had coursed between star and boy. "Are you real?" he asked in a wondering voice.

The creature gave a silver neigh which translated itself into the boy's mind as "I am not real. And yet in a sense I am that which is the only reality."

"Why have you come?" The boy's own breath was rapid, not so much with apprehension as with excitement and anticipation.

"You called on me."

"The rune—" Charles Wallace whispered. He looked with loving appreciation at the glorious creature standing beside him on the star-watching rock. One silver-shod hoof pawed lightly, and the rock rang with clarion sound. "A unicorn. A real unicorn."

"That is what you call me. Yes."

"What are you, really?"

"What are *you*, really?" the unicorn countered. "You called me, and because there is great need, I am here."

"You know the need?"

"I have seen it in your mind."

"How is it that you speak my language?"

The unicorn neighed again, the sound translucent as silver bubbles. "I do not. I speak the ancient harmony."

"Then how is it that I understand?"

"You are very young, but you belong to the Old Music."

"Do you know my name?"

"Here, in this When and Where, you are called Charles Wallace. It is a brave name. It will do."

Charles Wallace stretched up on tiptoe to reach his arms about the beautiful beast's neck. "What am I to call you?"

"You may call me Gaudior." The words dropped on the rock like small bells.

Charles Wallace looked thoughtfully at the radiance of the horn. "Gaudior. That's Latin for *more joyful*."

The unicorn neighed in acquiescence.

"That joy in existence without which . . ."

Gaudior struck his hoof lightly on the rock, with the sound of a silver trumpet. "Do not push your understanding too far."

"But I'm not wrong about Gaudior?"

"In a sense, yes; in a sense, no."

"You're real and you're not real; I'm wrong and I'm right."

"What is real?" Gaudior's voice was as crystal as the horn.

"What am I supposed to do, now that I've called on all Heaven with its power and you've come?"

Gaudior neighed. "Heaven may have sent me, but my powers are closely defined and narrowly limited. And I've never been sent to your planet before. It's considered a hardship assignment." He looked down in apology.

Charles Wallace studied the snow-dusted rock at his feet. "We haven't done all that well by our planet, have we?"

"There are many who would like to let you wipe yourselves out, except it would affect us all; who knows what might happen? And as long as there are even a few who belong to the Old Music, you are still our brothers and sisters."

Charles Wallace stroked Gaudior's long, aristocratic nose. "What should I do, then?"

"We're in it together." Gaudior knelt delicately and indicated that Charles Wallace was to climb up onto his back. Even with the unicorn kneeling, it was with difficulty that the boy clambered up and sat astride, up toward the great neck, so that he could hold on to the silver mane. He pressed his feet in their rubber boots as tightly as he could against the unicorn's flanks.

Gaudior asked, "Have you ridden the wind before?"

"No."

"We have to be careful of Echthroi," Gaudior warned. "They try to ride the wind and throw us off course."

"Echthroi—" Charles Wallace's eyes clouded. "That means *the enemy.*"

"Echthroi," Gaudior repeated. "The ancient enemy. He who distorted the harmony, and who has gathered an army of destroyers. They are everywhere in the universe."

Charles Wallace felt a ripple of cold move along his spine.

"Hold my mane," the unicorn advised. "There's always the possibility of encountering an Echthros, and if we do, it'll try to unseat you."

Charles Wallace's knuckles whitened as he clutched the heavy mane. The unicorn began to run, skimming over the tops of the grasses, up, over the hills, flinging himself onto the wind and riding with it, up, up, over the stars . . .

THREE

The sun with its brightness

In her attic bedroom Meg regarded Ananda, who thumped her massive tail in a friendly manner. "What's this about?" Meg demanded.

Ananda merely thudded again, waking the kitten, who gave a halfhearted *brrtt* and stalked across the pillow.

Meg looked at her battered alarm clock, which stood in its familiar place on the bookcase. The hands did not seem to have moved. "Whatever's going on, I don't understand."

Ananda whined softly, an ordinary whine coming from an ordinary dog of questionable antecedents, a mongrel like many in the village.

"Gaudior," Meg murmured. "More joyful. That's a good name for a unicorn. *Gaudior, Ananda*: that joy without which the universe will fall apart and collapse. Has the world lost its joy? Is that why we're in such a mess?" She stroked Ananda thoughtfully, then held up the hand which had been pressing against the dog's flank. It glowed with radiant warmth. "I told Charles Wallace I'm out of practice in kything. Maybe I've been settling for the grownup world. How did you know we needed you, Ananda? And when I touch you I can kythe even more deeply than I've ever done before." She put her hand back on the comfortable flank and closed her eyes, shivering with the strain of concentration.

She saw neither Charles Wallace nor the unicorn. She saw neither the familiar earth with the star-watching rock, the woods, the hills, nor the night sky with its countless galaxies. She saw nothing. Nothing. There was no wind to ride or be blown by.

Nothing was. She was not. There was no dark. There was no light. No sight nor sound nor touch nor smell nor taste. No sleeping nor waking. No dreaming, no knowing.

Nothing.

And then a surge of joy.

All senses alive and awake and filled with joy.

Darkness was, and darkness was good. As was light.

Light and darkness dancing together, born together, born of each other, neither preceding, neither following, both fully being, in joyful rhythm.

The morning stars sang together and the ancient harmonies were new and it was good. It was very good.

And then a dazzling star turned its back on the dark, and it swallowed the dark, and in swallowing the dark it became the dark, and there was something wrong with the dark, as there was something wrong with the light. And it was not good. The glory of the harmony was broken by screeching, by hissing, by laughter which held no merriment but was hideous, horrendous cacophony.

With a strange certainty Meg knew that she was experiencing what Charles Wallace was experiencing. She saw neither Charles Wallace nor the unicorn, but she knew through Charles Wallace's knowing.

The breaking of the harmony was pain, was brutal anguish, but the harmony kept rising above the pain, and the joy would pulse with light, and light and dark once more knew each other, and were part of the joy.

Stars and galaxies rushed by, came closer, closer, until many galaxies were one galaxy, one galaxy was one solar system, one solar system was one planet. There was no telling which planet, for it was still being formed. Steam boiled upward from its molten surface. Nothing could live in this primordial caldron.

Then came the riders of the wind when all the riders sang the ancient harmonies and the melody was still new, and the gentle breezes cooled the burning. And the boiling, hissing, flaming, steaming, turned to rain, aeons of rain, clouds emptying themselves in continuing torrents of rain which covered the planet with healing darkness, until the clouds were nearly emptied and a dim light came through their veils and touched the water of the ocean so that it gleamed palely, like a great pearl.

Land emerged from the seas, and on the land green began to spread. Small green shoots rose to become great trees, ferns taller than the tallest oaks. The air was fresh and smelled of rain and sun, of green of tree and plant, blue of sky.

The air grew heavy with moisture. The sun burned like brass behind a thick gauze of cloud. Heat shimmered on the horizon. A towering fern was pushed aside by a small greenish head on a long, thick neck, emerging from a massive body. The neck swayed sinuously while the little eyes peered about.

Clouds covered the sun. The tropical breeze heightened, became a cold wind. The ferns drooped and withered. The dinosaurs struggled to move away from the cold, dying as their lungs collapsed from the radical change in temperature. Ice moved inexorably across the land. A great white bear padded along, snuffling, looking for food.

Ice and snow and then rain again and at last sunlight breaking through the clouds, and green again, green of grass and trees, blue of sky by day, sparkle of stars by night.

* * *

Unicorn and boy were in a gentle, green glade, surrounded by trees.

"Where are we?" Charles Wallace asked.

"We're here," the unicorn replied impatiently.

"Here?"

Gaudior snorted. "Don't you recognize it?"

Charles Wallace looked around at the unfamiliar landscape. Tree ferns spread their fronds skyward as though drinking blue. Other trees appeared to be lifting their branches to catch the breeze. The boy turned to Gaudior. "I've never been here before."

Gaudior shook his head in puzzlement. "But it's your own Where, even if it's not your own When."

"My own what?"

"Your own Where. Where you stood and called on all Heaven with its power and I was sent to you."

Again Charles Wallace scanned the unfamiliar landscape and shook his head.

"It's a very different When," Gaudior conceded. "You're not accustomed to moving through time?"

"I've moved through fifteen years' worth of time."

"But only in one direction."

"Oh—" Understanding came to the boy. "This isn't my time, is it? Do you mean that Where we are now is the same place as the star-watching rock and the woods and the house, but it's a different time?"

"For unicorns it is easier to move about in time than

in space. Until we learn more what we are meant to do, I am more comfortable if we stay in the same Where."

"You know Where we are, then? I mean—When we are? Is it time gone, or time to be?"

"It is, I think, what you would call Once Upon a Time and Long Ago."

"So we're not in the present."

"Of course we are. Whenever we are is present."

"We're not in my present. We're not When we were when you came to me."

"When I was called to you," Gaudior corrected. "And When is not what matters. It's what happens in the When that matters. Are you ready to go?"

"But—didn't you say we're right here? Where the star-watching rock was—I mean, will be?"

"That's what I said." Gaudior's hoof pawed the lush green of the young grass. "If you are to accomplish what you have been asked to accomplish, you will have to travel in and out."

"In and out of time?"

"Time, yes. And people."

Charles Wallace looked at him in startlement. "What?"

"You have been called to find a Might-Have-Been, and in order to do this, you will have to be sent Within."

"Within—Within someone else? . . . But I don't know if I can."

"Why not?" Gaudior demanded.

"But—if I go Within someone else—what happens to my own body?"

"It will be taken care of."

"Will I get it back?"

"If all goes well."

"And if all does not go well?"

"Let us hold firmly to all going well."

Charles Wallace wrapped his arms about himself as though for warmth. "And you wonder that I'm frightened?"

"Of course you're frightened. I'm frightened, too."

"Gaudior, it's a very scary thing just to be told casually that you're going to be inside someone else's body. What happens to *me*?"

"I'm not entirely sure. But you don't get lost. You stay you. If all goes well."

"But I'm someone else, too?"

"If you're open enough."

"If I'm in another body, do I have to be strong enough for both of us?"

"Perhaps," Gaudior pointed out, "your host will be the stronger of the two. Are you willing?"

"I don't know . . ." He seemed to hear Meg warning him that it was always disastrous when he decided that he was capable of taking on, singlehanded, more than anyone should take on.

"It would appear," Gaudior said, "that you have been

called. And the calling is never random, it is always according to the purpose."

"What purpose?"

Gaudior ignored him. "It appears that you are gifted in going Within."

"But I've never—"

"Are you not able to go Within your sister?"

"When we kythe, then, yes, a little. But I don't literally go Within Meg, or become Meg. I stay me."

"Do you?"

Charles Wallace pondered this. "When I'm kything with Meg, I'm wholly aware of her. And when she kythes with me, then she's more aware of me than she is of herself. I guess kything is something like your going Within—that makes it sound a little less scary."

Gaudior twitched his beard. "Now you have been called to go Within in the deepest way of all. And I have been called to help you." The light in his horn pulsed and dimmed. "You saw the beginning."

"Yes."

"And you saw how a destroyer, almost since the beginning, has tried to break the ancient harmonies?"

"Where did the destroyer come from?"

"From the good, of course. The Echthros wanted all the glory for itself, and when that happens the good becomes not good; and others have followed that first Echthros. Wherever the Echthroi go, the shadows follow, and try to ride the wind. There are places where no one has ever heard the ancient harmonies. But there is always a moment when there is a Might-Have-Been. What we must do is find the Might-Have-Beens which have led to this particular evil. I have seen many Might-Have-Beens. If such and such had been chosen, then this would not have followed. If so and so had been done, then the light would partner the dark instead of being snuffed out. It is possible that you can move into the moment of a Might-Have-Been and change it."

Charles Wallace's fingers tightened in the silver mane. "I know I can't avert disaster just because Mrs. O'Keefe told me to. I may be arrogant, but not that arrogant. But my sister is having a baby, and I can be strong enough to attempt to avert disaster for her sake. And Mrs. O'Keefe gave me the rune . . ." He looked around him at the fresh green world. Although he was still wearing boots and the warm Norwegian anorak, he was not uncomfortable. Suddenly song surrounded him, and a flock of golden birds settled in the trees. "When are we, then? How long ago?"

"Long. I took us all the way back before this planet's Might-Have-Beens, before people came and quarreled and learned to kill."

"How did we get to here—to long ago?"

"On the wind. The wind blows where it will."

"Will it take us Where—When—you want us to go?"

The light of the unicorn's horn pulsed, and the light in the horn, holding the blue of the sky, was reflected in Charles Wallace's eyes. "Before the harmonies were broken, unicorns and winds danced together with joy and no fear. Now there are Echthroi who are greedy for the wind, as for all else, so there are times when they ride the wind and turn it into a tornado, and you had better be grateful we didn't ride one of those—it's always a risk. But we did come to When I wanted, to give us a little time to catch our breaths."

The golden birds fluttered about them, and then the sky was filled with a cloud of butterflies which joined the birds in patterned flight. In the grass little jeweled lizards darted.

"Here the wind has not been troubled," Gaudior said. "Come. This glimpse is all I can give you of this golden time."

"Must we leave so soon?"

"The need is urgent."

Yes, the need was indeed urgent. Charles Wallace looked up at the unicorn. "Where do we go now?"

Gaudior pawed the lush green impatiently. "Not Where; can you not get that through your human skull? When. Until we know more than we know now, we will stay right here in your own Where. There is something to be learned here, and we have to find out what."

"You don't know?"

"I am a mere unicorn." Gaudior dropped his silver lashes modestly. "All I know is that there is something important to the future right here in this place where you watch stars. But whatever it was did not happen until the ancient music of the spheres was distorted. So now we go to a When of people."

"Do you know when that When is?"

The light in Gaudior's horn dimmed and flickered, which Charles Wallace was beginning to recognize as a sign that the unicorn was troubled or uncertain. "A far When. We can ride this wind without fear, for here the ancient harmonies are still unbroken. But it may roughen if the When we enter is a dissonant one. Hold on tight. I will be taking you Within."

"Within—who am I going Within?" Charles Wallace twined the mane through his fingers.

"I will ask the wind."

"You don't know?"

"Questions, questions." Gaudior stomped one silver hoof. "I am not some kind of computer. Only machines have glib answers for everything." The light in the horn pulsed with brilliance; sparks flew from Gaudior's hoofs, and they were off and up. The smooth flanks became fluid, and slowly great wings lifted and moved with the wind.

The boy felt the wind swoop under and about them. Riding the unicorn, riding the wind, he felt wholly in freedom and joy; wind, unicorn, boy, merged into a single swiftness.

Stars, galaxies, circled in cosmic pattern, and the joy of unity was greater than any disorder within.

And then, almost without transition, they were in a place of rocks and trees and high grasses and a large lake. What would, many centuries later, become the star-watching rock was a small mountain of stone. The woods behind the rock was a forest of towering fern trees and giant umbrageous trees he did not recognize. In front of the rock, instead of the valley of Charles Wallace's When, there was a lake stretching all the way to the hills, sparkling in the sunlight. Between the rock and the lake were strange huts of stone and hide, half house, half tent, forming a crescent at the lake's edge.

In front of and around the dwellings was activity and laughter, men and women weaving, making clay from the lake into bowls and dishes, painting the pottery with vivid colors and intricate geometrical designs. Children played at the water's edge, splashing and skipping pebbles.

A boy sat on an outcropping of rock, whittling a spear with a sharp stone. He was tanned and lean, with shining hair the color of a blackbird's wing, and dark eyes which sparkled like the water of the lake. His cheekbones were high, and his mouth warm and full. He gave the making of the spear his full concentration. He looked across the glinting waters of the lake and sniffed the scent of fish. Then he turned back to his spear, but his sensitive nostrils quivered almost imperceptibly as he smelled in turn the green of grass, the blue of sky, the red blood of an animal in the forest. He did not appear to notice the unicorn standing behind him on the hill of stone, or if he did, he took the beautiful creature completely for granted. Gaudior's wings were folded back into the flanks now, so that they were invisible; the light in the horn was steady.

Meg pressed her hand intently against Ananda. The big dog turned her head and licked her hand reassuringly with her warm, red tongue.

Meg felt her senses assailed with an awareness she had never experienced with such intensity before, even in childhood. The blue of sky was so brilliant it dazzled her inner eye. Although it was cold in the attic, she could feel the radiant warmth of the day; her skin drank the loveliness of sun. She had never before smelled rock, nor the richness of the dark earth, nor the wine of the breeze, as she smelled them now.

Why? How? She could see the unicorn, but she could not see Charles Wallace. Where was he?

Then she understood.

Charles Wallace was Within the boy on the rock. In some strange way, Charles Wallace *was* the boy on the rock, seeing through his eyes, hearing through his ears (never had bird song trilled with such sparkling clarity), smelling through his nose, and kything all that his awakened senses received.

Gaudior neighed softly. "You must be careful," he warned. "You are not Charles Wallace Murry. You must lose yourself as you do when you kythe with your sister. You must become your host."

"My host—"

"Harcels, of the People of the Wind. You must not know more than he knows. When you think thoughts outside his thoughts, you must keep them from him. It is best if you do not even think them."

Charles Wallace stirred timidly within Harcels. How would he, himself, accept such an intrusion by another? Had he ever been so intruded?

"No," Gaudior replied, speaking only to that part of Charles Wallace which was held back from complete unity with Harcels. "We do not send anyone Within unless the danger is so great that—"

"That—"

The light in the horn flickered. "You know some of the possibilities if your planet is blown up."

"A few," Charles Wallace said starkly. "It just might throw off the balance of things, so that the sun would burst into a supernova."

"That is one of the possibilities, yes. Everything that happens within the created Order, no matter how small, has its effect. If you are angry, that anger is added to all the hate with which the Echthroi would distort the melody and destroy the ancient harmonies. When you are loving, that lovingness joins the music of the spheres."

Charles Wallace felt a ripple of unease wash over him. "Gaudior—what am I supposed to do—Within Harcels?"

"You might start by enjoying being Within him," Gaudior suggested. "In this When, the world still knows the Old Music."

"Does he see you, as I do?"

"Yes."

"He is not surprised."

"To joy, nothing is surprising. Relax, Charles. Kythe with Harcels. Be Harcels. Let yourself go." He struck one hoof against rock, drawing sparks, leapt from the rock in a great arc, and galloped into the woods.

Harcels rose, stretched languorously. He, too, leapt from the rock with the gravity-defying ease of a ballet dancer, landed on the springy grass, rolled over in merriment, sprang to his feet, and ran to the water's edge, calling to the children, the weavers, the potters.

At the edge of the lake he stood very still, isolating himself from the activity around him. He pursed his lips and whistled, a long sweet summons, and then called softly, "Finna, Finna, Finna!"

Halfway across the lake there was a disturbance in the water and a large creature came swimming, leaping, flying, toward Harcels, who in turn flung himself into the water and swam swiftly to meet it.

Finna was akin to a dolphin, though not as large, and her skin was an iridescent blue-green. She had the gracious smile of a dolphin, and the same familiarity with sea and air. As she met Harcels she sent a small fountain of water through her blowhole, drenching the boy, who shouted with laughter.

For a few moments they wrestled together, and then Harcels was riding Finna, leaping through the air, holding tight as Finna dove down, down deep below the surface, gasping as she flashed again up into the sunlight, sending spray in every direction.

It was sheer joy.

What Charles Wallace had known in occasional flashes of beauty was Harcels's way of life.

In the attic bedroom Meg kept her hand on Ananda. A shudder moved like a wave over them both. "Oh, Ananda," Meg said, "why couldn't it have stayed that way? What happened?"

* * *

—When? Charles Wallace wondered.—When are we?

For Harcels, all Whens were Now. There was yesterday, which was gone, which was only a dream. There was tomorrow, which was a vision not unlike today. When was always Now, for there was little looking either backward or forward in this young world. If Now was good, yesterday, though a pleasurable dream, was not necessary. If Now was good, tomorrow would likely continue to be so.

The People of the Wind were gentle and harmonious. On the rare occasions when there was a difference of opinion, it was mediated by the Harmonizer, and his judgment was always accepted. Fish were caught, flesh shot with bow and arrow, never more than needed. Each person in the tribe knew what he was born to do, and no gift was considered greater or less than another. The Harmonizer held a position no more lofty than the youngest cook just learning to build a fire or clean a fish.

One day a wild boar of monstrous size chased a small party of hunters, and the smallest and slowest among them was gored in the side. Harcels helped carry him home, and knelt all through the night with the Healer, bringing fresh cool moss to lay against the fevered wound, singing the prayers of healing as each star moved in its own ordained dance across the sky.

In the morning there was great rejoicing, for not only

was the fiery wound cooling but it was recognized that Harcels had found his gift and would be apprenticed to the Healer, and when the Healer went to dwell with those who move among the stars, Harcels would take his place.

The melody was clear and pure. The harmony was undistorted. Time was still young and the sun was bright by day and moved without fear to rest in the realm of distant stars by night.

Harcels had many friends among his people, but his heart's companions were beasts: Finna, and Eyrn, a great bird something between an eagle and a giant gull, and large enough for Harcels to ride. Eyrn's feathers were white, tipped with rose, shading to purple. She was crowned with a tuft of rosy feathers, and her eyes were ruby. With Harcels firmly astride she would fly high, high, higher, until the air was thin and the boy gasped for breath. She flew far and high, so that he could see the dwellings of distant tribes, could see the ocean that stretched, it seemed, across all the rest of the world.

Harcels asked the Teller of Tales about the other tribes.

"Leave them be," the Teller of Tales said in the sharpest voice he had ever been heard to use.

"But it might be fun to know them. They might have things to teach us."

"Harcels," the Teller of Tales said, "I, too, have ridden a creature like your Eyrn, and I have had my steed descend in a hidden place, that I might watch unseen. I saw a man kill a man."

"But why? Why ever would one man kill another?"

The Teller of Tales looked long into the clear eyes of the boy. "Let us hope you will never have to know."

It was easy for Charles Wallace to live Within Harcels, in the brightness of the young sun, where darkness was the friend of light. One day when Harcels was astride Eyrn, they flew over a cluster of dwellings and the boy started to ask Eyrn to descend, but Charles Wallace gently drew his thoughts to the pleasure of flight as Eyrn threw himself upon a stream of wind and glided with the merest motion of wings. Charles Wallace was not certain that this small interference was permissible; he knew only that if Harcels learned the ways of the tribes who knew how to kill, his joy would vanish with his innocence.

—It was the right thing to do, Meg kythed to him fiercely.—It has to be the right thing.

She looked again at the clock. The hands had barely moved. While the seasons were following each other in swift succession in that Other Time where Charles Wallace lived Within Harcels, time was arrested in her own present moment. Time was moving only in that When in which the land so familiar and dear to her was different, where the flat star-watching rock was a hill of stone, the green valley a lake, and the little woods a dark forest.

She sighed achingly for a time so full of joy that it was difficult to realize it had once been real.

Ananda whined and looked at Meg with great anxious eyes.

"What is it?" Meg asked in alarm. She heard Gaudior's neigh, and saw a pulsing of silver light, the diamond-brilliant light which lit the unicorn's horn.

Charles Wallace was astride Gaudior's great neck, looking from within his own eyes at Harcels, Within whom he had known such spontaneity and joy that his own awareness would evermore share in it. He rubbed his cheek gently against the unicorn's silver neck. "Thank you," he whispered.

"Don't thank me," Gaudior snorted. "I'm not the one to decide whom you go Within."

"Who does, then?"

"The wind."

"Does the wind tell you?"

"Not until you are Within. And don't expect it to be this way every time. I suspect that you were sent Within Harcels to help get you accustomed to Within-ing in the easiest way possible. And you must let yourself go even more deeply into your hosts if you are to recognize the right Might-Have-Beens."

"If I let myself go, how can I recognize?"

"That you will have to discover for yourself. I can only tell you that this is how it works."

"Am I to be sent Within again now?"

"Yes."

"I'm not as afraid as I was, but, Gaudior, I'm still afraid."

"That's all right," Gaudior said.

"And if I let more of myself go, how can I kythe properly with Meg?"

"If you're meant to, you will."

"I'm going to need her . . ."

"Why?"

"I don't know. I just know that I am."

Gaudior blew three iridescent bubbles. "Hold tight, tight, tight. We're off on the wind, and there may be Echthroi this time who will try to take you from my back and throw you off the rim of the world."

FOUR

The snow with
its whiteness

The great unicorn flung himself into the wind and they were soaring among the stars, part of the dance, part of the harmony. As each flaming sun turned on its axis, a singing came from the friction in the way a finger moved around the rim of a crystal goblet will make a singing, and the song varies in pitch and tone from glass to glass.

But this song was exquisite as no song from crystal or wood or brass can be. The blending of melody and harmony was so perfect that it almost made Charles Wallace relax his hold on the unicorn's mane.

"No!" Meg cried aloud. "Hold on, Charles! Don't let go!"

A blast of icy cold cut across the beauty of the flight, a cold which carried a stench of death and decay.

Retching, Charles Wallace buried his face in Gaudior's mane, his fingers clenching the silver strands as the

Echthroid wind tried to drag him from the unicorn's back. The stench was so abominable that it would have made him loosen his grasp had not the pungent scent of Gaudior's living flesh saved him as he pressed his face against the silver hide, breathing the strangeness of unicorn sweat. Gaudior's bright wings beat painfully against invisible wings of darkness beating at them. The unicorn neighed in anguish, his clear tones lost in the howling of the tempest.

Suddenly his hoofs struck against something solid. He whinnied with anxiety. "Hold on tightly, don't let go," he warned. "We've been blown into a Projection."

Charles Wallace could hardly be clutching the mane with more intensity. "A what?"

"We've been blown into a Projection, a possible future, a future the Echthroi want to make real." His breath came in gasping gulps; his flanks heaved wildly under Charles Wallace's legs.

The boy shivered as he remembered those darkly flailing wings and the nauseous odor. Whatever the Echthroi wanted to make real would be something fearful.

They were on a flat plain of what appeared to be solidified lava, although it had a faint luminosity alien to lava. The sky was covered with flickering pink cloud. The air was acrid, making them cough. The heat was intense and he was perspiring profusely under the light anorak, which held in the heat like a furnace.

"Where are we?" he asked, wanting Gaudior to tell him that they were not in his own Where, that this could not possibly be the place of the star-watching rock, of the woods, only a few minutes' walk from the house.

Gaudior's words trembled with concern. "We're still here, in your own Where, although it is not yet a real When."

"Will it be?"

"It is one of the Projections we have been sent to try to prevent. The Echthroi will do everything in their power to make it real."

A shudder shook the boy's slight frame as he looked around the devastated landscape. "Gaudior—what do we do now?"

"Nothing. You mustn't loosen your hold on my mane. They want us to do something, and anything we do might be what they need to make this Projection real."

"Can't we get away?"

The unicorn's ears flicked nervously. "It's very difficult to find a wind to ride when one has been blown into a Projection."

"But what do we do?"

"There is nothing to do but wait."

"Is anybody left alive?"

"I don't know."

Around them a sulfurous wind began to rise. Both boy

and unicorn were convulsed with paroxysms of coughing, but Charles Wallace did not loosen his grasp. When the seizure was over, he dried his streaming eyes on the silver mane.

When he looked up again, his heart lurched with horror. Waddling toward them over the petrified earth was a monstrous creature with a great blotched body, short stumps for legs, and long arms, with the hands brushing the ground. What was left of the face was scabrous and suppurating. It looked at the unicorn with its one eye, turned its head as though calling behind it to someone or something, and hurried toward them as fast as its stumps would take it.

"Oh, Heavenly Powers, save us!" Gaudior's neigh streaked silver.

The anguished cry called Charles Wallace back to himself. He cried,

> "With Gaudior in this fateful hour
> I call on all Heaven with its power
> And the sun with its brightness,
> And the snow with its whiteness . . ."

He took a deep breath and hot air seared his lungs and again he was assailed by an unquellable fit of coughing. He buried his face in the unicorn's mane and tried to control the spasm which shook him. It was not until the racking had nearly passed that he became aware of something cool brushing his burning face.

He raised his eyes and with awed gratitude he saw snow, pure white snow drifting down from the tortured sky, covering the ruined earth. The monster had stopped its ponderous approach and was staring up at the sky, mouth open to catch the falling flakes.

With the snow came a light wind, a cool wind. "Hold!" Gaudior cried, and raised his wings to catch the wind. His four hoofs left the ground and he launched himself into the wind with a surge of power.

Charles Wallace braced, trying to tighten the grip of his legs about the unicorn's broad neck. He could feel the wild beating of Gaudior's heart as with mighty strokes he thrust along the wind through the darkness of outer space, until suddenly they burst into a fountain of stars, and the stench and the horror were gone.

The unicorn's breath came in great gulps of star-lit air; the wings beat less frantically; and they were safely riding the wind again and the song of the stars was clear and full.

"Now," said Gaudior, "we go."

"Where?" Charles Wallace asked.

"Not Where," Gaudior said. "When."

Up, up, through the stars, up to the far reaches of the universe where the galaxies swirled in their starry dance, weaving time.

Exhausted, Charles Wallace felt his eyelids drooping.

"Do not go to sleep," Gaudior warned.

Charles Wallace leaned over the unicorn's neck. "I'm not sure I can help it," he murmured.

"Sing, then," Gaudior commanded. "Sing to keep yourself awake." The unicorn opened his powerful jaws and music streamed out in full and magnificent harmony. Charles Wallace's voice was barely changing from a pure treble to a warm tenor. Now it was the treble, sweet as a flute, which joined Gaudior's mighty organ tones. He was singing a melody he did not know, and yet the notes poured from his throat with all the assurance of long familiarity.

They moved through the time-spinning reaches of a far galaxy, and he realized that the galaxy itself was part of a mighty orchestra, and each star and planet within the galaxy added its own instrument to the music of the spheres. As long as the ancient harmonies were sung, the universe would not entirely lose its joy.

He was hardly aware when Gaudior's hoofs struck ground and the melody dimmed until it was only a pervasive beauty of background. With a deep sigh Gaudior stopped his mighty song and folded his wings into his flanks.

Meg sighed as the beauty of the melody faded and all she heard was the soft movement of the wind in the bare trees. She realized that the room was cold, despite the electric heater which augmented the warm air coming up the attic stairs from the radiators below. She reached over Ananda to the foot of the bed and pulled up her old eiderdown and wrapped it around them both. A gust of wind beat at the window, which always rattled unless secured by a folded piece of cardboard or a sliver of wood stuck between window and frame.

"Ananda, Ananda," she said softly, "the music—it was more—more real than any music I've ever heard. Will we hear it again?"

The wind dropped as suddenly as it had risen, and once again she could feel the warmth coming from the little heater. "Ananda, he's really a very small boy . . . Where is Gaudior going to take him now? Whom is he going to go Within?" She closed her eyes, pressing the palm of her hand firmly against the dog.

It was the same Where as the Where of Harcels, but there were subtle differences, though it was still what Gaudior had called Once Upon a Time and Long Ago, so perhaps men still lived in peace and Charles Wallace would be in no danger. But no: time, though still young, was not as young as that, she felt.

The lake lapped close to the great rock and stretched across the valley to the horizon, a larger lake than the lake of Harcels's time. The rock itself had been flattened by wind and rain and erosion, so that it looked like an enormous, slightly tilted tabletop. The forest was dark and deep, but the trees were familiar, pine and hemlock and oak and elm.

Dawn.

The air was pure and blue and filled with the fragrance of spring. The grass around the rock looked as though it had been covered with a fall of fresh snow, but the snow was a narcissus-like flower with a spicy scent.

On the tabletop stood a young man.

She did not see Charles Wallace. She did not see the unicorn. Only the young man.

A young man older than Charles Wallace. Harcels had been younger. This young man was older, perhaps not as old as Sandy and Dennys, but more than fifteen. She saw no hint of Charles Wallace within the man, but she knew that somehow he was there. As Charles Wallace had been himself and yet had been Harcels, so Charles Wallace was Within the young man.

He had been there all night, sometimes lying on his back to watch the stars swing slowly across the sky; sometimes with his eyes closed, as he listened to the lapping of the small waves on the pale sand, the clunkings of frogs and the hoot of a night bird, the sound of an occasional fish slipping through the water. Sometimes he neither heard nor saw; he did not sleep, but abandoned his senses and lay on the rock patiently opening himself to the wind.

Perhaps it was his gift of kything practiced with Meg that helped Charles Wallace slip more and more deeply into the being of another.

Madoc, son of Owain, king of Gwynedd.

Madoc, on the dawning of his wedding day.

Meg's eyes slowly lowered; her body relaxed under the warmth of the eiderdown; but her hand remained on Ananda as she slid into sleep.

Madoc!

It was for Charles Wallace as though a shuttered window had suddenly been opened. It was not a ballad or a song he was trying to remember, it was a novel about a Welsh prince named Madoc.

He heard Gaudior's warning neigh. "You are Within Madoc. Do not disturb him with outside thoughts."

"But, Gaudior, Madoc was the key figure in the book—oh, why can't I remember more!"

Again Gaudior cut him off. "Stop trying to think. Your job now is to let yourself go into Madoc. Let go."

Let go.

It was almost like slipping down, deeper and deeper, into the waters of a pool, deeper and deeper.

Let go.

Fall into Madoc.

Let go.

Madoc rose from the rock and looked to the east, awaiting the sunrise with exalted anticipation. His fair skin was tanned, with a reddishness which showed that he was alien to so fierce a sun. He looked toward the indigo line of horizon between lake and sky, with eyes so blue that the sky paled in comparison. His hair, thick and gold as a lion's mane, was nearly covered with an elaborate crown of early spring flowers. A lavish chain of flowers was flung over his neck and one shoulder. He wore a kilt of ferns.

The sky lightened, and the sun sent its fiery rays over the edge of the lake, reaching up into the sky, pulling itself, dripping, from the waters of the night. As the sun seemed to make a great leap out of the dark, Madoc began to sing in a strong, joyful baritone.

> "Lords of fire and earth and water,
> Lords of rain and wind and snow,
> When will come the Old Man's daughter?
> Time to come, or long ago?
> Born of friend or borne by foe?
>
> Lords of water, earth, and fire,
> Lords of wind and snow and rain,
> Where is found the heart's desire?

> Has she come? will come again?
> Born, as all life's born, with pain?"

When he finished, still looking out over the water, his song was taken up as though by an echo, a strange, thin, cracked echo, and then an old man, dressed with the same abundance of flowers as Madoc, came out of the forest.

Madoc bent down and helped the old man up onto the rock. For all the Old One's age, his stringy-looking muscles were strong, and though his hair was white, his dark skin had a glow of health.

> "Lords of snow and rain and wind,
> Lords of water, fire, and earth,
> Do you know the one you send?
> Does it call for tears or mirth?
> Shall we sing for death or birth?"

When the strange duet was ended, the old man held up his hand in a gesture of blessing. "It is the day, my far-sent son."

"It is the day, my to-be-father. Madoc, son of Owain, king of Gwynedd, will be Madoc, son of Reschal, Old One of the Wind People."

"A year ago today, you sang the song in your delirium," Reschal said, "and it was the child of my old age who found you in the forest."

"And it is mirth that is called for," the young man affirmed, "and we shall sing today for birth, for the birth of the new One which Zyll and I will become when you join us together."

"On the night that Zyll was born," the Old One said, "I dreamed of a stranger from a distant land, across a lake far greater than ours—"

"From across the ocean"—the young man put his hand lightly on the Old One's shoulder—"from the sea which beats upon the shores of Cymru, the sea which we thought went on and on until a ship would fall off at the end of the world."

"The end of the world—" the old man started, but broke off, listening.

The young man listened, too, but heard nothing. "Is it the wind?"

"It is not the wind." Reschal looked at the young man and put a gnarled hand on the richly muscled arm. "Madoc, son of Owain, king of Gwynedd—how strange those syllables sounded to us. We did not know what is a king, nor truly do we yet."

"You have no need of a king, Old One of the People of the Wind. Owain, my father, is long buried: I am a lifetime away from Gwynedd in Cymru. When the soothsayer looked into the scrying glass and foretold my father's death, he saw also that I would live my days far from Gwynedd."

The old man again lifted his head to listen.

"Is it the wind?" Still, Madoc could hear nothing beyond the sounds of early morning, the lapping of the lake against the shore, the stirring of the wind in the hemlocks which made a distant roaring which always reminded him of the sea he had left behind him.

"It is not the wind." There was no emotion in the old man's face, only a continuing, controlled listening.

The young man could not hide the impatience in his voice. "When is Zyll coming?"

The dark Old One smiled at him with affection. "You have waited how many years?"

"I am seventeen."

"Then you can wait a while longer, while Zyll's maidens make her ready. And there are still questions I must ask you. Are you certain in your heart that you will never want to leave Zyll and this small, inland people and go back to the big water and your ship with wings?"

"My ship was broken by wind and wave when we attempted to land on the rocky shores of this land. The sails are torn beyond mending."

"Another ship could be built."

"Old One, even had I the tools to fell the trees for lumber for a new ship, even had my brother and my companions not perished, I would never wish to leave Zyll and my new brethren."

"And your brother and your companions?"

"They are dead," Madoc said bleakly.

"Yet you hold them back so that they cannot continue their journey."

"We were far from home." Madoc spoke softly. "It is a long journey for their spirits."

"Are the gods of Gwynedd so weak they cannot care for their own?"

Madoc's blue eyes were dark with grief. "When we left Gwynedd in Cymru because of the quarreling of my brethren over our father's throne, it seemed to us the gods had already abandoned us. For brothers to wish to kill each other for the sake of power is to anger the gods."

"Perhaps," the old man said, "you must let the gods of Gwynedd go, as you must free your companions from your holding."

"I brought them to their death. When my father died, and my brothers became drunk with lust for power, as no wine can make a man drunk, I felt the gods depart. In a dream I saw them turn their backs on our quarreling, saw them as clearly as anything the soothsayers see in their scrying glass. When I awoke, I took Gwydyr aside and said that I would not stay to watch brother against brother, but that I would go find the land the Wise Ones said was at the farther end of the sea. Gwydyr demurred at first."

"He thought he might become king?"

"Yes, but Gwydyr and I were the youngest. The throne was not likely to be ours while the other five remained alive."

"Yet you, Madoc, the seventh son, were the favored of the people."

"Had I let them proclaim me king, there would have been no way to avoid bloodshed. I left Gwynedd to prevent the horror of brother against brother."

"Have you"—the old man regarded Madoc keenly— "in fact left it?"

"I have left it. Gwynedd in Cymru is behind me. It will be ruled by whomever the gods choose. I do not wish to know. For now I am Madoc, son-to-be of Reschal, soon to be husband of Zyll of the People of the Wind."

"And Gwydyr? Have you let him go?"

Madoc gazed across the lake. "In many ways it seemed that I was older than he, though there were seven years between us. When we came to the tribe on the Far Side of the Lake he was afraid of their dark skins and hair and their strange singing that was full of hoots and howls, and he ran from them. They kept me as guest, yet I was a prisoner, for they would not let me go into the forest to look for my brother. They sent a party of warriors to search for him, and when they returned they carried only the belt with the jeweled buckle which marked him as the son of a king. They told me he had been killed by a snake; Gwydyr did not know what a snake is, for we have none in Gwynedd. They told me that he had called my name before he died, and that he had left me the Song of the King's Sons. And they buried him out in the forest. Without me, they buried my brother, and I do not even know the place where he is laid."

"That is the way of the People on the Far Side of the Lake," the old man said. "They fear the dead and try to escape the ancient terror."

"The ancient terror?"

Reschal looked at the tender sky of early morning. "That which went wrong. Once there were no evil spirits to blight the crops, to bring drought or flood. Once there was nothing to fear, not even death."

"And what happened to bring fear?"

"Who knows? It was so long ago. But is it not in Gwynedd, too?"

"It is in Gwynedd," Madoc replied soberly, "or brother would not have turned against brother. Yes, we too know what you call the ancient terror. Death, it is thought, or at least the fear of death, came with it. Reschal, I would that I knew where those across the lake had laid my brother, that I may say the prayers that will free his soul."

"It is their way to put the dead far from them and then to lose the place. They hide the dead, even from themselves, that their spirits may not come to the lake and keep the fish away."

"And your people?"

The old man pulled himself up proudly. "We do not fear the spirits of our dead. When there has been love during life, why should that change after death? When one of us departs we have a feast of honor, and then we send the spirit to its journey among the stars. On clear nights we feel the singing of their love. Did you not feel it last night?"

"I watched the stars—and I felt that they accepted me."

"And your brother? Did you feel his light?"

Madoc shook his head. "Perhaps if I could have found the place where they buried him . . ."

"You must let him go. For the sake of Zyll you must let him go."

"*When will come the Old Man's daughter?*" Madoc asked. "I felt the People on the Far Side of the Lake to try to find my brother's grave, and in the forest I was quickly lost. For days I wandered, trying to make my way back, straying farther and farther from them. I was nearly dead when Zyll came hunting the healing herbs which are found only in the deepest part of the forest. *When will come the Old Man's daughter? Where is found the heart's desire?* Here, Reschal."

"You will let Gwydyr go to his place among the stars?"

"*Does it call for tears or mirth? Shall we sing for death or birth?*" Madoc sang softly. "I have shed my tears for the past. Today is for mirth. Why have you dragged me through tears again?"

"So that you may leave them behind you," Reschal said, and raised his withered arms to the sun. The lake, the shore, the rock, the forest behind, were bathed in golden light, and as though in response to Reschal's gesture there came a sound of singing, a strange wild song of spring and flowers and sunlight and growing grass and the beating of the heart of all of those young and in love. And Madoc's tears were dried, and thoughts of his lost companions and brother receded as the singing filled him with expectancy and joy.

The children of the tribe came first, wearing chains of flowers which flapped against their brown bellies as they danced along. Madoc, shining with delight, turned from the children to the Old One. But Reschal's eyes were focused on the unseen distance across the lake and he was listening, not to the children, but to that sound for which he had been straining before. And now Madoc thought that he, too, heard a throbbing like a distant heartbeat. "Old One, I hear it now. What is it?"

Reschal gazed across the water. "It is the People Across the Lake. It is their drums."

Madoc listened. "We have heard their drums before, when the wind blows from the south. But today the wind blows from the north."

The old man's voice was troubled. "We have always

lived in peace, the People of the Wind and those Across the Lake."

"Perhaps," Madoc suggested, "they come to my wedding celebration?"

"Perhaps."

The children had gathered around the rock and were looking expectantly at Madoc and Reschal. The Old One raised his arm again, and singing drowned out the steady beating of the drums, and the men and women of the tribe, ranging from coltish girls and boys to men and women with white hair and wrinkled skin, came dancing toward the great rock. In their midst, circled by a group of young women, was Zyll. She wore a crown on her head to match Madoc's, and a short skirt made entirely of spring flowers. Her copper skin glowed as though lit by the sun from within, and her eyes met Madoc's with a sparkle of love.

Nowhere, Madoc thought, could wedding garments be more beautiful, no matter how much gold was woven into the cloth, nor with how many jewels the velvets and satins were decorated.

The flower-bedecked crowd parted to let Zyll come to the rock. Madoc stooped for her upraised hands, and gently lifted her so that she stood between him and Reschal. She bowed to her father, and then began to move in the ritual wedding dance. Madoc, during the year he had spent with the Wind People, had seen Zyll dance many times before: at the birth of each moon; at the feast of the newborn sun in winter; at the spring and autumn equinox, dance for the Lords of the lake, the sky, the rain and rainbow, the snow and the wind.

But for the Wind Dancers, as well as for all the other Wind People with their various gifts, there was only one Wedding Dance.

Madoc stood transfixed with joy as Zyll's body moved with the effortless lightness of the spring breeze. Her body leapt upward and it seemed that gravity had no power to pull her down to earth. She drifted gently from sky to rock as the petals fall from flowering trees.

Then she held out her hands to Madoc, and he joined in the dance, marveling as he felt some of Zyll's effortlessness of movement enter his own limbs.

At first, when Zyll had found Madoc half dead in the forest, and had brought him to the Wind People, they had been afraid of him. His blue eyes, his pale skin, reddened by exposure, his tawny hair, were unlike anything they had ever seen. They approached him shyly, as though he were a strange beast who might turn on them. As they became accustomed to his presence, some of the Wind People proclaimed him a god. But then his anger flashed like lightning, and though there were some who said that his very fieriness announced him the Lord of the storm, he would have none of their attempts to set him apart.

"Stay with your own wind gods," he commanded.

"You have served them well, and you live in the light of their favor. I, too, will serve the Lords of this place, for it is their pleasure that I am still alive."

Gradually the Wind People began to accept him as one of themselves, to forget his outer differences. The Old One said, "It is not an easy thing to refuse to be worshipped."

"When people are worshipped, then there is anger and jealousy in the wake. I will not be worshipped, nor will I be a king. People are meant to worship the gods, not themselves."

"You are wise beyond your years, my son," Reschal said.

"My father did not want to be worshipped. But some of his sons did. That is why I am here."

Across the lake the drums were silent.

The Old One watched Madoc and Zyll as their bodies slowly ceased the motions of the dance. Then he lifted Madoc's hand and placed it over Zyll's, and then put a hand on each of their heads. And as he did so, the sound of drums came again. Loud and close. Threatening.

A ripple went through the Wind People as they saw three dugout canoes approaching swiftly, each paddled by many men. Standing in the bow of the middle and largest dugout was a tall, fair-skinned, blue-eyed man.

With a glad shout Madoc leapt from the rock and ran to the water's edge. "Gwydyr!"

FIVE

The fire with all the strength it hath

In the attic Meg lay quietly in bed, her eyes closed. Her hand continued to rub rhythmically against Ananda, receiving the tingling warmth. Behind her lids her eyes moved as though she were dreaming. The kitten stood up, stretched its small back into a high arch, yawned, and curled up at her feet, purring.

Charles Wallace-within-Madoc felt the young man's surge of joy at seeing his brother alive, the brother he had thought dead and buried in a forgotten part of the forest.

The man in the dugout jumped overboard and ran splashing to shore.

"Gwydyr! You are alive!" Madoc held out his arms to his brother.

Gwydyr did not move into the embrace. His blue eyes were cold, and set close together. It was then that Madoc noticed the circlet around his brother's head, not of flowers, but of gold.

"Gwydyr, my elder brother." The joy slowly faded from the sunny blue of Madoc's eyes. "I thought you dead."

Gwydyr's voice was as cold as his eyes. "It was my wish that you should think so."

"But why should you wish such a thing!"

At the pain in Madoc's voice, Zyll dropped lightly from the rock and came to stand close by him.

"Did you not learn in Gwynedd that there is room for one king only?"

Madoc's eyes kept returning to Gwydyr's golden crown. "We left Gwynedd for that reason, to find a place of peace."

Gwydyr gestured behind him, and the drummers began to beat slowly on the taut skins. The paddles were rested and the men splashed into the shallow water, and pulled the dugouts onto the shore.

Gwydyr raised the corners of his lips into what was more a grimace than a smile. "I have come to claim the Old Man's daughter."

The sound of the drums was an aching pain in Madoc's ears. "My brother, I wept for your death. I thought to rejoice to see you alive."

Gwydyr spoke with grim patience as though to a dimwitted child. "There is room for no more than one king in this place, little brother, and I, who am the elder, am that king. In Gwynedd I had no hope against six brothers. But here I am king and god and I have come to let the Wind People know that I reign over the lake and all the lands around. The Old Man's daughter is mine."

Zyll pressed against Madoc, her fingers tight on his arm.

Reschal spoke in his cracked voice. "The People of the Wind are people of peace. Always we have lived in amity with those Across the Lake."

Again Gwydyr's lips distorted into a smile. "Peace will continue as long as you give us half of your fish and half of all you hunt and if I take with me across the water the princess who stands beside my brother."

Zyll did not move from Madoc's side. "You come too late, Elder Brother. Madoc of Reschal and I have been made One."

"Madoc of Reschal. Ha! My laws are stronger than your laws." Gwydyr gestured imperiously. The men with the paddles pulled the blades off the shafts, and stood holding dangerously pointed spears.

A united cry of disbelief, then anger, came from the Wind People.

"No!" Madoc cried, outrage giving his voice such volume that it drowned out the beating of the drums, the shouting of the warriors with the spears, the anger of the Wind People. "There will be no bloodshed here because of the sons of Owain." He stepped away from Zyll and

Reschal and confronted Gwydyr. "Brother, this is between you and me." And now he smiled. "Unless, of course, you are afraid of Madoc and need your savages with spears to protect you."

Gwydyr made an enraged gesture. "And what of your peaceable Wind People?"

Then Madoc saw that the festive garlands were gone from the young men, flung in a heap in front of the great rock. Instead of flowers they carried spears, bows and arrows.

Reschal looked at him gravely. "I have been hearing the war drums since last sundown. I thought it better to be prepared."

Madoc flung his arms wide. There was grim command in his voice. "Put down your arms, my brothers. I came to you in peace. I will not be the cause of war."

The young men looked first at Madoc, then at the People Across the Lake, their spears threatening.

"Brother," Madoc said to Gwydyr, "have your men put down their spears. Or do you fear to fight me in fair combat?"

Gwydyr snarled an order, and the men on the shore behind him placed their spears carefully on the sand in easy reach.

Then the Old One nodded at the young men, and they, too, put down their weapons.

Gwydyr shouted, "If we are to fight for the Old Man's daughter, little brother, I choose the weapon."

"That is fair," Madoc replied.

Zyll made a soft moan of anxiety and placed her hand on his arm.

"I choose fire," Gwydyr announced.

Madoc sang:

> "Lords of water, earth, and fire,
> Where is found the heart's desire?"

"Fire it shall be, then. But in what form?"

"You must make fire, little brother," Gwydyr said. "If your fire cannot overcome mine, then I will be king of the Wind People as well as those Across the Lake, and I will claim the Old Man's daughter for my own." His close-set eyes flickered greedily.

Reschal walked slowly toward him. "Gwydyr, sixth son of Owain, pride has turned the light behind your eyes to ice, so that you can no longer see clearly. You will never take my daughter."

Gwydyr gave the old man a mighty shove, so that he fell sprawling on the beach, face down. Zyll screamed, and her scream was arrested in midair, to hang there.

Madoc sprang to help the old man, and bent down on one knee to raise Reschal from the sand. But his eyes followed the Old One's to a small pool of water in a declivity in the sand, and his movements, like Zyll's scream, were suspended. Only the reflection in the small pool of water moved. Gwydyr's face was quivering in the wind-stirred puddle, his face so like and so unlike Madoc's. The eyes were the same blue, but there was no gold behind them, and they turned slightly in to a nose pinched with cruelty and lust. This was not, Madoc thought, the brother who had come with him to the New World. Or was it? and he had never truly seen his brother before, only Gwydyr as he hoped him to be.

Ripples moved over the shallow oval and the reflection shimmered like the reflections in the soothsayers' scrying glass in Gwynedd.

Madoc had always feared the scrying glass; so he feared the small oval of water which reflected Gwydyr's face, growing larger and larger, and darker and darker, quivering until it was no longer the face of a man but of a screaming baby. The face receded until Madoc saw a black-haired woman holding and rocking the baby. "You shall be great, little Madog," she said, "and call the world your own, to keep or destroy as you will. It is an evil world, little Madog." The baby looked at her, and his eyes were set close together, like Gwydyr's, and turned inward, just so, and his mouth pouted with discontent. Again the face grew larger and larger in the dark oval and was no longer the face of a baby, but a man with an arrogant and angry mien. "We will destroy, then, Mother," the man said, and the face rippled until it was a small, slightly pear-shaped sphere, and on the sphere were blotches of green and brown for land, and blue and grey for seas, and a soft darkness for clouds, and from the clouds came strange dark objects which fell upon the land and fell upon the sea, and where they fell, great clouds arose, umbrellaing over the earth and the sea; and beneath the bulbous clouds was fire, raging redly and driven wild by wind.

Gwydyr's voice rippled across the scrying oval of water. "I choose fire, little brother. Where is your fire?"

The flames vanished and the oval was only a shallow pool reflecting nothing more than the cloud that moved across the sun.

Time resumed, and Zyll's scream continued as though it had never been broken. Madoc raised Reschal from the beach, stepping into the oval as he did so, splashing the shallow water onto the sand. "Stand back, Old One," he said. "I will break the scry." And he stamped once more on the water left in the puddle, until there was not enough to hold the least reflection.

From the central dugout came one of the warriors, carrying a smoking brazier. Gwydyr took one of the spears and held the sharp end over the coals. "You must make your own fire, Madoc!" He laughed derisively.

Madoc turned to the rock where the young men had

laid their chains of flowers. He gathered the flowers in his arms and placed them in a heap over the oval where the water had been. Then he took the crown of flowers from his head and added it to the garlands. As though responding to a signal, Zyll cast hers on the fragrant pile. One by one all the men, women, children of the Wind People threw their headpieces onto the heap of flowers, Reschal last of all.

"What do you think you're doing?" Gwydyr screamed, dancing about on the sand, thrusting his flaming spear at his brother.

Madoc leapt aside. "Wait, Gwydyr. You chose fire. You must let me fight fire with fire."

"You, you alone must make the fire. These are my rules."

Madoc replied quietly, "You were always one for making your own rules, Brother Gwydyr."

"I am the king, do you hear me, I am the king!" Gwydyr's voice rose hysterically.

Madoc, moving as though in a dream, pushed his brother's words aside, and focused the blue fire of his eyes on the great pyre of flowers. The scent of crushed blossoms rose like smoke. Madoc thrust his arms shoulder-deep into the garlands and pushed them aside so that once more he could see the oval. A thin film of water had bubbled up from the sand.

"No more of Gwydyr's nightmares," he commanded, staring fixedly at the water, which sparkled from the sun. The water rippled and shimmered and resolved itself once again into a mother holding a baby, but a different baby, eyes wide apart, with sunlight gleaming through the blue, a laughing, merry baby. "You will do good for your people, El Zarco, little Blue Eyes," the mother crooned. "Your eyes are an omen, a token for peace. The prayer has been answered in you, blue for birth, blue for mirth."

Then the oval broke into shimmering, and all that was reflected was the cloudy sky. Madoc looked heavenward then, and cried in a loud voice,

> "I, Madoc, in this fateful hour
> Place all Heaven with its power
> And the sun with its brightness,
> And the snow with its whiteness,
> And the fire with all the strength it hath . . ."

The sun burst from behind the clouds and shafted directly onto the garlands. The scent of roses mingled with the thin wisp of smoke which rose from the crushed petals. When the smoke was joined by a small tongue of flame, Madoc leapt toward his brother. "There is my fire, Gwydyr." He wrenched the spear from his brother and threw it with all his might into the lake. "Now we will fight in fair combat." And he clasped Gwydyr to him as though in love.

For time out of time the two brothers wrestled by the lake, both panting with exertion, but neither seeming to tire beyond the other. Their bodies swayed back and forth in a strange dance, and the People of the Wind and those Across the Lake watched in silence.

The sun completed its journey across the sky and dropped into the forest for the night's rest, and still the brothers held each other in an anguished grip and their breathing was louder than the wind in the trees.

The fire slowly consumed the garlands, and when there was nothing left but a handful of ashes, Madoc forced Gwydyr into the lake, and held him down under the water until rising bubbles told him that his brother was screaming for mercy. Then he raised him from the lake and water spewed from Gwydyr's mouth as dark as blood, and he hung limply in Madoc's arms.

Madoc gestured to the People Across the Lake. "Bring out your boats and take your king back to your own land." His voice held scorn and it held pain and his blue eyes were softened by tears.

The three boats pushed into the water. The spear-oars were returned to their blades. Madoc dumped Gwydyr like a sack of grain into the center dugout. "Go. Never let us hear the sound of the war drums again." He reached into the canoe and took the golden circlet from Gwydyr's head and tossed it far out into the lake.

Then he turned his back on his brother and splashed ashore.

Zyll was waiting for him.

Madoc looked at her and sang,

> "Lords of water, earth, and fire
> Lords of rain and snow and water,
> Nothing more do I aspire,
> For I have the Old Man's daughter,
> For I have my heart's desire."

And to him Zyll sang,

> "Now we leave our tears for mirth.
> Now we sing, not death, but birth."

Madoc held her close in his arms. "Tomorrow I will mourn for my brother, for this death is far worse than the other. But tonight we rejoice."

The children lifted their voices and began to sing, and then all the People of the Wind were singing, and Reschal said softly to Madoc, "That which your brother wanted us to believe from the scry is part of his nightmare. Perhaps our dreams will be stronger than his."

"Yes, Old One," Madoc said, but he thought of the

things he had seen falling from the sky, and the strange mushrooming clouds and the fire, and shuddered. He looked at the water that had seeped into the oval. But all that he saw was the smiling face of the moon.

The moon slipped behind the trees to join, briefly, her brother, sun. The stars danced their intricate ritual across the sky. The People Across the Lake looked at Gwydyr, and his golden crown was gone, and so was his power.

Madoc's arms encircled Zyll and he cried out in his sleep and tears slid through his closed eyelids and wet his lashes, and while he still slept, Zyll held him and kissed the tears away.

"Come," Gaudior said.

Charles Wallace stood by the unicorn, blinking. "Was it a dream?" He looked at the dark lake lapping the shore, at the tilted rock; it was empty.

Gaudior blew silver bubbles that bounced off his beard. "You were Within Madoc, deep Within this time."

"Madoc, son of Owain, king of Gwynedd. The Madoc of the book. And hasn't there been a recurring theory that Welsh sailors came here before Leif Ericson? . . . Something about Indians with blue or grey eyes . . ."

"You should know," Gaudior chided. "You were Within Madoc."

"It can't all have been real."

"Reality was different in those days," Gaudior said. "It was real for Madoc."

"Even the fire among the garlands?"

"Roses often burn. Theirs is the most purifying flame of all."

"And the scry—what Madoc saw in the water—was that a kind of Projection?"

The light in Gaudior's horn flickered. "Gwydyr was on the side of evil, and so he was open to the Projections of the Echthroi."

"So the terrible baby was a Projection the Echthroi want to have happen?"

"I'm never entirely sure about Projections," Gaudior admitted.

"And there was the other baby . . ." Charles Wallace closed his eyes to try to visualize the scry. "The blue-eyed baby, the answer to prayer, who was going to bring peace. So he's equally possible, isn't he?"

"It's all very confusing"—Gaudior shook his mane— "because we move in different dimensions, you and I."

Charles Wallace rubbed his fingers over his forehead as he had done in Meg's room. "It's all in the book somewhere. Why am I being blocked on that book?" The unicorn did not reply. "A book against war, a book about the legend of Madoc and Gwydyr, who came from Wales to this land . . . and what else? I can't get it . . ."

"Leave it alone," Gaudior advised.

Charles Wallace leaned against the unicorn, pressing his forehead against the silver hide, thinking out loud. "All we know is that a Welsh prince named Madoc did come to the New World with his brother Gwydyr and that Madoc married Zyll of the People of the Wind. Gaudior, if, unknowing, while I was Within Madoc I gave him, the rune, would that have been changing a Might-Have-Been?"

The unicorn replied unhelpfully, "It's all very complicated."

"Or—did Madoc have the rune himself? How could he, if it came from Ireland and St. Patrick?"

Gaudior raised his head and pulled back the dark silver of his lips in a ferocious grimace, baring his dangerous teeth. But all he did was open his mouth and drink wind as though quenching a terrible thirst.

Charles Wallace looked about, and as he looked, the scene rippled like the waters in the scrying oval on the beach, and the lake receded until he was looking across a wintry valley, and the rock was no longer a slightly tilted table but the flat star-watching rock, thinly crusted with snow.

Gaudior lowered his head and licked wind from his lips. "Gwydyr did not stay with the People Across the Lake."

"I wouldn't think he would, but how do you know?"

Gaudior raised tufted brows. "I have just been talking with the wind. Gwydyr left the lake in disgrace, and moved southward, ending up in South America."

Charles Wallace clapped his hand to his forehead. "That's it! It's in the book, too. Gwydyr going to Patagonia. And Vespugia is part of Patagonia. And there was a connection that was lost and had to be found, but what *was* it? I keep almost remembering, and then it's as if someone slams a door on my memory."

Gaudior sniffed. "Echthroi, probably. They'll try to block anything that might be a clue to the Might-Have-Been they don't want you to discover."

Charles Wallace nodded. "Mad Dog Branzillo was born in Vespugia. But right here, where we stand, Madoc came and married Zyll and made the roses burn for peace. What happened to the Wind People? Where are they now?"

"They were lovers of peace," Gaudior replied shortly. "Your planet does not deal gently with lovers of peace."

Charles Wallace sat on the rock, the thin rim of snow crackling beneath him. He put his head down on his knees. "I think I have to find out what the connection is between Wales and Vespugia, between Madoc and Gwydyr and Mad Dog Branzillo."

* * *

Meg stirred and opened her eyes. Her hand lay lightly on Ananda. "Such dreams, Fortinbras," she murmured, "such strange dreams." Her sleepy gaze drifted toward the clock and suddenly she was wide awake. "Ananda! For a moment I thought you were Fort. And it wasn't dreaming, was it? It was kything, but not clear and sharp, the way it was when Charles Wallace was Within Harcels. He was deeper Within Madoc, and so I have to dig deeper to find the kythe. And Charles wants me to find something out for him . . . but what?" She pushed her fingers through her hair, closed her eyes tightly, and concentrated, her hand pressing against Ananda. "Something about a lake . . . about burning roses . . . and two brothers fighting . . . yes . . . and Mad Dog Branzillo and Wales. That's it. He wants me to find a connection between Mad Dog Branzillo and Wales. And that hardly seems possible, much less likely." She listened to the sounds within the silence of the night, the sounds which were so familiar that they were part of the silence. The old house creaked comfortably. The wind brushed softly against the window.—Nobody's likely to be asleep, not tonight. And Sandy's a history buff. I'll go ask him.

She got out of bed, pushed her feet into furry slippers, and went downstairs. There was light shining under the door of the twins' room, so she knocked.

"What are you doing up, Sis?" Dennys asked. "You need your sleep."

"So do you, doc. I'm up for the same reason you are."

"I often study late," Dennys said. "What can we do for you?"

"What do you know about Vespugia?"

Dennys said, "With your hair down like that, you look about fifteen."

"I'm an old married woman. What about Vespugia?"

Sandy replied, "I was just reading about it in the encyclopedia. It's part of what used to be called Patagonia. Sort of between Argentina and Chile."

"Branzillo was born there?"

"Yes."

"Who colonized Vespugia?"

"Oh, the usual mishmash. Spaniards, a few English, and a group from Wales while it was still part of Patagonia."

Madoc was from Wales. She asked carefully, "Wales—when was that?"

"There's a legend that some Welshmen came to North America even before Leif Ericson, and that one of them went south, looking for a warm climate, and eventually settled in Vespugia—or where Vespugia is now. But that's only legend. However, it's fact that in 1865 a party left Wales for Patagonia and settled in the open wastelands near the Chubut River."

"So maybe Mad Dog Branzillo has some Welsh blood in him?"

"It's perfectly possible, although Branzillo hardly sounds Welsh."

"What year did you say the group left Wales?"

"1865."

"Are those the only times Wales is mentioned in connection with Vespugia?"

"In this encyclopedia."

She thought for a minute. "All right. What happened in 1865 that I ought to know about?"

Dennys said, "Meg, sit down if you're going to get Sandy to give you a history lesson. Is this something to do with being pregnant, like a passion for strawberries?"

"Raspberries. And I don't think it has much to do with being pregnant."

"Let me get *The Time Tables of History*." Sandy reached for the bookcase and pulled out a large and battered volume, and began turning the pages. "Aha. 1865. Appomatox was on April 9, and Lincoln was assassinated on the fourteenth. The Civil War ended on May 26."

"Quite a year."

"Yup. In England, Lord Palmerston died, and was succeeded as Prime Minister by Lord John Russell."

"I don't know much about him."

"And back to the once-more-United States, the Thirteenth Amendment abolished slavery."

"Would there have been slavery in Vespugia?"

"Not sure. Bolivar died in 1830, and his influence would likely have filtered through to Vespugia. So I doubt if there'd have been slaves."

"Well, good."

"Okay, and also in 1865 the Atlantic cable was finally completed. Oh, and here's something for you, Den: Lister caused a scandal by insisting on antiseptic surgery and using carbolic acid on a compound wound."

Dennys applauded. "You're almost as veritable an encyclopedia as Charles Wallace."

"Charles has it in his head and I have to look it up in a reference book. My sphere of knowledge is considerably more limited. Mendel came out with his law of heredity that year"—he peered down at the book again—"and the Ku Klux Klan was founded, and Edward Whymper climbed the Matterhorn. And Lewis Carroll wrote *Alice's Adventures in Wonderland*."

"Indeed, 1865 was quite a year," Dennys said. "What have you learned, Meg?"

"I think maybe a lot. Thanks, both of you."

"Get back into bed," Dennys chided. "You don't want to get chilled wandering around this drafty old barn in the middle of the night."

"I'm warm." She indicated her heavy robe and slippers. "I'm taking care. But thanks."

"If we made you some hot chocolate, would you drink it?"

"I'm off hot chocolate."

"Some consommé or bouillon?"

"No, thanks, really, I don't want anything. I'll get back into bed."

Sandy called after her, "And also in 1865 Rudyard Kipling was born, and Verlaine wrote *Poèmes saturniens*, and John Stuart Mill wrote *Auguste Comte and Positivism*, and Purdue, Cornell, and the universities of Maine were founded."

She waved back at him, then paused as he continued, "And Matthew Maddox's first novel, *Once More United*, was published."

She turned back, asking in a carefully controlled voice, "Maddox? I don't think I've ever heard of that author."

"You stuck to math in school."

"Yeah, Calvin always helped me with my English papers. Did this Matthew Maddox write anything else?"

Sandy flipped through the pages. "Let's see. Nothing in 1866, 1867. 1868, here we are, *The Horn of Joy*."

"Oh, that," Dennys said. "I remember him now. I had to take a lit course my sophomore year in college, and I took nineteenth-century American literature. We read that, Matthew Maddox's second and last book, *The Horn of Joy*. My prof said if he hadn't died he'd have been right up there with Hawthorne and James. It was a strange book, passionately antiwar, I remember, and it went way back into the past, and there was some weird theory of the future influencing the past—not my kind of book at all."

"But you remember it," Meg remarked.

"Yeah, I remember it, for some reason. There was a Welsh prince whose brothers were fighting for the throne. And he left Wales with one of his brothers, and was shipwrecked and landed somewhere on the New England coast. There was more, but I can't think of it right now."

"Thanks," Meg said. "Thanks a lot."

Ananda greeted her joyfully at the head of the stairs. Meg fondled the dog's floppy ear. "I really would have liked something hot to drink, but I didn't want Sandy and Dennys coming up to the attic and staying to talk when we have to concentrate on kything with Charles Wallace." She got back into bed and Ananda jumped up beside her and settled down. The clock's hands had moved ahead fifteen minutes, the length of time she had spent with Sandy and Dennys. And time was of the essence. But she felt that the trip downstairs had been worth it. She had found the author and the title of the book for Charles Wallace. And she had found a connection between Wales and Vespugia in 1865. But what did the connection mean? Madoc was Welsh, but he didn't go to Vespugia, he came here, and married here.

She shook her head. Maybe Charles Wallace and Gaudior could make something out of it.

And how any of this could connect with Mrs. O'Keefe was a mystery.

SIX

The lightning
with its rapid wrath

Thanks, Meg," Charles Wallace whispered. "Oh, Gaudior, she really did help us, she and the twins." He leaned forward to rest his cheek against the unicorn's neck. "The book was by Matthew Maddox. I don't think I ever read it, but I remember Dennys talking about it. And Mrs. O'Keefe was a Maddox, so she's got to be descended from Matthew."

"Descended," Gaudior snorted. "You make it sound like a fall."

"If you look at Mrs. O'Keefe, that's what it's like," Charles Wallace admitted. "1865. Can we go there?"

"Then," the unicorn corrected. "When. We can try, if you think it's important. We'll hope for a favorable wind."

Charles Wallace looked alarmed. "You mean we might get blown into another Projection?"

"It's always a risk. We know the Echthroi are after us, to stop us. So you must hold on."

"I'll hold on for dear life. The last thing I want is to get blown into another Projection."

Gaudior blew softly through his teeth. "I find our most recent information not very helpful."

"But it could be important, a group of Welshmen going to South America in 1865. I think we should try to go to Vespugia."

"That's a long way, and unicorns do not travel well to different Wheres. And to try to move in *both* space and time—I don't like it." He flicked his tail.

"Then how about trying to move to 1865, right here, the year Matthew Maddox published his first novel? Then we could try to move from 1865 here to 1865 in Vespugia. And maybe we could learn something from Matthew Maddox."

"Very well. It's less dangerous to go elsewhen first than to try to go elsewhen and elsewhere simultaneously." He began to gallop, and as he flung himself onto a gust of wind, the wings lifted and they soared upward.

The attack, just as they went through a shower of stars, was completely unexpected. A freezing gust blasted the wind on which they were riding, taking away Charles Wallace's breath. His knuckles whitened as he clenched the mane, which seemed to strengthen into steel wire to help him hold his grasp. He had a horrible sense of Gaudior battling with a darkness which was like an anti-unicorn, a flailing of negative wings and iron hoofs. The silver mane was torn from his hands as he was assailed by the horrible stench which accompanied Echthroi. Dark wings beat him from the unicorn's back and he felt the burning cold of outer space. This was more horrible than any Projection. His lungs cracked for lack of air. He would become a burnt-out body, a satellite circling forever the nearest sun . . .

A powerful wrench, and air rushed into his battered lungs. He felt a sharp tug at the nape of his neck, and the blue anorak tightened against his throat. The agonizing stench was gone and he was surrounded by the scent of unicorn breath, smelling of stars and frost. Gaudior was carrying him in his mouth, great ivory teeth clamped on the strong stuff of the anorak.

Gaudior's iridescent wings beat against the dark. Charles Wallace held his breath. If Gaudior dropped him, the Echthroi would be waiting. His armpits were cut from the pulling of the anorak, but he knew that he must not struggle. Gaudior's breath gusted painfully from between clenched teeth.

Then the silver hoofs touched stone, and they were safely at the star-watching rock. Gaudior opened his teeth and dropped the boy. For the first moments Charles Wallace was so weak that he collapsed onto the rock. Then he struggled to his feet, still trembling from the near disaster. He stretched his arms to ease his sore armpits and shoulders. Gaudior was breathing in great, panting gusts, his flanks heaving.

The soft breeze around them filled and healed their seared lungs.

Gaudior rolled his lips, and took a deep draught of clear air. Then he bent down and nuzzled Charles Wallace in the first gesture of affection he had shown. "I wasn't sure we were going to get away. The Echthroi are enraged that the wind managed to send you Within Madoc, and they're trying to stop you from going Within anyone else."

Charles Wallace stroked the unicorn's muzzle. "You saved me. I'd be tumbling in outer space forever if you hadn't grabbed my anorak."

"It was one chance in a million," Gaudior admitted. "And the wind helped me."

Charles Wallace reached up to put his arms around Gaudior's curving neck. "Even with help, it wasn't easy. Thank you."

Gaudior made a unicorn shrug; his curly beard quivered. "Unicorns find it embarrassing to be thanked. Please desist."

It was a hot, midsummer's day, with thunderheads massed on the horizon. The lake was gone, and the familiar valley stretched to the hills. The woods were a forest of mighty elms and towering oaks and hemlock. In the far distance was what looked like a cluster of log cabins.

"I don't think this looks like 1865," he told Gaudior.

"You'd know more about that than I would. I didn't have much opportunity to learn earth's history. I never expected this assignment."

"But, Gaudior, we have to know When we are."

"Why?"

Charles Wallace tried to quell his impatience, which was all the sharper after the terror of the attack. "If there's a Might-Have-Been we're supposed to discover, we have to know When it is, don't we?"

Gaudior's own impatience was manifested by prancing. "Why? We don't have to know everything. We have a charge laid on us, and we have to follow where it leads. You've been so busy trying to do the leading that we almost got taken by the Echthroi."

Charles Wallace said nothing.

"Perhaps," Gaudior granted grudgingly, "it wasn't entirely your fault. But I think we should not try to control the Whens and the Wheres, but should go Where we're sent. And what with all that contretemps with the Echthroi, you're still in your own body, and you're supposed to be Within."

"Oh. What should I do?"

Gaudior blew mightily through flared nostrils. "I will

have to ask the wind." And he raised his head and opened his jaws. Charles Wallace waited anxiously until the unicorn lowered his head and raised one wing, stretching it to its full span. "Step close to me," he ordered.

Charles Wallace moved under the wing and leaned against Gaudior's flank. "Did the wind say When we are?"

"You make too many demands," Gaudior chided, and folded his wing until Charles Wallace felt smothered. Gasping for breath, he tried to push his way out into the air, but the wing held him firmly, and at last his struggling ceased.

When he opened his eyes the day had vanished, and trees and rock were bathed in moonlight.

He was Within. Lying on the rock, looking up at the moon-bathed sky. Only the most brilliant stars could compete with the silver light. Around him the sounds of summer sang sweetly. A mourning dove complained from her place deep in the darkest shadows. A grandfather frog boomed his bull-call. A pure trilling of bird song made him sit up and call out in greeting, "Zylle!"

A young woman stepped out from the shadows of the forest. She was tall and slender, except for her belly, which was heavy with child. "Thanks for meeting me, Brandon."

Charles Wallace-within-Brandon Llawcae gave her a swift hug. "Anything I do with you is fun, Zylle."

Again, as when he was Within Harcels, he was younger than fifteen, perhaps eleven or twelve, still very much a child, an eager, intelligent, loving child.

In the moonlight she smiled at him. "The herbs I need to ease the birthing of my babe are found only when the moon is full, and only here. Ritchie fears it would offend Goody Adams, did she know."

Goody, short for Goodwife. That's what the Pilgrims said, instead of Mrs. This was definitely not 1865, then. More than a century earlier, perhaps even two centuries. Brandon Llawcae must be the son of early settlers . . .

"Let yourself go," Gaudior knelled. "Let yourself be Brandon."

"But why are we here?" Charles Wallace demurred. "What can we learn here?"

"Stop asking questions."

"But I don't want to waste time . . ." Charles Wallace said anxiously.

Gaudior whickered irritably. "You are here, and you are in Brandon. Let go."

Let go.

Be Brandon.

Be.

"So," Zylle continued, "it is best that Ritchie not know, either. I can always trust you, Brandon. You don't open your mouth and spill everything out when to do so would bring no good."

Brandon ducked his head shyly, then looked swiftly up at Zylle's eyes, which were a startling blue in her brown face. "I have learned from the People of the Wind that 'tis no harm to hold a secret in the heart."

Zylle sighed. "No, it is no harm. But it grieves me that you and I may not share our gifts with those we love."

"My pictures." Brandon nodded. "My parents want me to try not to see my pictures."

"Among my people," Zylle said, "you would be known as a Seer, and you would be having the training in prayer and trusting that would keep your gift very close to the gods, from whom the gift comes. My father had hoped that Maddok might have the gift, because it is rare to have two with blue eyes in one generation. But my little brother's gift is to know about weather, when to plant and when to harvest, and that is a good gift, and a needed one."

"I miss Maddok." Bran scowled down at the rock. "He never comes to the settlement any more."

Zylle placed her hand lightly on his shoulder. "It's different in the settlement now that there are more families. Maddok no longer feels welcome."

"I welcome him!"

"He knows that. And he misses you, too. But it isn't only that the settlement is larger. Maddok is older, and has to do more work at home. But he will always be your friend."

"And I'll always be his. Always."

"Your pictures—" Zylle looked at him intently. "Are you able to stop seeing them?"

"Not always. When I look at something that holds a reflection, sometimes the pictures come, whether I will or no. But I try not to ask them to come."

"When you see your pictures, it is all right to tell me what you see, the way you used to tell Maddok."

"Ritchie is afraid of them."

She pressed his shoulder gently. "Life has been nothing but hard work for Ritchie, with no time for seeing pictures or dreaming dreams. Your mother tells me that in Wales there are people who are gifted with the second sight, and that these people may be feared for their gift but they are not frowned on."

"Ritchie says I would be frowned on. It is different here than in Wales. Especially since Pastor Mortmain came and built the church and scowled whenever Maddok visited the settlement or I went to the Indian compound."

"Pastor Mortmain would try to separate the white people from the Indians."

"But *why?*" Brandon demanded. "We were friends."

"And still are," Zylle assured him. "When did you last see a picture?"

"Tonight," he told her. "I saw the reflection of a candle on the side of the copper kettle Mother had just polished, and I saw a picture of here, this very place, but the rock was much higher, and there"—he pointed to the valley—"it was all a lake, with the sun sparkling on the water."

She looked at him wonderingly. "My father, Zillo, says that the valley was once a lake bed."

"And I saw Maddok—at least, it wasn't Maddok, because he was older, and his skin was fair, but he looked so like Maddok, at first I thought it was."

"The legend," she murmured. "Oh, Brandon, I feel we are very close, you and I. Perhaps it is having to keep our gifts hidden that brings us added closeness." While they were talking she had been gathering a small plant that grew between the grasses. She held the blossoms out to the moonlight. "I know where to find the healing herbs, herbs that will keep babies from choking to death in the winter, or from dying of the summer sickness when the weather is hot and heavy as it is now. But your mother warns me that I must not offer these gifts; they would not be well received. But for myself, and the birthing of Ritchie's and my baby, I will not be without the herbs which will help give me a good birthing and a fine child." She began to spread the delicate blossoms on the rock. As the moonlight touched them, petals and leaf alike appeared to glow with inner silver. Zylle looked up at the moon and sang,

> "Lords of fire and earth and water,
> Lords of moon and wind and sky,
> Come now to the Old Man's daughter,
> Come from fathers long gone by.
> Bring blue from a distant eye.
>
> Lords of water, earth, and fire,
> Lords of wind and snow and rain,
> Give to me my heart's desire.
> Life as all life comes with pain,
> But blue will come to us again."

Then she knelt and breathed in the fragrance of the blossoms, took them up in her hands, and pressed them against her forehead, her lips, her breasts, against the roundness of her belly.

Brandon asked, "Do we take the flowers home with us?"

"I would not want Goody Adams to see them."

"When Ritchie and I were born, there wasn't a midwife in the settlement."

"Goody Adams is a fine midwife," Zylle assured him. "Had she been here, your mother might not have lost those little ones between you and Ritchie. But she would not approve of what I have just done. We will leave the birthing flowers here for the birds and moon and the wind. They have already given me their help."

"When—oh, Zylle, do you know when the baby will come?"

"Tomorrow." She stood. "It's time we went home. I would not want Ritchie to wake and find me not beside him."

Brandon reached for her long, cool fingers. "It was the best day in the world when Ritchie married you."

She smiled swiftly, concealing a shadow of worry in her eyes. "The people of the settlement look with suspicion on an Indian in their midst, and a blue-eyed Indian at that."

"If they'd only listen to our story that comes from Wales, and to your story—"

She pressed his fingers. "Ritchie warns me not to talk about our legend of the white man who came to us in the days when there were only Indians on this continent."

"Long ago?"

"Long, long ago. He came from across the sea, from a land at the other end of the world, and he was a brave man, and true, who lusted neither after power nor after land. My little brother is named after him."

"And the song?" Brandon asked.

"It's old, very old, the prayer for a blue-eyed baby to keep the strength of the prince from over the sea within the Wind People, and the words may have changed over the years. And I have changed, for I have made my life with the white people, as the Golden Prince made his with the Wind People. For love he stayed with the princess of a strange land, and made her ways his ways. For love I leave my people and stay with Ritchie, and my love is deep, deep, for me to be able to leave my home. I sing the prayer because it is in my blood, and must be sung; and yet I wonder if my child will be allowed to know the Indian half of himself?"

"He?"

"It will be a boy."

"How do you know?"

"The trees have told me in the turning of their leaves under the moonlight. I would like a girl baby, but Ritchie will be pleased to have a son."

The footpath through the grasses led them to a brook, which caught the light of the moon and glimmered in the shifting shadows of the leaves. The brook was spanned by a natural stone bridge, and here Zylle paused, looking down at the water.

Brandon, too, looked at their reflections shifting and shimmering as the wind stirred the leaves. While he looked at Zylle's reflection, the water stirring her mouth into a tender smile, he saw, too, a baby held close in her arms, a black-haired, blue-eyed baby with gold behind its eyes.

Then, while he gazed, the eyes changed in the child and turned sullen, and the face was no longer the face of a baby but the face of a man, and he could not see Zylle anywhere. The man wore a strange-looking uniform with many medals, and his jowls were dark, jutting pridefully. He was thinking to himself, and he was thinking cruel thoughts, vindictive thoughts, and then Brandon saw fire, raging fire.

His body gave a mighty shudder and he gasped and turned toward Zylle, then glanced fearfully at the brook. The fire was gone, and only their two faces were reflected.

She asked, "What did you see?"

Eyes lowered, gazing on the dark stone of the bridge, he told her, trying not to let the images reappear in his mind's eye.

She shook her head somberly. "I make nothing out of it. Certainly nothing good."

Still looking down, Brandon said, "Before I was made to feel afraid of my pictures, they were never frightening, only beautiful."

Zylle squeezed his hand reassuringly. "I'd like to tell my father about this one, for he is trained in the interpretation of visions."

Brandon hesitated, then: "All right, if you want to."

"I want him to give me comfort," she said in a low voice.

They turned from the brook and walked on home in silence, to the dusty clearing with its cluster of log cabins.

The Llawcaes' cabin was the first, a sizable building with a central room for sitting and eating, and a bedroom at either end. Brandon's room was a shed added to his parents' room, and was barely large enough to hold a small bed, a chest, and a chair. But it was all his, and Ritchie had promised that after the baby was born he would cut a fine window in the wall, as people were beginning to do now that the settlement was established.

Brandon's cubbyhole was dark, but he was used to his own room's night and moved in it as securely as though he had lit a candle. Without undressing, he lay down on the bed. In the distance the thunder growled, and with the thunder came an echo, a low, rhythmic rumbling which Brandon recognized as the drums of the Wind People as they sang their prayers for rain.

In the morning when he wakened, he heard bustling in the central room, and went in to find his mother boiling water in the big black kettle suspended from a large hook in the fireplace. Goody Adams, the midwife, was bustling about, exuding importance.

"This is a first birth," she said. "We'll need many kettles of water for the Indian girl."

"Zylle is our daughter," Brandon's mother reminded the midwife.

"Once an Indian, always an Indian, Goody Llawcae. Not forgetting that we're all grateful that her presence among us causes us to live in peace with the savage heathen."

"They're not—" Brandon started fiercely.

But his mother said, "The chores are waiting, Brandon."

Biting his lip, he went out.

The morning was clear, with a small mist drifting across the ground and hazing the outline of the hills. When the sun was full, the mist would go. The settlers were grateful for the mist and the heavy dews, which were all that kept the crops from drying up and withering completely, for there had been no rain for more than a moon.

Brandon went to the small barn behind the cabin to let their cow out into the daylight. She would graze with the other cattle all day, and at dusk Brandon would ride out on his pony to bring her home for milking. He gave the pony some oats, then fed the horse. In the distance he could hear hammering. Goodman Llawcae and his son Ritchie were the finest carpenters for many miles around, and were always busy with orders.

—I'm glad Ritchie didn't hear Goody Adams call

Zylle's people savage heathens, he thought.—It's a good thing he was in with Zylle. Then he started back to the house. The picture he had seen in the brook the night before troubled him. He was afraid of the dark man with cruel thoughts, and he was afraid of the fire. Since he had tried to repress the pictures, they had become more and more frightening.

When he reached the cabin and went in through the door, which was propped open to allow all the fresh air possible to enter, his mother came out of the bedroom and spoke to Ritchie, who was pacing up and down in front of the fireplace.

"Your father needs you, Ritchie. Zylle is resting now, between pains. I will call you at once should she need you."

Goody Adams muttered, "The Indian girl does not cry. It is an omen."

Ritchie flung back his head. "It is the mark of the Indian, Goody. Zylle will shed no tears in front of you."

"Heathen—" Goody Adams started.

But Goody Llawcae cut her short. "Ritchie. Brandon. Go to your father."

Ritchie flung out the door, not deigning to look at the midwife. Brandon followed him, calling, "Ritchie—"

Ritchie paused, but did not turn around.

"I hate Goody Adams!" Brandon exploded.

Now Ritchie looked at his young brother. "Hate never

did any good. Everyone in the settlement feels the lash of Goody Adams's tongue. But her hands bring out living babies, and there's been no childbed fever since she's been here."

"I liked it better when I was little and there was only us Llawcaes, and the Higginses, and Davey and I used to play with Maddok."

"It was simpler then," Ritchie agreed, "but change is the way of the world."

"Is change always good?"

Ritchie shook his head. "There was more joy when there were just the two families of us, and no Pastor Mortmain to put his dead hand on our songs and stories. I cannot find it in me to believe that God enjoys long faces and scowls at merriment. Get along with you now, Bran. I have work to do, and so do you."

When Brandon finished his chores and hurried back to the cabin, walking silently, one foot directly in front of the other, as Maddok had taught him, Ritchie, too, had returned, and was standing in the doorway. The sun was high in the sky and beat fiercely on the cabins and the dusty compound. The grass was turning brown, and the green leaves had lost their sheen.

Ritchie shook his head. "Not yet. It's fiercely hot. Look at those thunderheads."

"They've been there every day." Brandon looked at

the heavy clouds massed on the horizon. "And not a drop of rain."

A low, nearly inaudible moan came from the cabin, and Ritchie hurried indoors. From the bedroom came a sharp cry, and Brandon's skin prickled with gooseflesh, despite the heat. "Oh God, God, make Zylle be all right." He focused on one small cloud in the dry blue, and there he saw a picture of Zylle and the black-haired, blue-eyed baby. And as he watched, both mother and child changed, and the mother was still black-haired, but creamy of skin, and the baby was bronze-skinned and blue-eyed, and the joy in the face of the mother was the same as in the picture of Zylle. But the fair-skinned mother was not in the familiar landscape but in a wild, hot country, and her clothes were not like the homespun or leather he was accustomed to, but different, finer than clothes he had seen before.

The baby began to cry, but the cry came not from the baby in the picture but from the cabin, a real cry, the healthy squall of an infant.

Goody Llawcae came to the door, her face alight. "It's a nephew you have, Brandon, a bonny boy, and Zylle beaming like the sun. Though sorrow endure for a night, joy cometh in the morning."

"It's afternoon."

"Don't be so literal, lad. Run to let your father know. Now!"

"But when may I see Zylle and the baby?"

"After his grandfather has had the privilege. Run!"

When Goody Adams had at last taken herself off, the Llawcaes gathered about the mother and child. Zylle lay on the big carved bed which Richard Llawcae had made for her and Ritchie as a wedding present. Light from the door to the kitchen-living room fell across her as she held the newborn child in her arms. Its eyes were tightly closed, and it waved tiny fists in searching gestures, and its little mouth opened and closed as though it were sipping its strange new element, air.

"Oh, taste and see," Zylle murmured, and touched her lips softly to the dark fuzz on the baby's head. His copper skin was still moist from the effort of birth and the humidity of the day. In the distance, thunder growled.

"His eyes?" Brandon whispered.

"Blue. Goody Adams says the color of the eyes often changes, but Bran's won't. No baby could ask for a better uncle. May we name him after you?"

Brandon nodded, blushing with pleasure, and reached out with one finger to touch the baby's cheek.

Richard Llawcae opened the big, much-used Bible, and read aloud, "I love the Lord, because he hath heard my voice and my supplications. The sorrows of death compassed me, and the pains of hell gat hold upon me: I found trouble and sorrow. Then called I upon the name of the Lord. Gracious is the Lord, and righteous. I was brought low, and he helped me. Return unto thy rest, O my soul; for the Lord hath dealt bountifully with thee."

"Amen," Zylle said.

Richard Llawcae closed the Book. "You are my beloved daughter, Zylle. When Ritchie chose you for his betrothed, his mother and I were uncertain at first, as were your own people. But it seemed to your father, Zillo, and to me that two legends were coming together in this union. And time has taught us that it was a blessed inevitability."

"Thank you, Father." She reached out to his leathery hand. "Goody Adams did not like it that I shed no tears."

Goody Llawcae ran her hand gently over Zylle's shining black hair. "She knows that it is the way of your people."

—Savages, heathen savages, Brandon thought.—That's what Goody Adams thinks of Zylle's people.

When Bran went to do his evening chores a shadow materialized from behind the great trunk of a pine tree. Maddok.

Brandon greeted him with joy. "I'm glad, glad to see you! Father was going to send me to the Indian compound after chores, but now I can tell you: the baby's come! A boy, and all is well."

The shadow of a smile moved across Maddok's face, in which the blue eyes were as startling as they were in

Zylle. "My father will be glad. Your family will allow us to come tonight, to see the baby?"

"Of course."

Maddok's eyes clouded. "It's not 'of course.' Not any more."

"It is with us Llawcaes. Maddok—how did you know to come, just now?"

"I saw Zylle yesterday. She told me it would be today."

"I didn't see you."

"You weren't alone. Davey Higgins was with you."

"But you and Davey and I always played together. It was the three of us."

"Not any more. Davey has been forbidden to leave the settlement and come to the compound. Your medicine man's gods do not respect our gods."

Brandon let his breath out in a sigh that was nearly a groan. "Pastor Mortmain. It's not our gods that don't respect your gods. It's Pastor Mortmain."

Maddok nodded. "And his son is courting Davey's sister."

Brandon giggled. "I'd love to see Pastor Mortmain's face if he heard himself referred to as a medicine man."

"He is not a good medicine man," Maddok said. "He will cause trouble."

"He already has. It's his fault Davey can't see you."

Maddok looked intently into Brandon's eyes. "My father also sent me to warn you."

"Warn? Of what?"

"We have had runners out. In the town there is much talk of witchcraft."

Witchcraft. It was an ugly word. "But not here," Brandon said.

"Not yet. But there is talk among your people."

"What kind of talk?" Brandon asked sharply.

"My sister shed no tears during the birth."

"They know that it is the way of the Indian."

"It is also the mark of a witch. They say that a cat ran screaming through the street at the time of the birth, and that Zylle put her pain into the cat."

"That is nonsense." But Brandon's eyes were troubled.

"My father says there are evil spirits abroad, hardening men's hearts. He says there is lust to see evil in innocence. Brandon, my friend and brother, take care of Zylle and the baby."

"Zylle and I picked herbs for the birthing," Brandon said in a low voice.

"Zylle was taught all the ways of a good delivery, and she has the healing gifts. But that, too, would be looked upon as magic. Black magic."

"But it's not magic—"

"No. It is understanding the healing qualities of certain plants and roots. People are afraid of knowledge that is not yet theirs. My father is concerned for Zylle, and for you."

Brandon protested. "But we are known as God-loving people. Surely they couldn't think—"

"Because you are known as such, they will wish to think," Maddok said. "My father says you should go more with the other children of the settlement, where you can see and hear. It's better to be prepared. I, too, will keep my ears open." Without saying goodbye, he disappeared into the forest.

Late in the evening, when most of the settlement was sleeping, Zylle's people came through the woods, silently, in single file, approaching the cabin from behind, as Maddok had done in the afternoon.

They clustered around Zylle and the baby, were served Goody Llawcae's special cold herb tea, and freshly baked bread, fragrant with golden cheese and sweet butter.

Zillo took his grandson into his arms, and a shadow of tenderness moved across his impassive face. "Brandon, son of Zylle of the Wind People and son of Ritchie of Llawcae, son of a prince from the distant land of Wales; Brandon, bearer of the blue," he murmured over the sleeping baby, rocking him gently in his arms.

Out of the corner of his eye, Brandon saw one of the Indian women go to his mother, talking to her softly. His mother put her hand to her head in a worried gesture.

And before the Indians left, he saw Zillo take his father aside.

Despite his joy in his namesake, there was heaviness in his heart when he went to bed, and it was that, as much as the heat, which kept him from sleeping. He could hear his parents talking with Ritchie in the next room, and he shifted position so that he could hear better.

Goody Llawcae was saying, "People do not like other people to be different. It is hard enough for Zylle, being an Indian, without being part of a family marked as different, too."

"Different?" Ritchie asked sharply. "We were the first settlers here."

"We come from Wales. And Brandon's gift is feared."

Richard asked his wife, "Did one of the Indians give you a warning?"

"One of the women. I had hoped this disease of witch-hunting would not touch our settlement."

"We must try not to let it start with us," Goodman Llawcae said. "At least the Higginses will stand by us."

"Will they?" Ritchie asked. "Goodman Higgins seems much taken with Pastor Mortmain. And Davey Higgins hasn't come to do chores with Brandon in a long time."

Richard said, "Zillo warned me of Brandon, too."

"Brandon—" Goody Llawcae drew in her breath.

"He saw one of his pictures last night."

On hearing this, Brandon hurried into the big room. "Zylle told you!"

"She did not, Brandon," his father said, "and eavesdroppers seldom hear anything pleasant. You did give Zylle permission to speak to her father, and it was he who told me. Are you ashamed to tell us?"

"Ashamed? No, Father, not ashamed. I try not to ask for the pictures, because you don't want me to see them, and I know it disturbs you when they come to me anyhow. That is why I don't tell you. I thought you would prefer me not to."

His father lowered his head. "It is understandable that you should feel this way. Perhaps we have been wrong to ask you not to see your pictures if they are God's gift to you."

Brandon looked surprised. "Who else would send them?"

"In Wales it is believed that such gifts come from God. There is not as much fear of devils there as here."

"Zylle and Maddok say my pictures come from the gods."

"And Zillo warned me," his father said, "that you must not talk about your pictures in front of anybody, especially Pastor Mortmain."

"What about Davey?"

"Not anybody."

"But Davey knows about my pictures. When we were little, I used to describe them to Davey and Maddok."

The parents looked at each other. "That was long ago. Let's hope Davey has forgotten."

Ritchie banged his fist against the hard wood of the bedstead. Richard held up a warning hand. "Hush. You will wake your wife and son. Once the heat breaks, people's temperaments will be easier. Brandon, go back to bed."

Back in his room, Brandon tossed hotly on his straw pallet. Even after the rest of the household was quiet, he could not sleep. In the distance he heard the drums. But no rain came.

The next evening when he was bringing the cow home from the day's grazing, Davey Higgins came up to him. "Bran, Pastor Mortmain says I am not to speak to you."

"You're speaking."

"We've known each other all our lives. I will speak as long as I can. But people are saying that Zylle is preventing the rain. The crops are withering. We do not want to offend the Indians, but Pastor Mortmain says that Zylle's blue eyes prove her to be not a true Indian, and that the Indians were afraid of her and wished her onto us."

"You know that's not true!" Brandon said hotly. "The Indians are proud of the blue eyes."

"I know it," Davey said, "and you know it, but we are still children, and people do not listen to children. Pastor Mortmain has forbidden us to go to the Indian compound, and Maddok is no longer welcome here. My father believes everything Pastor Mortmain says, and my sister is being courted by his son, that pasty-faced Duth-

bert. Bran, what do your pictures tell you of all this?"
Davey gave Brandon a sidewise glance.

Brandon looked at him directly. "I'm twelve years old
now, Davey. I'm no longer a child with a child's pictures." He left Davey and took the cow to the shed, feeling that denying the pictures had been an act of betrayal.

Maddok came around the corner of the shed. "My father
has sent me to you, in case there is danger. I am to follow
you, but not be seen. But you know Indian ways, and
you will see me. So I wanted you to know, so that you
won't be afraid."

"I am afraid," Brandon said flatly.

"If only it would rain," Maddok said.

"You know about weather. Will it rain?"

Maddok shook his head. "The air smells of thunder,
but there will be no rain this moon. There is lightning in
the air, and it turns people's minds. How is Zylle? and
the baby?"

Now Brandon smiled. "Beautiful."

At family prayers that evening the Llawcae faces were
sober. Richard asked for wisdom, for prudence, for rain.
He asked for faithfulness in friendship, and for courage.
And again for rain.

The thunder continued to grumble. The heavy night
was sullen with heat lightning. And no drop fell.

* * *

The children would not talk with Brandon. Even Davey shamefacedly turned away. Mr. Mortmain, confronting Brandon, said, "There is evil under your roof. You had better see to it that it is removed."

When Brandon reported this, Ritchie exploded. "The evil is in Mr. Mortmain's own heart."

The evil was as pervasive as the brassy heat.

Pastor Mortmain came in the evening to the Llawcaes' cabin, bringing with him his son, Duthbert, and Goodman Higgins. "We would speak with the Indian woman."

"My wife—" Ritchie started, but his father silenced him.

"It is late for this visit, Pastor Mortmain," Richard said. "My daughter-in-law and the baby have retired."

"Then they must be wakened. It is our intention to discover if the Indian woman is a Christian, or—"

Zylle walked into the room, carrying her child. "Or what, Pastor Mortmain?"

Duthbert looked at her, and his eyes were greedy.

Goodman Higgins questioned her gently. "We believe you to be a Christian, Zylle. That is true, is it not?"

"Yes, Goodman Higgins. When I married Ritchie I accepted his beliefs."

"Even though they were contrary to the beliefs of your people?" Pastor Mortmain asked.

"But they are not contrary."

"The Indians are pagans," Duthbert said.

Zylle looked at the pasty young man over the baby's head. "I do not know what pagan means. I only know that Jesus of Nazareth sings the true song. He knows the ancient harmonies."

Pastor Mortmain drew in his breath in horror. "You say that our Lord and Saviour sings! What more do we need to hear?"

"But why should he not sing?" Zylle asked. "The very stars sing as they turn in their heavenly dance, sing praise of the One who created them. In the meeting house do we not sing hymns?"

Pastor Mortmain scowled at Zylle, at the Llawcaes, at his son, who could not keep his eyes off Zylle's loveliness, at Goodman Higgins. "That is different. You are a heathen and you do not understand."

Zylle raised her head proudly. "Scripture says that God loves every man. That is in the Psalms. He loves my people as he loves you, or he is not God."

Higgins warned, "You must not blaspheme, child."

"Why," demanded Pastor Mortmain, "are you holding back the rain?"

"Why ever should I wish to hold back the rain? Our corn suffers as does yours. We pray for rain, twice daily, at morning and at evening prayer."

"The cat," Duthbert said. "What about the cat?"

"The cat is to keep rodents away from house and barn, like all the cats in the settlement."

Pastor Mortmain said, "Goody Adams tells us the cat is to help you fly through the air."

Duthbert's mouth dropped slightly, and Ritchie shouted with outrage. But Zylle silenced him with a gesture, asking, "Does your cat help you to fly through the air, Pastor Mortmain? No more does mine. The gift of flying through the air is given to only the most holy of people, and I am only a woman like other women."

"Stop, child," Goodman Higgins ordered, "before you condemn yourself."

"Are you a true Indian?" Pastor Mortmain demanded.

She nodded. "I am of the People of the Wind."

"Indians do not have blue eyes."

"You have heard our legend."

"Legend?"

"Yes. Though we believe it to be true. My father has the blue eyes, too, as does my little brother."

"Lies!" Pastor Mortmain cried. "Storytelling is of the devil."

Richard Llawcae took a step toward the small, dark figure of the minister. "How strange that you should say that, Pastor Mortmain. Scripture says that Jesus taught by telling stories. *And he spake many things unto them in parables . . . and without a parable spake he not unto them.* That is in the thirteenth chapter of the Gospel according to Matthew."

Pastor Mortmain's face was hard. "I believe this Indian woman to be a witch. And if she is, she must die like a witch. That, too, is in Scripture." He gestured to Goodman Higgins and Duthbert. "We will meet in church and make our decision."

"Who will make the decision?" Ritchie demanded, not heeding his father's warning hand. "All the men of the settlement, in fair discussion, or you, Pastor Mortmain?"

"Be careful," Goodman Higgins urged. "Ritchie, take care."

"David Higgins," Richard Llawcae said, "our two cabins were the first in this settlement. You have known us longer than anyone else here. Do you believe that my son would marry a witch?"

"Not knowingly, Richard."

"You were here with us during the evenings when the Indians came to listen to our stories, and we heard their own legend that matched ours. You saw how the Indian legend and the Welsh one insured peace between us and the People of the Wind, did you not, now, David?"

"Yes, that is so."

Pastor Mortmain intervened. "Goodman Higgins has told me of the storytelling which preceded the sop of reading from Scripture."

"Scripture was never a sop for us, Pastor. Those early years were hard. Goody Higgins died birthing Davey, and after her death in one week three of David's children died of diphtheria, and another only a year later coughed his life away. My wife lost four little ones between Richard and Brandon, one at birth, the other three as children. We were sustained and strengthened by Scripture then, as we are still. As for the stories, the winter evenings were long, and it was a pleasant way to while away the time as we worked with our hands."

Goodman Higgins shuffled his feet. "There was no harm in the stories, Pastor Mortmain. I have assured you of that."

"Perhaps not for you," Pastor Mortmain said. "Come."

Goodman Higgins did not look up as he followed Pastor Mortmain and Duthbert out of the cabin.

Nightmare. Brandon wanted to scream, to make himself wake up, but he was not asleep, and the nightmare was happening. When he did his chores he was aware that Maddox was invisibly there, watching over him. Sometimes he heard him rustling up in the branches of a tree. Sometimes Maddok let Brandon have a glimpse of him behind a tree trunk, behind the corner of a barn or cabin. But wherever he went, Maddok was there, and that meant that the Indians knew all that was happening.

A baby in the settlement died of the summer sickness, which had always been the chief cause of infant mortality during the hot months, but it was all that was needed to convict Zylle.

Pastor Mortmain sent to the town for a man who was said to be an expert in the detection of witches. He had sent many people to the gallows.

"And that's supposed to make him an expert?" Ritchie demanded.

The settlement crackled with excitement. It seemed to Brandon that people were enjoying it. The Higgins daughter walked along the dusty street with Duthbert, and did not raise her eyes, but Pastor Mortmain's son smiled, and it was not a pleasant smile. People lingered in their doorways, staring at Pastor Mortmain and the expert on witches as they stood in front of the church. Davey Higgins stayed in his cabin and did not come out, though the other children were as eager as their parents to join in the witch hunt.

It was part of the nightmare when the man from the city who had hanged many people gave Pastor Mortmain and the elders of the village his verdict: there was no doubt in his mind that Zylle was a witch.

A sigh of excitement, of horror, of pleasure, went along the street.

That evening when Brandon went to the common pasture to bring the cow home, one of the other boys spat on the ground and turned away. Davey Higgins, tying the halter on the Higgins cow, said, "It is the Lord's will that the witch should die."

"Zylle is not a witch."

"She's a heathen."

"She's a Christian. A better one than you are."

"She's a condemned witch, and tomorrow they take her to the jail in town, though she'll be brought back here to be hanged—"

"So we can all see." One of the boys licked his lips in anticipation.

"No!" Brandon cried. "No!"

Davey interrupted him. "You'd better hold your tongue, or I could tell things about you to make Pastor Mortmain condemn you as a witch, too."

Brandon looked levelly at Davey while the others teased him to tell.

Davey flushed. "No. I didn't mean anything. Brandon is my friend. It's not his fault his brother married a witch."

"How could you let them take Zylle and the baby away?" Brandon demanded of Ritchie and his parents. "How could you!"

"Son," Richard Llawcae said, "Zylle is not safe here, not now with feelings running high. There are those who would hang her immediately. Your brother and I are going to town tomorrow to speak to people we know there. We think they will help us."

But the witch-hunting fever was too high. There was no help. There was no reason. There was only nightmare.

Goody Llawcae stayed in the town to tend Zylle and the baby; that much was allowed, but it was not through kindness; there were those who feared that Zylle might try to take her own life, or that something might happen to prevent them seeing a public hanging.

Richard and Ritchie refused to erect the gallows.

Avoiding their eyes, Goodman Higgins pleaded, "You must not refuse to do this, or you, too, will be accused. In the town they have convicted entire families."

Richard said, "There was another carpenter, once, and he would have refused to do this thing. Him I will follow."

There were others more than willing to erect a crude gallows. A gallows is more easily built than a house, or a bed, or a table.

The date for the hanging was set.

On the eve, Brandon went late to bring the cow in from the pasture, in order to avoid the others. When he got to the barn. Maddok was waiting there in the shadows.

"My father wants to see you."

"When?" Bran asked.

"Tonight. After the others are asleep, can you slip away without being seen?"

Bran nodded. "You have taught me how to do that. I will come. It has meant much to me to know that you have been with me."

"We are friends," Maddok said without a smile.

"Is it going to rain soon?" Brandon asked.

"No. Not unless prayer changes things."

"You pray every night. So do we."

"Yes. We pray," Maddok said, and slipped silently into the woods.

In the small hours of the morning, before dawn, when he was sure everybody in the settlement would be asleep, Brandon left the cabin and ran swiftly as a young deer into the protecting shadows of the woods.

Maddok was standing at the edge of the forest, waiting. "Come. I know the way in the dark more easily than you."

"Zillo knows everything? You've told him?"

"Yes. But he wants to meet with you."

"Why? I'm still only a child."

"You have the gift of seeing."

Brandon shivered.

"Come," Maddok urged. "My father is waiting."

They traveled swiftly, Brandon following Maddok as he led the way, over the brook, through the dark shadows of the forest.

At the edge of the Indian clearing, Zillo stood. Maddok nodded at his father, then vanished into the shadows.

"You won't let it happen?" Brandon begged. "If Zylle is harmed, Ritchie will kill."

"We will not let it happen."

"The men of the settlement expect the Indians to

come. They have guns. They are out of their right minds, and they will not hesitate to shoot."

"They must be prevented. Have you seen anything in a vision lately?"

"I have tried not to. I am afraid."

"No one knows you are here?"

"Only Maddok."

Zillo pulled a polished metal sphere from a small pouch and held it out to catch the light of the late moon. "What do you see?"

Brandon hesitantly looked into it. "This is right for me to do, when my father . . . ?"

Zillo's eyes were expressionless. "I have held this action in prayer all day. It is not your father's wish to deny a gift of the gods, and at this time we have no one in the tribe with the gift of seeing."

As Brandon looked, the light in the metal sphere shifted, and he saw clouds moving swiftly across the sky, clouds reflected in water. Not taking his eyes from the scrying metal he said, "I see a lake where the valley should be, a lake I have seen before in a picture. It is beautiful."

Zillo nodded. "It is said there was a lake here in long-gone days. In the valley people have found stones with the bones of fish in them."

"The sky is clouding up," Brandon reported. "Rain is starting to fall, spattering into the water of the lake."

"You see no fire?"

"Before, I saw fire, and I was afraid. Now there is only rain."

The severity of Zillo's face lifted barely perceptibly.

"That is good, that picture. Now I will teach you some words. You must learn them very carefully, and you must make sure that you do not use them too soon. Only the blue-eyed children of the Wind People are taught these words, and never before have they been given to one not of the tribe. But I give them to you for Zylle's saving."

On the morning of the execution Zylle was returned to the settlement. Infant Brandon was taken from her and given to Goody Llawcae.

"He is too young to be weaned," Goody Llawcae objected. "He will die of the summer sickness."

"The witch will not harm her own child," Pastor Mortmain said.

It took six of the strongest men in the settlement to restrain Ritchie and Richard.

"Tie the witch's hands," the man from the city ordered.

"I will do it," Goodman Higgins said. "Hold out your hands, child."

"Show her no gentleness, Higgins," Pastor Mortmain warned, "unless you would have us think you tainted, too. After all, you have listened to their tales."

Goody Llawcae, holding the crying baby, said, "Babies

have died of the summer sickness for years, long before Zylle came to dwell among us, and no one thought of witchcraft."

Angry murmurs came from the gathered people. "The witch made another baby die. Let her brat die as well."

Ritchie, struggling compulsively, nearly broke away.

Pastor Mortmain said, "When the witch is dead, you will come back to your senses. We are saving you from the evil."

The people of the settlement crowded about the gallows in ugly anticipation of what was to come. Davey Higgins stayed in the doorway of his cabin.

Goodman Higgins and Pastor Mortmain led Zylle across the dusty compound and up the steps to the gallows.

Brandon thought his heart would beat its way out of his body. He felt a presence beside him, and there was Maddok, and he knew that the rest of the tribe was close by.

"Now," Maddok whispered.

And then Brandon cried aloud the words which Zillo had taught him.

> "With Zylle in this fateful hour
> I call on all Heaven with its power
> And the sun with its brightness,
> And the snow with its whiteness,
> And the fire with all the strength it hath,
> And the lightning with its rapid wrath—"

Thunderstorms seldom came till late afternoon. But suddenly the sky was cleft by a fiery bolt, and the church bore the power of its might. The crash of thunder was almost simultaneous. The sky darkened from a humid blue to a sulfurous dimness. Flame flickered about the doorway of the church.

The Indians stepped forward until the entire settlement was aware of their presence, silent and menacing. Several men raised guns. As Duthbert fired, lightning flashed again and sent Duthbert sprawling, a long burn down his arm, his bullet going harmlessly into the air. Flames wreathed the belfry of the church.

Zillo sprang across the compound and up the steps to the gallows. "No guns," he commanded, "or the lightning will strike again. And this time it will kill."

Duthbert was moaning with pain. "Put down the guns—don't shoot—"

Pastor Mortmain's face was distorted. "You are witches, all of you, witches! The Llawcae boy has the Indian girl's devil with him that he can call lightning! He must die!"

The Indians drew in closer. Maddok remained by Brandon. And then Davey Higgins came from the door of his cabin and stood on Brandon's other side.

Ritchie broke away from the men who were holding him, and sprang up onto the gallows. "People of the settlement!" he cried. "Do you think all power is of the devil? What we have just seen is the wrath of God!"

He turned his back on the crowd and began to untie Zylle.

The mood of the people was changing. Richard was let loose and he crossed the dusty compound to Pastor Mortmain. "Your church is burning because you tried to kill an innocent woman. Our friends and neighbors would never have consented to this madness had you not terrified them with your fire and brimstone."

Goodman Higgins moved away from Pastor Mortmain. "That is right. The Llawcaes have always been God-fearing people."

The Indians drew closer.

Ritchie had one arm about Zylle. He called out again: "The Indians have always been our friends. Is this how we return their friendship?"

"Stop them—" Pastor Mortmain choked out. "Stop the Indians! They will massacre us—stop them—"

Ritchie shouted, "Why should we? Do you want us to show you more compassion than you have shown us?"

"Ritchie!" Zylle faced him. "You are not like Pastor Mortmain. You have a heart in you. Show them your compassion!"

Zillo raised a commanding hand. "This evil has been stopped. As long as nothing like this ever happens again, you need not fear us. But it must never happen again."

Murmurs of "Never, never, we are sorry, never, never," came from the crowd.

Pastor Mortmain moaned, "The fire, the fire, my God, the church, the church is burning."

Ritchie led Zylle down the steps and to his mother, who put the baby into her daughter-in-law's waiting arms. Brandon, standing between Maddok and Davey, watched as his mother and Zylle, his father and brother, turned their backs on the burning church and walked across the compound, past their chastened neighbors, past the watchful Indians, and went into their cabin. He stayed, his feet rooted to the ground as though he could not move, while the people of the settlement brought ineffectual buckets of water to try to control the flames and keep the fire from spreading to the cabins around the church. He watched the belfry collapse, a belfry erected more to the glory of Pastor Mortmain than to the glory of God.

And then he felt the rain, a gentle rain which would fall all day and sink into the thirsty ground, a rain which would continue until the deepest roots of plant and tree had their chance to drink. A rain which put out the fire before it spread to any of the dwellings.

Behind the three boys the People of the Wind stood silently, watching, as the people went slowly into their cabins. When there was no one left by the empty gallows except the three children, Zillo barked a sharp command and the Indians quickly dismantled the ill-built platform and gallows, threw the wood on the smoking remains of the church, and left, silently.

* * *

The horror was over, but nothing would ever be the same again.

When Brandon and Maddok went into the Llawcae cabin, Zillo was there, holding the baby. The kettle was simmering, and Goody Llawcae was serving herb tea, "to quieten us."

"I am angry." Ritchie looked past Brandon to his mother. "Your herbs will not stop my anger."

"You have cause to be angry," his father said. "Anger is not bitterness. Bitterness can go on eating at a man's heart and mind forever. Anger spends itself in its own time. Small Brandon will help to ease the anger."

Zillo handed the baby to Ritchie, who took his son and held him against his strong shoulder. Ritchie looked, then, at his brother. "Where did you get those words you called out just before the storm?"

"From Zillo."

"When?"

"Last night. He sent for me."

Zillo looked at Richard and Ritchie, his eyes fathomless. "He is a good lad, your young one."

Richard Llawcae returned Zillo's gaze, and put his arm lightly around Brandon's shoulders. "The ways of the Lord are mysterious, and we do not need to understand them. His ways are not our ways—though we would like them to be. We do not need to understand Brandon's gifts, only to know that they are given to him by God." He turned to the Bible and leafed through the pages until he had found the passage he wanted. "The Lord is faithful, who shall establish you, and keep you from evil. And the Lord direct your hearts into the love of God. Now the Lord of peace himself give you peace always by all means . . ."

Brandon, worn out by lack of sleep, by terror and tension, put his head down on his arms and slid into sleep, only half hearing as Ritchie said that he could not continue to live in the settlement. He would take Zylle and the baby and return to Wales, where they could start a new life . . .

The world was bleak for Brandon when Ritchie and Zylle and the baby left.

One day as he was doing his chores, Maddok appeared, helped him silently, and then together they went through the woods toward the Indian compound.

Under the great shadowing branches of an oak, Maddok paused. He looked long at Brandon. "It is right that Zylle should have gone with Ritchie."

Brandon looked at Maddok, then at the ground.

"And it is right that you and I should become brothers. My father will perform the ceremony tonight, and you will be made one of the People of the Wind."

A spark of the old light appeared in Brandon's face. "Then no one can keep us apart."

"No one. And perhaps you will marry one of the People of the Wind. And perhaps our children will marry, so that our families will be united until eternity."

Brandon reached for Maddok's hands. "Until eternity," he said.

SEVEN

The winds with their swiftness

And Charles Wallace was on Gaudior's back.

"I've read about the Salem trials, of course," he mused aloud. "Is there—oh, Gaudior, do other planets have the same kind of horror as ours?"

"There are horrors wherever the Echthroi go."

"Brandon: he's younger than I. And yet—am I like Brandon? Or is he like me?"

"I do not think you would be accepted by a host who is alien to what you are—Gwydyr, for instance."

"I hate to think I caused Brandon so much pain—"

"Do not take too much on yourself," Gaudior warned. "We don't know what would have happened had you not been Within Brandon."

"What did we learn Within? It's a strange triangle: Wales and here; Wales and Vespugia; Vespugia and here. It's all interconnected, and we have to find the connections—

oh!" He stepped back from Gaudior with a startled flash of comprehension.

"What now?" Gaudior asked.

Charles Wallace's voice rose with excitement. "When Madoc is spelled the Welsh way, it's Madog! Get it?"

Gaudior blew a small bubble.

"Madog. Mad Dog. It's a play on words. Mad Dog Branzillo may really be Madog. El Rabioso. Mad Dog. It's a ghastly sort of pun. Madoc: Madog: Mad Dog."

The unicorn looked down his long nose. "You may have something there."

"So there's another connection! Gaudior, we have to go to Patagonia, to Vespugia. I understand that it isn't easy for unicorns to move in both time and space, but you've got to try."

Gaudior raised his wings and stretched them up toward the sky. "The last time we gave explicit directions to the wind, look what happened."

"We didn't get to 1865. But we did learn important things about Madoc's descendants."

"Is that all you remember?" The unicorn folded his wings.

"It's in the book, Matthew Maddox's—"

"Somehow or other," Gaudior said, "we are blundering closer and closer to the Might-Have-Been which the Echthroi don't want us to get to, and the closer we get, the more they will try to prevent us. Already you have changed small things, and they are angry."

"What have I changed?"

"Don't you know?"

Charles Wallace bowed his head. "I tried to stop Harcels from seeing the ways of other men."

"And . . ."

"Zylle—I tried to stop them from hanging her. Would she have been hanged—without the rune?"

"There are many things unicorns do not feel they need to know."

"And there are some things we do need to know if we're to succeed in doing what Mrs. O'Keefe asked me to do." For a moment he looked startled, remembering Calvin's mother. "How strange that it should have come from Mrs. O'Keefe—the charge. And the rune."

"That should teach you something."

"It does. It teaches me that we have to go to Vespugia to find the connection between Mom O'Keefe and Mad Dog Branzillo."

The light in Gaudior's horn flickered rapidly.

"I know—" Charles Wallace stroked the unicorn's neck. "The Echthroi nearly got us when we were aiming for 1865 in our own Where. Perhaps we have to leave the star-watching rock and aim for 1865 in Patagonia, when the Welsh group arrived there. Perhaps they met Gwydyr's descendants. I think we have no choice now except to go to Patagonia."

"They may attack us again." Gaudior's anxious neigh broke into silver shards. "It might be a good idea for you to tie yourself to me. If the Echthroi tear you from my back again, it isn't likely that I'd be able to catch you a second time."

Charles Wallace looked all around him, carefully, and saw nothing but the woods, the rock, the valley, the mountains beyond. Then: "I know!" He slid off Gaudior's back to the rock. "I forgot to bring in the hammock this autumn. Meg usually does it. It's just a few yards along the path, between two old apple trees. It's a woven rope one, and it's hung on good stout laundry rope, from Mortmain's General Store—Mortmain! Gaudior, do you suppose—"

"We don't have time for suppositions," Gaudior warned. "Bind yourself to me."

Charles Wallace hurried along the path, with the unicorn following, prancing delicately as bare blackberry canes reached across the path and tore at his silver hide.

"Here we are. Mother likes the hammock to be far away from the house so that she can't possibly hear the telephone." He started untying one end of the hammock. The branches of the apple trees were bare of leaves, but a few withered apples still clung palely to the topmost branches. The earth around the trees and under the hammock smelled of cider vinegar and mulching leaves.

"Make haste slowly," Gaudior advised, as Charles Wallace's trembling fingers fumbled with the knots. The air was cold, and the unicorn bent his neck so that he could breathe on Charles Wallace's fingers to warm them. "Think only about untying the knots. The Echthroi are near."

Warmed by the unicorn's breath, the boy's fingers began to lose their stiffness, and he managed to untie the first knot. Two more knots, and one end of the hammock dropped to the leafy ground, and Charles Wallace moved to the second tree, where the hammock seemed even more firmly secured to the gnarled trunk. He worked in silence until the hammock was freed. "Kneel," he told the unicorn.

Charles Wallace dragged one end of the hammock under the unicorn, so that the heavy webbing was under Gaudior's great abdomen. With difficulty he managed to fling the rope up over Gaudior's flanks. He clambered up and bound the rope securely around his waist. "It's a good thing Mother always uses enough rope for five hammocks."

Gaudior whickered. "Are you tied on securely?"

"I think so. The twins taught me to make knots."

"Hold on to my mane, too."

"I am."

"I don't like this," Gaudior objected. "Are you sure you think we ought to try to go to Patagonia?"

"I think it's what we have to do."

"I'm worried." But Gaudior began to run, until he had gathered enough speed to launch himself.

The attack came almost immediately, Echthroi surrounding boy and unicorn. Charles Wallace's hands were torn from Gaudior's mane, but the rope held firm. The breath was buffeted out of him, and his eyelids were sealed tight against his eyes by the blasting wind, but the Echthroi did not succeed in pulling him off Gaudior's back. The rope strained and groaned, but the knots held.

Gaudior's breath came in silver streamers. He had folded his wings into his flanks to prevent the Echthroid wind from breaking them. Boy and unicorn were flung through endless time and space.

A cold, stenching wind picked them up and they were flung downward with a violence over which the unicorn had no control. Helplessly they descended toward a vast darkness.

They crashed.

They hit with such impact that Charles Wallace thought fleetingly, just before he lost consciousness, that the Echthroi had flung them onto rock and this was the end.

But the descent continued. Down down into blackness

and cold. No breath. A feeling of strangling, a wild ringing in the ears. Then he seemed to be rising, up, up, and light hit his closed eyes with the force of a blow, and clear cold air rushed into his lungs. He opened his eyes.

It was water and not rock they had been thrown against.

"Gaudior!" he cried, but the unicorn floated limply on the surface of the darkness, half on his side, so that one of Charles Wallace's legs was still in the water. The boy bent over the great neck. No breath came from the silver nostrils. There was no rise and fall of chest, no beat of heart. "Gaudior!" he cried in anguish. "Don't be dead! Gaudior!"

Still, the unicorn floated limply, and small waves plashed over his face.

"Gaudior!" With all his strength Charles Wallace beat against the motionless body.—The rune, he thought wildly,—the rune . . .

But no words came, except the unicorn's name. "Gaudior! Gaudior!"

A trembling stirred the silver body, and then Gaudior's breath came roaring out of him like an organ with all the stops pulled out. Charles Wallace sobbed with relief. The unicorn opened eyes which at first were glazed, then cleared and shone like diamonds. He began to tread water. "Where are we?"

Charles Wallace bent over the beautiful body, stroking neck and mane in an ecstasy of relief. "In the middle of an ocean."

"Which ocean?" Gaudior asked testily.

"I don't know."

"It's your planet. You're supposed to know."

"Is it my planet?" Charles Wallace asked. "The Echthroi had us. Are you sure we aren't in a Projection?"

Unicorn and boy looked around. The water stretched to the horizon on all sides. Above them the sky was clear, with a few small clouds.

"It's not a Projection." Gaudior whickered. "But we could be anywhere in Creation, on any planet in any galaxy which has air with oxygen and plenty of water. Does this seem to you like an ordinary earth ocean?" He shook his head, and water sprayed out from his mane. "I am not thinking clearly yet . . ." He gulped air, then regurgitated a large quantity of salt water. "I have drunk half this ocean."

"It looks like a regular ocean," Charles Wallace said tentatively, "and it feels like winter." His drenched anorak clung to his body in wet folds. His boots were full of water, which sloshed icily against his feet. "Look!" He pointed ahead of them to a large crag of ice protruding from the water. "An iceberg."

"Which direction is land?"

"Gaudior, if we don't even know what galaxy or

planet we're on, how do you expect me to know where land is?"

With difficulty Gaudior stretched his wings to their fullest extent, so that they shed water in great falls that splashed noisily against the waves. His legs churned with a mighty effort to keep afloat.

"Can you fly?" Charles Wallace asked.

"My wings are waterlogged."

"Can't you ask the wind where we are?"

A shudder rippled along the unicorn's flanks. "I'm still half winded—the wind—the wind—we hit water so hard it's a wonder all our bones aren't broken. The wind must have cushioned our fall. Are you still tied on?"

"Yes, or I wouldn't be here. Ask the wind, please."

"Winded—the wind—the wind—" Again Gaudior shook water from his wings. He opened his mouth in his characteristic gesture of drinking, gulped in the cold, clear breeze, his lips pulled back to reveal the dangerous-looking teeth. He closed his eyes and his long lashes were dark against his skin, which had paled to the color of moonlight. He opened his eyes and spat out a great fountain of water. "Thank the galaxies."

"Where are we?"

"Your own galaxy, your own solar system, your own planet. Your own Where."

"You mean this is the place of the star-watching rock? Only it's covered by an ocean?"

"Yes. And the wind says it's midsummer."

Charles Wallace looked at the iceberg. "It's a good thing it's summer, or we'd be dead from cold. And summer or no, we'll die of cold if we don't get out of water and onto land, and soon."

Gaudior sighed. "My wings are still heavy with water and my legs are tiring."

A wave dashed over them. Charles Wallace swallowed a mouthful of salty water and choked, coughing painfully. His lungs ached from the battering of the Echthroid wind and the cold of the sea. He was desperately sleepy. He thought of travelers lost in a blizzard, and how in the end all they wanted was to lie down in the snow and go to sleep, and if they gave in to sleep they would never wake up again. He struggled to keep his eyes open, but it hardly seemed worth the effort.

Gaudior's legs moved more and more slowly. When the next wave went over them, the unicorn did not kick back up to the surface.

As water and darkness joined to blot out Charles Wallace's consciousness, he heard a ringing in his ears, and through the ringing a voice calling, "The rune, Chuck! Say it! Say the rune!"

But the weight of the icy water bore him down.

Ananda's frantic whining roused Meg.

"Say it, Charles!" she cried, sitting bolt-upright.

Ananda whined again, then gave a sharp bark.

"I'm not sure I remember the words—" Meg pressed both hands against the dog, and called out,

> "With Ananda in this fateful hour
> I place all Heaven with its power
> And the sun with its brightness,
> And the snow with its whiteness,
> And the fire with all the strength it hath,
> And the lightning with its rapid wrath,
> And the winds with their swiftness along their path . . ."

The wind lifted and the whitecaps were churned into rolling breakers, and unicorn and boy were raised to the surface of the water and caught in a great curling comber and swept along with it across the icy sea until they were flung onto the white sands of dry land.

EIGHT

The sea with its deepness

Unicorn and boy vomited sea water and struggled to breathe, their lungs paining them as though they were being slashed by knives. They were sheltered from the wind by a cliff of ice onto which the sun was pouring, so that water was streaming down in little rivulets. The warmth of the sun which was melting the ice also melted the chill from their sodden bodies, and began to dry the unicorn's waterlogged wings. Gradually their blood began to flow normally and they breathed without choking on salt water.

Because he was smaller and lighter (and billions of years younger, Gaudior pointed out later), Charles Wallace recovered first. He managed to wriggle out of the still-soaking anorak and drop it down onto the wet sand. Then with difficulty he kicked off the boots. He looked at the ropes which still bound him to the unicorn; the knots were pulled so tight and the cord was by now so sodden that it was impossible to untie himself. Exhausted, he bent over Gaudior's neck and felt the healing sun send its rays deep into his body. Warmed and soothed, his nose pressed against wet unicorn mane, he fell into sleep, a deep, life-renewing sleep.

When he awoke, Gaudior was stretching his wings out to the sun. A few drops of water still clung to them, but the unicorn could flex them with ease.

"Gaudior," Charles Wallace started, and yawned.

"While you were sleeping," the unicorn reproved gently, "I have been consulting the wind. Praise the Music that we're in the When of the melting of the ice or we could not have survived." He, too, yawned.

"Do unicorns sleep?" Charles Wallace asked.

"I haven't needed to sleep in aeons."

"I feel all the better for a nap. Gaudior, I'm sorry."

"For what?"

"For making you try to get us to Patagonia. If I hadn't, we might not have been nearly killed by the Echthroi."

"Apology accepted," Gaudior said briskly. "Have you learned?"

"I've learned that every time I've tried to control things we've had trouble. I don't know what we ought to do now, or Where or When we ought to go from here. I just don't know . . ."

"I think"—Gaudior turned his great head to look at the boy—"that our next step is to get all these knots untied."

Charles Wallace ran his fingers along the rope. "The knots are all sort of welded together from wind and water and sun. I can't possibly untie them."

Gaudior wriggled against the pressure of the ropes. "They appear to have shrunk. I am very uncomfortable."

After a futile attempt at what looked like the most pliable of the knots, Charles Wallace gave up. "I've got to find something to cut the rope."

Gaudior trotted slowly up and down the beach. There were shells, but none sharp enough. They saw a few pieces of rotting driftwood, and some iridescent jellyfish and clumps of seaweed. There were no broken bottles or tin cans or other signs of mankind, and while Charles Wallace was usually horrified at human waste and abuse of nature, he would gladly have found a broken beer bottle.

Gaudior turned inland around the edge of the ice cliff, moving up on slipping sand runneled by melting ice. "This is absurd. After all we've been through, who would have thought I'd end up like a centaur with you permanently affixed to my back?" But he continued to struggle up until he was standing on the great shoulder of ice.

"Look!" Charles Wallace pointed to a cluster of silvery plants with long spikes which had jagged teeth along the sides. "Do you think you could bite one of those off, so I can saw the rope with it?"

Gaudior splashed through puddles of melted ice, lowered his head, and bit off one of the spikes as close to the root as his large teeth permitted. Holding it between his teeth he twisted his head around until Charles Wallace, straining until the rope nearly cut off his breath, managed to take it from him.

Gaudior wrinkled his lips in distaste. "It's repellent. Careful, now. Unicorn's hide is not as strong as it looks."

"Stop fidgeting."

"It itches." Gaudior flung his head about with uncontrollable and agonized laughter. "Hurry."

"If I hurry I'll cut you. It's coming now." He moved the plant-saw back and forth with careful concentration, and finally one of the ropes parted. "I'll have to cut one more, on the other side. The worst is over now."

But when a second rope was severed, Charles Wallace was still bound to the unicorn, and the plant was limp and useless. "Can you bite off another spike?"

Gaudior bit and grimaced. "Nothing really has to taste that disagreeable. But then, I am not accustomed to any food except starlight and moonlight."

At last the ropes were off boy and beast, and Charles Wallace slid to the surface of the ice cliff. Gaudior was attacked by a fit of sneezing, and the last of the sea water flooded from his nose and mouth. Charles Wallace looked at the unicorn and drew in his breath in horror. Where the lines of rope had crossed the flanks there were red welts, shocking against the silver hide. The entire abdominal area, where the webbed hammock had rubbed, was raw and oozing blood. The water which had flooded from Gaudior's nostrils was pinkish.

The unicorn in turn inspected the boy. "You're a mess," he stated flatly. "You can't possibly go Within in this condition. You'd only hurt your host."

"You're a mess, too," Charles Wallace replied. He looked at his hands, and the palms were as raw as Gaudior's belly. Where the anorak and his shirt had slipped, the rope had cut into his waist as it had cut Gaudior's flanks.

"And you have two black eyes," the unicorn informed him. "It's a wonder you can see at all."

Charles Wallace squinted, first with one eye, then the other. "Things are a little blurry," he confessed.

Gaudior shook a few last drops from his wings. "We can't stay here, and you can't go Within now, that's obvious."

Charles Wallace looked at the sun, which was moving toward the west. "It's going to be cold when the sun goes down. And there doesn't seem to be any sign of life. And nothing to eat."

Gaudior folded his wings across his eyes and appeared to contemplate. Then he returned the wings to the bleeding flanks. "I don't understand earth time."

"What's that got to do with it?"

"Time is of the essence, we both know that. And yet it will take weeks, if not months, for us to heal."

When the unicorn stared at him as though expecting a response, Charles Wallace looked down at a puddle in the ice. "I don't have any suggestions."

"We're both exhausted. The one place I can take you without fear of Echthroi is my home. No mortal has ever been there, and I am not sure I should bring you, but it's the only way I see open to us." The unicorn flung back his mane so that it brushed against the boy's bruised face with a silver coolness. "I have become very fond of you, in spite of all your foolishness."

Charles Wallace hugged the unicorn. "I have become fond of you, too."

Joints creaking painfully, Gaudior knelt. The boy clambered up, wincing as he inevitably touched the red welts which marred the flanks. "I'm sorry. I don't want to hurt you."

Gaudior neighed softly. "I know you don't."

The boy was so exhausted that he was scarcely aware of their flight. Stars and time swirled about him, and his lids began to droop.

"Wake up!" Gaudior ordered, and he opened his eyes to a world of starlit loveliness. The blurring of his vision had cleared, and he looked in awe at a land of snow and ice; he felt no cold, only the tenderness of a soft breeze which touched his cuts and bruises with healing gentleness. In the violet sky hung a sickle moon, and a smaller, higher moon, nearly full. Mountains heaved snow-clad shoulders skyward. Between the ribs of one of the foothills he saw what appeared to be a pile of enormous eggs.

Gaudior followed his gaze. "The hatching grounds. It has been seen by no other human eyes."

"I didn't know unicorns came from eggs," the boy said wonderingly.

"Not all of us do," Gaudior replied casually. "Only the time travelers." He took in great draughts of moonlight, then asked, "Aren't you thirsty?"

Charles Wallace's lips were cracked and sore. His mouth was parched. He looked longingly at the moonlight and tentatively opened his mouth to it. He felt a cool and healing touch on his lips, but when he tried to swallow he choked.

"I forgot," Gaudior said. "You're human. In my excitement at being home it slipped my mind." He cantered off to one of the foothills and returned with a long blue-green icicle held carefully in his teeth. "Suck it slowly. It may sting at first, but it has healing properties."

The cool drops trickled gently down the boy's parched throat, like rays of moonlight, and at the same time that they cooled the burning, they warmed his cold body. He gave his entire concentration to the moonsicle, and when he had finished the last healing drops he turned to thank Gaudior.

The unicorn was rolling in the snow, his legs up in the air, rolling and rolling, a humming of sheer pleasure coming from his throat. Then he stood up and shook himself, flinging splashes of snow in all directions. The red welts were gone; his hide was smooth and glistening perfection. He looked at the sore places on Charles Wallace's waist and hands. "Roll, the way I did," he ordered.

Charles Wallace threw himself into the snow, which was like no other snow he had ever felt; each flake was separate and tingly; it was cool but not chilling, and he felt healing move not only over the rope burns but deep within his sore muscles. He rolled over and over, laughing with delight. Then came a moment when he knew that he was completely healed, and he jumped up. "Gaudior, where is everybody? all the other unicorns?"

"Only the time travelers come to the hatching grounds, and during the passage of the small moon they can be about other business, for the small moon casts its warmth on the eggs. I brought you here, to this place, and at this moon, so we'd be alone."

"But why should we be alone?"

"If the others saw you they'd fear for their eggs."

Charles Wallace's head came barely halfway up the unicorn's haunches. "Creatures your size would be afraid of me?"

"Size is immaterial. There are tiny viruses which are deadly."

"Couldn't you tell them I'm not a virus and I'm not deadly?"

Gaudior blew out a gust of air. "Some of them think mankind *is* deadly."

Charles Wallace, too, sighed, and did not reply.

Gaudior nuzzled his shoulder. "Those of us who have been around the galaxies know that such thinking is foolish. It's always easy to blame others. And I have learned, being with you, that many of my preconceptions about mortals were wrong. Are you ready?"

Charles Wallace held out his hands to the unicorn. "Couldn't I see one of the eggs hatch?"

"They won't be ready until the rising of the third moon, unless . . ." Gaudior moved closer to the clutch, each egg almost as long as the boy was tall. "Wait—" The unicorn trotted to the great globular heap, which shone with inner luminosity, like giant moonstones. Gaudior bent his curved neck so that his mane brushed softly over the surface of the shells. With his upper teeth he tapped gently on one, listening, ears cocked, the short ear-hairs standing up and quivering like antennae. After a moment he moved on to another shell, and then another, with unhurried patience, until he tapped on one shell twice, thrice, then drew back and nodded at the boy.

This egg appeared to have rolled slightly apart from the others, and as Charles Wallace watched, it quivered, and rolled even farther away. From inside the shell came a sound of tapping, and the egg began to glow. The tapping accelerated and the shell grew so bright the boy could scarcely look at it. A sharp cracking, and a flash of brilliance as the horn thrust up and out into the pearly air, followed by a head with the silver mane clinging damply to neck and forehead. Dark silver-lashed eyes opened slowly, and the baby unicorn looked around, its eyes reflecting the light of the moons as it gazed on its fresh new environment. Then it wriggled and cracked the rest of the shell. As fragments of shell fell onto the snowy ground they broke into thousands of flakes, and the shell became one with the snow.

The baby unicorn stood on new and wobbly legs, neighing a soft moonbeam sound until it gained its balance. It stood barely as tall as Charles Wallace, testing one forehoof, then the other, and kicking out its hind legs. As Charles Wallace watched, lost in delight, the baby unicorn danced under the light of the two moons.

Then it saw Gaudior, and came prancing over to the big unicorn; by slightly lowering the horn it could have run right under the full-grown beast.

Gaudior nuzzled the little one's head just below the horn. Again the baby pranced with pleasure, and Gaudior began to dance with it, leading the fledgling in steps ever more and more intricate. When the baby began to tire, Gaudior slowed the steps of the dance and raised his head to the sickle moon, drew back his lips in an exaggerated gesture, and gulped moonlight.

As the baby had been following Gaudior in the steps of the dance, so it imitated him now, eagerly trying to drink moonlight, the rays dribbling from its young and inexperienced lips and breaking like crystal on the snow. Again it tried, looking at Gaudior, until it was thirstily and tidily swallowing the light as it was tipped out from the curve of the moon.

Gaudior turned to the nearly full moon, and again with exaggerated gestures taught the little one to drink. When its flanks were quivering with fullness, Gaudior turned to the nearest star, and showed it the pleasures of finishing a meal by quenching its thirst with starlight. The little one sipped contentedly, then closed its mouth with its tiny, diamond-like teeth, and, replete, leaned against Gaudior.

Only then did it notice Charles Wallace. With a leap of startlement, it landed on all four spindly legs, squealed in terror and galloped away, tail streaming silver behind it.

Charles Wallace watched the little creature disappear over the horizon. "I'm sorry I frightened it. Will it be all right?"

Gaudior nodded reassuringly. "It's gone in the direction of the Mothers. They'll tell it you're only a bad dream it had coming out of the shell, and it'll forget all about you." He knelt.

Reluctantly Charles Wallace mounted and sat astride the great neck. Holding on to a handful of mane, he looked about at the wild and peaceful landscape. "I don't want to leave."

"You human beings tend to want good things to last forever. They don't. Not while we're in time. Do you have any instructions for me?"

"I'm through with instructions. I don't even have any suggestions."

"We'll go Where and When the wind decides to take us, then?"

"What about Echthroi?" Charles Wallace asked fearfully.

"Because we're journeying from the home place the wind should be unmolested, as it was when we came here. After that we'll see. We've been in a very deep sea, and I never thought we'd get out of it. Try not to be afraid. The wind will give us all the help it can." The wings stretched to their full span and Gaudior flew up between the two moons, and away from the unicorn hatching grounds.

Meg sighed with delight.

"Oh, Ananda, Ananda, that was the most beautiful kythe! How I wish Charles Wallace could have stayed there longer, where he's safe . . ."

Ananda whined softly.

"I know. He has to leave. But the Echthroi are after him, and I feel so helpless . . ."

Ananda looked up at Meg, and the tufts of darker fur above the eyes lifted.

Meg scratched the dog between the ears. "We did send him the rune when he was in the Ice Age sea, and the wind came to help." Anxiously she placed her hand on Ananda, and closed her eyes, concentrating.

She saw the star-watching rock, and two children, a girl and a boy, perhaps thirteen and eleven, the girl the elder. The boy looked very much like a modern Brandon Llawcae, a Brandon in blue jeans and T-shirt—so it was definitely not 1865.

Charles Wallace was Within the boy, whose name was not Brandon.

Chuck.

Mrs. O'Keefe had called Charles Wallace Chuck.

Chuck was someone Mrs. O'Keefe knew. Someone Mrs. O'Keefe had said was not an idiot.

Now he was with a girl, yes, and someone else, an old woman. Chuck Maddox, and his sister, Beezie, and their grandmother. They were laughing, and blowing dandelion clocks, counting the breaths it took for the lacy white spores to leave the green stem.

Beezie Maddox had golden hair and bright blue eyes and a merry laugh. Chuck was more muted, his hair a soft brown, his eyes blue-grey. He smiled more often than laughed. He was so much like Brandon that Meg was sure he must be a direct descendant.

"Ananda, why am I so terribly frightened for him?" Meg asked.

"Let's blow dandelion clocks," Beezie had suggested.

"Not around the store you don't," their father had said. "I'll not have my patch of lawn seeded with more dandelion spore than blows here on its own."

So Chuck and Beezie and the grandmother came on a Sunday afternoon, across the brook, along to the flat rock. In the distance they could hear the sound of trucks on the highway, although they could not see them. Occasionally a plane tracked across the sky. Otherwise, there was nothing to remind them of civilization, and this was one of the things Chuck liked best about crossing the brook and walking through the woods to the rock.

Beezie handed him a dandelion. "Blow."

Chuck did not much like the smell of the spore; it was heavy and rank, and he wrinkled his nose with distaste.

"It doesn't smell all that bad to me," Beezie said. "When I squish the stem it smells green, that's all."

The grandmother held the snowy fronds to her nose. "When you're old, nothing smells the way it used to." She blew, and the white snowflakes of her dandelion flew in all directions, drifting on the wind.

Chuck and his sister had to blow several times before the clock told its time. The grandmother, who was quickly out of breath, and who had pressed her hand against her heart as she struggled up the fern-bordered path from the brook, blew lightly, and all the spores flew from the stem, danced in the sunny air, and slowly settled.

Chuck looked at Beezie, and Beezie looked at Chuck.

"Grandma, Beezie and I huff and puff and you blow no stronger than a whisper and it all blows away."

"Maybe you blow too hard. And when you ask the time, you mustn't fear the answer."

Chuck looked at the bare green stem in his grandmother's fingers. "I blew four times, and it isn't nearly four yet. What time does your dandelion tell, Grandma?"

The spring sun went briefly behind a small cloud, veiling the old woman's eyes. "It tells me of time past, when the valley was a lake, your pa says, and a different people roamed the land. Do you remember the arrowhead you found when we were digging to plant tulip bulbs?" Deftly she changed the subject.

"Beezie and I've found lots of arrowheads. I always carry one. It's better'n a knife." He pulled the flat chipped triangle from his jeans pocket.

Beezie wore jeans, too, thin where her sharp knees were starting to push through the cloth. Her blue-and-white-checked shirt was just beginning to stretch tightly across her chest. She dug into her pockets like her brother, pulling out an old Scout knife and a bent spoon. "Grandma, blowing the dandelion clocks—that's just superstition, isn't it?"

"And what else would it be? Better ways there are of telling the time, like the set of the sun in the sky and the shadows of the trees. I make it out to be nigh three in the afternoon, and near time to go home for a cup of tea."

Beezie lay back on the warm ledge of rock, the same kind of rock from which the arrowhead had been chipped. "And Ma and Pa'll have tea with us because it's Sunday, and the store's closed, and nobody in it but Pansy. Grandma, I think she's going to have kittens again."

"Are you after being surprised? What else has Pansy to do except frighten the field mice away."

Despite the mention of tea, Chuck too lay back, putting his head in his grandmother's lap so she could ruffle his hair. Around them the spring breeze was gentle; the leaves whispered together; and in the distance a phoebe called wistfully. The roaring of a truck on the distant highway was a jarring note.

The grandmother said, "When we leave the village and cross the brook it's almost as though we crossed out of time, too. And then there comes the sound of the present"—she gestured toward the invisible highway—"to remind us."

"What of, Grandma?" Beezie asked.

The old woman looked into an unseen distance. "The world of trucks isn't as real to me as the world on the other side of time."

"Which side?" Chuck asked.

"Either side, though at the present I know more about the past than the future."

Beezie's eyes lit up. "You mean like in the stories you tell us?"

The grandmother nodded, her eyes still distant.

"Tell us one of the stories, Grandma. Tell us how Queen Branwen was taken from Britain by an Irish king."

The old woman's focus returned to the children. "I may have been born in Ireland, but we never forgot we came from Branwen of Britain."

"And I'm named after her."

"That you are, wee Beezie, and after me, for I'm Branwen, too."

"And Zillah? I'm Branwen Zillah Maddox." Beezie and Chuck knew the stories of their names backwards and forwards but never lost pleasure in hearing them.

Meg opened her eyes in amazement.

Branwen Zillah Maddox. B.Z. Beezie.

Mrs. O'Keefe.

That golden child was Mrs. O'Keefe.

And Chuck was her brother.

* * *

"Zillah comes from your Maddox forebears," the grand-mother told the children, "and a proud name it is, too. She was an Indian princess, according to your pa, from the tribe which used to dwell right here where we be now, though the Indians are long gone."

"But you don't know as much about Zillah as you do about Branwen."

"Only that she was an Indian and beautiful. There are too many men on your father's side of the family, and stories come down, nowadays, through women. But in Branwen's day there were men who were bards."

"What's bards?" Chuck asked.

"Singers of songs and tellers of tales. Both my grand-ma and my grandpa told me the story of Branwen, but mostly my grandma, over and over, and her grandma told her before that, and the telling goes back beyond memory. Britain and Ireland have long misunderstood each other, and this misunderstanding goes back be-yond memory, too. And in the once upon a time and long ago when the Irish king wooed the English prin-cess, 'twas thought there might at last be peace between the two green and pleasant lands. There was feasting for many moons at the time of the nuptials, and then the Irish king sailed for Ireland with his wife."

"Wouldn't Branwen have been homesick?" Beezie asked.

"And of course she'd have been homesick. But she was born a princess and now she was a queen, and queens know how to mind their manners—or did in those days."

"And the king? What was he like?"

"Oh, and handsome he was, as the Irish can be, as was my own sweet Pat, who bore well the name of the blessed saint, with black hair and blue eyes. Branwen knew not that he was using her to vent his spleen against her land and her brethren, knew it not until he trumped up some silly story of her sitting in the refectory and casting her eye on one of his men. So, to punish her—"

"For what?" Chuck asked.

"For what, indeed? For his own jealous fantasies. So, to punish her, he sent her to tend the swine and barred her from the palace. So she knew he had never loved her, and her heart burned within her with anguish. Then she thought to call on her brother in England, and she used the rune, and whether she and hers gave the rune to Patrick, or whether their guardian angels gave it to each of them, she called on all Heaven with its power—"

The children chanted the rune with her.

> *"And the sun with its brightness,*
> *And the snow with its whiteness,*
> *And the fire with all the strength it hath,*
> *And the lightning with its rapid wrath,*
> *And the winds with their swiftness along their path,*

And the sea with its deepness,
And the rocks with their steepness,
And the earth with its starkness,
All these I place
By God's almighty help and grace
Between myself and the powers of darkness!"

The grandmother continued, "And the sun shone on her fair hair and warmed her, and the gentle snow fell and made all clean the sty in which the Irish king had set her, and the fire burst from the fireplace of his wooden palace and the lightning struck it and it burned with mighty rage and all within fled the fury. And the wind blew from Britain and the sails of her brother Bran's ship billowed as it sped over the deep sea and landed where the rocks were steep and the earth stark. And Bran's men scaled the rock and rescued their beloved Branwen."

"Is it a true story, Grandma," Beezie asked, "really?"

"To those with the listening ear and the believing heart."

"Chuck has the believing heart," Beezie said.

The grandmother patted his knee. "One day maybe you will be the writer your father wanted to be. He was not cut out for a storekeeper."

"I love the store," Beezie said defensively. "It smells good, of cinnamon and fresh bread and apples."

"I'm hungry," Chuck said.

"And wasn't I after saying before we got into story-telling that we should get along home for tea? Pull me up, both of you."

Chuck and Beezie scrambled to their feet and heaved the old woman upright. "We'll pick a bouquet for Ma and Pa on the way," Beezie said.

The narrow path was rough with rocks and hummocks of grass, and walking was not easy. The grandmother leaned on a staff which Chuck had cut for her from a grove of young maples which needed thinning. He went ahead, slowing down when he saw Beezie and his grandmother lagging behind him. A bouquet of field flowers was growing in Beezie's hands, for she paused whenever she saw that the old woman was out of breath. "Look, Chuck! Look, Grandma! Three more jacks-in-the-pulpit!"

Chuck was hacking away with his arrowhead at a strand of bittersweet snaking around a young fir tree, strangling it with coils strong as a boa constrictor's. "Ma used to have us looking for bittersweet a year or so ago, and now it's taking over. It'll kill this tree unless I cut through it. You two go along and I'll catch up."

"Want my knife?" Beezie offered.

"No. My arrowhead's sharp."

For a moment he stared after his sister and grandmother as they wended their slow way. He sniffed the fragrance of the air. Although the apple trees were green, the pink and white blossoms were still on the ground. The scent of lilac mingled with the mock orange. He might be able to hear the trucks on the road and see the planes in the sky, but at least here he couldn't smell them.

Chuck liked neither the trucks nor the planes. They all left their fumes behind them, blunting the smell of sunlight, of rain, of green and growing things, and Chuck "saw" with his nose almost more than with his eyes. Without looking he could easily tell his parents, his grandmother, his sister. And he judged people almost entirely by his reaction to their odor.

"I don't smell a thing," his father had said after Chuck had wrinkled his nose at a departing customer.

Chuck had said calmly, "He smells unreliable."

His father gave a small, surprised laugh. "He is unreliable. He owes me more than I can afford to be owed, for all his expensive clothes."

When the strand of bittersweet was severed, Chuck stood leaning against the rough bark of the tree, breathing in its resiny smell. In the distance he could see his grandmother and Beezie. The old woman smelled to him of distance, of the sea, which was fifty or more miles away, but perhaps it was a farther sea which clung to her. "And you smell green," he had told her. "Ah, and that's because I come from a far green country and the scent of it will be with me always."

"What color do I smell?" Beezie had asked.

"Yellow, like buttercups and sunlight and butterfly wings."

Green and gold. Good smells. Home smells. His mother was the blue of sky in early morning. His father was the rich mahogany of the highboy in the living room, with the firelight flickering over the polished wood. Comfortable, safe smells.

And suddenly the thought of the odor of cookies and freshly baked bread called to him, and he ran to catch up.

The family lived over the store in a long, rambling apartment. The front room, overlooking the street, was a storeroom, filled with cartons and barrels. Behind it were three bedrooms: his parents', his own little cubbyhole, and the bigger room Beezie shared with the grandmother. Beyond these were the kitchen and the large long room which served as living and dining room.

There was a fire crackling in the fireplace, for the spring evenings were apt to be chilly. The family was seated about a large round table set for tea, with cookies and bread still warm from the oven, a pitcher of milk, and a big pot of tea covered with the cozy the grandmother had brought with her from Ireland.

Chuck took his place, and his mother poured his tea. "Did you save another tree?"

"Yes. I really should take Pa's big clippers with me next time."

Beezie pushed the plate of bread and butter to him. "Take your share quickly or I'll eat it all up."

Chuck's sensitive nostrils twitched. There was a smell in the room which was completely unfamiliar to him, and of which he was afraid.

The father helped himself to a cookie. "This is one of the times I wish Sunday afternoons came more than once a week."

"You've been acting tired lately." His wife looked at him anxiously.

"Being tired is the natural state of a country store-keeper who doesn't have much business sense."

The grandmother moved creakily from her chair at the table to her rocker. "Hard work's not easy. You need more help."

"Can't afford it, Grandma. How about telling us a story?"

"You've heard them all as many times as there are stars in the sky."

"I never tire of them."

"I'm told out for today."

"Oh, come on, Grandma," Mr. Maddox cajoled. "You never tire of storytelling, and you know you make most of it up as you go along."

"Stories are like children. They grow in their own way." She closed her eyes. "I will just take a small snooze."

"You tell me about the Indian princess, then, Pa," Beezie ordered.

"I don't know much about her as far as provable facts are concerned. My illustrious forebear, Matthew Maddox, from whom I may have inherited an iota of talent, wrote about her in his second novel. It was a best-seller in its day. Sad he couldn't have known about its success, but it was published posthumously. It was a strange sort of fantasy, with qualities which make some critics call it the first American science-fiction novel, because it played with time, and he'd obviously heard of Mendel's theories of genetics. Anyhow, Beezie love, it's a fictional account of the two brothers from ancient Wales who came to this country after their father's death, the first Europeans to set foot on these uncharted shores. And, as the brothers had quarreled in Wales, so they quarreled in the New World, and the elder of the two made his way to South America. Madoc, the younger brother, stayed with the Indians in a place which is nameless but which Matthew Maddox implies is right around here, and he married the Indian princess Zyll, or Zillah, and in the novel it is his strain which is lost, and must be found again."

"Sounds interesting," Chuck said.

Beezie wrinkled her nose. "I don't much like science fiction. I like fairy tales better."

"The Horn of Joy has elements of both. The idea that the proud elder brother must be defeated by the inconsequential but honest younger brother is certainly a fairytale theme. There was also a unicorn in the story, who was a time traveler."

"Whyn't you tell us about it before?" Beezie asked.

"Thought you'd be too young to be interested. Anyhow, I sold my copy when I was offered an outrageously large sum for it when I . . . it was too large an amount to turn down. Matthew Maddox, for a nineteenth-century writer, had an uncanny intuition about the theories of space, time, and relativity that Einstein was to postulate generations later."

"But that's not possible," Beezie protested.

"Precisely. But it's all in Matthew's book, nevertheless. It's an evocative, haunting novel, and since Matthew Maddox assumed that he was descended from the younger Welshman, the one who stayed here, and the Indian princess, I've followed his fancy that the name Maddox comes from Madoc." A shadow moved across his face. "When my father had a stroke and I had to leave my poet's garret in the city and come help out with the store, I had to give up my dream of following in Matthew's footsteps."

"Oh, Pa—" Chuck said.

"I'm mainly sorry for you children. I never had a

chance to prove whether or not I could be a writer, but I'm a failure as a merchant." He rose. "I'd better go down to the store for an hour or so and work on accounts."

When he left, holding on to the banister as he went down the steep stairs, the smell that made Chuck afraid went with him.

Chuck told no one, not even Beezie, about the smell which was in his father but was not of his father.

Twice that week, Chuck had nightmares. When he cried out in terror his mother came hurrying, but he told her only that he had had a bad dream.

Beezie wasn't put off so easily. "You're worried about something, Chuck."

"There's always something to worry about. Lots of people owe Pa money, and he's worried about bills. I heard a salesman say he couldn't give Pa any more credit."

Beezie said, "You're too young to worry about things like that. Anyhow, it isn't the kind of thing you worry about."

"I'm getting older."

"Not that old."

"Pa's giving me more to do. I know more about the business now."

"But that's not what you're worried about."

He tried another tack. "I don't like the way Paddy O'Keefe's always after you in school."

"Paddy O'Keefe's repeated sixth grade three times. He may be good at baseball, but I'm not one of the girls who thinks the sun rises and sets on him."

"Maybe that's why he's after you." He had succeeded in deflecting her attention.

"I don't let him near me. He never washes. What does he smell like, Chuck?"

"Like a dandruffy woodchuck."

One evening after supper Beezie said, "Let's go see if the fireflies are back." It was Friday, and no school in the morning, so they could go to bed when they chose.

Chuck felt an overwhelming desire to get out of the house, away from the smell, which nearly made him retch. "Let's go."

It was still twilight when they reached the flat rock. They sat, and the stone still held the warmth of the day's sun. At first there were only occasional sparkles, but as it got darker Chuck was lost in a daze of delight as a galaxy of fireflies twinkled on and off, flinging upward in a blaze of light, dropping earthward like falling stars, moving in continuous effervescent dance.

"Oh, Beezie!" he cried. "I'm dazzled with gorgeousness."

Behind them the woods were dark with shadows. There was no moon, and a thin veil of clouds hid the stars. "If it were a clear night," Beezie remarked, "the fireflies wouldn't be as bright. I've never seen them this beautiful." She lay back on the rock, looking up at the shadowed sky, then closing her eyes. Chuck followed suit.

"Let's feel the twirling of the earth," Beezie said. "That's part of the dance the fireflies are dancing, too. Can you feel it?"

Chuck squeezed his eyelids tightly closed. He gave a little gasp. "Oh, Beezie! I felt as though the earth had tilted!" He sat up, clutching at the rock. "It made me dizzy."

She gave her bubbling little giggle. "It can be a bit scary, being part of earth and stars and fireflies and clouds and rocks. Lie down again. You won't fall off, I promise."

He leaned back, feeling the radiance soak into his body. "The rock's still warm."

"It's warm all summer, because the trees don't shade it. And there's a rock in the woods that's always cool, even on the hottest day, because the leaves are so close together that the sun's fingers never touch it."

Chuck felt a cold shadow move over him and shuddered.

"Someone walk over your grave?" Beezie asked lightly.

He jumped up. "Let's go home."

"Why? What's wrong? It's so beautiful."

"I know—but let's go home."

When they got back, everything was in confusion. Mr. Maddox had collapsed from pain, and been rushed to the hospital. The grandmother was waiting for the children.

The frightening smell had exploded over Chuck with the violence of a mighty wave as he entered.

The grandmother pulled the children to her and held them.

"But what is it? What's wrong with Pa?" Beezie asked.

"The ambulance attendant thought it was his appendix."

"But he will be all right?" she pleaded.

"Dear my love, we'll have to wait and pray."

Chuck pressed against her, quivering, not speaking. Slowly the smell was dissipating, leaving a strange emptiness in its wake.

Time seemed to stand still. Chuck would glance at the clock, thinking an hour had passed, only to find it barely a minute. After a long while Beezie fell asleep, her head in her grandmother's lap. Chuck was watchful, looking from the clock to the telephone to the door. But at length he, too, slept.

In his sleep he dreamed that he was lying on the flat rock, and feeling the swing of the earth around the sun, and suddenly the rock tilted steeply, and he was sliding off, and he scrabbled in terror to keep from falling off the precipice into a sea of darkness. He cried out, "Rocks—steep—" and the grandmother put her hand on the rock and steadied it and he stopped dreaming.

But when he woke up he knew that his father was dead.

NINE

The rocks
with their steepness

The sudden shrilling of the telephone woke Meg with a jolt of terror. Her heart began to thud, and she pushed out of bed, hardly aware of Ananda. Her feet half in and half out of her slippers, one arm shoved into her robe, she stumbled downstairs and into her parents' bedroom, but they were not there, so she hurried on down to the kitchen.

Her father was on the phone, and she heard him saying, "Very well, Mrs. O'Keefe. One of us will be right over for you."

It was not the president.

But Mrs. O'Keefe? In the middle of the night?

The twins, too, were in the doorway.

"What was that about?" Mrs. Murry asked.

"As you gathered, it was Mrs. O'Keefe."

"At this time of night!" Sandy exclaimed.

"She's never called us before," Dennys said, "at any time."

Meg breathed a sigh of relief. "At least it wasn't the president. What did she want?"

"She said she's found something she wants me to see, and ordered me to go for her at once."

"I'll go," Sandy said. "You can't leave the phone, Dad."

"You've got the weirdest mother-in-law in the world," Dennys told Meg.

Mrs. Murry opened the oven door and the fragrance of hot bread wafted out. "How about some bread and butter?"

"Meg, put your bathrobe on properly," Dennys ordered.

"Yes, doc." She put her left arm into the sleeve and tied the belt. If she stayed in the kitchen with the family, then time would pass with its normal inevitability. The kythe which had been broken by the jangling of the telephone was lost somewhere in her unconscious mind. She hated alarm clocks, because they woke her so abruptly out of sleep that she forgot her dreams.

In the kything was something to do with Mrs. O'Keefe. But what? She searched her mind. Fireflies. Something to do with fireflies. And a girl and a boy, and the smell of fear. She shook her head.

"What's the matter, Meg?" her mother asked.

"Nothing. I'm trying to remember something."

"Sit down. A warm drink won't hurt you."

It was important that she see Mrs. O'Keefe, but she couldn't remember why, because the kythe was gone.

"I'll be right back," Sandy assured them, and went out the pantry door.

"What on earth . . ." Dennys said. "Mrs. O'Keefe is beyond me. I'm glad I'm not going in for psychiatry."

Their mother set a plateful of fragrant bread on the table, then turned to put the kettle on. "Look!"

Meg followed her gaze. Coming into the kitchen were the kitten and Ananda, single file, the kitten with its tail straight up in the air, mincing along as though leading the big dog, whose massive tail was wagging wildly. They all laughed, and the laughter froze as the two creatures came past the table with the telephone. Twice since the president's call the phone had rung, first Calvin, then his mother. When would it ring again, and who would call?

It surprised Meg that the warm bread tasted marvelous, and the tea warmed her, and she was able, at least for the moment, to relax. Ananda whined beseechingly, and Meg gave her a small piece of toast.

Outside came the sound of a car, the slamming of a door, and then Sandy came in with Mrs. O'Keefe. The old woman had cobwebs in her hair, and smudges of dirt on her face. In her hand she held some scraps of paper.

"Something in me told me to go to the attic," she announced triumphantly. "That name—Mad Dog Branzillo—it rang a bell in me."

Meg looked at her mother-in-law and suddenly the kythe flooded back. "Beezie!" She cried.

Mrs. O'Keefe lunged toward her as though to strike her. "What's that?"

Meg caught the old woman's hands. "Beezie, Mom. You used to be called Beezie."

"How'd you know?" the old woman demanded fiercely. "You couldn't know! Nobody's called me Beezie since Chuck."

Tears filled Meg's eyes. "Oh, Beezie, Beezie, I'm so sorry."

The family looked at her in astonishment. Mr. Murry asked, "What is this, Meg?"

Still holding her mother-in-law's hands, Meg replied, "Mrs. O'Keefe used to be called Beezie when she was a girl. Didn't you, Mom?"

"It's best forgotten," the old woman said heavily.

"And you called Charles Wallace Chuck," Meg persisted, "and Chuck was your little brother and you loved him very much."

"I want to sit down," Mrs. O'Keefe said. "Leave the past be. I want to show you something." She handed a yellowed envelope to Mr. Murry. "Look at that."

Mr. Murry pushed his glasses up his nose. "It's a letter from a Bran Maddox in Vespugia to a Matthew Maddox right here."

The twins looked at each other. Sandy said, "We were just talking about Matthew Maddox tonight when we were looking something up for Meg. He was a nineteenth-century novelist. Is there a date on the letter?"

Mr. Murry carefully drew a yellowed sheet of paper from the old envelope. "November 1865."

"So the Matthew Maddox could be the one whose book Dennys studied in college!"

"Let Father read the letter," Dennys stopped his twin.

My beloved brother, Matthew, greetings, on this warm November day in Vespugia. Is there snow at home? I am settling in well with the group from Wales, and feel that I have known most of them all our lives. What an adventure this is, to start a colony in this arid country where the children can be taught Welsh in school, and where we can sing together as we work.

The strangest thing of all is that our family legend was here to meet me. Papa and Dr. Llawcae will be wild with excitement. We grew up on the legend of Madoc leaving Wales and coming to the New World, the way other children grew up on George Washington and the cherry tree. Believe it or not— but I know you'll believe it, because it's absolutely true—there is an Indian here with blue eyes who says he is descended from a Welsh prince who came to America long before any other white men. He does not know how his forebears got to South America, but he swears that his mother sang songs to him about being the blue-eyed descendant of a Welsh prince. He is called Gedder, though that is not his real name. His mother died when he and his sister were small, and they were brought up by an English sheep rancher who couldn't pronounce his Welsh name, and called him Gedder. And his sister's name—that is perhaps the most amazing of all: Zillie. She does not have the blue eyes, but she is quite beautiful, with very fine features, and shining straight black hair, which she wears in a long braid. She reminds me of my beloved Zillah.

Gedder has been extraordinarily helpful in many ways, though he has a good deal of arrogance and a tendency to want to be the leader which has already caused trouble in this community where no man is expected to set himself above his brothers.

But how wonderful that the old legend should be here to greet me! As for our sister Gwen, she shrugs and says, "What difference does a silly old story make?" She is determined not to like it here, though she's obviously pleased when all the young men follow her around.

Has Dr. Llawcae decided to let Zillah come and

join me in the spring? The other women would welcome her, and she would be a touch of home for Gwen. I'm happy here, Matthew, and I know that Zillah would be happy with me, as my wife and life's companion. Women are not looked down on here—Gwen has to admit that much. Perhaps you could come, and bring Zillah with you? The community is settled enough so that I think we could take care of you, and this dry climate would be better for you than the dampness at home. Please come, I need you both.

Your affectionate brother,

Bran

Mr. Murry stopped. "It's very interesting, Mrs. O'Keefe, but why is it so important for me to see it?"—that you called in the middle of the night, he seemed to be adding silently.

"Don't you see?"

"No, sorry."

"Thought you was supposed to be so brilliant."

Mrs. Murry said, "The letter was mailed from Vespugia. That's strange enough, that you should have a letter which was mailed from Vespugia."

"Right," the old woman said triumphantly.

Mr. Murry asked, "Where did you find this letter, Mrs. O'Keefe?"

"Told you. In the attic."

"And your maiden name was Maddox." Meg smiled at the old woman. "So they were forebears of yours, this Bran Maddox, and his brother, Matthew, and his sister, Gwen."

She nodded. "Yes, and likely his girlfriend, Zillah, too. Maddoxes and Llawcaes in my family all the way back."

Dennys looked at his sister's mother-in-law with new respect. "Sandy was looking up about Vespugia tonight, and he told us about a Welsh colony in Vespugia in 1865. So one of your ancestors went to join it?"

"Looks like it, don't it? And that Branzillo, he's from Vespugia."

Mr. Murry said, "It's a remarkable coincidence—" He stopped as his wife glanced at him. "I still don't see how it can have any connection with Branzillo, or what it would mean if it did."

"Don't you?" Mrs. O'Keefe demanded.

"Please tell us," Mrs. Murry suggested gently.

"The names. Bran. Zillah. Zillie. Put them together and they aren't far from Branzillo."

Mrs. Murry looked at her with surprised admiration. "How amazing!"

Mr. Murry asked, "Are there other letters?"

"Were. Once."

"Where are they?"

"Gone. Went to look. Began thinking about this

Branzillo when I went home. Remembered Chuck and me—"

"Chuck and you what, Mom?" Meg probed.

Mrs. O'Keefe pushed her cobwebby hair away from her eyes. "We used to read the letters. Made up stories about Bran and Zillah and all. Played games of Let's Pretend. Then, when Chuck—didn't have the heart for Let's Pretend any more, forgot it all. Made myself forget. But that name, Branzillo, struck me. Bran. Zillah. Peculiar."

Mr. Murry looked bemusedly at the yellowed paper. "Peculiar, indeed."

"Where's your little boy?" Mrs. O'Keefe demanded.

Mr. Murry looked at his watch. "He went for a walk."

"When?"

"About an hour ago."

"In the middle of the night, and at his age?"

"He's fifteen."

"No. Twelve. Chuck was twelve."

"Charles Wallace is fifteen, Mrs. O'Keefe."

"A runt, then."

"Give him time."

"And you don't take care of him. Chuck needs special care. And people criticize me for not taking care of my kids!"

Dennys, too, looked at his watch. "Want me to go after him, Dad?"

Mr. Murry shook his head. "No. I think we have to

trust Charles Wallace tonight. Mrs. O'Keefe, you'll stay awhile?"

"Yes. Need to see Chuck."

Meg said, "Please excuse me, everybody. I want to go back to bed." She tried to keep the urgency from her voice. She felt a panicky need to get back to the attic with Ananda. "Chuck *was* twelve," Mrs. O'Keefe had said. Chuck was twelve when what? Anything that happened to Chuck was happening to Charles Wallace.

Mrs. Murry suggested, "Would you like to take a cup of tea with you?"

"No, thanks, I'm fine. Someone call me when Charles gets in?"

Ananda followed her upstairs, contentedly licking her lips for the last buttery crumbs.

The attic felt cold and she got quickly into bed and wrapped the quilt around herself and the dog.—Charles Wallace wanted me to find a connection between Wales and Vespugia, and Dennys found one in his reference books. But it's a much closer connection than that. The letter Mrs. O'Keefe brought was from 1865, and from Vespugia, so the connection is as close as her attic.

Despite the warm glow of the electric heater, she shivered.

—Those people in the letter must be important, she thought,—and the Bran who wrote the letter, and his sister Gwen. Certainly the name Zillie must have some connection with Madoc's Zyll, and Ritchie Llawcae's Zylle, who was nearly burned for witchcraft.

—And then, the Matthew he wrote to must be the Matthew Maddox who wrote the books. There's something in that second book that matters, and the Echthroi don't want us to know about it. It's all interconnected, and we still don't know what the connections mean.

—And what happened to Beezie, that she should end up as Mom O'Keefe? Oh, Ananda, Ananda, whatever happened?

She lay back against the pillows and rubbed her hand slowly back and forth over the dog's soft fur, until the tingling warmth moved up her arm and all through her.

"But why Pa?" Beezie demanded over and over again. "Why did Pa have to die?"

"There's never an answer to that question, my Beezie," the grandmother replied patiently. "It's not a question to be asking."

"But I do ask it!"

The grandmother looked tired, and old. Chuck had never before thought of her as old, as being any age at all. She was simply Grandma, always there for them. Now she asked, not the children, but the heavens, "And why my Patrick, and him even younger than your father. Why anything?" A tear slid down her cheek, and Beezie and Chuck put their arms around her to comfort her.

Mrs. Maddox went over the ledgers so patiently kept up to date by her husband. The more she looked, the more slowly her hands turned the pages. "I knew it was bad, but I didn't know it was this bad. I should have realized when he sold Matthew Maddox's book . . ."

Chuck crawled up into the dark storage spaces under the eaves, looking for treasure. He found a bottle full of pennies, but no gold or jewels to give his mother. He found an old *Encyclopaedia Britannica*, the pages yellow, the bindings cracked, but still useful. He found a set of china wrapped in old newspapers dated long before he and Beezie were born, which he hoped they might be able to sell. He found a strongbox, locked.

He brought his findings to the living room. His mother was in the store, but Beezie and the grandmother were there, doing the week's baking.

"The pennies are old. They may be worth something. The china's good. It may pay for our fuel for a month or so. What's in the box?"

"There isn't a key. I'm going to break it." He took hammer and screwdriver and wrench, and the old lock gave way and he was able to lift the lid. In the box was a sheaf of letters and a large notebook with a crumbling blue leather binding. He opened the book to the first page, and there was a watercolor sketch, faded only slightly, of the spring countryside.

"Grandma! It's our rock, our picnic rock!"

The old woman clucked. "And so it is."

The rock was shaded in soft blues and lavenders merging into grey. Behind it the trees were lush with spring green. Above it flew a flock of butterflies, the soft blues of the spring azures complemented by the gold and black of the tiger swallowtails. Around the rock were the familiar spring flowers, dappling the grass like the background of a tapestry.

Chuck exclaimed in delight, "Oh, Beezie, oh, Grandma!" Reverently he turned the page. In beautiful script was written, *Madrun, 1864, Zillah Llawcae.*

The grandmother wiped her floury hands carefully and put on her spectacles, bending over the book. Together they read the first page.

Madrun.

Past ten o'clock. Through my bedroom window I can look down the hill to the Maddoxes' house. Mr. and Mrs. Maddox will be asleep. They get up at five in the morning. Gwen Maddox—who knows? Gwen has always considered herself a grownup and me a child, though we're separated by only two years.

The twins, my dear twins, Bran and Matthew. Are they awake? When Bran lied about his age, so afraid was he he'd miss the war, and went to join the cavalry, I feared he might be killed in battle. When I dreamed of his homecoming, as I did each night when I looked at his diamond on my finger and prayed for his safety, I never thought it could be like this, with Bran withdrawn and refusing to communicate with anyone, even his twin. If I try to speak to him about our marriage, he cuts me short, or turns away without a word. Matthew says there have been others who have suffered this sickness of spirit because of the horrors of war.

I am, and have been for nearly seventeen years, Zillah Llawcae. Will I ever be Zillah Maddox?

They continued to turn the pages, more quickly now, not pausing to read the journal entries, but looking at the delicate paintings of birds and butterflies, flowers and trees, squirrels and wood mice and tree toads, all meticulously observed and accurately reproduced.

A shiver ran up and down Chuck's spine. "Pa's mother was a Llawcae. This Zillah could be one of our ancestors . . . and she was alive when she painted all this, and it's just the way it is now, just exactly the same."

He turned another page; his eye was caught, and he read:

This is my seventeenth birthday, and a sorry one it has been, though Father and I were invited to the Maddoxes' for dinner. But Bran was there and yet he wasn't there. He sat at the table, but he hardly ate the delicious dishes which had been especially prepared, to tempt him as much as in honor of me, and if anyone asked him a question he answered in monosyllables.

He turned the page and paused again.

Matthew says Bran almost had a conversation with him last night, and he is hopeful that the ghastly war wounds of his mind and spirit are beginning to heal. I wear his ring with its circle of hope, and I will not give up hoping. What would I do without Matthew's friendship to comfort and sustain me? Had it not been for Matthew's accident, I wonder which twin would have asked for my hand? A question better not raised, since I love them both so tenderly.

The grandmother took the top letter from the packet. "It's from Bran Maddox, the one Zillah's talking about, but it's from some foreign place, Vespugia? Now where would that be?"

"It's part of what used to be Patagonia."

"Pata—?"

"In South America."

"Oh, then." She drew the letter out of its envelope.

My beloved brother, Matthew, greetings, on this warm November day in Vespugia. It there snow at home? I am settling in well with the group from Wales, and feel that I have known most of them all our lives . . .

When she finished reading the letter, she said, "Your poor pa would have been thrilled at all this."

Chuck, nodding, continued to turn the pages, reading a line here and there. As well as the nature pictures, the young Zillah Llawcae had many sketches of people, some in ink, some in watercolor. There was an ink drawing of a tall man in a stovepipe hat, carrying a black bag and looking not unlike Lincoln, standing by a horse and buggy. Underneath was written, "Father, about to drive off to deliver a baby."

There were many sketches of a young man, just beyond boyhood, with fair hair, a clear, beardless complexion, and wide-apart, far-seeing eyes. These were labeled, "My beloved Bran," "My dearest Bran," "My heart's love." And there were sketches of someone who looked like Bran and yet not like Bran, for the face was etched with lines of pain. "My dear Matthew," Zillah had written.

"It's so beautiful," Beezie said. "I wish I could paint like that."

But the old woman's thoughts had shifted to practicality. "I wonder, would this notebook bring a few dollars?"

"Grandma, you wouldn't sell it!" Chuck was horrified.

"We need money, lad, if we're to keep a roof over our heads. Your ma'll sell anything she can sell."

The antiques dealer who bought the pennies and the set of china for what seemed to Chuck and Beezie a staggering sum was not interested in Zillah's notebook.

Mrs. Maddox looked at it sadly. "I know it's worth something. Your father would know where I should take it. If only I could remember the name of the person who bought Matthew Maddox's book."

But Chuck could not feel it in his heart to wish the beautiful journal sold. His grandmother took an old linen pillowcase and made a cover to protect the crumbling leather binding, and on it Beezie embroidered two butterflies, in blue and gold. She was as entranced with the journal as was Chuck.

They shared the notebook and the letters with the grandmother, reading aloud to her while she did the ironing or mending, until they had her as involved as they were. The present was so bleak that all three found relief in living the long past.

Beezie and Chuck looked at the old foundation behind the store. "That's where the Maddoxes' house must have been. They didn't live above the store, the way we do."

"Our apartment was all part of the store."

"I wonder what happened to the house?"

"We'll never know," Beezie said drearily.

"I tried to check one of Matthew Maddox's books out of the library," Chuck said. "But the librarian said they haven't been around in a long time. She thinks somebody must have lifted them. But I did get some books on Vespugia. Let's go upstairs and look at them."

They compared the photographs in the books with the watercolors in the final pages of the journal, where Zillah had tried to reproduce in ink and paint what Bran had described in his letters. Zillah's painting of vast plains rising terrace-fashion up to the foot of the Andes gave them a feeling of a world so different it might have been another planet.

Beezie had turned back to Zillah's notebook, to a painting of a tall and handsome Indian, with strange blue eyes set rather too close to his aquiline nose. The caption read: "This is how I think Gedder must look, the Indian who Bran writes is descended from Madoc's brother."

Chuck reached for one of Bran's letters and read:

I wish I was more drawn to Gedder, who is so obviously drawn to Gwen. I feel an ingrate when I think of all he has done for us. Building is completely different in Vespugian weather than at home—or in Wales, and I shudder to think what kind of houses we might have built had Gedder not shown us how to construct dwellings to let the wind in, rather than to keep it out. And he showed us what crops to plant, hardy things like cabbage and carrots, and how to make windbreaks for them. All the Indians have helped us, but Gedder more than the others, and more visibly. But he never laughs.

"I don't trust people who don't laugh." He put the letter down.

Beezie got a baby-sitting job that began right after school, so Chuck took her place at the cash register, pretending that he was Matthew Maddox and that the store was big and flourishing. The grandmother took in ironing and sewing, and her old hands were constantly busy. There was no time for leisurely cups of tea and the telling of tales. Chuck moved more and more deeply into his games of Let's Pretend. Matthew and Zillah, Bran and Gwen, Gedder and Zillie, all were more alive for him than anyone except Beezie and the grandmother.

One evening Mrs. Maddox stayed late downstairs in the store. When Chuck came home from chopping wood for one of their neighbors, he found Beezie and his grandmother drinking herb tea. "Grandma, I'm hungry." He could feel his belly growling. Supper had been soup and dry toast.

Seeming to ignore his words, the old woman looked at him. "Duthbert Mortmain's been calling on your ma. He's downstairs now."

"I don't like him," Beezie said.

"You may have to," the grandmother told her.

"Why?" Chuck asked. He remembered Duthbert Mortmain as a lumbering, scowling man who did small plumbing jobs. How did he smell? Not a pleasant smell. Hard, like a lump of coal.

"He's offered to marry your ma and take over the store."

"But Pa—"

"The funeral baked meats are long cold. Duthbert Mortmain's got a shrewd business head, and no one's bought the store, nor likely to. Your ma's not got much choice. And for all her hard work and heavy heart, she's still a pretty woman. Not surprising Duthbert Mortmain should fall for her."

"But she's our *mother*," Beezie protested.

"Not to Duthbert Mortmain. To him she's a desirable woman. And to your mother, he's a way out."

"Out of what?" Chuck asked.

"Your mother's about to lose the store and the roof over our heads. Another few weeks and we'll be out on the street."

Chuck's face lit up. "We could go to Vespugia!"

"Going anywhere takes money, Chuck, and money's

what we don't have. You and Beezie'd be put in foster homes, and as to your ma and me . . ."

"Grandma!" Beezie clutched the old woman's sleeve. "You don't want Ma to marry him, do you?"

"I don't know what I want. I'd like to know that she was taken care of, and you and Chuck, before I die."

Beezie flung her arms about the old woman. "You're not going to die, Grandma, not ever!"

Chuck's nostrils twitched slightly. The scent of dandelion spore was strong.

The old woman untangled herself. "You've seen how death takes the ready and unready, my Beezie. Except for my concern about your future, and your mother's, I'm ready to go home. It's been a long time I've been separated from my Patrick. He's waiting for me. The last few days I've kept looking over my shoulder, expecting to see him."

"Grandma"—Beezie pushed her fingers through her curls—"Ma doesn't *love* Duthbert Mortmain. She can't! I hate him!"

"Hate hurts the hater more'n the hated."

"Didn't Branwen?"

"Branwen hated not. Branwen loved, and was betrayed, and cried the rune for help, and not for hate or revenge. And the sun melted the white snow so that she could sleep warm at night, and the fire in her little stove did not burn out but flickered merrily to keep her toasty, and the lightning carried her message to her brother, Bran, and her Irish king fled to his ship and the wind blew him across the sea and his ship sank in its depths and Bran came to his sister Branwen and blessed the stark earth so that it turned green and flowering once more."

Beezie asked, "Did she ever love anybody again, after the Irish king?"

"I've forgotten," the old woman said.

"Grandma! Why don't we use the rune? Then maybe Ma won't have to marry Duthbert Mortmain."

"The rune is not to be used lightly."

"This wouldn't be lightly."

"I don't know, my Beezie. Patterns have to be worked out, and only the very brash tamper with them. The rune is only for the most dire emergency."

"Isn't this an emergency?"

"Perhaps not the right one." The old woman closed her eyes and rocked back and forth in silence, and when she spoke it was in a rhythmic singsong, much as when she intoned the words of the rune. "You will use the rune, my lamb, you will use the rune, but not before the time is ripe." She opened her eyes and fixed Beezie with a piercing gaze which seemed to go right through her.

"But how will I know when the time is ripe? Why isn't it ripe now?"

The old woman shook her head and closed her eyes

and rocked again. "This moment is not the moment. The night is coming and the clouds are gathering. We can do nothing before they are all assembled. When the time is ripe, Chuck will let you know. From the other side of darkness, Chuck will let you know, will let you know, will let . . ." Her words trailed off, and she opened her eyes and spoke in her natural voice. "To bed with both of you. It's late."

"Horrid old Duthbert Mortmain," Beezie said to Chuck one fine summer's day. "I won't call him Pa."

"Nor I."

Duthbert Mortmain seemed quite content to have them call him Mr. Mortmain.

He ran the store with stern efficiency. With their mother he was gentle, occasionally caressing her soft hair. People remarked on how he doted on her.

A sign over the cash register read NO CREDIT. Beezie and Chuck helped out in the afternoons and on Saturdays as usual. And their mother still did not smile, not even when Duthbert Mortmain brought her a box of chocolates tied with a lavender ribbon.

She no longer smelled of fear, Chuck thought, but neither did she smell of the blue sky of early morning. Now it was the evening sky, with a thin covering of cloud dimming the blue.

Duthbert Mortmain saved his pleasantries for the customers. He laughed and made jokes and gave every appearance of being a hearty, kindly fellow. But upstairs in the evenings his face was sour.

"Don't be noisy, children," their mother warned. "Your—my husband is tired."

Beezie whispered to Chuck, "Pa was tired, too, but he liked to hear us laugh."

"We were his own children," Chuck replied. "We don't belong to Duthbert Mortmain, and he doesn't like what doesn't belong to him."

Duthbert Mortmain did not show his vicious temper until the following spring. There was never a sign of it in the store, even with the most difficult customers or salesmen, but upstairs he began to let it have its way. One morning his wife ("I hate it when people call her Mrs. Mortmain!" Beezie exploded) came to breakfast with a black eye, explaining that she had bumped into a door in the dark. The grandmother, Beezie, and Chuck looked at her, but said nothing.

And it became very clear that Duthbert Mortmain did not like children, even when they were quiet. Whenever Chuck did anything which displeased his stepfather, which was at least once a day, Mortmain boxed his ears, so that at last they rang constantly.

When Beezie sat at the cash register, her stepfather pinched her arm every time he passed, as though in affection. But her arms were so full of black and blue marks that she kept her sweater on all the time to hide the bruises.

One day at recess in the schoolyard, Chuck saw Paddy O'Keefe come up to Beezie, and hurried over to them to hear Paddy asking, "Old Mortmain after you?"

"What do you mean?"

"You know what I mean."

"No. I don't." But she shivered.

Chuck intervened, "You leave my sister alone."

"Better tell old Mortmain to leave her alone, runt. You ever need any help, Beezie, you just let me know. Li'l ole Paddy'll take care of you."

That night Duthbert Mortmain's temper flared totally out of control.

They had finished the evening meal, and when Beezie was clearing the table, her stepfather reached out and pinched her bottom, and Chuck saw the look of cold hatred she turned on him.

"Duthbert—" their mother protested.

"Duthbert Mortmain, take care." The grandmother gave him a long, level gaze. She spoke not another word, but warning was clear in her eyes. She put cups and glasses on a tray, and started for the sink.

Mortmain, too, left the table, and as the old woman neared the stairway he raised his arm to strike her.

"No!" Beezie screamed.

Chuck thrust himself between his grandmother and stepfather and took the full force of Mortmain's blow.

Again Beezie screamed, as Chuck fell, fell down the steep stairs in a shower of broken china and glass. Then she rushed after him.

Chuck lay in a distorted position at the foot of the stairs, looking up at her with eyes that did not see. "Gedder pushed me. He pushed me. Don't let him marry Gwen. Zillah, don't let Gedder, don't let . . ."

TEN

The earth with its starkness

A field of dandelions. Yellow. Yellow. Exploding into white, into a blizzard of white, a terror of white. Green stems, sickly trickling ooze.

Grandma.

Grandma.

Grandma, you're not going to die. Not ever.

Gedder.

Smell. Bad smell.

Gun. Gedder's gun. Stop him

terrible fall

Gwen   Zillah

head hurts

hurts

crystal horn heals
Matthew's unicorn comes
tip touches head with light   heals

Beezie! Grandma! Ma! Pa!

Two stones in the cemetery.
A fight at the edge of the cliff, like Gwydyr and Madoc
at the edge of the lake. Bad. Bad.
Beezie, never let him touch you.

From inside himself Charles Wallace watched as the unicorn lowered his head and the blazing tip of the horn
touched Chuck's head, pouring light into it. He kept the
horn there until the light had poured itself out, and the
spasms of pain subsided and the boy stopped babbling
and slept.

"Charles Wallace!"
He listened. The voice sounded like Gaudior, and yet it
was not Gaudior, and he no longer saw the silver beauty
of the unicorn nor the light of the horn. Nothing was
visible, not even darkness. Something was happening,
and he did not know what. He was still Within Chuck,
and yet he was intensely conscious of himself as Charles
Wallace, and something was pulling him.

Meg sat up, blinking and rubbing her hand against Ananda's fur. The kitten had returned and was sleeping on the pillow. At first Meg did not know why there were tears on her cheeks, or why she was frightened.

She closed her eyes in sadness and saw the unicorn standing motionless by the star-watching rock. A pear-shaped drop of crystal slid from Gaudior's eye and shattered into a thousand fragments on the stone. The unicorn looked up at the sky. The stars were sparkling brilliantly. Small wisps of starlit cloud moved in the rapid north wind. She thought she heard Gaudior saying, "The Old Music was in them once. That was a victory for the Echthroi."

Meg thought of Mrs. O'Keefe waiting downstairs. Yes. That was a victory for the enemy, indeed. That Beezie, the golden child, should have become the old hag with missing teeth and resentful eyes was unbearable.

There's more to her than meets the eye.

Infinitely more.

And what now? What's going to happen?

To Chuck?

To Charles Wallace?

"Charles Wallace!"

He listened. Was it Gaudior? He could hear, but he could not see, and the voice echoed as though coming from a great distance.

"Charles Wallace." The voice was compassionate. "You don't have to stay Within Chuck now that this has happened. We did not expect this."

Charles Wallace felt cold and confused and therefore cross. "But I *am* Within Chuck."

"Yes. And Chuck is unconscious, and when he comes to, he will not be the same. His skull has been fractured. Although the healing of the horn has taken away the worst of the pain it could not repair the brain damage. And so there have been instructions that you are to be released now if you so desire."

Charles Wallace felt weighed down by darkness and pain.

The almost-Gaudior voice continued. "Within Chuck as he is now, you will have no control over his actions. His brain is short-circuited. If there is a Might-Have-Been which you should alter in order to avert disaster, you will have no ability either to recognize it or to change it."

"If you release me from Within Chuck, then what?"

"You will be sent Within someone else, and then you will be better able to accomplish your mission. Time is of the essence, as you understand. And we do not know what may happen while you are trapped Within this injured child."

"Who are you?" Charles Wallace asked the invisible voice. "You sound like Gaudior, but you aren't Gaudior."

The voice laughed gently. "No, I am not Gaudior. All

the healing light went from his horn, but he could not cure Chuck, though he kept him from dying—and that may not have been a kindness. He has gone home to dip his horn in the pools of healing to replenish it."

"Then who are you?"

Again the voice laughed. "You saw me when Gaudior took you home after you nearly drowned in the Ice Age sea. I am the unicorn you saw come forth from the shell."

"Why can't I see you? Why can't I see anything?" The words of the voice had reassured him, and yet he still felt foreboding.

"While you are in Chuck, you see only what Chuck sees, and he is unconscious, and will be for several days. Come, Charles Wallace, there's no time to be lost. Let us help you out of Chuck. If Mad Dog Branzillo is to be prevented from starting a holocaust you must not dally."

"I have to think—" Something was wrong, and he did not know what.

"Charles Wallace. Gaudior will corroborate what I have told you. Chuck's brain has been damaged. He's little better than an idiot. Come out."

"If I come out, will I see you?" There was something about the voice which was inconsistent with the visual image of the baby unicorn; but of course it would no longer be a baby.

"Of course you'll see me. Hurry. There's a terrible urgency about what you are to accomplish."

"I?"

"Of course, you. You were selected, weren't you?"

"No. Beezie—Mrs. O'Keefe—laid a charge on me."

"Because you're the only one who can prevent Branzillo."

"But I can't—"

"Of course you can." The voice was tenderly patient. "Why do you think you were chosen?"

"Well—Gaudior seemed to think it was that I might be able to go Within people, because of the way Meg and I kythe."

"Exactly. You were chosen because of your special gifts, and your unusual intelligence. You know that yourself, don't you?"

"Well—I can kythe. And I know my I.Q.'s high, as far as that goes. But that's not enough—"

"Of course it is. And you have the ability to see the difference between right and wrong, and to make the correct decisions. You were selected because you are an extraordinary young man and your gifts and your brains qualify you. You are the only one who can control the Might-Have-Been."

Charles Wallace's stomach was churning.

"Come, Charles Wallace. You have been chosen. You are in control of what is going to happen. You are needed. We must go."

Charles Wallace began to throw up. Was it in reaction to

the tempting words, or because Chuck, with his bashed-in skull, was vomiting? But he knew that whatever the voice looked like, it was not a unicorn. When he had stopped retching he said, "I don't know who you are, but you're not like Gaudior. Gaudior would never say what you've just said. It was trying to use my high I.Q. and trying to control things that got us into trouble in the first place. I don't know what I'm supposed to use, but it's not my intellect or strength. For better or worse, I'm Within Chuck. And I've never come out of Within on my own. It's always happened to me. I'm staying Within."

Meg let out a long sigh. "He made the right choice, didn't he?"

Ananda's warm tongue gently touched Meg's hand.

Meg closed her eyes, listening. She thought she heard a howl of defeat, and she whiffed the ugly stench of Echthroi.

So they had been trying to get at Charles Wallace in a much more subtle way than by trying to snatch him from Gaudior's back or throw him into Projections.

Duthbert Mortmain had nearly killed Chuck. Nothing went in straight lines for him any more, not time, not distance. His mind was like the unstable earth, full of faults, so that layers shifted and slid. It was like being in a nightmare from which there was no possibility of waking. She ached for him, and for Charles Wallace Within him.

* * *

Pain and panic

the world tilting

twirling on its axis, out of control

spinning off away from the sun into the dark

light bursting against his eyes, an explosion of light

a kaleidoscope of brilliant colors assailing his nostrils

"Chuck!" The voice came echoing from a vast distance, echoing along the unseen walls of a dark tunnel.

"Chuck! It's Beezie, your sister. Chuck, can you hear me?"

He was weighted down by the vast heaviness of the atmosphere, but he managed to lift one finger in response to Beezie's calling, afraid, as he did so, that if the weight lifted he would fall off the wildly tilting earth . . .

"He hears me! Ma, Chuck moved his finger!"

Slowly the rampant, out-of-control speed lessened, and the planet resumed its normal pace. Colors stopped their kaleidoscopic dance and stayed in place. Smells became identifiable once more: coffee; bread; apples. Beezie: the gold was not as brilliant as it had been, but it was still Beezie. And their mother: the blue was cloudy now, hardly blue at all, closer to the grey of rain clouds. Grandma: where is Grandma's smell? Why is there emptiness? Where is the green?

"Grandma!"

"She's dead, Chuck. Her heart gave out."

"Gedder pushed her. He killed her."

"No, Chuck." Beezie's voice was bitter, and the bitterness further muted the gold. "Duthbert Mortmain. He was furious with her, and he was going to strike her, but you saved her, and he hit you instead, and you fell all the way down the stairs and fractured your skull. And Grandma—she just . . ."

"What? Did Gedder—"

"No, no, not Gedder, Chuck, Duthbert Mortmain. He felt as awful as he's capable of feeling. He and Ma drove you to the hospital, and I stayed home with Grandma, and she looked at me and said, 'I'm sorry, Beezie, I can't wait any longer. My Patrick's come for me.' And she gave a little gasp, and that was all."

He heard her, but between the stark words came other sounds and the smell of a hot and alien wind. Time's layers slipped and slid under him. "But Gwen shouldn't marry Gedder. Gwydyr's children shouldn't marry Madoc's."

There was panic in Beezie's voice. "What are you talking about? Chuck, please don't. You scare me. I want you to get all the way well."

"Not Let's Pretend. Real. Gwen and Gedder—it would be bad, bad . . ."

The cliff loomed high over him, dark, shadowing. Gedder was at the top of the cliff, waiting, waiting . . . who was he waiting for?

* * *

Chuck slowly improved, until he could put cans and boxes on the store shelves. Even though he could not manage school, he recovered enough to mark the prices on the store's stock. He seldom made a mistake, and when he did, Duthbert Mortmain did not box his ears.

Sometimes Chuck saw him as Mortmain, sometimes as Gedder, when his worlds warped. "Gedder is nicer than he used to be," he reported to Beezie. "He's nicer to Ma. And to Grandma and me."

"Grandma—" A sob choked Beezie's voice. "Chuck, how can you! How can you play Let's Pretend about that?" Her voice rose with outrage. "How can you go away from me like this when I need you? Don't leave me!"

He heard and he did not hear. He was caught between the layers and he could not get into the right layer so that he could be with Beezie. "Grandma says I'm not to let him hear me call him Gedder, because that's not his real name, so I won't." He had intended to say, he thought he was saying, "I'll never leave you, Beezie," but the words of the other layer came out of his mouth. "Where's Matthew? I want to talk to him. He has to get Zillah to Vespugia."

Sometimes the earth started to tilt again and he could not stand upright against the velocity. Then he had to stay in bed until the tilting steadied.

He climbed the attic stairs one day when the earth was

firm under his feet, and crawled into all the dimmest and most cobwebby corners, until his hands felt a packet. At first he thought it was an old tobacco pouch, but then he saw that it was oilskin wrapped about some papers. Letters. And newspaper clippings.

Letters from Bran to Zillah, to Matthew. Urgent letters.

He looked at them and the words danced and flickered. Sometimes they seemed to say one thing, sometimes another. He could not read the small print. He pushed the heels of his hands against his eyeballs and everything sparkled like fireworks. He sobbed with frustration, and took the letters and clippings downstairs and put them under his pillow.

—I'll tell Grandma. She'll help me read them.

The kythe came to Meg in distorting waves.

One minute she understood, and the next she was caught up in Chuck's shifting universe. She pulled herself away from the kythe to try to think.

—What's coming clear, she thought,—is that it's important to know whether Mad Dog Branzillo is from Madoc's or Gwydyr's line. Somehow or other, it's between the two babies in the scry, the scry which both Madoc and Brandon Llawcae saw.

We don't know much about Gwydyr's line. He was disgraced, and he went to Vespugia eventually, and we think Gedder is his descendant.

We know a little more about Madoc's line. From each time Charles Wallace has gone Within, we know that most of Madoc's ancestors stayed around here.

So Branzillo's ancestors matter. And it's all in Matthew Maddox's book that Charles Wallace can't get at because the Echthroi are blocking him. But what can Charles Wallace do about it, even if he and Gaudior ever do get to Patagonia?

Slowly, she moved back into the kythe.

"Chuck." It was Beezie's voice.

"Here I am."

"How do you feel?"

"Dizzy. The earth's spinning, like the night we saw the fireflies."

"The night Pa died."

"Yes. Like then."

"You remember?" she asked in surprise.

"Of course."

"Lots of things you don't remember. That's why you can't go to school any more. Chuck—"

"What?"

"Ma's going to have a baby."

"She can't. Pa's dead."

"She's married again."

"She and Gedder can't have a baby. It would be bad."

"I thought you were talking the way you used to. I

thought you were all right!" Her voice rose in frustration and outrage. "Not Gedder! Mortmain!"

He tried to come back to her, but he could not. "Same difference. Same smell. The baby has to come from Madoc. Bran and Zillah have to have the baby because of the prayer."

"What prayer?" she shouted.

> "Lords of blue and Lords of gold,
> Lords of winds and waters wild,
> Lords of time that's growing old,
> When will come the season mild?
> When will come blue Madoc's child?"

"Where'd you learn that?"

"The letters."

"What letters?"

He became impatient. "Bran's letters, of course."

"But we've read them all. There wasn't anything like that in them."

"Found some more."

"When? Where?"

"In the attic. Grandma helps me read them."

"Where are they?" she demanded.

He fumbled under his pillow. "Here."

* * *

Chuck walked through a spring evening, smelling of growing grass, and blossoms drifting from the trees. He walked over the fields, over the brook, drinking the water rushing with melting snow, lifting his head, clambering to his feet, going on to the flat rock. Pain walked with him, and there was a dark veil of cloud between his eyes and the world. If a chair was pulled out of place he walked into it. Trees and rocks did not move; he felt safer at the rock than anywhere else.

He did not tell anybody about the veil.

He began to make mistakes in stamping the prices on the stock, but Duthbert Mortmain assumed it was because the fall had made him half-witted.

The baby came, a boy, and the mother no longer worked in the store. Paddy O'Keefe had dropped out of school and came in to help. Chuck followed Paddy's instructions, marking the cans with the stamp which Paddy set for him. He heard Paddy say, "He's more trouble than he's worth. Whyn't you send him to the nuthouse?"

Mortmain muttered something about his wife.

"Aren't you afraid he'll hurt the baby?" Paddy asked.

After that, Chuck stayed out of the way as much as possible, spending the warm days at the flat rock, the cold ones curled up in the attic. He saw Beezie to talk to only in the evenings, and Sunday afternoons.

"Chuck, what's wrong with your eyes?"

"Nothing."

"You're not seeing properly."

"It's all right."

"Ma—"

"Don't tell Ma!"

"But you ought to see a doctor."

"No! All they want is any excuse to put me away. You must have heard them, Paddy and Duthbert. They want to put me in an institution. For my own good, Mortmain said to Ma. He said I'm an idiot and I might hurt the baby."

Beezie burst into tears and flung her arms around her brother. "You wouldn't!"

"I know I wouldn't. But it's the one thing Ma might listen to."

"And you're not an idiot!"

His cheeks were wet with Beezie's tears. "If you tell them about my eyes they'll put me in an insane asylum for my own good and the baby's. I'm trying to keep out of the way."

"I'll help you, oh, Chuck, I'll help you," Beezie promised.

"I have to stay long enough to make sure Matthew sends Zillah to Vespugia. He's saving the money."

"Oh, Chuck," Beezie groaned. "Don't let them hear you talk like this."

* * *

As the veil deepened and darkened, his inner vision lightened. When the weather was fine he lay out on the flat rock all day, looking up toward the sky and seeing pictures, pictures more vivid than anything he had seen with unveiled eyes. His concentration was so intense that he became part of all that was happening in the pictures. Sometimes in the evenings he told Beezie about them, pretending they were dreams, in order not to upset her.

"I dreamed about riding a unicorn. He was like moonlight, and so tall I had to climb a tree to get on his back, and we flew among the fireflies, and the unicorn and I sang together."

"That's a lovely dream. Tell me more."

"I dreamed that the valley was a lake, and I rode a beautiful fish sort of like a porpoise."

"Pa said the valley was a lake, way back in prehistory. Archaeologists have found fish fossils in the glacial rocks. Maybe that's why you dreamed it."

"Grandma told us about the lake, the day we blew dandelion clocks."

"Oh, Chuck, you're so strange, the way you remember some things . . ."

"And I dreamed about a fire of roses, and—" He reached gropingly for her hand. "I can move in and out of time."

"Oh, Chuck!"

"I can, Beezie."

"Please—please stop."

"It's only dreams," he comforted.

"Well, then. But don't tell Ma."

"Only you and Grandma."

"Oh, Chuck."

He knew the route to the rock so well that it was easier for him to go in the dark, when he could see nothing, than in sunlight when shafts of brilliance penetrated the veil like spears and hurt his eyes and confused his sense of direction.

Time. Time. There wasn't much time.

Time. Time was as fluid as water.

He stood by Matthew's couch. "You can't wait any longer. You have to get Zillah to Vespugia now, or it will be too late."

Matthew is writing, writing against time. It's all in the book Pa talked about. They don't want me to see the book.

Ritchie is cutting a window in Brandon's room, before leaving for Wales . . .

But Zillah isn't there . . . Why is there an Indian girl instead?

Because it isn't Zillah's time. She comes later, in Matthew's time

Unicorns can move in time

and idiots

space is more difficult

Paddy wants me out of the way. Paddy and Mortmain.
Not much time

> Lords of space and Lords of time,
> Lords of blessing, Lords of grace,
> Who is in the warmer clime?
> Who will follow Madoc's rhyme?
> Blue will alter time and space.

Did you not learn in Gwynedd that there is room for
one king only?

You will be great, little Madog, and call the world your
own, to keep or destroy as you will. It is an evil world,
little Madog.

You will do good for your people, El Zarco, little Blue
Eyes. The prayer has been answered in you, blue for
birth, blue for mirth

Which blue will it be

They are fighting
up on the cliff
on the steep rock

the world
it's tilting
it's going too fast
I'm going to fall

ELEVEN

All these I place

The light came back slowly. There had been shadows, nothing but deepening shadows, and pain, and slowly the pain began to leave and healing light touched his closed lids. He opened them. He was on the star-watching rock with Gaudior.

"The wind brought you out of Chuck."

"What happened to him?"

"Mortmain had him institutionalized. Are you ready? It's time—" A ripple of tension moved along the unicorn's flanks.

Charles Wallace felt the wind all about them, cold, and yet strengthening. "What Chuck saw—two men fighting—was it real?"

"What is real?" Gaudior replied infuriatingly.

"It's important!"

"We do not always know what is important and what

is not. The wind sends a warning to hurry, hurry. Climb up, and hold very tight."

"Should I bind myself to you again?"

"The wind says there's no time. We'll fly out of time and through galaxies the Echthroi do not know. But the wind says it may be difficult to send you Within, even so. Hold on, and try not to be afraid."

Charles Wallace felt the wind beneath them as Gaudior spread his wings. The flight at first was serene. Then he began to feel cold, a deep, penetrating cold far worse than the cold of the Ice Age sea. This was a cold of the spirit as well as the body. He did not fall off the unicorn because he was frozen to him; his hands were congealed in their clenched grasp on the frozen mane.

Gaudior's hoofs touched something solid, and the cold lifted just enough so that the boy was able to unclench his hands and open his frozen lids. They were in an open square in a frozen city of tall, windowless buildings. There was no sign of tree, of grass. The blind cement was cracked, and there were great chunks of fallen masonry on the street.

"Where—" Charles Wallace started, and stopped.

The unicorn turned his head slowly. "A Projection—"

Charles Wallace followed his gaze and saw two men in gas masks patrolling the square with machine guns. "Do they see us?"

The question was answered by the two men pausing,

turning, looking through the round black eyes of their gas masks directly at unicorn and boy, and raising their guns.

With a tremendous leap Gaudior launched upward, wings straining. Charles Wallace pressed close to the neck, hands twined in the mane. But for the moment they had escaped the Echthroi, and when Gaudior's hoofs touched the ground, the Projection was gone.

"Those men with guns—" Charles Wallace started. "In a Projection, could they have killed us?"

"I don't know," Gaudior said, "and I didn't want to wait to find out."

Charles Wallace looked around in relief. When he had left Chuck, it was autumn, the cold wind stripping the trees. Now it was high spring, the old apple and pear trees in full blossom, and the smell of lilac on the breeze. All about them, the birds were in full song.

"What should we do now?" Charles Wallace asked.

"At least you're asking, not telling." Gaudior sounded unusually cross, so the boy knew he was unusually anxious.

Meg shivered. Within the kythe she saw the star-watching rock and a golden summer's day. There were two people on the rock, a young woman, and a young man—or a boy? She was not sure, because there was something wrong with the boy. But from their dress she was positive that it was the time of the Civil War—around 1865.

* * *

The Within-ing was long and agonizing, instead of immediate, as it had always been before. Charles Wallace felt intolerable pain in his back, and a crushing of his legs. He could hear himself screaming. His body was being forced into another body, and at the same time something was struggling to pull him out. He was being torn apart in a battle between two opposing forces. Sun blazed, followed by a blizzard of snow, snow melted by raging fire, and violent flashings of lightning, driven by a mighty wind, which whipped across sea and land . . .

His body was gone and he was Within, Within a crippled body, the body of a young man with useless legs like a shriveled child's . . . Matthew Maddox.

From the waist up he looked not unlike Madoc, and about the same age, with a proud head and a lion's mane of fair hair. But the body was nothing like Madoc's strong and virile one. And the eyes were grey, grey as the ocean before rain.

Matthew was looking somberly at the girl, who appeared to be about his age, though her eyes were far younger than his. "Croeso f'annwyl, Zillah." He spoke the Welsh words of endearment lovingly. "Thank you for coming."

"You knew I would. As soon as Jack O'Keefe brought your note, I set off. How did you get here?"

He indicated a low wagon which stood a little way from the rock.

She looked at the powerful torso, and deeply muscled shoulders and arms. "By yourself, all the way?"

"No. I can do it, but it takes me a long time, and I had to go over the store ledgers this morning. When I went to the stables to find Jack to deliver the note, I swallowed my pride and asked him to bring me."

Zillah spread her billowing white skirts about her on the rock. She wore a wide-brimmed leghorn hat with blue ribbons, which brought out the highlights in her straight, shining black hair, and a locket on a blue ribbon at her throat. To Matthew Maddox she was the most beautiful, and desirable, and—to him—the most unattainable woman in the world.

"Matt, what's wrong?" she asked.

"Something's happened to Bran."

She paled. "How do you know? Are you sure?"

"Last night I woke out of a sound sleep with an incredibly sharp pain in my leg. Not my own familiar pain, Bran's pain. And he was calling out to me to help him."

"O dear Lord. Is he going to be all right?"

"He's alive. He's been reaching out to me all day."

She buried her face in her hands, so that her words were muffled. "Thank you for telling me. You and Bran— you've always been so close, even closer than most twins."

He acknowledged this with a nod. "We were always close, but it was after my accident that—it was Bran who brought me back into life, Zillah, you know that."

She dropped her hand lightly on his shoulder. "If Bran is badly wounded, we're going to need you. As once you needed Bran."

After the accident, five years earlier, when his horse had crashed into a fence and rolled over on him, crushing his pelvis and legs and fracturing his spine, Bran had shown him no pity; instead, had fiercely tried to push his twin brother into as much independence as possible, and refused to allow him to feel sorry for himself.

"But Rollo jumps fences twice as high with ease."

"He didn't jump that one."

"Bran, just before he crashed, there was a horrible, putrid stink—"

"Stop going back over things. Get on with it."

They continued to go everywhere together—until the war. Unlike Bran, Matthew could not lie about his age and join the cavalry.

"I lived my life through Bran, vicariously," Matthew told Zillah. "When he went to war, it was the first time he ever left me out." Then: "When you and Bran fell in love, I knew that I had to start letting him go, to try to find some kind of life of my own, so that he'd be free. And it was easier to let go with you than with anyone else in the world, because you've always treated me like a complete human being, and I knew that the two of you would not exclude me from your lives."

"Dear Matt. Never. And you are making your own life. You're selling your stories and poems, and I think they're as good as anything by Mark Twain."

Matthew laughed, a warm laugh that lightened the pain lines in his face. "They're only a beginner's work."

"But editors think they're good, too, and so does my father."

"I'm glad. I value Dr. Llawcae's opinion as much as anybody's in the world."

"And he loves you and Bran and Gwen as though you were my brothers and sister. And your mother has been a second mother to me since my own dear mama died. As for our fathers—they may be only distant kin, but they're like as two peas in a pod with their passion for Wales. Matt—have you said anything about Bran to Gwen or your parents?"

"No. They don't like the idea that Bran and I can communicate without speech or letters the way we do. They pretend it's some kind of trick we've worked out, the way we used to change places with each other when we were little, to fool people. They think what we do isn't real."

"It's real, I don't doubt that." Zillah smiled. "Dear Matt, I think I love you nearly as much as Bran does."

* * *

A week later, Mr. Maddox received official news that his son had been wounded in battle and would be invalided home. He called the family into the dark, book-lined library to inform them.

Mrs. Maddox fanned herself with her black lace fan. "Thank God."

"You're glad Bran's been wounded!" Gwen cried indignantly.

Mrs. Maddox continued to fan herself. "Of course not, child. But I'm grateful to God that he's alive, and that he's coming home before something worse than a bullet in the leg happens to him."

—It is worse, Mama, Matthew thought silently.—Bran has been shutting me out of his thoughts and he's never done that before. All I get from him is a dull, deadening pain. Gwen is more right than she knows, not to be glad.

He looked thoughtfully at his sister. She was dark of hair and blue of eye like Zillah, making them appear more like sisters than distant cousins. But her face did not have Zillah's openness, and her eyes were a colder blue and glittered when she was angry. After Matthew's accident she had pitied him, but had not translated her pity into compassion. Matthew did not want pity.

Gwen returned his gaze. "And how do you feel about your twin's coming home, Matthew?"

"He's been badly hurt, Gwen," he said. "He's not going to be the same debonair Bran who left us."

"He's still only a child." Mrs. Maddox turned toward her husband, who was sitting behind the long oak library table.

"He's a man, and when he comes home the store will become Maddox and Son," her husband said.

—Maddox and Son, Matthew thought without bitterness—not Maddox and Sons.

He turned his wheelchair slightly away. He was totally committed to his writing; he had no wish to be a partner in Maddox's General Store, which was a large and prosperous establishment in the center of the village, and had the trade of the surrounding countryside for many miles. The first story of the rambling frame building was filled with all the foodstuffs needed for the village. Upstairs were saddles and harnesses, guns, plows, and even a large quantity of oars, as though Mr. Maddox remembered a time when nearly all of the valley had been a great lake. A few ponds were all that remained of the original body of water. Matthew spent most mornings in the store, taking care of the ledgers and all the accounts.

Behind the store was the house, named Merioneth. The Llawcae home, Madrun, stood beyond Merioneth, slightly more ostentatious, with white pillars and pink-brick façade. Merioneth was the typical three-storied white frame farmhouse with dark shutters which had replaced the original log cabins.

"People think we're putting on airs, giving our houses names," Bran had complained one day, before the accident, as he and Matthew were walking home from school.

Matthew did a cartwheel. "I like it," he said as he came right side up. "Merioneth is named in honor of a distant cousin of ours in Wales."

"Yah, I know, Michael Jones, a congregational minister of Bala in Merioneth."

"Cousin Michael's pleased that we've given the house that name. He mentions it almost every time he writes to Papa. Weren't you listening yesterday when he was telling us about Love Jones Parry, the squire of Madrun, and his plan to take a trip to Patagonia to inspect the land and see if it might be suitable for a colony from Wales?"

"That's the only interesting bit," Bran had said. "I love to travel, even just to go with Papa to get supplies. Maybe if the squire of Madrun really does take that trip, we could go with him."

It was not long after this that the accident happened, and Matthew remembered how Bran had tried to rouse him from despair by telling him that Love Jones Parry had actually gone to Patagonia, and reported that although the land was wild and desolate, he thought that the formation of a Welsh colony where the colonists would be allowed to teach their native tongue in school might be possible. The Spanish government paid scant attention to that section of Patagonia, where there were only a few Indians and a handful of Spaniards.

But Matthew refused to be roused. "Exciting for you. I'm not going to get very far from Merioneth ever again."

Bran had scowled at him ferociously. "You cannot afford the luxury of self-pity."

—It is still an expensive luxury, Matthew thought—and one I can ill afford.

"Matt!" It was Gwen. "A penny for your thoughts."

He had been writing when his father had summoned them, and still had his note pad on his lap. "Just thinking out the plot for another story."

She smiled at him brightly. "You're going to make the name of Maddox famous!"

"My brave baby," Mrs. Maddox said. "How proud I am of you! That was the third story you've sold to *Harper's Monthly*, wasn't it?"

"The fourth—Mama, Papa, Gwen: I think I must warn you that Bran is going to need all our love and help when he comes home."

"Well, of course—" Gwen started indignantly.

"No, Gwen," he said quietly. "Bran is hurt much more than just the leg wound."

"What are you talking about?" his father demanded.

"You might call it Bran's soul. It's sick."

* * *

Bran returned, limping and withdrawn. He shut Matthew out as effectively as though he had slammed a door in his twin's face.

Once again Matthew sent a note to Zillah to meet him at the flat rock. This time he did not ask Jack O'Keefe for help, but lying on the wagon, he pulled himself over the rough ground. It was arduous work, even with his powerful arms, and he was exhausted when he arrived. But he had allowed more than enough time. He heaved himself off the wagon and dragged over to the rock, stretched out, and slept under the warm autumn sun.

"Matt—"

He woke up. Zillah was smiling down at him. "F'annwyl." He pushed the fair hair back from his eyes and sat up. "Thanks for coming."

"How is he today?"

Matthew shook his head. "No change. It's hard on Papa to have another crippled son."

"Hush. Bran's not a cripple!"

"He'll limp from that leg wound for the rest of his life. And whether or not his spirit will heal is anybody's guess."

"Give him time, Matt . . ."

"Time!" Matthew pushed the word away impatiently. "That's what Mama keeps saying. But we've given him time. It's three months since he came home. He sleeps half the day and reads half the night. And he's still keeping himself closed to me. If he'd talk about his experiences it might help him, but he won't."

"Not even to you?"

"He seems to feel he has to protect me," Matthew said bitterly, "and one of the things I've always loved most in Bran was his refusal to protect or mollycoddle me in any way."

"Bran, Bran," Zillah murmured, "the knight in shining armor who went so bravely to join the cavalry and save the country and free the slaves . . ." She glanced at the ring on her finger. "He asked me to return his ring. To set me free, he said."

Matthew stretched out his hand to her, then drew it back.

"There has to be time for me as well as for Bran. When he gave me this ring I promised I'd be here for him when he returned, no matter what, and I intend to keep that promise. What can we do to bring him out of the slough of despond?"

Matthew ached to reach out to touch her fair skin, to stroke her hair as black as the night and as beautiful. He spread his hand on the warm rock. "I tried to get him to take me riding. I haven't ridden since he went away."

"And?"

"He said it was too dangerous."

"For you? Or for him?"

"That's what I asked him. And he just said, 'Leave me alone. My leg pains me.' And I said, 'You never used to let me talk about it when my legs and back hurt.' And he just looked at me and said, 'I didn't understand pain then.' And I said, 'I think you understood it better then than you do now.' And we stopped talking because we weren't getting anywhere, and he wouldn't open an inch to let me near him."

"Father says his pain should be tolerable by now, and the physical wound is not the problem."

"That's right. We've got to get him out of himself somehow. And Zillah, something else happened that I need to talk to you about. Yesterday when I hoped I could get Bran to take me riding I wheeled out to the stable to check on my saddle, and when I pushed open the stable door there were Jack and—and—"

"Gwen?"

"How did you guess?"

"I've noticed him looking at her. And she's looked right back."

"They were doing more than looking. They were kissing."

"Merchant's daughter and hired hand. Your parents would not approve. How about you?"

"Zillah, that's not what I mind about Jack O'Keefe. He's a big and powerful man and he has nothing but scorn for me—or anything with a physical imperfection. I saw him take a homeless puppy and kill it by flinging it against the wall of the barn."

She put her hands over her eyes. "Matt! Stop!"

"I think it's his enormous physical healthiness that attracts Gwen. I'm a total cripple, and Bran's half a one, at least for now. And Jack is life. She doesn't see the cruelty behind the wide smile and loud laugh."

"What are you going to do about it?"

"Nothing. For now. Mama and Papa have enough on their minds, worrying their hearts out over Bran. And if I warn Gwen, she'll just think I'm jealous of all that Jack can do and all that I cannot. I'll try to talk to Bran, but I doubt he'll hear."

"Dear Matt. It comforts me that you and I can talk like this." Her voice was compassionate, but it held none of the pity he loathed. "My true and good friend."

One night after dinner, while the men lingered over the port, Mr. Maddox looked at Bran over the ruby liquid in his glass. "Matthew and Zillah would like you to join them in their Welsh lesson this week."

"Not yet, Papa."

"Not yet, not yet, that's all you've been saying for the past three months. Will Llawcae says your wound is healed now, and there's no reason for your malingering."

To try to stop his father, Matthew said, "I was remarking today that Gwen looks more Indian than Welsh, with her high cheekbones."

Mr. Maddox poured himself a second glass of port, then stoppered the cut-glass decanter. "Your mother does not like to be reminded that I have Indian blood, though it's generations back. The Llawcaes have it, too, through our common forebears, Brandon Llawcae and Maddok of the People of the Wind, whose children intermarried. Maddok was so named because he had the blue eyes of Welsh Madoc—but then, I don't need to repeat the story."

"True," Bran agreed.

"I like it." Matthew sipped his wine.

"You're a romanticizer," Bran said. "Keep it for your writing."

Mr. Maddox said stiffly, "As your mother has frequently pointed out, black hair and blue eyes are far more common in people of Welsh descent than Indian, and Welsh we indubitably are. And hard-working." He looked pointedly at Bran.

Later in the evening Matthew wheeled himself into Bran's room. His twin was standing by the window, holding the velveteen curtains aside to look across the lawn to the woods. He turned on Matthew with a growl. "Go away."

"No, Bran. When I was hurt I told you to go away, and you wouldn't. Nor will I." Matthew wheeled closer to his brother. "Gwen's in love with Jack O'Keefe."

"Not surprised. Jack's a handsome brute."

"He's not the right man for Gwen."

"Because he's our hired hand? Don't be such a snob."

"No. Because he is, as you said, a brute."

"Gwen can take care of herself. She always has. Anyhow, Papa would put his foot down."

There was an empty silence which Matthew broke. "Don't cut Zillah out of your life."

"If I love Zillah, that's the only thing to do. Free her."

"She doesn't want to be free. She loves you."

Bran walked over to his bed with the high oak bedstead and flung himself down. "I'm out of love with everything and everybody. Out of love with life."

"Why?"

"Do you have to ask me?"

"Yes, I do. Because you aren't telling me."

"You used to know without my having to tell you."

"I still would, if you weren't shutting me out."

Bran moved his head restlessly back and forth on the pillow. "Don't you be impatient with me, twin. Papa's bad enough."

Matthew wheeled over to the bed. "You know Papa."

"I'm no more cut out to be a storekeeper than you are. Gwen's the one who has Papa's hard business sense. But I don't have a talent like yours to offer Papa as an alternative. And he's always counted on me to take over the business. And I don't want to. I never did."

"What, then?" Matthew asked.

"I'm not sure. The only positive thing the war did for me was confirm my enjoyment of travel. I like adventure—but not killing. And it seems the two are seldom separated."

It was the nearest they had come to a conversation since Bran's return, and Matthew felt hopeful.

Matthew was writing on his lap desk in a sunny corner of the seldom-used parlor.

There Bran found him. "Twin, I need you."

"I'm here," Matthew said.

Bran straddled a small gilt chair and leaned his arms on the back. "Matt, nothing is the way I thought it was. I went to war thinking of myself as Galahad, out to free fellow human beings from the intolerable bondage of slavery. But it wasn't as simple as that. There were other, less pure issues being fought over, with little concern for the souls which would perish for nothing more grand than political greed, corruption, and conniving for power. Matt, I saw a man with his face blown off and no mouth to scream with, and yet he screamed and could not die. I saw two brothers, and one was in blue and one was in grey, and I will not tell you which one took his saber and ran it through the other. Oh God, it was brother against brother, Cain and Abel all over again. And I was turned into Cain. What would God have to do with a nation where brothers can turn against each other with such brutality?" Bran stopped speaking as his voice broke on a sob.

Matthew put down his lap desk and drew his twin to him, and together they wept, as Bran poured out all the anguish and terror and nightmare he had lived through. And Matthew held him and drew the pain out and into his own heart.

When the torrent was spent, Bran looked at his twin. "Thank you."

Matthew held him close. "You're back, Bran. We're together again."

"Yes. Forever."

"It's good to have you coming back to life."

"Coming back to life hurts. I need to take my pain away."

Matthew asked, startled, "What?"

"Matt, twin, I'm going away."

"What!" Matthew looked at Bran standing straight and strong before him. The yellow satin curtains warmed the light and brightened Bran's hair. "Where?"

"You'll never guess."

Matthew waited.

"Papa had a letter from Wales, from Cousin Michael. A

group left for Patagonia to start a colony. They're there by now. I'm going to join them. How's that for an old dream come true?"

"We were going together . . ."

"Dear my twin, you're making a name for yourself here with your pen. I know that the creation of a story is work, even if Papa doesn't. But you couldn't manage a life of physical hardship such as I'll be having in the Welsh colony."

"You're right," Matthew acknowledged. "I'd be a burden."

"I won't be far from you, ever again," Bran assured him, "even in Patagonia. I promise to share it with you, and you'll be able to write stories about it as vividly as though you'd been there in body. Cousin Michael writes that the colony is settling in well, in a small section known as Vespugia, and I'll tell you everything about it, and describe a grand cast of characters for you."

"Have you told Zillah?"

Bran shook his head.

"Twin, this affects Zillah too, you know. She wears your ring."

"I'll tell everyone tonight at dinner. I'll get Mama to ask the Llawcaes."

Dinner was served in the dining room, a large, dark, oak-paneled chamber that seemed to drink in the light from the crystal chandelier. Heavy brown curtains like the ones in the library were drawn against the cold night. The fire burning brightly did little to warm the vast cavern.

During the meal, conversation was largely about the Welsh expedition to Patagonia, with both Mr. Maddox and Dr. Llawcae getting vicarious excitement out of the adventure.

"What fun," Gwen said. "Why don't you go, Papa? If I were a man, I would."

Matthew and Bran looked at each other across the table, but Bran shook his head slightly.

After dessert, when Mrs. Maddox pushed back her chair, nodding to Gwen and Zillah to follow her, Bran stopped them. "Wait, please, Mama. I have something to tell everybody. We've all enjoyed discussing the Patagonian expedition, and the founding of the colony in Vespugia, Years ago, before Matt's accident, we dreamed of joining the squire of Madrun when he made his journey to see if it would be a suitable place for a colony. So perhaps it won't surprise you that I have decided to join the colonists and make a new life for myself in Vespugia. Today I've written Cousin Michael and Mr. Parry in Wales, and sent letters to Vespugia."

For a moment there was stunned silence.

Bran broke it, smiling. "Dr. Llawcae says a warmer climate will be better for me."

Mr. Maddox asked, "Isn't going to Patagonia rather an excessive way to find a warmer climate? You could go south, to South Carolina or Georgia."

Bran's lips shut in a rigid expression of pain. "Papa, do you forget where I've come from and what I've been doing?"

Mrs. Maddox said, "No, son, your father does not forget. But the war is over, and you must put it behind you."

"In the South? I doubt I would be welcome in the Confederate states."

"But Vespugia—so far away—" Tears filled Mrs. Maddox's eyes. Zillah, her face pale but resolute, drew a fresh handkerchief from her reticule and handed it to her. "If you'd just continue to regain your strength, and go on studying Welsh with Matthew, and come into the business with your father—"

Bran shook his head. "Mama, you know that I cannot go into the business with Papa. And I have no talent, like Matthew's, which I could use here. It seems that the best way to pull myself together is to get out, and what better way to learn Welsh than to be with people who speak it all the time?"

Mr. Maddox spoke slowly, "You took me by surprise, son, but it does seem to be a reasonable solution for you, eh, Will?" He looked at the doctor, who was tamping his pipe.

"In a way, I identify with Madoc, Papa," Bran said. "Matt and I were rereading T. Gwynn Jones's poem about him this evening." He looked at Gwen. "Remember it?"

She sniffled. "I never read Welsh unless Papa forces me."

"Madoc left Wales in deep despair because brother was fighting against brother, just as we did in this ghastly war, 'until it seemed as if God himself had withdrawn his care from the sons of men.' . . . *ymdroi gyda diflastod as anobaith Madog wrth ystried cyflwr gwlad ei ededigaeth, lle'r oedd brawd un ymladd yn erbyn brawd hyd nes yr oedd petal Duw ei hun wedi peidio â gofalu am feibion dynion.*"

Mr. Maddox drew on his pipe. "You do remember."

"Good lad," Dr. Llawcae approved.

"I remember, and too well I understand, for there were many nights during the war when God withdrew from our battlefields. When the sons of men fight against each other in hardness of heart, why should God not withdraw? Slavery is evil, God knows, but war is evil, too, evil, evil."

Zillah pushed her empty dessert plate away and went to kneel by Bran, impulsively taking his hand and pressing it against her cheek.

He took her hand in his. "I went to war thinking that mankind is reasonable, and found that it is not. But it has always been so, and at last I am growing up, as Matthew grew up long before me. I know that he would give a great deal to come to Vespugia with me, and I to have him, but we both know that it cannot be."

Mrs. Maddox was still weeping into the handkerchief Zillah had given her. "Never again can there be a war that can do such terrible things to people."

Mr. Maddox said, "My dear, it is not good for us to keep reminding Bran of the war. Perhaps getting away from Merioneth and going to Vespugia will be the best way for him to forget."

Matthew looked at his father and saw him letting his dream of *Maddox and Son* disappear into the wilderness of Vespugia.

"Bran." Zillah rose and looked down at him.

"Little Zillah."

"I'm not little Zillah any more, Bran. You changed that the night before you went to war when you put this ring on my finger."

"Child," Dr. Llawcae remonstrated, "it is the dearest wish of my heart that Llawcaes and Maddoxes be once more united in marriage. I gave Bran my blessing when he came to me to ask for your hand. But not yet. You're only seventeen."

"Many women are married and mothers at seventeen. I want to go to Vespugia with Bran, as his wife."

"Zillah," Dr. Llawcae said, "you will wait. When Bran is settled, in a year or two, he can send for you."

Bran pressed Zillah's hand. "It needn't all be decided tonight."

In the end, Bran went with Gwen, not with Zillah. Mr. Maddox caught Gwen and Jack O'Keefe kissing behind the stable door, and announced flatly that she was to accompany her brother to Vespugia. No amount of tears, of hysterics from Gwen, of pleading from Mrs. Maddox, could change his stand.

Gwen and Zillah wept together. "It's not fair," Gwen sobbed. "A woman has no say in her own life. I hate men!"

Matthew tried to intercede with Dr. Llawcae for Zillah, but the doctor was adamant that she should wait at least until she was eighteen, and until Bran had suitable living arrangements.

Store and house were empty after they left. Matthew spent the morning working on accounts, and in the afternoon and evenings he stayed in his corner of the empty parlor, writing. His first novel was published and well received and he was hard at work on his second. It was this, and conversations with Zillah, who came frequently to Merioneth from Madrun, which kept him going.

"Bran's all right," he assured Zillah. "He sends love."

"They can't even have reached Vespugia yet," Zillah protested. "And there's certainly been no chance for him to send a letter."

"You know Bran and I don't need letters."

She sighed. "I know. Will Bran and I ever be like that?"

"Yours will be a different kind of unity. Better, maybe, but different."

"Will he send for me?"

"You must give him time, Zillah—time once again. Time to settle into a new world and a new way of life. And time for your father to get used to the idea of having his only child go half the way across the world from him."

"How's Gwen?"

"Part sulking and feeling sorry for herself, and part enjoying all the sailors on the ship making cow's eyes at her and running to do her bidding. But she's not going to be happy in Vespugia. She's always hated hot weather, and she's never liked roughing it."

"No, she wasn't a tomboy, like me. She thought Father was terrible to let me run wild and play rough games with you and Bran. Will your father relent and let her come home?"

"Not while Jack's around. There's no second-guessing Papa, though, when he latches on to an unreasonable notion." He paused. "Remember the old Indian verses, Zillah?"

"About black hair and blue eyes?"

"Yes. They've been singing around in my head, and I can't get them out, especially one verse:

"Lords of spirit, Lords of breath,
Lords of fireflies, stars, and light,
Who will keep the world from death?
Who will stop the coming night?
Blue eyes, blue eyes, have the sight."

"It's beautiful," Zillah said, "but I don't really know what it means."

"It's not to be taken literally. The Indians believed that as long as there was one blue-eyed child in each generation, all would be well."

"But it wasn't, was it? They've been long gone from around here."

"I think it was a bigger all-rightness than just for their tribe. Anyhow, both you and Gwen have at least a drop of Indian blood, and you both have the blue eyes of the song."

"So, in a way," Zillah said dreamily, "we're the last of the People of the Wind. Unless—"

Matthew smiled at her. "I think you're meant to have a black-haired, blue-eyed baby."

"When?" Zillah demanded. "Bran's a world away from me. And I'll be old and white-haired and wrinkled before Papa realizes I'm grown up and lets me go." She looked at him anxiously.

* * *

Matthew's work began to receive more and more critical acclaim, and Mr. Maddox began thinking of it as something "real," rather than fanciful scribbling not to be taken seriously. One of the unused downstairs rooms was fixed up as a study, and Dr. Llawcae designed a larger and more efficient lap desk.

The study was at the back of the house and looked across the lawn to the woods, and in the autumn Matthew feasted on the glory of the foilage. The room was sparsely furnished, at his request, with a black leather couch on which he could rest when sitting became too painful. As the cold weather set in, he began more and more often to spend the nights there. In front of the fireplace was a butler's table and a comfortable lady chair upholstered in blue, the color of Zillah's eyes: Zillah's chair, he thought of it.

It was midsummer before letters began to arrive on a regular basis. True to his promise, Bran sent Matthew vivid descriptions:

How amazingly interconnected everything is, at least to us who have Welsh blood in our veins. My closest friends here are Richard Llawcae, his wife, and his son Rich. They must be at least distant kin to all of us, for Llawcae is not a common name, even in Wales. Richard says they have forebears who emigrated to the New World in the very early days, and then went back to Wales, for nothing there was as bad as the witch-hunting in the Pilgrim villages and towns. One of their ancestors was burned, they think, or nearly so. They don't know exactly where they came from, but probably around Salem.

Rich has eyes for no one but Gwen, and I wish she would see and return his love, for I can think of no one I'd rather have as a brother-in-law. But Gwen sees Gedder before Rich. Gedder is taller and bigger and stronger—perhaps—and certainly more flamboyant. He worries me. Zillie has told me of his fierce ambitions, and his manner toward all of us becomes a little more lordly every day. God knows he is helpful—if it weren't for the Indians, I'm not sure the colony would have survived, for everything is different from at home—times for planting, what to plant, how to irrigate, etc. We are grateful indeed that the Indians not only have been friendly but have given us all the help they could. Yet I could wish Gedder had been more like his brethren and not so pushy and bossy. None of us likes the way Gedder treats his sister, as though she were his slave and inferior.

It is astounding how Zillie has the same features as Gwen and Zillah, the wide-apart eyes with the faintest suggestion of a tilt—though hers are a warm brown, and not blue—and the high cheek-bones and delicate nose. And, of course, the straight, shining black hair. People have remarked on the likeness between Gwen and Zillie. I haven't talked with anyone except the Llawcaes about the Madoc legend following us to Vespugia, and they don't laugh it away. Truly, truth is stranger than fiction. Put it into a story for me, Matt.

—I will, Matthew promised silently.—I will. But you must tell me more.

My house is nearly finished, large and airy, with verandas. Everyone knows that it is being built for my bride, and for our children. Zillie often comes and stands, just out of the way, and looks, and that makes me uncomfortable. I don't think she comes of her own volition. I think Gedder sends her. I talk much about my Zillah, and how I long for the day when she will arrive. Matthew, twin, use your influence on Dr. Llawcae to let her come soon. Why is he keeping her with him? I need her, now.

As winter closed in and Matthew could not go out of doors, Zillah began to come from Madrun to Merioneth nearly every day at teatime, and Matthew missed her more than he liked to admit when she did not appear. He was hurrying to finish his second novel, considerably more ambitious than the first, but he tired quickly, and lay on the black couch, reaching out to Bran and Vespugia, all through the winter, the summer, and into a second winter. He felt closer to his twin than ever, and when he neared the shallows of sleep he felt that he actually was in arid Vespugia, part of all that was happening in the tight-knit colony.

In the mornings, when he worked with his soft, dark pencil and large note pad, it was as though he were setting down what he had seen and heard the night before.

"You're pale, Matt," Zillah said one afternoon as she sat in the lady chair and poured his tea.

"It's this bitter cold. Even with the fire going constantly, the damp seeps into my bones."

He turned away from her concern and looked out the window at the night drawing in. "I have to get my book finished, and there's not much time. I have a large canvas, going all the way back to the Welsh brothers who fought over Owain of Gwynedd's throne. Madoc and his brother, Gwydyr, left Wales, and came to a place which I figure to have been somewhere near here, when the valley was still a lake left from the melting of the ice. And once again brothers fought. Gwydyr wanted power, wanted adulation. Over and over again we get caught in fratricide, as Bran was in that ghastly war. We're still bleeding from the wounds. It's a primordial pattern, left us from Cain and Abel, a net we can't seem to break out of. And unless it is checked it will destroy us entirely."

She clasped her hands. "Will it be checked?"

He turned back toward her. "I don't know, Zillah. When I sleep I have dreams, and I see dark and evil things, children being killed by hundreds and thousands in terrible wars which sweep over them." He reached for her hand. "I do not croak doom casually, f'annwyl. I do not know what is going to happen. And irrationally, perhaps, I am positive that what happens in Vespugia is going to make a difference. Read me the letter from Bran that came today once more, please."

She took the letter from the tea table and held it to the lamp.

Dear my twin, and dear my Zillah, when are you coming? Matthew, if you cannot bring Zillah to me, then Zillah must bring you. She writes that the winter is hard on you, and she is worried. There would be much to hold your attention here. Llewellyn Pugh languishes for love of Zillie, and I think she would turn to him did Gedder not keep forcing her on me, no matter how loudly I say that I am betrothed, and that my Zillah is coming to join us any day now. Do not make me a liar!

We have had our first death, and a sad one it was, too. The children are forbidden to climb up onto the cliff which protects the colony from the winds, but somehow or other, one of them managed the steep climb, and fell. We all grieve. It may be a good thing that there is so much work for everybody that there is little idle time, and this helps us all, particularly the parents of the little one. Rich has been a tower of strength. He was the one of us who was able to bring tears from the mother, partly because he was not ashamed to weep himself.

"He is a good man, that Rich," Matthew said. "He'd do anything in the world for Gwen."

"You talk as though you know him."

Matthew smiled at her. "I do. I know him through Bran. And through my novel. What happens with Rich, with Bran, with Gwen, with Zillie—it matters to my story. It could even change it." She looked at him questioningly. "This book is pushing me, Zillah, making me write it. It excites me, and it drives me. In its pages, myth and matter merge. What happens in one time can make a difference in what happens in another time, far more than we realize. What Gedder does is going to make a difference, to the book, perhaps to the world. Nothing, no one, is too small to matter. What you do is going to make a difference."

In the early winter Matthew caught a heavy chest cold, which weakened him, and Dr. Llawcae came daily. Matthew spent the days on the black leather couch, wrapped in blankets. He continued to work on his novel and sold several more stories. He kept his earnings, which were considerable, in a small safe in his study. And now he left the study not at all.

When he was too exhausted to write, he slid into a shallow sleep, filled with vivid dreams in which Bran and the Vespugian colony were more real than chilly Merioneth.

He was at the flat rock in his dream, the rock where he used to meet Zillah when he sought privacy. But instead of Zillah there was a boy, perhaps twelve years old, dressed in strange, shabby clothes. The boy was lying on the rock, and he, too, was dreaming, and his dream and Matthew's merged.

Gedder is after Gwen. Stop him. The baby must come from Madoc. Gwydyr's line is tainted. There is nothing left but pride and greed for power and revenge. Stop him, Matthew.

He saw his twin, but this was not Bran in Vespugia . . . Was it Bran? It was a young man, about their age, standing by a lake. Behind him stood another, a little older, who looked like Bran and yet not like Bran, for there was resentment behind the eyes. Like Gedder. The two began to wrestle, to engage in mortal combat.

At the edge of the lake a huge pile of flowers smoldered, with little red tongues of flame licking the petals of the roses—

"Matthew!"

He opened his eyes and his mother was hovering over him with a cup of camomile tea.

Beside the growing pages of the manuscript lay a genealogy which he had carefully worked out, a genealogy which could go in two different directions, like a double helix. In one direction there was hope; in the other, disaster. And the book and Bran and the Vespugian colony were intertwined in his mind and heart.

The winter was bitter cold.

"As the days begin to lengthen, the cold begins to strengthen," Matthew said to Dr. Llawcae, who listened gravely to Matthew's heart and his chest.

He leaned back and looked at the young man. "Matthew, you are encouraging Zillah."

Matthew smiled. "I've always encouraged Zillah, from the days when we were all children and she wanted to climb trees as high as Bran and I did."

"That's not what I mean. You're encouraging her in this wild-goose chase to go to Vespugia and join Bran."

"When Bran asked you for Zillah's hand, you gave him your blessing," Matthew reminded the doctor.

"That was with the understanding that Bran would stay here and become his father's partner."

"Once a blessing is given, Dr. Llawcae, it cannot be withdrawn." Matthew urged, "Zillah's heart is in Vespugia with Bran. I understand how she has taken her mother's place in your house and at your table. But she is your daughter, Dr. Llawcae, and not your wife, and you must not keep her tied to you."

The doctor's face flushed darkly with anger. "How dare you!"

"Because I love Zillah with all my heart, and I always have. I will miss her as much as you. Without Zillah, without Bran, I would be bereft of all that makes life worthwhile. But I will not hold them back out of selfishness."

The doctor's face grew darker. "You are accusing me of selfishness?"

"Inadvertent, perhaps, but selfishness, nonetheless."

"You—you—if you weren't a cripple, I'd—" Dr. Llawcae dropped his raised hand, turned, and left the room.

One afternoon in March, with occasional splatters of rain coming down the chimney and hissing out in the fire, Matthew looked intensely at Zillah, presiding over the tea tray. "Zillah. It's time. You must go to Vespugia."

"You know I want to." She reached out to hold his thin fingers. "Father says maybe next year."

"Next year's too late. Bran needs you now. What are you going to do about your father? Next year will always be next year. He'll not let you go."

She stared into the fire. "I'd rather go with Father's blessing, but I'm afraid you're right, and he's not going to give it. The problem is money, and finding a ship, and booking passage—all the things that are difficult, if not impossible, for a girl."

"You must go, this spring as soon as the ice breaks and ships can sail."

"Why, Matt, such urgency, all of a sudden?"

"Bran reached out to me last night—"

"Is something wrong?"

"Not with Bran. But Gedder—Rich—" He was seized with a fit of coughing, and when he leaned back he was too weak to talk.

Zillah continued to come daily to sit in the lady chair by the fire, to preside over the tea tray, and warm him with her smile. For the next few weeks he did not mention her going to Vespugia. Then one day, when the bare outlines of the trees were softened with coming buds, he greeted her impatiently.

He could hardly wait for her to sit down behind the tea tray. "Zillah, open the safe." Carefully, he gave her the combination, watching her fingers twirl the dial as she listened. "All right. Good. Bring out that big manila envelope. It's for you."

She looked at him in surprise. "For me?"

"I've been busy these last weeks."

"Father says you're pushing yourself too hard. Is the book done?"

"To all intents and purposes. There's some deepening to do, and a certain amount of revision. But I've been busy in other ways. Open the envelope."

She did so. "Money, and—what's this, Matt?"

"A ticket. There's a ship sailing for South America in four days. You must be on it."

"But, Matthew, I can't let you—"

"I've earned the money by my writing. It's mine to do with what I will Zillah, Bran needs you. You must go. You will swing the balance."

"What balance?"

"The line must be Madoc's and not Gwydyr's—"

"I don't understand. You're flushed. Are you—"

"I'm not feverish. It's part of the book . . . You do love Bran?"

"With all my heart."

"Enough to leave Madrun without your father's blessing, and secretly?"

She held the manila envelope to her breast.

"You'll go?"

"I'll go." She took his cold hand and held it to her cheek.

"All will be well," he promised. "When thou passest through the waters, I will be with thee; and through the rivers, they shall not overflow thee: when thou walkest through the fire, thou shalt not be burned; neither shall the flame kindle upon thee. For the fire is roses, roses . . ."

He did not see her again. Neither could bear the pain of parting.

Dr. Llawcae came storming over to Merioneth. Matthew could hear him shouting, "Where did she get the money? How did she get the passage?"

Matthew smiled, fleetingly grateful that Dr. Llawcae considered him such a cripple that he could not possibly have made the necessary arrangements.

When the doctor came into the study to check Matthew's heart, his temper had cooled enough so that he was no longer shouting. "I suppose you're pleased about this?"

"Zillah and Bran love each other," Matthew replied quietly. "It is right that they be together. And you have always been so interested in your Welsh heritage, and in this colony, that you will end up feeling differently. You can visit them—"

"Easy enough to say. What about my practice?"

"You haven't taken a vacation in years. You've earned a few weeks away."

Dr. Llawcae gave him only a cursory examination, saying, "You'll feel better when warmer weather comes."

Summer was slow in coming.

Matthew sent the book off to his publisher. The pain in his back was worse each day, and his heart skipped and galloped out of control. In his dreams he was with Bran, waiting for Zillah. He was with Gwen, still resentful, but beginning to laugh again with Rich, to respond to his steadfast love, his outgoing ways. At the same time she was still intrigued by Gedder, by his fierce dark looks and the hiddenness behind his eyes, so unlike Rich's candid ones. She knew that Rich loved her, but Gedder's strangeness fascinated her.

She's playing with Rich and Gedder and it will make trouble, the boy on the rock told Matthew as he slipped deeper into the dream.

Gedder and Bran. Standing on the cliff and looking down at the houses of the settlement. Gedder urging Bran to marry Zillie, to give Gwen in marriage to him, in order to secure the future.

"What future?" Bran asked.

Gedder looked appraisingly down at the prospering colony. "Ours."

And Zillie came and looked adoringly at Bran, Zillie so like and so unlike Zillah.

Wait, twin! Wait for Zillah! Do not trust Gedder—

Matthew was jolted out of the dream as his supper tray was brought. He ate a few bites, then pushed the tray away and slid back into the dream

Felt the Vespugian heat, warming his chilled bones

Bran, if only I could have come with Zillah

Gedder again. Gedder in his favorite place up on the cliff's lip, looking down on the colony, the colony he wants for his own.

Someone's with him. Not Bran. Rich.

Quarreling. Quarreling over Gwen, over the colony. Quarreling at the cliff's edge.

Danger.

Matthew stirred restlessly on the couch, his eyes tightly closed. The boy was there, the child from another time, urging him. "Matthew, you must help Rich. Please . . ."

Once upon a time and long ago, men did not quarrel in this way, when the morning stars sang together and the children of men shouted for joy

But dissonance came

Madoc and Gwydyr fought

Gedder and Rich

Rich, watch out! Gedder has a knife—

Rich sees, sees in time, grasps the knife hand, twists it,

so that the knife drops. Gedder reaches after it, snarling with anger, reaching for the knife so that he loses his balance and falls—falls after the knife, over the edge of the cliff, falls, falls . . .

Zillie screams and cannot stop screaming.

Matthew waited for the next letter from Bran, but it did not come until the lilac bushes were in full bloom.

My very dear twin,

Zillah is here, at last she is here, but my dearest heart has arrived to a community in confusion and desolation. Gwen weeps and will not stop. Zillie's tears no longer flow, but her eyes hold anguish. Gedder is dead, and—inadvertently—by Rich's hand. Gedder provoked a quarrel, and drew a knife. Rich took the knife from him, and Gedder, lunging after it, lost his balance and fell from the cliff to his death. It was an accident; nobody blames Rich, even Zillie. But Rich feels he cannot stay here with us, not with blood on his hands.

Will it ever cease, the turning of brother against brother? Gedder wanted power, and I cannot grieve for his death, only for his life, with its inordinate lust and pride. Why does Gwen weep? I do not think she knows. "I am homesick," she cries, "I want to go home." So Rich will take her home. And what will happen then, who knows?

Gwydyr fought Madoc and lost and the battle continued through to Gedder, brother against brother

And the ship which brought Zillah carried Gwen and Rich to the Northern continent, to lilies of the valley and lilacs in the dooryard, to Merioneth and the store, and Papa will at last have his partner, and the store will be Maddox and Llawcae

Oh, Zillah, my Zillah

> Lords of melody and song,
> Lords of roses burning bright,
> Blue will right the ancient wrong,
> Though the way is dark and long,
> Blue will shine with loving light.

A coughing fit jerked Matthew awake, away from Vespugia, from Bran and Zillah.

"Gwen—" he gasped, "Rich—Can't wait—sorry—"

Then the coughing took him, and when the racking had passed, there was nothing but agony. His back was an explosion of pain and the room began to get dark, and a rank stink like spoiling flowers choked him. There was no longer any light or warmth in the crackling flames . . .

"Matthew!" Meg opened her eyes, and she was calling the name aloud. The kitten, disturbed, jumped down from the bed. Ananda did not move.

—What happened? What happened to Matthew? to Charles Wallace? Is Charles Wallace all right?

—Strange, she thought,—the kythe with Matthew was clearer than any since Harcels. Maybe because Matthew and Bran were kythers.

She reached out to Charles Wallace, and felt only absence. Nor did she sense Gaudior. Always, when Charles Wallace was brought out of Within, she could see him, could see the unicorn.

"I'm going downstairs," she said aloud, and pushed her feet into her slippers.

Ananda followed her downstairs, stepping on the seventh step so that it let out a loud groan, and the dog yelped in surprise. Behind them the kitten padded softly, so light that the seventh step made the merest sigh.

The kitchen fire was blazing, the kettle humming. Everything looked warm and comfortable and normal, except for Mrs. O'Keefe in the rocking chair. The kitten padded across to her and jumped up on her lap, purring, and flexing its sharp little claws.

Meg asked, "Charles Wallace isn't back yet?"

"Not yet. Are you all right, Meg?" her mother asked.

"I'm fine."

"You look pale."

"Maybe I'll take Sandy and Dennys up on their offer of bouillon, if it's still good."

"Sure, Sis," Sandy said. "I'll make it. Chicken or beef?"

"Half a spoon of each, please, and a slosh of lemon juice." She looked at the twins with fresh comprehension. Was she closer to Charles Wallace than to the twins because they were twins, sufficient unto themselves? She glanced at the phone, then at her mother-in-law. "Mom—Beezie, do you remember Zillah?"

Mrs. O'Keefe looked at Meg, nodded her head, shook it, closed her eyes.

"Mom, Zillah really did get to Vespugia, didn't she?" Meg looked at the old woman, needing reassurance.

Mrs. O'Keefe huddled her arms about herself and rocked. "I forget. I forget."

Mrs. Murry looked anxiously at her daughter. "Meg, what is this?"

"It makes all the difference who Branzillo's forebears were."

Sandy handed Meg a steaming cup. "Sis, the past has happened. Knowing who Branzillo's ancestors were can't change anything."

"There was a time when it hadn't happened yet," Meg tried to explain, realizing how strange she sounded. "It's the Might-Have-Been Charles Wallace was to change, and I think he's changed it. It's the charge Mom O'Keefe laid on him when she gave him the rune."

"Stop talking!" Mrs. O'Keefe pushed herself up out of the rocking chair. "Take me to Chuck. Quickly. Before it's too late."

TWELVE

Between myself and the powers of darkness

They ran, pelting across the frozen ground, which crunched under their feet, Meg and the twins and Mrs. O'Keefe. They ran across the rimed lawn and through the aisles of the twins' Christmas trees to the stone wall.

Meg held her hand out to Mrs. O'Keefe and helped her over the low wall. Then, still holding her mother-in-law's hand, pulling her along, she ran down the path, past the two large glacial rocks, to the star-watching rock.

Charles Wallace was lying there, eyes closed, white as death.

"Beezie!" Meg cried. "The rune! Quickly!"

Mrs. O'Keefe was panting, her hand pressed to her side. "With me . . ." She gasped. "Grandma . . ."

Dennys knelt on the rock, bending over Charles Wallace, feeling for his pulse.

"With Chuck in this fateful hour," Mrs. O'Keefe gasped, and Meg joined in, her voice clear and strong:

"I place all Heaven with its power
And the sun with its brightness,
And the snow with its whiteness,
And the fire with all the strength it hath,
And the lightning with its rapid wrath,
And the winds with their swiftness along their path,
And the sea with its deepness,
And the rocks with their steepness,
And the earth with its starkness,
All these I place
By God's almighty help and grace
Between myself and the powers of darkness!"

Light returned slowly. There had been pain, and darkness, and all at once the pain was relieved, and light touched his lids. He opened them, to the sharpness of starlight. He was lying on the star-watching rock, with Gaudior anxiously bending over him, tickling his cheek with the curly silver beard.

"Gaudior, what happened?"

"We barely got you out in time."

"Did Matthew—"

"He died. We didn't expect it quite so soon. The Echthroi—"

"I guess we got to 1865 after all." Charles Wallace looked up at the stars.

"Stand up." Gaudior sounded cross. "I don't like to see you lying there. I thought you were never going to open your eyes."

Charles Wallace scrambled to his feet, lifted one leg, then the other. "How strange to be able to use my legs again—how wonderful."

Gaudior knelt beside him. "Climb."

Charles Wallace, legs shaky as though from long disuse, clambered onto the great back.

He rode a Gaudior who had become as tiny as a dragonfly, rode among the fireflies, joining their brilliant dance, twinkling, blinking, shooting over the star-watching rock, over the valley, singing their song, and he was singing, too, and he was himself, and yet he was all he had learned, he carried within himself Brandon and Chuck and their song and the song was glory . . .

And he rode a Gaudior who had become as large as a constellation, rode among the galaxies, and he was himself, and he was also Madoc, and he was Matthew, Matthew flying through showers of stars, caught up in the joy of the music of the spheres . . .

part of the harmony, part of the joy

The silver neigh of the unicorn sounded all about the star-watching rock, rippling over Meg and the twins, Mrs. O'Keefe and Charles, and the night was illumined by the flash of the horn, blinding them with oblivion as it pointed at each of them in turn.

Meg thought she heard Charles Wallace call, "Gaudior, goodbye—oh, Gaudior, goodbye . . ."

Who was Gaudior?

She knew once who Gaudior was.

Again she heard his silver knell ringing in farewell.

Sandy asked, "Hey, did you see lightning?"

Dennys looked bewildered. "It's too cold. And look at all the stars."

"What was that flash, then?"

"Beats me. Like everything else tonight. Charles, what was with you? I couldn't find a pulse and then suddenly it throbbed under my fingers."

Slowly, color was returning to the boy's cheeks. "You came just in time." He looked at Mrs. O'Keefe, who still had her hand to her side and was breathing with painful gasps. "Beezie. Thank you." There was infinite sadness in his voice.

"That's what Meg called her," Sandy said. "What is all this?"

"Mom O'Keefe laid a charge on me . . ."

Dennys said, "We told you it was nuts for you to think you could stop Branzillo single-handed. Did you fall asleep or something? You could have got frostbite." He sounded concerned and uncertain.

"Come on in, now," Sandy added, "and no more of this nonsense."

"After the president's call, you call it nonsense?" Meg demanded fiercely.

"Meg, you shouldn't be out in the cold," Dennys objected.

"I'm all right."

Charles Wallace took Mrs. O'Keefe's hands in his. "Thank you."

"Chuck's no idiot." Mrs. O'Keefe thumped Charles Wallace on the shoulder.

"Come on," Sandy urged. "Let's get moving."

Dennys held Mrs. O'Keefe's arm. "We'll help you."

They returned to the house, Sandy and Dennys supporting Mrs. O'Keefe; Meg holding Charles Wallace's hand as though they were both small children once more.

Ananda greeted them ecstatically.

Mrs. Murry hurried to her youngest son, but refrained from touching him. "She's really adopted us, hasn't she? You'd think she'd been with us forever."

"Watch out for that tail." Mr. Murry moved between the dog and the model of the tesseract. "A couple of indiscriminate wags and you could undo years of work." He turned to his daughter. "Meg, you shouldn't have gone out in this weather with your cold."

"It's all right, Father. My cold's better and I didn't get chilled. Did the president—"

"No. Nothing yet."

Meg tried to think. What did she remember? The president's call, of course. Mrs. O'Keefe's rune, and the response of the weather. The coming of Ananda. Kything with Charles Wallace in the attic, kything through aeons of time, kything which had faded to dreams because the unicorn—

A unicorn. That was absurd.

There was Mrs. O'Keefe's phone call in the middle of the night. Sandy went for her and brought her back to the house, and she had an old letter—who was it from? What did it say?

"Well, Charles." Mr. Murry regarded his son gravely. "How about the charge?"

Charles Wallace did not reply immediately. He was studying the model of the tesseract, and he touched one of the Lucite rods carefully, so that the entire model began to vibrate, to hum softly, throwing off sparkles of brilliance. "We still don't know much about time, do we? I think—" He looked bewildered. "Father, I think it's going to be all right. But not because I was intelligent, or brave, or in control. Meg was right, earlier this evening, when she talked about everything, everywhere, interreacting."

"You were gone longer than we expected."

"I was gone a long time. An incredibly long time."

"But what did you do?" Sandy asked.

"And where did you go?" Dennys added.

"Mostly I stayed right by the star-watching rock—"

"Father!" Meg exclaimed. "The letter Mom O'Keefe brought. Charles hasn't seen it."

Mrs. O'Keefe held out the yellowed paper to Mr. Murry.

"Please read it to me, Father." Charles Wallace looked pale and exhausted.

"My dear Gwen and Rich," Mr. Murry read,

Thank you for writing us so promptly of Papa's death. Zillah and I are grateful that he died peacefully in his sleep, with none of the suffering he feared. I know that you both, and little Zillah, are a consolation for Mama. And Papa had the satisfaction of having Rich for his partner, and of knowing that the name of Maddox and Llawcae will not be lost, for our young Rich talks with great enthusiasm about going to Merioneth when he is old enough.

Our little Matthew is a rapidly growing boy. I had hoped that as he grew out of babyhood he would be called Matthew, but he keeps the nickname given him by the Indian children, Branzillo, a combination of my name and Zillah's. Little Rich tries to keep up with his big brother in every way . . .

Mr. Murry looked up. "The letter breaks off there. Strange—it seems diff—is that what I read before?"

Mrs. Murry frowned slightly. "I'm not sure. It didn't sound quite—but we're all exhausted with strain and lack of sleep. Memory plays queer tricks at times like this."

"It has to be what Father read before," Sandy said flatly. "It offends my reasonable mind, but it really does seem possible that Branzillo's forebears came from around here."

"The letter did come from Mrs. O'Keefe's attic," Dennys said. "So it's even likely that he's distantly descended from her forebears, and that would make them umpteenth cousins."

Sandy protested, "But what effect could that have on his starting a nuclear war? Or—we hope—on not starting one?"

Charles Wallace turned away from the argument, looked once more at the tesseract, then went to Mrs. O'Keefe, who was once again huddled in the rocking chair in front of the fire. Meg left the twins and followed Charles Wallace.

"Beezie," he asked softly, "what happened to Chuck?"

—Beezie, Chuck. They were in the vanishing kythe. Meg stepped closer to the rocker to hear Mrs. O'Keefe's reply.

"He died," she said bleakly.

"How?"

"They took him away and put him in an institution. He died there, six months later."

Charles Wallace expelled a long, sad breath. "Oh, Beezie, Beezie. And the baby?"

"Took after Duthbert Mortmain. Died in the State Penitentiary. Embezzlement. Let it be. What's done's done. What's gone's gone."

Ananda pressed against Meg, and she stroked the raised head.

Beezie. Chuck. Paddy O'Keefe. The kythe flickered briefly in Meg's mind. Beezie must have married Paddy for more or less the same reasons that her mother had married Duthbert Mortmain. And she learned not to feel, not to love, not even her children, not even Calvin. Not to be hurt. But she gave Charles Wallace the rune, and told him to use it to stop Mad Dog Branzillo. So there must be a little of the Old Music left in her.

"Matthew's book," Charles Wallace said. "It's happening, all that he wrote."

The phone rang.

Mrs. Murry looked toward her husband, but did not speak.

They waited tensely.

"Yes, Mr. President?" Mr. Murry listened, and as he listened, he smiled. "El Zarco is setting up a Congress for the working out of peace plans and the equitable distribution and preservation of the earth's resources. What's that, Mr. President? He wants me to come as an advisor on the use of space for peace? Well, yes, of course, for a few weeks . . . This is splendid news. Thank you for calling." He put down the receiver and turned to his family.

"El Zarco—" Meg whispered.

"Madog Branzillo's favorite nickname, you know that," her father said. "The Blue-eyed."

"But his threats—"

Her father looked at her in surprise. "Threats?"

"Of war—"

Everybody except Charles Wallace and Mrs. O'Keefe was looking at her.

"The phone call before dinner—" she said. "Wasn't the president afraid of war?"

"El Zarco has put down the militant members of his cabinet. He's always been known as a man of peace."

Charles Wallace spoke softly, so only Meg could hear. "They haven't traveled with a unicorn, Meg. There was no El Rabioso for them. When Matthew sent Zillah to marry Bran, and when Gedder was killed, that was the Might-Have-Been. El Rabioso was never born. It's always been El Zarco." He held her hand so tightly that it hurt.

Mrs. O'Keefe looked at Meg, nodding. "Baby will be born."

"Oh, Mom," Meg cried. "Will you be glad to be a grandmother?"

"Too late," the old woman said. "Take me home. Chuck and Grandma are waiting for me."

"What's that?" Mr. Murry asked.

"Chuck and Grandma—never mind. Just take me home."

"I'll drive you," Mr. Murry said.

Meg kissed her mother-in-law good night. It was the first time she had ever kissed her. "See you, Mom. See you soon."

When the car drove off, Dennys turned to his sister. "I'm not sure she'll make it to be a grandmother, Meg. I think her heart's running out."

"Why?"

"Badly swollen ankles. Blue tinge to her fingernails and lips. Shortness of breath."

"She ran all the way to the star-watching rock."

"She was short of breath before then. It's a wonder it didn't kill her. And what all that was about I'll never know."

"This whole evening's confusing," Sandy agreed. "I suggest we just forget it and go to bed. And Mrs. O'Keefe would never have made it back without Dennys and me, Meg. But you're right, Mother, she's quite an old girl."

"She is, indeed," Mrs. Murry agreed. "And I agree with you, Sandy, about getting to bed. Meg, you need your sleep."

The baby within Meg stirred. "You're more than right about Mom O'Keefe, Mother, more right than any of us could possibly have imagined. There's much much more to her than meets the eye. I hate the thought of losing her, just as we're discovering her."

Charles Wallace had once again been contemplating the intricate model of the tesseract. He spoke softly to his sister. "Meg, no matter what happens, even if Dennys is right about her heart, remember that it was herself she placed, for the baby's sake, and yours, and Calvin's, and all of us—"

Meg looked at him questioningly.

Charles Wallace's eyes as he returned her gaze were the blue of light as it glances off a unicorn's horn, pure and clear and infinitely deep. "In this fateful hour, it was herself she placed between us and the powers of darkness."

GOFISH

QUESTIONS FOR THE AUTHOR

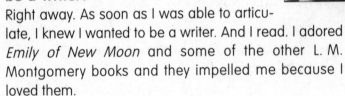

What did you want to be when you grew up?
A writer.

When did you realize you wanted to be a writer?
Right away. As soon as I was able to articulate, I knew I wanted to be a writer. And I read. I adored *Emily of New Moon* and some of the other L. M. Montgomery books and they impelled me because I loved them.

When did you start to write?
When I was five, I wrote a story about a little "gurl."

What was the first writing you had published?
When I was a child, a poem in *CHILD LIFE*. It was all about a lonely house and was very sentimental.

Where do you write your books?
Anywhere. I write in longhand first, and then type it. My first typewriter was my father's pre–World War One machine. It was the one he took with him to the war. It had certainly been around the world.

What is the best advice you have ever received about writing?
To just write.

What's your first childhood memory?
One early memory I have is going down to Florida for a couple of weeks in the summertime to visit my grand-mother. The house was in the middle of a swamp, sur-rounded by alligators. I don't like alligators, but there they were, and I was afraid of them.

What is your favorite childhood memory?
Being in my room.

As a young person, whom did you look up to most?
My mother. She was a storyteller and I loved her stories. And she loved music and records. We played duets together on the piano.

What was your worst subject in school?
Math and Latin. I didn't like the Latin teacher.

What was your best subject in school?
English.

What activities did you participate in at school?
I was president of the student government in boarding school and editor of a literary magazine, and also belonged to the drama club.

Are you a morning person or a night owl?
Night owl.

What was your first job?
Working for the actress Eva La Gallienne, right after college.

What is your idea of the best meal ever?
Cream of Wheat. I eat it with a spoon. I love it with butter and brown sugar.

Which do you like better: cats or dogs?
I like them both. I once had a wonderful dog named Touche. She was a silver medium-sized poodle, and quite beautiful. I wasn't allowed to take her on the subway, and I couldn't afford to get a taxi, so I put her around my neck, like a stole. And she pretended she was a stole. She was an actor.

What do you value most in your friends?
Love.

What is your favorite song?
"Drink to Me Only with Thine Eyes."

What time of the year do you like best?
I suppose autumn. I love the changing of the leaves.
I love the autumn goldenrod, the Queen Anne's lace.

What was the original title of *A Wrinkle in Time*?
"Mrs Whatsit, Mrs Who and Mrs Which."

How did you get the idea for *A Wrinkle in Time*?
We were living in the country with our three kids on this
dairy farm. I started reading what Einstein wrote about
time. And I used a lot of those principles to make a universe that was creative and yet believable.

**How hard was it to get *A Wrinkle in Time*
published?**
I was kept hanging for two years. Over and over again I
received nothing more than the formal, printed rejection
slip. Eventually, after twenty-six rejections, I called my
agent and said, "Send it back. It's too different. Nobody's
going to publish it." He sent it back, but a few days later
a friend of my mother's insisted that I meet John Farrar,

the publisher. He liked the manuscript, and eventually decided to publish it. My first editor was Hal Vursell.

Which of your characters is most like you?
None of them. They're all wiser than I am.

THE L'ENGLE CAST

Books featuring the Murry-O'Keefes:

A Wrinkle in Time (WT)

A Wind in the Door (WD)

A Swiftly Tilting Planet (STP)

Many Waters (MW)

The Arm of the Starfish (AS)

Dragons in the Waters (DW)

A House Like a Lotus (HL)

An Acceptable Time (AT)

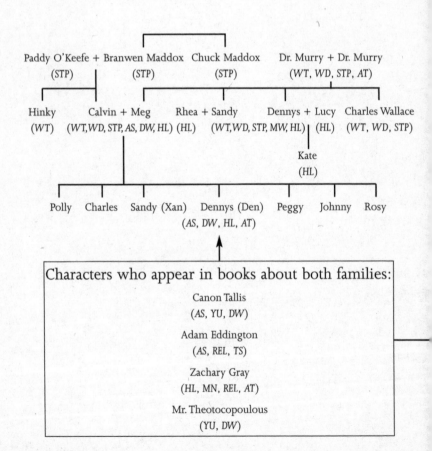

Paddy O'Keefe + Branwen Maddox   Chuck Maddox   Dr. Murry + Dr. Murry
(STP)   (STP)   (STP)   (WT, WD, STP, AT)

Hinky   Calvin + Meg   Rhea + Sandy   Dennys + Lucy   Charles Wallace
(WT)   (WT,WD, STP, AS, DW, HL)   (HL)   (WT,WD, STP, MW, HL)   (HL)   (WT, WD, STP)

Kate
(HL)

Polly   Charles   Sandy (Xan)   Dennys (Den)   Peggy   Johnny   Rosy
                              (AS, DW, HL, AT)

Characters who appear in books about both families:

Canon Tallis
(*AS*, YU, *DW*)

Adam Eddington
(*AS*, REL, TS)

Zachary Gray
(HL, MN, REL, *AT*)

Mr. Theotocopoulous
(YU, *DW*)

OF CHARACTERS

Books featuring the Austins:

Meet the Austins (MA)

The Moon by Night (MN)

The Twenty-four Days Before Christmas (TDC)

The Young Unicorns (YU)

A Ring of Endless Light (REL)

Troubling a Star (TS)

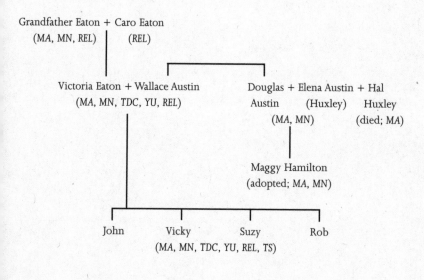

Grandfather Eaton + Caro Eaton
(MA, MN, REL)   (REL)

Victoria Eaton + Wallace Austin
(MA, MN, TDC, YU, REL)

Douglas + Elena Austin + Hal
Austin   (Huxley)   Huxley
      (MA, MN)   (died; MA)

Maggy Hamilton
(adopted; MA, MN)

John   Vicky   Suzy   Rob
(MA, MN, TDC, YU, REL, TS)

Dot.Cloud

Actual photo of Dubai City, taken from atop the Berj Tower. Dubai is a classic example of a hydrocarbon-economy leader that wants to become an epicenter of the Cloud economy.

-------------*What They Are Saying*--------------

Peter Fingar does it again. His uncanny knack for bringing technology and society together to extrapolate the future never ceases to amaze me. Reading sections of *Dot.Cloud* had me picturing him with a crystal ball, reading the minds and secret product plans of cloud computing's finest visionaries. Every business executive should read this book. **—George Barlow,** CEO, Cloud Harbor

This 21ˢᵗ century business platform represents a new paradigm for coordination, collaboration, and decision making that will result in new discoveries, combinatory innovations, and significantly enhanced operations. *Dot.Cloud* elegantly and methodically lays open and describes the vital elements that form the new business platform, and provides the understanding you'll need to fully realize the business potential that it makes possible.

—Bryan Maizlish, IT Architect and author,

IT Portfolio Management: Unlocking the Business Value of Technology

Landmark Books by Peter Fingar

EXTREME COMPETITION:
INNOVATION AND THE GREAT 21ST CENTURY
BUSINESS REFORMATION

BUSINESS PROCESS MANAGEMENT:
THE THIRD WAVE

IT DOESN'T MATTER:
BUSINESS PROCESSES DO

THE REAL-TIME ENTERPRISE:
COMPETING ON TIME

THE DEATH OF 'E' AND
THE BIRTH OF THE REAL NEW ECONOMY

ENTERPRISE E-COMMERCE

THE BLUEPRINT FOR BUSINESS OBJECTS

NEXT GENERATION COMPUTING:
DISTRIBUTED OBJECTS FOR BUSINESS

Acclaim for our books:
Featured book recommendation
Harvard Business School's *Working Knowledge,*
Book of the Year, *Internet World*

Meghan-Kiffer Press
Tampa, Florida, USA
www.mkpress.com
Innovation at the Intersection of Business and Technology

Dot.Cloud

The 21st Century
Business Platform
Built on
Cloud Computing

Peter Fingar

Meghan-Kiffer Press
Tampa, Florida, USA, www.mkpress.com
Innovation at the Intersection of Business and Technology

Publisher's Cataloging-in-Publication Data

Fingar, Peter.
Dot Cloud: The 21st Century Business Platform Built on Cloud Computing /
Peter Fingar, - 1st ed.
 p. cm.
 Includes bibliographic entries, appendices, and index.
 ISBN-10: 0-929652-49-5   ISBN-13: 978-0-929652-49-8
 1. Management 2. Technological innovation. 3. Diffusion of innovations.
 4. Globalization—Economic aspects. 5. Information technology. 6. Information Society. 7. Organizational change. I. Fingar, Peter. II. Title

HM48.F75 2009   Library of Congress No. 2009923534
303.48'33–dc22   CIP

Published by Meghan-Kiffer Press
310 East Fern Street — Suite G
Tampa, FL 33604 USA

Any product mentioned in this book may be a trademark of its company.

Meghan-Kiffer books are available at special quantity discounts for
corporate education and training use. For more information, write
Special Sales, Meghan-Kiffer Press, Suite G, 310 East Fern Street,
Tampa, Florida 33604, or email mkpress@tampabay.rr.com

Meghan-Kiffer Press
Tampa, Florida, USA
Innovation at the Intersection of Business and Technology
Printed in the United States of America.   SAN 249-7980
MK Printing 10 9 8 7 6 5 4 3 2 1

Table of Contents

Foreword by Jim Sinur

It is amazing how Peter Fingar manages to aggregate streams of evolving behaviors, business trends and enabling technologies in a way that captures the imagination. *Dot.Cloud* is both visionary and realistic in that each of the pieces of the vision have working examples today, but not woven together like in this writing. The goal of the virtual business platform is not just a dream, but attainable once all the contributing pieces are brought together. Peter brings them together here in a way that will work under any number of situations, across just about any industry.

Peter's *Dot.Cloud* vision supports the tenets of shared processes that are enabled, optimized, tuned and changed to meet changing business demands while balancing the needs of multiple and diverse business partners and collaborators. All of this is leveraged with powerful technologies and shared infrastructures that, in the past, were only available to large organizations that had sufficient capital to invest in large-scale information technology, making them exclusive and unattainable for the average business or individual. But now with cloud computing, I can see, for instance, the opportunity to link super computing to analytic driven optimization for small businesses that would not dream of having this kind of resource and the supporting infrastructure.

To say that we are living in an exciting time is an understatement, and Peter has captured, in large part, the essence of how business will work going forward. Don't just skim through this book, for it is certainly worth the time to consume and digest the business insights found throughout its pages.

—**Jim Sinur,** Vice President, Gartner

Foreword by Bryan Maizlish

Supply-side opportunities for cost savings and efficiency enabled by cloud computing receive the majority of attention and focus. But now, *Dot.Cloud* explores the demand side and reveals the game-changing opportunities for businesses large and small. Market leaders understand that in today's hypercompetitive and cost optimization environment, a key differentiator is time-based competition. Time-based competition is centered on optimizing the time from innovation to operations, and gaining the agility needed to sense and respond to customer demands with speed and precision. This requires that traditional organizational hierarchies be replaced with dynamic self-managed, self-organizing teams. Cloud computing provides the infrastructure foundation required to support this new organizational dynamic.

Cloud computing enables a new business operations platform that combines key aspects of Web 2.0, human interaction management, business process management and real-time business intelligence. This 21st century business platform represents a new paradigm for coordination, collaboration, and decision making that will result in new discoveries, combinatory innovations, and significantly enhanced operations.

Dot.Cloud elegantly and methodically lays open and describes the vital elements that form the new business platform, and provides the understanding you'll need to fully realize the business potential that it makes possible.

—**Bryan Maizlish,** author, *IT Portfolio Management: Unlocking the Business Value of Technology*

Preface

I first became interested in the intersection of "technology and business" in 1968. What a remarkable journey it has been since then. I was a kid then, and now I'm a grandpa, but for some reason, I stay young—at least partly by not coming from a *position of knowing*, but from a *position of learning*.

In addition to my research and writing, I now give keynote talks around the world and do consulting for leading-edge companies in the U.S. and abroad. I've held technical and management positions, including at the earth's largest oil company and the second largest telecommunications company; taught graduate computing studies in the U.S. and abroad; coauthored a landmark book on distributed object computing, and later a book cited as the seminal work on business process management—but so what?

The "so what" is that when I see something really new, something I know is game-changing, I start writing as a way of learning. Lately, I've been researching and writing about the next generation of the *business* Internet, the Cloud. Although I explain the main ideas of Cloud Computing in lay terms, and quote several other experts to round out perspectives, this is not a technical book about Cloud Computing technologies; it's a business book.

- It's about what the Cloud portends for business.
- It's about transformation in the ways companies are managed.
- It's about business models for the 21st century.

These are interesting times, and I'd like to share my discoveries with you.

Tampa Florida, 2009

One

Prolog

Someday soon you will look into a computer screen and see reality. Some part of your world—the town you live in, the company you work for, your school system, the city hospital, or a picture that sketches the state of an entire far-flung corporation at this second—will hang there in a sharp color image, abstract but recognizable, moving subtly in a thousand places. This Mirror World you are looking at is fed by a steady rush of new data pouring in through cables. It is infiltrated by your own software creatures, doing your own business."
—David Gelernter, Department of Computer Science, Yale University, *Mirror Worlds: or the Day Software Puts the Universe in a Shoebox*, Oxford University Press, 1992.

Key Points: Shift Happens. The Unexpected Matters.

There's an interesting relationship between business and technology. Technology changes, business adapts—business changes, technology adapts. Sometimes, changes are small; sometimes exponential. Sometimes changes can be foreseen; sometimes they are totally unexpected. Grappling with unexpected and exponential change is now upon us, as businesses and individuals. This chapter provides a quick snapshot of the business, economic and technological changes that now surround us in order to set a context for the Cloud and what it portends.

Technology advances don't roll along undisturbed.
Business advances don't roll along undisturbed.
    … The two interact in most interesting, intertwined ways.
- Shift happens.
- The unexpected matters.

We are witnessing a seismic shift in information technology—the kind that comes around every decade or so. Years ago, Yale computer expert and Unabomber victim, David Gelernter saw quantum leap on the horizon, where local-scale software programs on your PC or company's servers were about to be joined by global public software works that would revolutionize computing and transform society as a whole.

In Gelernter's Mirror Worlds, you interact with reality, transforming computers from handy tools to crystal balls that will allow us to see the world more vividly and see into it more deeply. Reality will be replaced gradually, piece-by-piece, by a software imitation. We will live inside the imitation, gaining control over our world, plus a huge new measure of insight and vision.

In Gelernter's Mirror Worlds, a hospital administrator might wander through an entire medical complex via a desktop computer. Any citizen might explore the performance of the local schools, chat electronically with teachers and other Mirror World visitors, plant software agents to report back on interesting topics; decide to run for the local school board, hire a campaign manager, and conduct the better part of the campaign itself (Barack Obama, 2008)—all by interacting with the Mirror World.

If you are thinking Gelernter makes for good sci-fi bedtime reading, think again. Across the globe, IT giants are frantically building out the infrastructure for Mirror Worlds. It's called the Cloud, and with Cloud Computing, all is changed, utterly.

But wait.

Fast forward from Gelernter's 1992 Mirror Worlds to 2008.

The year 2008 began on a Tuesday.
Matters went downhill swiftly from there.
Starbucks closed 600 coffee shops in the U.S.,
Fed Chairman Ben Bernanke assured Congress that neither
Fannie May nor Freddie Mac were in danger of failing, and
GOP Sen. Ted Stevens of Alaska was indicted.

Now we're in the midst of another crisis, the worst since the 1930s.
—Nobel Laureate, Paul Krugman, *New York Times*, Nov. 2008.[1]

> *This is a mental recession as well as an economic one.*
> *Solving it means getting more and more people involved*
> *in a fundamental rebirth.*
> —David Brooks, *New York Times*, Nov. 2008.[2]
>
> *Crises are the ultimate in painful learning experiences.*
> —Stephen S. Roach, Chairman, Morgan Stanley Asia, Nov. 2008.[3]

So here we are in 2008 with IT giants (IBM, Google, Microsoft, Amazon, Oracle, to name a few) building a whole new business computing platform while the world economy burns and there's talk of putting the big "D" in recession, as in, "depression."

But build it they will. In fact they must, as we face a whole new world of economic challenges of the "creative destruction" kind. We faked our way out of the dot-com boom collapse by Alan Greenspan and company giving away "free" money to pump up a housing bubble. But now that sucking sound of three trillion dollars evaporating from stock markets, made when the dot-com collapse happened, could sound like a breeze. That sound could now turn into a roar. We will not get out of the downward economic spiral by doing more of the same things we've done before. We need new ideas, new business models. In short we are going to have to innovate our way out of the mess and reinvent our future.

Gathering Clouds

In a lengthy conversation the other day, I was asked what it really takes for an organization to make "deep" change and bring about true transformation. Is it top-down? Bottom-up? I thought with some pause, then answered that I think the real trigger point is "pain." You've got to really feel the heat to make significant change. And starting with the Crash of 2008, pain motivators abound.

In my work in business process management, I've seen "islands of change," but very few strategic, enterprise or value-chain wide examples of deep change. Sure, there are lots of ROI stories to tell about this or that business improvement, but please tell me, "Has your company made deep change and built a 'killer company' for the 21st century?"

It seems that we humans will resist change until the pain becomes acute. It's the old story of putting the frog into a cold pan of water, gradually turning up the heat, and watching the frog boil to death. If that frog was a newcomer to an already boiling pot of water it would, of course, jump right away.

Perhaps that's why we see so many newcomers disrupt industries, while those incumbents feeling the rising heat don't make significant moves until it's too late. And, it seems that the newcomers disrupt established industries with *management innovation,* business model innovation that not only incorporates their suppliers, and their suppliers' suppliers, but also places their customers at the very center of their business processes—and taps the creative abilities of all employees to meet the ever-changing needs of their customers.

Putting the customer at the center, and providing customer experiences that delight, drives all the rest. By taking such an outside-in versus inside-out view, such companies are no longer *sellers* to their customers, they become *buyers* for their customers, going to the ends of the earth to find the most cost-effective sources of high-quality goods and services to deliver to their customers. Amazon applied these principles in retailing, as did Dell with direct-to-customer PC sales where the customer was put to work configuring their own machines.

Not all incumbents are doomed to boil to death. GE's former CEO, Jack Welch, first saw his former wife, Jane, shopping on the Internet. She as much as had shown him the water was coming to a boil, and, unlike many top frogs in huge organizations, he jumped. He embraced economist Joseph Schumpeter's notion of creative destruction. Welch launched a major corporate-wide initiative, "Destroy Your Business.com, before some upstart in a Silicon Valley garage does!" So, newcomer or incumbent, the smart frogs are those whose who can see, *and* feel it, when "shift happens"—and then act.

And, right now, shift is happening on a scale so vast that it's hidden in plain sight.

Shift Happens

No company is an island. It's just a player in a larger society, in a larger world. Today, the heat is rising in that larger world. Aronica and Ramdoo write in their book, *The World is Flat?*, "Globalization is the most profound reorganization of the world since the Industrial Revolution."[4] The water (globalization) is coming to a boil, with three billion new capitalists from China, India and the former Soviet Union providing the heat.

Did you know?[5]

☑ No one knows the exact population of China. Some estimate 1.2 billion; others 1.5 billion. Considering those numbers, the entire U.S. population is just a rounding error.

☑ The 25% of the population in China with the highest IQs is greater than the total population of North America.

☑ If you are one in a million, in China there are 1,300 people just like you.

☑ The country with the most English-speaking people is not the U.S. ... It's China.

☑ In the 1980s, capitalism supposedly triumphed over communism. By the year 2050, communist China is expected to have a gross domestic product (GDP) twice that of the United States.

☑ The world's greatest debtor nation is ... America. In 2008, Americans spent $438 billion more than it earned, and the most recent report from the Commerce Department found savings rates at a negative one percent, the lowest since the Great Depression, and down from 11 percent after WWII.

☑ The United States' national debt is currently over $10.6 trillion, and has increased an average of $3.45 billion *per day* since September 28, 2007. Add to that, corporate, state and local, and consumer debt and you get a whopping total that may exceed $70+ trillion. America owes more money than any other country in the world, and by a huge amount.

☑ To finance its current account deficit with the rest of the world, America has to import $2.6 billion in cash—every working day. That is an amazing 80 percent of the entire world's net savings.

☑ In 1900, the titles of: richest country in the world, largest military, center of world business and finance, strongest education system, world's center of innovation and invention, the world standard currency, and highest standard of living belonged to … England.

☑ The U.S. is 20th in the world in broadband Internet penetration (tiny Luxembourg just passed America).

☑ As of September 2006, there were over 106 million registered users of MySpace. If MySpace were a country, it would be the 11th largest in the world (between Japan and Mexico).

☑ It is estimated that 1.5 exabytes (1.5×10^{18}) of unique, new information will be generated worldwide this year. That's estimated to be more than in the previous 5,000 years.

☑ The amount of new technical information is doubling every two years. For students starting a four-year technical or college degree, this means that half of what they learn in their first year of study will be outdated by their third year of study. It is predicted to double every 72 hours by 2010.

☑ Third-generation fiber optics has recently been tested by both NEC and Alcatel that pushes 10 trillion bits per second down one strand of fiber. That's 1,900 CDs, or 150 million simultaneous phone calls, every second. It's currently tripling about every 6 months and is expected to do so for at least the next 20 years. The fiber is already there. They're just improving the switches on the ends.

☑ 47 million laptops were shipped worldwide last year. The $100 laptop project is expecting to ship between 50 to 100 million laptops a year to children in underdeveloped countries with the one laptop per child (OLPC) project.

☑ By 2023, when 1st graders will be just 23 years old and beginning their (first) careers, it only will take a $1,000 computer to exceed the information-handling capabilities of the human brain.

☑ The U.S. Department of Labor estimates that today's learner will have 10 to 14 jobs . . . by age 38.

☑ India's Tata is introducing a $2,200 car. China's Chery plans to introduce a $10,000 luxury car in the U.S. market.

Shift happens. With the scale of shift happening in the larger world, right before our very eyes, all is changed in the world of business, changed utterly. How can your company compete in the brave new world of high-change, total global competition?

Innovations needed to reach the bottom of the pyramid in emerging countries have profound business consequences. It's called *blowback*. With China's highly educated workforce, the "Made-in-China" label will mean products that are not just low cost, but also high quality. Will America soon be importing its green technology from Suntech Power Co., Ltd., China's leading solar cell manufacturer, in the same way America is now importing its hybrid automobile engines from Japan? Will mighty America become the stand-in for England circa 1900? Psst. "Little frog. The temperature is rising:"

- Can your consulting firm compete on quality with India's Wipro or Infosys who have huge pools of Six-Sigma certified consultants?
- Can your electronics factory compete with iPod City, north of Shanghai, where factory workers are paid $50/month turning out the high-tech iPods?
- Can your bank compete with BOB (Bank of Baroda, India's International Bank) with its world-class staff and rock-bottom infrastructure costs?
- Can your computer company compete with Novatium's $70 NetPC?
- Can your car company compete with the Chinese Chery $10,000 luxury car?

Novatium's CEO, Rajesh Jain, who wrote the insightful foreword to *Extreme Competition: Innovation and the Great 21st Century Business Reformation,*[6] and India's first Internet billionaire, wants to get his NetPC down to $70. That's innovation. That's also blowback, as he'll take his innovation global. Jain wrote, "Google was a black swan. No one expects the next Microsoft or Intel or Cisco to come out of India, but I believe it is entirely possible."

In contrast, many U.S. companies are spending their time dreaming up ways to extract more money from their customers without giving any value in return (e.g., complicated telco service plans, credit-card "gotcha" charges, non-interchangeable printer cartridges from the same brand, and other consumer rip offs). Caveat competitor. Consumers are now more fully informed than ever, and will no longer put up with companies that can't or won't deliver *true* value.

Change, Inc.

It's instructive to read what Michael Hugos wrote in *The Greatest Innovation Since The Assembly Line,*[7] "Responsiveness now trumps efficiency in the high-change global economy." It's time for a business innovation flip-flop. Instead of insiders continuing to *push* business innovation, it's time for companies that want to survive to *pull* innovation into their hearts and souls, into their very DNA, for "responsiveness" is all in the brave new world of total global competition. So let's cut the small talk, let's cut out the management theory platitudes. The real issue is how your company responds to the greatest shift since the Industrial Revolution—*globalization.*

Most Western companies have but one real competitive asset left in this new world of abundant, low-cost supply sources—their *customers.* Delivering successful customer outcomes and meeting customer expectations without exception is the goal. As a company transforms from being a seller to becoming a buyer for its customers, it will desperately seek business innovation. That means taking innovation beyond the walls of the enterprise, beyond the internal R&D group, and beyond the borders of nations—it's called open innovation. It is business innovation that will determine the winners and losers in the brave new world of total global competition, and only truly innovative enterprises will still be standing as this great shift plays itself out.

It seems that no one is immune when shift happens. Companies aren't going to deal with the maelstrom I've described by squeezing another 1% of cost savings out of their invoice settlement processes. If you take Pareto's rule seriously and want to deal with the 20% of exceptions, that require 80% of the real work of the enterprise, you'll need human interaction management, for it's people who do the work of a company. If you want the kind of responsiveness Hugos speaks of, you won't get it via traditional management structures and paradigms. Agility in the high-change global economy is all about human-driven business processes, human-to-human interactions that include unique case management, ad-hoc collaborations, the wisdom of crowds, marketplaces of ideas, dynamic and just-in-time sourcing from networks of far-flung suppliers, complex sales proposals, open innovation collaborations, new product development and the like.

Consider what Jon Pyke, chairman of the Workflow Management Coalition recently wrote, "It comes back to the need to understand that business processes [how work gets done for customers] exist at two levels (the people and the systems). Being able to grasp that fundamental point provides us with clues as to where the next innovative developments in business evolution will come from. Allowing for the unpredictable actions of the human components in any given operation is essential. These actions are not ad-hoc processes, nor are they transaction exception handling. We need to tackle the unstructured interactions between people—in particular knowledge workers. These unstructured and unpredictable interactions can, and do, take place all the time—and it's only going to get worse! The advent of Web 2.0, social computing, SaaS [software as a service] etc., is already having, and will continue to have, a profound effect on the way we manage and do business."

A Prescription for Business Pain

Jane Welch, sound the alarm! The temperature is rising!

So it is that *pain* is indeed the great motivator when shift happens. When your enterprise feels the acute pain of the great shift, it's time to turn to your doctor, Dr. Jeffrey Sterllings, who is the lead character in Kiran Garimella's book, *The Power of Process,*[8] for a business process management prescription:

Bepium, qty365, tid.
Unlimited refills

Dr. Sterllings' prescription is the only known cure for the ancient Chinese curse, "May you live in interesting times." And as Robert F. Kennedy said in a 1966 speech in Capetown, South Africa, after quoting the Chinese curse, "Like it or not we live in interesting times. They are times of danger and uncertainty; but they are also more open to the creative energy of men than any other time in history." Hmm, 1966 seems somewhat calm from today's perspective. To adjust to the times, we must change how we do our work, how we deliver value, how we manage our companies, how we get so close to our customers that we can anticipate their needs even before they do. Garimella's "bepium" is an abstruse reference to business process management (BPM). As we'll learn, business processes are how work gets done, by whom and for whom, and the Cloud will become the place where those processes reside and are managed. Business processes are at the center of how we collaborate, how we innovate, how we sense and respond, and how we operate and manage our companies with our customers at the center of everything we do. We'll touch on each of these issues throughout this book.

Cloud Computing Means More Than a Supercomputer

We do indeed live in very interesting times, and this book describes how a whole new "business operations platform" in the Cloud can open a whole new set of possibilities for conducting business in the brave new world of total global competition. We'll begin with a brief description, in layman terms, of the Cloud, and then examine:

- The new innovation imperative (Innovation's Child)
- How work gets done in the 21st century—business process management in the Cloud
- Where work gets done—the business operations platform in the Cloud, not an office building or skyscraper
- Work 2.0: Connect-and-Collaborate with Human Interaction Management in the Cloud, and
- The End of Management and the rise of self-organizing, self-managed Bioteams.

This book is not a technical treatment of Cloud Computing. It is, instead, about the business implications of an emerging business platform and what it portends for businesses that want to survive and thrive in the 21st century. Let's begin with a brief overview of Cloud Computing.

References.

[1] http://www.nytimes.com/2008/11/28/opinion/28krugman.html

[2] http://www.nytimes.com/2008/11/28/opinion/28brooks.html

[3] http://www.nytimes.com/2008/11/28/opinion/28roach.html

[4] www.mkpress.com/flat

[5] Many of these factoids are from Karl Fisch, Director of Technology for Arapahoe High School in Centennial, Colorado. Watch a remix of his powerful video at www.mkpress.com/shifthappens

[6] www.mkpress.com/extreme

[7] www.mkpress.com/greatestinnovation

[8] http://www.mkpress.com/#Power

Two

The Gathering Storm: Get Your Head into the Clouds

The Next IT Platform Shift and a Really Big Question:
"Why is Consumer IT so simple and Enterprise IT so complex?"

Key Points: What Exactly Is the Cloud?

Just as it was with that new-fangled "Internet" thing a decade ago, the Cloud and Cloud Computing suffer from confusion and hype. Sorry, but pat definitions won't do when it comes to understanding these two new buzzwords. But, as they are game-changing phenomena, business leaders—and the rest of us—must gain an understanding of what these terms really mean and how they will affect us. Remember how the Internet affected the retail book industry that was slow to grasp an understanding of the Internet before it got *Amazoned?* To gain a wide perspective, we will turn to some reporting, bringing together the ideas of the movers and shakers who are actively building the Cloud and delivering Cloud Computing.

What is the Cloud?

> "It's complete gibberish. It's insane.
> When is this idiocy going to stop?"
> —Larry Ellison, CEO, Oracle[1]

> Cloud Computing was originally defined by
> John Gage of Sun Microsystems—way back in 1984!
> "The Network is the Computer."

> Fast forward to the 21st century:
> "In Cloud Computing: The data center is the computer."
> —Lew Tucker, CTO, Cloud Computing, Sun Microsystems

> What is the Cloud?
> In short, it's the "*Real* Internet," or what the Internet was really meant to be in the first place—An endless computer made up of networks of networks of computers.

> Who coined the term Cloud Computing?
> In May 1997, NetCentric tried to trademark "cloud comput-ing" but later abandoned it in April 1999. So much for that.
> In 2006 , Google's Eric Schmidt used the term in response to Amazon's Jeff Bezo's Elastic Compute Cloud, originally named Elastic Compute Capability—but "cloud" sounded sexier.
> Correct answer: Who cares? It doesn't matter.

> For Venture Capitalists (VCs) the Cloud means
> "no more having to build one data center per startup!"
> In short, the Cloud is a profit center, not an IT cost center.

Cloud Computing is poised to change the way we access tech-nology, and it may be as game-changing as the commercialization of the Internet over a decade ago. Definitions of Cloud Computing vary widely, but the big idea is that:

> For geeks, Cloud Computing means grid computing, utility com-puting, software as a service, virtualization, Internet-based applica-tions, autonomic computing, peer-to-peer computing, on-demand and remote processing—and various combinations of these terms.
> Information factories anyone?
> For non-geeks, Cloud Computing is simply a platform where individuals and companies use the Internet to access endless hardware, software and data resources for most of their computing needs, leaving the mess to their Cloud Service Providers (CSPs).

Carl Howe, director of Anywhere Consumer Research at the analysis firm Yankee Group, explains, "It's things that you can use from your desktop computer or from your mobile phone—that you don't have to spend a lot of deployment money to make happen; they are just *services* that you can use."[2]

How about the Cloud as your PC? Sure, why not? Citrix, the 26th largest software company in the world, known by Windows users across the globe for it's GoToMyPC and GoToMeeting (in the Cloud), and New Delhi startup, Nivio, among others, are ready to become your virtual Desktop in the Cloud. That means they take care of the typical PC messes: crashes, lost data, viruses, upgrades, et al. And it doesn't matter what you use to connect to your virtual desktop in the sky: Windows, Mac or Linux. Word, Powerpoint, Excel and other PC applications are "just there." Companies with thousands of PCs to keep up and running and loaded with current versions of software just had their lives made easier with the Desktop in the Cloud.

A really big game changer for businesses is that they will need to make only minimal hardware and software investments to achieve a new level of IT cost savings as the entire spectrum of business technologies and services becomes accessible in the Cloud. But it won't be just cost savings.

Cloud Computing makes it possible to create new "business operations platforms" that will allow companies to change their business models and collaborate in powerful new ways with their customers, suppliers and trading partners —stuff that simply could not be done before.

Cloud Computing is the next step in the evolution of the Internet as a source of "services." It's those services that users are interested in, not the underlying technologies.

While most people have become accustomed to using services such as emailing or searching or shopping on the Internet, by extension, it makes sense that business technologies should be accessible in the same way.

When small and midsized businesses learn of the potential benefits
of Cloud Computing, they will be able to tap
IT infrastructures, platforms and software
that only huge enterprises could deploy in the past,
making the Cloud the great *leveler.*
The Cloud opens a new world of entrepreneurial opportunities,
not just to those in the industrialized world,
but also to emerging economies across the globe,
including three billion new capitalists from
China, India, Brazil, and the former Soviet Union.
Even you and I as individuals
will be able to use one of the world's largest supercomputers,
without having to house it, manage it, power it,
administer it, provision it—or buy it.

ET, call home!

Seti@home is an example of how distributed computing can
add up to something really big, really powerful. A big processing
job gets split up into lots of little jobs and distributed out to different PCs to get the power of a supercomputer without having to
build or buy a supercomputer.

The Search for Extra-Terrestrial Intelligence (SETI) is a collective set of projects that gives you an idea of how a swarm of
millions of home computers can make for one big "virtual supercomputer." SETI@home is a computing project that was launched
by U.C. Berkeley in 1999.

Ordinary people like you and me contribute to SETI research
by downloading and running the SETI@home software package
onto their PCs. Harnessed by the Internet, over 5 million computer
users in more than 200 countries have signed up for SETI@home
and have collectively contributed over 19 billion hours of computer processing time.

As of January 29, 2008 the Seti@home achieves an average
throughput of 387 Teraflops, making it equivalent to the second
fastest supercomputer on Earth.

This platform shift in technology to networks of interlinked
computers enables a *business platform shift* to networks of intercon-

nected companies that will create new winners and losers as the world rises from the ashes of the Crash of 2008. The importance of swift and deep cost-cutting, of focusing scarce resources on core activities, and of convincing investors that your business can adapt to unexpected change are but three reasons companies will put their heads into the Cloud.

Sure, there will be "oops" along the way, for example, SWIFT, the organization that manages international bank transfers, is planning to build a data center in neutral Switzerland. That will allow it to keep data about European transfers on the old continent, where it cannot be subpoenaed by the American government.

In addition to many forthcoming technical challenges, there will be political challenges. Let the law suits begin. Bring on the technical challenges of privacy, security, availability and reliability. So it is with any technological advancement.

The Technologies Behind the Cloud

Look! Up in the sky! It's a bird! It's a plane!
No. It's Hadoop, the elephant in the Cloud!

Doug Cutting, a search specialist, named his new creation Hadoop, after his son's stuffed elephant. Cutting's creation, Hadoop, is an Apache Lucene sub-project in a Free Java software framework that supports distributed applications running on large clusters of commodity computers that process huge amounts of data. It's a globally accessible fabric of resources, rather than local machines or remote server farms. The driver has been making hundreds of petabytes of data searchable.

Now, what search pioneers like Cutting have been pursuing has turned into general-purpose computing platforms, vastly more powerful than any ever built before—a massively parallel, scalable architecture that happily accommodates multifarious software.

> In short, the Cloud is the Computer.

Here's a simplified definition of cloud computing from Wikipedia, "Cloud Computing is a computing paradigm shift where computing is moved away from personal computers or an individual application server to a "cloud" of computers. Users of the Cloud only need to be concerned with the computing *service* being asked for, as the underlying details of how it is achieved are hidden. This method of distributed computing is done through pooling all computer resources together and being managed by software rather than a human." All this new capability is driving the need to manage these advances as a *unified* Cloud.

> The Cloud is in its infancy,
> as was the Internet in the early 1990s.
> But considering how the Internet transformed the world,
> buckle up and get ready for the ride ahead.

It seems we could be moving from computing-on-a-chip to computing-on-a-planet. Did you know that Google chose the little Oregon town of The Dalles, at the end of the fabled Oregon Trail along the Columbia River Gorge, to build a new 30-acre campus?

The Dalles campus will be the base for a server farm of unprecedented scale. You see, there's a dam there with a 1.8-gigawatt power station serving up electricity at one fifth the cost of Silicon Valley electricity, plus a fiber-optic hub linked to Harbour Pointe, Washington, the connection point of PC-1, a fiber-optic super pipe that was built to handle 640 Gbps between Asia and the U.S., and taps into the Northwest Open Access Network, a node of the experimental Internet2 (Yeah, I know Alaskan Senator Stevens calls them "tubes").

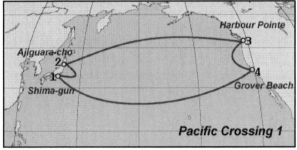

Update! It won't be just The Dalles in Google's next generation data center plans; it's also the high seas, where the company is planning data centers powered by wave farms.[3]

Google is pondering a floating data center that could be powered and cooled by the ocean. These offshore data centers could sit 3 to 7 miles offshore and reside in about 50 to 70 meters of water. Google filed for a patent that outlines a concept that would not only be savvy engineering, but deliver great financial returns.

Google is talking about self-contained units that would sit offshore much like oil rigs—and, "look Ma, no property taxes!"

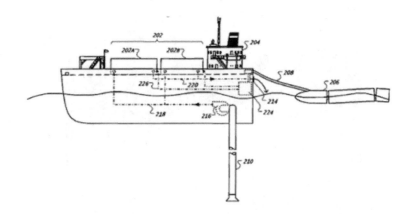

Hmm, is Google the only one that gets it? Not a chance!

Debra J. Chrapaty, Corporate Vice President, Global Foundation Services of Microsoft, isn't about to let Google take over the clouds in the sky. She says, "Google has done a great job of hyping its prowess, but we're neck and neck with them."[4] Her group is on a building spree to create some 20 one-billion-dollar data centers that already includes a huge complex in rural Quincy, Washington that taps cheap energy provided by the Grand Coulee Dam. "We're going to reinvent the infrastructure of our industry," she says. Microsoft packages 2,500 servers into preconfigured shipping containers, and each hyper scale data center can hold up to 224 containers or 560,000 servers. Danny Kim, the chief technology officer at FullArmor Corp. in Boston, has already moved his company to Microsoft's Windows Azure, and he isn't alone.

Meahwhile, IBM has recently invested in data centers specifically geared for the delivery of cloud services. It has new centers in Sao Paulo, Brazil; Bangalore, India; Seoul, Korea; and Hanoi, Vietnam, bringing the total number of its hubs to 13.[5]

And let's not forget Salesforce.com and its on-demand platform, Force.com, one of the original purveyors of the Cloud via its customer relationship management systems offered as a service; no hardware needed. Its latest messaging is, "It's the fastest way to get from ideas to applications. It's about more innovation and less infrastructure. It's about running your business in the Cloud." Salesforce.com was founded in 1999 by former Oracle executive Marc Benioff, who pioneered the concept of delivering enterprise applications via a simple Web site. Salesforce.com is building on its legacy and its AppExchange directory of on-demand applications. By the way, it's not all about corporate greed. Benioff is coauthor of *Compassionate Capitalism: How Corporations Can Make Doing Good an Integral Part of Doing Well* and *The Business of Changing the World.*

And this just in from the company that coined the term, "the network is the computer." Sun Microsystems' CEO, Jonathan Schwartz, gleefully explained, "As it turns out, midway through our due diligence in the acquisition of StorageTek, we learned they were the owners of Network.com. They hadn't really ever used it—a hidden gem. In hindsight, it may end up being one of the most valuable domain names in the history of computing."

The Way Back Machine

If computers of the kind I have advocated become the computers of the future, then computing may someday be organized as a public utility just as the telephone system is a public utility... The computer utility could become the basis of a new and important industry.
—John McCarthy, MIT Centennial in 1961

The key ideas behind Cloud Computing aren't new. So, before continuing, let's set some historical context, via the WayBack-Machine, and go back to GTE Data Services (GTEDS) in 1969. General Telephone and Electronics, one of the largest telephone providers in the world, took to heart the ideas of *Grosch's* law, "Computer performance increases as the square of the cost. If you want to do it twice as cheaply, you have to do it four times faster. The law can also be interpreted as meaning that computers present economies of scale: Bigger computers are more economical."

According to Dr. Herbert R. J. Grosch, "Grosch's Law was originally intended as a means for pricing computing services. IBM's Tom Watson Jr. ordered me to start a service bureau in Washington. The first question was 'how much do I charge.' So I developed what became known as Grosch's Law." While Grosch's law was far more pertinent to the 1960s and 1970s mainframe era, the underpinnings of "utility computing" were quite the same as today's rationale for Cloud Computing. In other words, rather than companies such as Savings and Loan institutions buying and maintaining their own mainframes, they could instead turn to a "computer utility," such as the one envisioned by GTEDS, and gain the efficiencies of Grosch's law. GTE could make a profit by consolidating its data centers and becoming a "service bureau," as it was called back them.

Being fresh out of college, my colleague Ken Bruggeman and I, along with our former IBMer boss, Ken Gold, went to downtown Tampa with a shovel and camera to take some pictures of ground being broken in front of the big billboard announcing the place where the GTEDS data center would be built. We were, of course, impatient youngsters with a passion for this new idea of a computer utility.

Tampa, Florida, USA

Oops. Darn. It sort of never really happened. Along came lower cost minicomputers (Dec's VAX, IBM's System/3, et al). Then came the PC revolution. Then the *almost* killer revolution proclaimed by Sun Microsystems' John Gage in 1984, "The Network is the Computer." Another oops, sorry, John, that didn't happen either, because the network wasn't fast enough in 1984. And oops, sorry, Larry Ellison of Oracle, the Network Computer (NC) was also before its time; the typical home had dialup Internet access in 1996—the network still wasn't fast enough.

As Eric Schmidt, former CTO of Sun Microsystems and now CEO of Google, observed,

> "When the network becomes as fast as the processor,
> the computer hollows out and spreads across the network."

Ah, so now that the overabundance of dark fiber laid down during the dot-com boom is being lit up, perhaps it's time for a "computer utility redux;" perhaps it's now time for the great computer in the sky; perhaps it's now time for Cloud Computing.

Who is leading the charge in massive-scale computing of the kind needed for Web 2.0 and beyond? All the titans shown in the figure below have stepped up to the plate, along with spades of smaller players such as Ribbit, "Silicon Valley's First Phone Company," the startup that wants to take your telephone to the Cloud.

IBM's Blue Cloud
Amazon's Elastic Compute Cloud
Sun Microsystems' Network.com
Google Apps TNG
Dell's Cloud Computing Solutions
Microsoft Office Live Workspace
Yahoo's M45
HP's Adaptive Infrastructure as a Service
... to name a few

Now, that's the gist of it, the gist of Cloud Computing. If, like many business people, that's more than you care to know, stop here before taking a closer look, and jump to Chapter 3: What's It For?.

A Closer Look

Russ Daniels, vice president and chief technology officer of Cloud Services Strategy at Hewlett Packard, writes in his blog, *Designing the Cloud,* 6 "It's impossible to overestimate the industry's ability to hype any new concept, stretching it to mean virtually everything, and so nothing. The Cloud is the latest example. Here I propose a narrow, limited definition, intentionally excluding as much as possible, because in that narrow definition something profound is occurring, something that will extend the reach of information technology to vast new markets, increase its value to existing ones, and ultimately transform the structure of our industry. The Cloud comprises three aspects:

- *Cloud Computing*, a design pattern that enables self-service automation, scaling , flexing, variable costs, and rich data analytics;
- *Cloud Platforms*, the tools, programming and information models, supporting software runtime components, and related technologies. Platforms facilitate implementing Cloud Services that depend on the Cloud Computing design pattern to meet their requirements, particularly those related to cost;
- *Cloud Services*, a delivery model for information services.

"The Cloud will not replace other forms of IT delivery any time soon. We'll still find value in software running and storing data on local devices, in complex mission-critical applications running on scale-up hardware, in virtualized and automated internal IT environments, in outsourced delivery, and so on. There are many reasons: today's inability of the Cloud to meet mission-critical requirements, the cost and risk of rewriting software to the Cloud Computing design pattern, and an unwillingness to change things that aren't broken among them. This means that most enterprises will execute in a hybrid model, providing and consuming Cloud Services, with those services integrated into traditionally delivered IT services as needed.

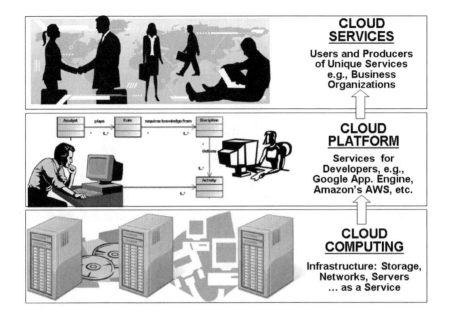

"If not to replace existing IT services, where will the Cloud fit? The best use of the Cloud will be to exploit its advantages and address un-served markets beyond the reach of traditional IT approaches. Because of their low-cost, pervasive accessibility, and ability to capture, persist, and analyze massive amounts of data, Cloud Services allow us to identify an individual's intentions, preferences, and circumstances and offer assistance. We can shift the focus of experience from an application/device pair to the user's concerns. Technology can provide continuity and consistency across services and devices, removing layers of complexity, serving more people in more circumstances.

"None of this will happen without the appropriate incentives for the businesses needed to enable it. The good news is that Cloud Services enable businesses to create richer, deeper relationships with customers, to treat each one as an individual, to customize offerings to meet the specific needs of each, and to integrate with the business partners to make this happen smoothly and affordably."

Shane Robison, executive vice president, chief strategy and

technology officer at HP, elaborates,[7]

> "The technology industry is in the early stages of a big shift
> —one that will transform how we access information,
> share content, and communicate."

"This next wave will be driven by a new model of computing: Instead of installing packaged software applications on their computers, people and businesses will use their browsers to access a wide range of cloud services available on-demand over the Internet. As this transition accelerates, the IT industry has an opportunity to drive a quantum-leap improvement in the user experience.

"Picture cloud services that are intelligent enough to anticipate your needs, based on a real-time understanding of your location, time of day, and preferences. In this next phase, the search for information will be done for you, not by you. You will have a seamless, consistent experience across all of the different devices you own, and all of the various on-demand services you care about.

"To realize the full potential of this new model, the technology industry needs to think about the cloud as a platform for creating new services and experiences that we have yet to imagine. We're moving to a future state where everything will be delivered to you as a service, from your work life to entertainment to various communities. We call this "Everything as a Service," and we believe this is where the world is headed. Individuals and businesses will have full control to customize their computing environments and to shape the experiences they want to have. This applies to individual consumers looking to personalize a variety of cloud services based on their lifestyle, as well as the largest global enterprises, which will increasingly turn to dynamic cloud-based offerings to meet their most demanding computing requirements.

"The true power of the cloud happens when you have continuous interaction between your device—your smartphone, laptop, TV—and the network, and they jointly act on your behalf. Here's a simple example: say it's 2 p.m. and your calendar shows you're booked on a flight to Toronto at 6 p.m. Your device should have the smarts to anticipate what information you'll need for this trip and then proactively gather it for you—a weather forecast for the Toronto area, a status update on your flight, a recommended route to the airport based on up-to-the-minute traffic conditions, and so on. In this scenario, the big step forward is the pervasive, proactive and highly personalized nature of cloud services.

> "Some may say they heard this before during the 1990's Internet bubble. But here is the difference: back then, we were living in a world of painfully slow Internet access. Despite all the hype, it simply wasn't possible to use the Internet as a platform for anything more than static pages."

"Fast forward to today. As broadband Internet access goes global and mobile, we have a legitimate opportunity to complete the transition from a web of static pages to a web of dynamic services. This can only happen if the IT industry does the hard work necessary to put the final pieces of the puzzle in place. That brings us back to the need for a higher level of intelligence built into our devices, our networks, and the software that ties it all together.

> "The shift to cloud computing will dramatically reduce the cost of information technology, but let's be clear —the implications of this shift go far beyond cost savings."

"The big disruptor over the next several years will be our ability to deliver a meaningful improvement in the user experience. If we are successful in doing that, we will create the next wave of growth for the technology industry. As we move from the desktop model to the cloud and a world where everything will be delivered as a service, there are five trends that are worth paying close attention to:

1. The digital world will converge with the physical world: Back in 1995, the mantra was, "Everything is virtual. Geography is irrelevant." But from now on, factors such as your physical location mean a lot. Cloud services will be increasingly aware of the context you're in, right down to details such as the time, the weather, where you're headed, and which friends or busi-

ness colleagues happen to be present nearby.

2.   The era of device-centric computing is over. Connectivity-centric computing will take center-stage: People often ask, "When am I going to get that one device that does everything I can imagine?" Flip that equation on its head. What you really want is the ability to use any number of devices, and have them all provide easy access to the services and content you care about. Devices will continue to play an important role, but in the next phase they become interchangeable — and the cloud services become the focal point.

3.   Publishing will be democratized. A global Internet population of 1.2 billion people now has the tools to produce everything from books and magazines to music and videos. This represents a massive disruption of old publishing models. People will soon have the ability to print on demand any book ever published. The concept of "out of print" will be a thing of the past. Similarly, warehouses of physical inventory in the publishing world will no longer be necessary.

4.   Crowd-sourcing is going mainstream and will change the rules of the game forever. Fortune 50 companies will access top talent on a global basis via the Internet, saving millions of dollars in professional services, from occupations as diverse as accountants, advertising experts, attorneys, and engineers. Reputation systems will lower the risks involved by exposing the poor performers. One example of this shift to crowd sourcing is HP's Logoworks service, which is transforming the graphics design industry.

5.   Enterprises will use radically different tools to make key business decisions, including systems to more accurately predict the future. A merger is taking place between the structured data that fuels business intelligence and the unstructured data of the web. This combination represents a kind of Holy Grail that will advance the state of the art in business intelligence. At the same time, market-based systems that enable companies to accurately predict the future will become common practice in the enterprise.

"As Everything as a Service evolves, we have an opportunity to reshape the computing industry forever and, more importantly, create more dynamic services that enrich our everyday lives and improve how we do business. To realize this potential, the technology industry must innovate by building a higher level of intelligence into the next generation of devices, networks and software. When we are successful in providing a dramatically better user experience, we will be poised for the next wave of growth."

Scalability

Utility computing and on-demand computing have been around for quite some time, and serve as foundations of Cloud Computing. Geva Perry, chief marketing officer at GigaSpace Technologies, explains, "The main benefit of utility computing is better economics. Corporate data centers are notoriously underutilized, with resources such as servers often idle 85 percent of the time. This is due to over provisioning—buying more hardware than is needed on average in order to handle peaks (such as the opening of the Wall Street trading day or the holiday shopping season), to handle expected future loads and to prepare for unanticipated surges in demand. Utility computing allows companies to only pay for the computing resources they need, when they need them."[8]

A special report in the *Economist* expands on the benefits to corporate data centers, "Before Ford revolutionized car making, automobiles were put together by teams of highly skilled craftsmen in custom-built workshops. Similarly, most corporate data centers today house armies of 'systems administrators,' the craftsmen of the information age. There are an estimated 7,000 such data centers in America alone, most of them one-off designs that have grown over the years, reflecting the history of both technology and the particular use to which it is being put. It is no surprise that they are egregiously inefficient. On average only 6% of server capacity is used, according to a study by McKinsey, a consultancy, and the Uptime Institute, a think-tank. Microsoft's data center in Northlake, just like Henry Ford's first large factory in Highland Park, Michigan, may one day be seen as a symbol of a new industrial era."[9]

Perry expands his discussion to Cloud Computing and what it means for corporate IT, "Cloud computing is a broader concept than utility computing and relates to the underlying architecture in which the services are designed. It may be applied equally to utility services and internal corporate data centers. Wall Street firms have been implementing internal clouds for years. They call it 'grid computing,' but the concepts are the same.

"Although it is difficult to come up with a precise and comprehensive definition of cloud computing, at the heart of it is the idea that applications run somewhere on the 'cloud' (whether an internal corporate network or the public Internet)—we don't know or care where. But as end users, that's not big news: We've been using web applications for years without any concern as to where the applications actually run.

"The big news is for application developers and IT operations. Done right, cloud computing allows them to develop, deploy and run applications that can easily grow capacity (scalability), work fast (performance), and never—or at least rarely—fail (reliability), all without any concern as to the nature and location of the underlying infrastructure.

"Taken to the next step, this implies that cloud computing infrastructures, and specifically their middleware and application platforms, should ideally have these characteristics:

- *Self-healing:* In case of failure, there will be a hot backup instance of the application ready to take over without disruption (known as failover). It also means that when I set a policy that says everything should always have a backup, when a failure occurs and my backup becomes the primary, the system launches a new backup, maintaining my reliability policies.

- *SLA-driven:* The system is dynamically managed by *service-level agreements* that define policies such as how quickly responses to requests need to be delivered. If the system is experiencing peaks in load, it will create new instances of the application on more servers in order to comply with the committed service levels—even at the expense of a low-priority application.

- *Multi-tenancy:* The system is built in a way that allows several customers to share infrastructure, without the customers being aware of it and without compromising the privacy and security of each customer's data.

- *Service-oriented:* The system allows composing applications out of discrete services that are loosely coupled (independent of each other). Changes to, or failure of, one service will not disrupt other services. It also means I can re-use services.
- *Virtualized:* Applications are decoupled from the underlying hardware. Multiple applications can run on one computer (virtualization a la VMWare) or multiple computers can be used to run one application (grid computing).
- *Linearly Scalable:* Perhaps the biggest challenge. The system will be predictable and efficient in growing the application. If one server can process 1,000 transactions per second, two servers should be able to process 2,000 transactions per second, etc.
- *Data, Data, Data:* The key to many of these aspects is management of the data: its distribution, partitioning, security and synchronization. New technologies, such as Amazon's SimpleDB, are part of the answer, not large-scale relational databases. And don't let the name fool you. As my colleague Nati Shalom rightfully proclaims, SimpleDB is not really a database. Another approach that is gaining momentum is in-memory data grids."

> While utility computing can change the economics of IT, Cloud Computing could change the economics of business, allowing companies to adapt and scale their business models and markets.

"It is a sign of lively 'combinatorial innovation,' made possible because entrepreneurs as well as incumbents can cheaply try new combinations of technology," says Google's Hal Varian in the *Economist*'s special report on Cloud Computing.

"Many start-ups would probably not even exist without the cloud. Take Animoto, a service that lets users turn photos into artsy MTV-like music videos using artificial intelligence. When it launched on Facebook, a social network, demand was such that it had to increase the number of its virtual machines on AWS from 50 to 3,500 within three days. 'You could give me unlimited funding,' says Adam Selipsky of Amazon Web Services (AWS), 'and I wouldn't know how to deploy that many servers in 72 hours.'"

"Combinatorial innovation should also be made easier by the fact that the cloud will be a huge collection of electronic services based on standards. But this service-oriented architecture will be even more important for existing firms because it should free their inner workings—their 'business processes'—from the straitjacket of their ERP systems and allow these processes to be more easily adapted, for instance to launch a new product."

The Cloud Isn't Just for Garage Startups; It's Also for the Fortune 500 and Beyond

Indeed, the Cloud isn't just for startups, its for incumbents as well. Just consider how Nasdaq and the New York Times have embraced the Cloud to augment their existing legacy IT systems. Both tapped into Amazon.com's Internet-provisioned computing and storage services (Elastic Compute Cloud (EC2) and Simple Storage Service (S3))to augment their own IT resources. The Times processed 4 terabytes of data through Amazon Web Services by simply using a credit card to get the service going. In a matter of minutes it converted scans of more than 15 million news stories into PDFs for online distribution—$240! Look, Ma, no New York Times IT infrastructure needed. Meanwhile, Nasdaq uses Amazons's S3 storage system to deliver historical stock and mutual fund information, rather than add the load to its own computing infrastructure.

In other examples of early Cloud Computing adopters, Infosolve Technologies uses Sun's Network.com to scrub customer addresses rather than implement the needed infrastructure internally. The medical robotics firm Intuitive Surgical and recruitment services provider Jobscience use the Cloud to provision their own applications. Both companies use the Force.com platform.

How about using a *galactic* internal, private cloud to gain economies of scale? GE seems more than interested in that idea. According to GE chief technology officer, Greg Simpson,

- "Three years ago, only a quarter of the money GE spent on computing power was allocated to its centralized data centers: the rest of it was spent by the group's individual operating companies. Today, that data center share has climbed to 45 per cent and GE's units 'buy' far more of their computing as a service from the center. Centralization has taken hold."

- "A year ago, in 85 per cent of the cases where it had a new computing task to handle, GE bought a new server to deal with the task. By last December 2008, that proportion had fallen to just 50 per cent. In place of all those extra computers are 'virtual machines,' using software from companies like VMware, GE is loading extra work on its existing computers, then moving it between computers as needs change."

But then comes an even bigger proposition. How about a huge company like GE blending both internal clouds and going beyond the firewall to reach out to customers and suppliers in the Cloud? GE's supply chain is huge, including 500,000 suppliers in more than 100 countries that cut across cultures and languages, buying up $55 billion a year. GE wanted to modernize its cumbersome home-grown sourcing system, the Global Supplier Library, build a single multi-language repository, and offer self-service capabilities so that suppliers could maintain their own data. So did CIO Gary Reiner and team start programming? The short answer is no, they looked to the Cloud for a solution. In 2008, GE engaged software-as-a-service (SaaS) vendor Aravo to implement its Supplier Information Management (SIM) SaaS that would ultimately become the largest SaaS deployment to date.

"They're using SaaS for 100,000 users and 500,000 suppliers in six languages: that's a major technology deployment shift," said Mickey North Rizza, research director at AMR Research. She said that the sheer volume of transactions, combined with the fact that GE supply chain and procurement employees around the world can now access the same sourcing partner information, all from one spot. It is significant not only for the supply chain management space, but also for the SaaS and cloud computing world.

"Finally we have a very large company tackling the data transparency issue by using a SaaS product," North Rizza continued. "It's a huge deal." When GE goes outside its "firewall" to innovate, you betcha, other CEOs will be asking their CIOs lots of questions about harnessing the Cloud, internally, with tightly controlled external clouds provisioned by third parties, and finally, with public clouds.

According to Forrester Research's 2008 survey of software IT decision-makers, just 16 percent of respondents said they were already using or currently piloting SaaS applications. Conversely, more than 80 percent were still on the sidelines—curious, for sure, but not yet completely sold or running SaaS applications right now. Forty-six percent said they were interested in SaaS or planning to pilot; 37 percent said they were "not at all interested." As news spreads about GE and other Fortune 500 companies innovating with private and public Clouds, interest in intra-, inter-, private and public clouds will likely skyrocket. And, of course all these cloud formations will need to interoperate to become one Intercloud, much as we have one Internet today.

As IT veteran and Cordys chief strategy officer, Jon Pyke, wrote in "Weathering the Perfect Storm," "There will be not just one cloud but a number of different sorts: private ones and public ones, which themselves will divide into general-purpose and specialized clouds. People are already using the term 'Intercloud' to mean a federation of all kinds of clouds, in the same way that the Internet is a network of networks. And all of those clouds will be full of applications and services."

> Yesterday, the Internet—tomorrow, the Intercloud.

Want more proof that the Cloud isn't just for garage dot.com types of startups? How about the super-sensitive, super-guarded military? Although many think Cloud Computing is nowhere ready for prime time or mission-critical usage, John Garing, the CIO of the Defense Information Systems Agency (DISA) at the Department of Defense (DoD) thinks otherwise. As reported in "On-Demand Enterprise," Garing called Cloud Computing something we absolutely have to do. "If you deploy a force somewhere in the world for disaster relief—or a special operations team, they ought to be able to connect to the network like you or I can from home, and bring together or compose—the services and information they need for what they're doing at that particular place and time, rather than have to connect to a bunch of applications." When DISA's RACE (Rapid Access Computing Environment) went live, and he saw someone experimenting on RACE to provision services in only seven minutes. he joked, "That's pretty impressive for the Department of Defense, or the federal government. Seven months would be more like it." Although RACE is a private cloud located entirely within DISA's walls, government customers still get the public cloud experience with a Web portal, 24-hour-a-day availability, and a service catalog.

Meanwhile, Kevin Jackson of Dataline, a technology solutions provider to DoD and federal agencies, emailed me and wrote that his company is working with DoD organizations to define and address tactical military requirements. These requirements have always been there, but shipboard compute and storage capacity limited the commander's ability to address them. The advent of cloud technologies, however, has led to the concept of a "Tactical Cloud" where battle group resources can be immediately pooled to run high fidelity models and simulations, the results of which are used in crafting a commander's decisions.

Jackson recalled that when Cloud Computing first came into vogue, there was a rather serious discussion about the private cloud concept. The whole idea of cloud computing seemed to argue against implementing such a capability behind organizational walls. Although in some circles, the idea of a private cloud is being subsumed by the more acceptable "Enterprise Cloud," Jackson used a different cloud concept, the "Tactical Cloud." In the view of many, the development of a private or Enterprise Cloud for the DoD is a fait accompli, so private clouds seems like an appropriate evolution. Enterprise Clouds, however, overlooked the need for military formations to simultaneously leverage this new IT approach and operate independently. Individual units could combine their IT infrastructure virtually using Cloud Computing concepts. One case hypothesized the use of high fidelity tactical simulations in faster than real-time to help commanders better evaluate tactical options before committing to a course of action. This Tactical Cloud would also need to seamlessly reach back and interact with the DoD's Enterprise Cloud. There could even be situations where the Tactical Cloud would link to a public cloud in order to access information or leverage a infrastructure-as-a-service. A naval formation seems to be the perfect environment for a tactical or "Battlegroup Cloud." Although each ship would normally operate its IT infrastructure independently, certain situations could be better served by linking all the resources into a virtual supercomputer. Even more interesting is the fact that the Tactical Clouds could go beyond DoD and meet the needs of police, firefighters, medical professionals and homeland security organizations. If the DoD could improve its operations with a Tactical Cloud couldn't these other organizations benefit as well? After all it was the DoD's Arpanet that gave us the Internet.

Managing resources in the Intercloud will be a technological challenge. Sun Microsystems' Lew Tucker said that Sun's acquisition of Q-layer, a Belgium cloud computing company was to gain the capability to automate the deployment and management of both public and private clouds. With Q-layer technology, Sun can provide a self-service virtual data center where companies can manage virtual components, via a management layer. Enterprises will be able to define a system architecture at Web scale, and Tucker explained that as businesses continue to rely more on technology to drive mission-critical processes, the agility of the data center will become more important to the flexibility of the entire company.

Geroge Barlow, CEO of Cloud Harbor, explains another aspect of cloud management, "Few people yet understand the major role enterprise software appliances will play in the upcoming cloud computing revolution. Appliance-based Software Delivery (AbSD) is an emerging technology that puts ready-to-run applications on a server (appliance) that is built specifically to be deployed on-premise, behind the firewall of an enterprise computing installation. These appliances will contain the same applications that run on servers in the cloud and be maintained exclusively by the cloud application vendors at the same application release level as the corresponding cloud offerings. The main advantage of AbSD applications is that they are securely connected to both the cloud and the organization's on-premise network concurrently. This affords the enterprise the safety and convenience of keeping data and connections to existing on-premise applications behind the organization's firewall while still allowing most of the advantages of the Software-as-a-Service or Platform-as-a-Service computing models."

Barlow also argues, "Some of the interesting ways On-Demand will appeal to larger businesses include budgeting the expenditures as operating expense rather than capital expenditures, creating business performance dashboards by combining information from cross-functional enterprise systems such as CRM and ERP, and collaborating across geographic and organizational boundaries to create core-function pilots and innovation projects. If there is an urgent need for an application, being able to assemble a team and begin creating processes or using available pre-created applications without having to incur the typical costs and delays can significantly impact strategic imperatives like time-to-market."

Jon Pyke summarizes, "There will be many ways in which the cloud will change businesses and the economy, most of them hard to predict, but one theme is already emerging. In the teeth of the Perfect Storm of the current economic turmoil and advancing technology, businesses will have to become more like the technology itself: more adaptable, more interwoven and more specialized. Organizations should use the Perfect Storm as an opportunity to get fit and healthy. There is an idiom that states 'a better built ship can weather a storm.' An organization should take a good look at what it does, but most importantly it should take a long hard look at how it does things."

From Then to Now

Just as GE's legendary CEO, Jack Welch, learned about the power of the Internet in the 1990s by watching his (now former) wife shopping online, consumers are out front of companies when it comes to using the Cloud and Web 2.0. Just think Google, Yahoo, eBay, Amazon, and Flickr—all with very sophisticated and powerful Cloud infrastructures. On the other hand, it's been tough to convince the largest enterprises that the Cloud represents the next infrastructure, the next computing platform.

As Sun Microsystems' CEO, Jonathan Schwartz blogged,

"I'm sure George Westinghouse was confounded
by the Chief Electricity Officers of the time that resisted buying
power from a grid, rather than building their own internal utilities."

He goes on to write, "We learned a lot, but mainly that most enterprises today define On Demand computing as hosting—they want to give their computers, software, networking and storage to a third party, and rent them back for a fixed price. But that'd be like an electricity company collecting generators and unique power requirements, and trying to build a grid out of them. That's not a business we're in (nor one in which technology plays much of a role—it's all about managing real estate and call centers, as far as we can tell). Grids are all about standardization and transparency—and building economies of scale."

Schwartz isn't too concerned about early adoption by large enterprises, ". . . rumor has it there's a good business in the long tail. My view—most computing will be purchased by that tail. There are, after all, far more small financial institutions than large. The same applies to movie studios, pharmaceutical companies, academic institutions, and nearly every other industry on earth. I'm very comfortable betting on the value in volume—and the willingness of those smaller firms to change culture, process and lifestyle to get a competitive advantage through network services." As with most new paradigms, Cloud Computing may start at the edges of enterprises and slowly be absorbed into more and more functions.

My very first experience touching a PC, I'm guessing around 1971 and way before "real" PCs were developed, was a Datapoint 2200, the device that also led to the development of the first 8-bit microprocessors, and whose specifications led to the creation of the Intel 8008 single chip microprocessor. Now, not so many years later, I'm waiting for the specification from OMG's Business Process Management Initiative, or whoever, that will make it possible to put business process management in the Cloud—with Web 2.0 simplicity. The time is ripe.

Over time, Cloud Computing could help IT managers dramatically reduce the complexities and costs of managing scale-out IT infrastructures in the Web 2.0 era, and could also help manage the complexities of scale-out inter-enterprise business process management—including requisite real-time petabyte-scale business intelligence, business rules via intelligent agents, inter-enterprise business process modeling, complex event processing, and human interaction management.

Old-line CIOs will certainly cling to their in-house infrastructures, claiming *security* as the major concern (and don't forget compliance: SOX, HIPAA, GLBA, FFIEC, PCI, COBIT, et al). Of course, security is, and always will be a major concern, even for in-house located systems, though one that can be overcome in the Cloud. For every major technology shift, commensurate new management controls and auditing procedures are needed, as I explained in a BPTrends column, "EDP Audit and Control Redux."[10] So, watch for FWaaS (firewalls) and VPNaaS (virtual private networks) as standard services in the Cloud.

As the *Economist* noted, "The Cloud lends itself to similar hyperbole [as Internet 1.0]. Yet so far there has not been much debate about its economic fallout—probably because the "new economy" ended badly and the newest one is currently doing even worse.

> "There will be many ways in which the Cloud will change businesses and the economy, most of them hard to predict, but one theme is already emerging. Businesses are becoming more like the technology itself: more adaptable, more interwoven and more specialized. These developments may not be new, but Cloud Computing will speed them up.

"Corporate IT has always promised to make companies more agile. In the 1990s many companies re-engineered their business processes when they started using a form of software called enterprise-resource planning (ERP), which does things such as managing a firm's finances and employees. But once these massive software packages were in place, it was exceedingly difficult to change them. Implementing SAP, the market leader in ERP, is like pouring concrete into your company, goes an old joke among IT types.

"This helps to explain why in many firms IT departments and business units have traditionally been at loggerheads. In recent years tensions have worsened. Companies must grapple with ever-changing markets and regulations, yet IT budgets are being cut. Many firms now have a huge backlog of IT projects."[11]

- Hello, business process management in the Cloud.
- Hello, business operations platform in the Cloud.

Bruce Richardson of AMR Research wrote in December 2008, "Executives from one of the best-known ERP vendors [enterprise systems] recently talked to us about their 2009 product plans and strategy. At the end of the call, I expressed my astonishment that there were no plans to offer any part of their company's product line as software as a service (SaaS) [in the Cloud].

"As they talked, I was transported back to the early 1980s, where I found myself in a room filled with mainframe and minicomputer vendors. They were screaming about the need to kill off internal PC development initiatives because these lower cost, limited function desktop boxes would cannibalize sales of higher margin systems. While it didn't exactly play out that way, the hardware landscape was changed forever. IBM reinvented the mainframe as a giant server. PCs spread like kudzu, obliterating dumb terminals and small business computers. The only remaining minis are in computer museums.

"Is the same about to happen to the enterprise applications market? Are the largest ERP vendors becoming the new mainframes by holding on to the traditional deployment model? Looking out five years, which applications will run on premises versus on demand or in the *cloud?*[12]

The forward-thinking CIO will no doubt put his or her head in the clouds, and change his or her title to CPO, Chief Process Officer, for it's agile business processes that companies want to manage, not technology infrastructures. And, it's not one size fits all. It will likely be a combination of private and public Cloud infrastructures. But it will be a new paradigm, surely as the PC was a new paradigm to mighty-mainframe IBM in days gone by. So here's a word of warning to those who have shrugged off Web 2.0 and the Cloud as its platform, "Do so at your own peril, even though where all this will end up is still up in the air." Let the dot connecting begin.

Takeaway

In its essence, Cloud Computing is about using swarms of computers to deliver unprecedented computing power to people and organizations across the globe. Because much of the power is about information management versus just computational power, many advances in Cloud Computing have come from researchers taking on the challenges posed by Internet searches (Google's MapReduce and the open-source Hadoop systems). In everyday terminology, cloud computing uses sophisticated tools to harness the Internet to:

1. spread computing tasks across multiple clusters of machines,
2. provide a platform for new tools and techniques that can make the computing ecosystem far simpler, thus, available to all,
3. provide a platform for human collaboration and interaction never before possible, and
4. make all the world's information accessible anywhere, anytime.

Cloud Computing can deliver *tens of trillions of computations per second* in a way that users can tap through the Web, making super-computing available to the masses. It can do so by networking groups of thousands of servers that use low-cost consumer PC technology, with advanced operating systems to spread computational chores across them. By contrast, the newest and most powerful desktop PCs process only about three billion computations a second.

The economic and innovation implications are game changing, for technology will not only be available to handle the worlds business and financial transactions, but will also open a whole new world of human interaction and collaboration on a scale never before possible. In the past, information technology was about productivity; now it's about collaboration, a shared information base and collective intelligence.

Cloud computing will take globalization to a whole new level, and globalization is indeed the greatest reorganization of the world since the Industrial Revolution.

One shared world; one shared computer; one shared information base.

References.

[1] http://news.cnet.com/8301-1001_3-10059361-92.html

[2] https://www-304.ibm.com/jct03004c/businesscenter/smb/us/en/contenttemplate/!!/gcl_xmlid=158147/

[3] http://blogs.zdnet.com/BTL/?p=9937

[4] http://www.businessweek.com/print/technology/content/nov2008/tc20081121_382269.htm

[5] http://news.cnet.com/8301-1001_3-10059361-92.html

[6] http://www.communities.hp.com/online/blogs/designing-the-cloud/default.aspx

[7] http://www.hp.com/hpinfo/execteam/articles/robison/08eaas.html

[8] http://gigaom.com/2008/02/28/how-cloud-utility-computing-are-different/

[9] http://www.economist.com/specialreports/displayStory.cfm?story_id=12411882

[10] http://bptrends.com/publicationfiles/11-07-COL-EDP%20Audit-Fingar-Final.pdf

[11] http://www.economist.com/specialreports/displayStory.cfm?story_id=12411882

[12] http://www.amrresearch.com/content/View.asp?pmillid=22150

Three

The Cloud: What's It For? What Do You Do With It?

Revolutions never go backward.
—Wendell Philips, American abolitionist.

Key Points: What Do You Do With the Cloud?

Having glimpsed at the trends and technologies of the Cloud as a new computing platform, it's only logical to ask, "What do you do with it? How do you use it?" To answer these questions we will need to briefly introduce some buzzwords and, uh oh, three-letter acronyms (TLAs): SOA, Web 2.0, and Web 3.0. Please bear with me.

SOA and Everything as a Service

Oh no, here we go again with yet another TLA: SOA.

Information technology has a notorious reputation for being a solution in search of a problem. A current case in point is Service-Oriented Architecture (SOA). It seems yet another technology being "pushed" on business, when in fact it's a demand "pull" that is driving companies to embrace SOA. The business itself is demanding the technology to address complex business problems.

So, what's the current state of SOA? In a January 2009 report, "The Four Big Myths of SOA" by AMR Research analyst, Ian Finley, one myth cited was that "SOA is dead!" Finley wrote, "Recently, some have said SOA is dead, killed off by overambitious zealots, underperforming products, and bloated service engagements. Perhaps the SOA of their dreams is dead, but the real SOA is very much alive. SOA will be with us for a long time because we don't have a better approach. It's the accumulation of techniques learned and relearned in our evolution from structured programming through to client/server and Web application design. It's a compendium of current best practices applied to the problem of a rapidly changing business world. Unless the world stops changing or some radical new paradigm is uncovered, SOA will be the cornerstone of our software for years to come—just look at what the world's software vendors are investing in. SOA permeates everything from Virtual Machine hypervisors to Facebook. If there was a better approach, systems developers would be investing in it already. Until a successor emerges, SOA will continue to reign." So, rumors of SOA's early demise are highly exaggerated.

The worlds of business and business technology are growing overwhelmingly complex. Companies are complex systems, business processes are complex systems, and computer programs are complex systems. SOA is a set of organizing principles that provide a comprehensible framework for modeling and constructing complex systems. In short, service orientation is a complexity buster.

Since the beginning, three great trends have shaped business computing: the development of software components, the decoupling of these components, and the raising of the levels of abstraction to ever more meaningful human forms. SOA brings the first principles of abstraction, componentization and decoupling to a new level. SOA is the latest advancement in distributed computing systems, where software components are essentially a collection of self-contained "services" that users can access and use without knowing the location or platform a given service is deployed on.

But here's what is really important about SOA, in the words of Sandy Carter, a Vice President at IBM, "SOA is a business-driven IT architectural approach that supports integrating your business as linked, repeatable business tasks or services. It helps companies increase the flexibility of their business processes. Service-oriented architecture begins with a service—a service being simply a business task, such as a potential customer's credit rating on opening a new account. It's important to note that we're talking about a part of a business process here. Think about what your company does on a day-to-day basis, and break up those business processes into repeatable business tasks or components."

Carter is describing reusable business process fragments that can be reused in many contexts and settings—the key is reusable business process segments, not just reusable software. Those reusable process segments can be tapped as companies design innovative business processes as "situational" business processes across multiple business channels. That is, they are adapted to completely new business situations. So it is that software flexibility and reuse enables business process flexibility and reuse. That's the stuff of business agility in hyper competitive markets of the 21st century.

Carter continues, "As companies use SOA to provide standardized services and business processes, the value of IT to the overall business mission grows exponentially. SOA is the supporting IT infrastructure that enables companies to become more flexible through a focus on business processes. The relationship of a service to a process is critical. A business process is a set of related business tasks spanning people, systems, and information to produce a specific outcome or product. With SOA, a process is made up of a set of services."[1]

How much should be included in any given "service" how

"big" should it be? Carter explains that granularity is key, "Granularity is the amount of function the service exposes. For example, a fine-grained service provides smaller units of a business process, and a coarse-grained service provides a larger business task that contains a number of sub steps. For me, it's like Goldilocks and the Holy grail. Services cannot be too big or too small, but must be just right. If the service is too big, that yields less reuse. If it is too small, you end up with performance hits and poor mapping between business tasks and the services that support them. So granularity is sort of the Holy Grail: that is, determining how big or how small to design a service is more a function of how atomic the composite function is. In loan origination, the granularity of the service might be quite coarse, as there are only so many different functions associated with loan origination."

One basic premise of SOA is simple. It's about avoiding the need to build new software from scratch and duplicating software, data and business rules that already exist—massive duplication is the current reality in most companies. Such "reuse" has been a Holy grail of software development throughout the past fifty years (from subroutines to objects, from objects to components), and SOA takes the pursuit one big step further.

SOA is a continuation of the request/respond, object-oriented programming approach that's been evolving since the 1960s (Simula), where one object (or component) requests a service from another object (to do something, or supply some data) without having to know the interworkings of the responding object. Just make a request and the object responds.

What's new about SOA is that technical standards for sending messages are now based on Internet protocols and break the restrictions of proprietary techniques for objects or components to interoperate.

Even more interesting is that the architecture of the services allows them to be used in many different contexts, even contexts the software developer didn't have in mind for the services.

To achieve more or less universal interoperability, certain architectural principles are used in the design of services so that they are:

- reusable,
- abstract,
- autonomous,
- stateless,
- discoverable,
- composable, and
- loosely coupled.

> The potential benefits of service-oriented computing include a major reduction in the cost of software development, and speed and agility in building new software as business needs change.
>
> Services become Lego blocks
> for building software, rapidly and efficiently.

Ultimately, everything—infrastructure, information, widgets and business processes—could be rendered as a service, and delivered via the Cloud:

- AaaS - Architecture as a Service
- BPMaaS - Business Process Management as a Service
- DaaS - Data as a Service
- FaaS - Frameworks as a Service
- GaaS - Globalization as a Service
- GaaS - Governance as a Service
- HaaS - Hardware as a Service
- IDaaS - Identity as a Service
- MaaS - Mashups as a Service
- PaaS - Platform as a Service
- VaaS - Voice as a Service
- FWaaS - Firewalls as a Service

Returning to George Barlow of Cloud Harbor, "In addition to changing the way organizations develop their own applications, business process management as a service (BPMaaS) will create a new model of development and distribution for value-added providers. This capability allows for a community of developers to create business processes that can be shared freely or through the platform's subscription facilities. Thus, a significant library of diverse process templates can be created, each defining a unique business process. When developers build templates with customization in mind, subscribers can acquire the pre-defined templates, customize them to their own organization's needs and rapidly deploy the automated processes. New and innovative processes could be running in a matter of hours or days."

If you aren't a techie, you needn't know about all these SOA-oriented things. If you are, this sure sounds like the greatest thing since sliced bread.

That's enough SOA technical discussion for this business book. Just remember this:

> SOA is about connecting dots, and there are many new dots to connect with Everything as a Service (EaaS).

SOA and Business Mashups: Walls Come Tumbling Down

Do you think what I think when you hear the word "mashup?" Service-oriented computing just could be the greatest thing since sliced bread, but like any technology there are possibilities for good and bad outcomes from using service-oriented computing to create mashups. That's why the word "architecture" in SOA is so important, and architectural "standards" will be needed for truly achieving interoperability of software services in the Cloud.

In Web development, the term "Mashup" is used to describe easy, fast integration of services to produce results service owners had no idea could be produced. An example is the use of cartographic data from Google Maps to add location information to real-estate data, thereby creating a new and distinct service that was not originally provided by either source.

> Mashups aren't just for software, they are for business too. Software mashups enable business mashups.

As Andy Mulholland, Chris Thomas and Paul Kurchina, write in *Mashup Corporations*, "Providing services to innovators, inside the company and out, profoundly changes the way it appears to customers, partners and competitors. Some of these new business processes create markets where none existed before; others change the role the company plays within the value chain.

"Most of these processes feel completely unnatural at first and arrive with a complete checklist of objections and excuses explaining why they will never work. Lightweight, reusable services offer the perfect building blocks for inexpensive experiments that may fail, as expected, or may create a massive opportunity.

"Mashups aren't invented during the IT department's annual offsite meetings, except for the rare exception in which an IT organization is promoting the reuse of commonly used corporate services. Instead, they spring from the minds of entrepreneurial virtuosos who are continually sifting through the services they discover on the Internet and imagining the emergent possibilities.

"Companies that 'get' SOA do everything in their power to turn their value-creating processes into services and then place them in the hands of their most innovative thinkers whose efforts become the company's bridge to new customers. To the outside world, the company becomes increasingly defined by the services it offers others to use as a springboard for innovation and creating new kinds of business relationships."

In a wired world, the possibilities for assembling, then disbanding, geographically scattered project teams are almost endless. A growing number of companies are relying on electronically connected virtual project teams to get things done.

In time, the primary work unit in the enterprise will be "the project," not "the function" performed somewhere in the Org Chart. Think "white space" when thinking about organization charts and where work really gets done.

> Virtual, matrixed teams, composed of diverse competencies, knowledge and capabilities, with traditional hierarchical structures replaced by multi-company teams,
> will be assembled as needed, sometimes "on the fly."
> Such dynamically formed teams will tackle specific projects to pursue specific opportunities and to counter specific threats
> in the brave new world of total global competition.

Okay, the Cloud is a super-scalable, global computing infrastructure available on demand at the lowest possible cost. The Cloud delivers hyper-scale Web applications anytime (24/7 availability) and anywhere (global reach) to all stakeholders: employees, suppliers, stockholders and customers, with ease of use and features that often go beyond what desktop-only apps can deliver. The walls separating organizations from their peers, their partners, their competitors and their customers will come tumbling down, changing what it means to be a company. That's where we'll go in this book, beyond the technology, and on to the business transformations it enables. What's really important is that SOA in the Cloud means a fundamental shift from information technology (IT) to business technology (BT), where a "service" represents a "unit of business," not a "unit of technology." Services will be bundled, unbundled and rebundled at the speed of business.

Web 2.0 and the Great Simplification

Now, what about that Web 2.0 thing? As it turns out, Web 2.0 is a key driver for the production and consumption of "services." It's likely you're already a Web 2.0 participant, controlling your own information and *contributing* to the information used by others:

- Flickr
- MySpace
- Gmail
- Blog participation
- Wikipedia
- YouTube
- Page Ranked searching
- Amazon reviews

No, Web 2.0 is *not* new Internet technology, as Tim Berners-Lee, inventor of the World Wide Web, would tell you.

On the other hand, Tim O'Reilly, publisher and coiner of the term Web 2.0, would counter with, "Web 2.0 is the network as platform, spanning all connected devices; Web 2.0 applications are those that make the most of the intrinsic advantages of that platform: delivering software as a continually-updated service that *gets better the more people use it* [e.g., Wikipedia], consuming and remixing data from multiple sources, including individual users, while providing their own data and services in a form that allows remixing by others, creating *network effects* through an 'architecture of participation,' and going beyond the page metaphor of Web 1.0 to deliver rich user experiences." In other words,

- Web 2.0 is about many-to-many connections (social networking) instead of the one-to-many connections of the past.
- It's about meaningful, two-way conversations that add value for all participants in those conversations.
- It's about social computing and tapping the wisdom of crowds, instead of computing as a means of processing the transactions of business.
- It's about business people devising their own creative solutions without waiting for their IT staff—call them "situational computer applications" if you will, as they meet the immediate and ever-changing needs of workers wanting to get their work done.

> Web 2.0 is not based on a technology shift,
> but rather a *usage* paradigm shift.
> That shift has come about largely by
> the *simplicity of use,* call it Consumer IT, if you will.

In the world of technology, we speak of computer "users." In the world of Web 1.0 people were users that basically had Web pages served up to them (the read-only Internet). In the world of Web 2.0, users become "participants," *prosumers* (producers and consumers) actively contributing to and co-creating the value of the information base with which they work and share with others (the read-write Internet). Think Facebook, YouTube, MySpace, Second Life, wikis, blogs, or Google Apps, where you don't need to write even one line of code to participate.

And, the more these easy-to-use services get used, the better they become, and the more value they deliver. In short, Web 2.0 provides a platform where everything is a *service*, not an application or software code. Which then leads to the question,

Why is Consumer IT so *simple* and Enterprise IT so *complex?*

He who uses this machine should be able to forget that it is a machine.
—Antoine de Saint-Exupery, *Wind, Sand and Stars*, 1940.

Answering the IT complexity question unfolds many challenges and opportunities for the worlds of business and society at large. Michael Hugos, author of *The Greatest Innovation Since the Assembly Line* and award winning CIO wrote, "You are going to have to own up to the fact that we in IT are addicted to complexity. And our addiction to the complex, the expensive and the clunky is increasingly indulged at our own peril. That's because business people have discovered that consumer IT is better than corporate IT. It has more features and is more responsive, easier to use, faster to install and a whole lot cheaper to operate."

This strikes at the heart of IT and the complexity that has grown up with computer technology. Web 2.0 is all about a quantum leap from complexity to simplicity, especially from the user's perspective. Business architect Gene Weng netted it out with a quote from Leonardo da Vinci, "Simplicity is the ultimate sophistication." Internally, however, it takes some very complex software to make its use simple.

From an ease of use perspective,
complex is simple, simple is complex.

So, as Albert Einstein once said,
"Make everything as simple as possible, but not simpler."

Einstein's message resonates with the current world of Enterprise IT. If you can build a vision of an agile and innovative company, and show how to interweave the easy-to-use Consumer IT and complex Enterprise IT systems, tools and techniques to go where neither has gone before, you'll become a true pioneer and help raise your company from the ashes of the Crash of 2008.

Because of its simplicity of use, Web 2.0 creates new "network effects" that have great implication for businesses. Example tools, including social software, blogs, wikis, Web syndication and tagging (folksonomies) all provide vehicles to build communal knowledge and collaboration.

As Andy Mulholland and Nick Earle write in, *Mesh Collaboration*, "Social networks are invaluable tools inside and outside the enterprise. Within the company, managers can gain valuable insights into how their employees are interacting and using various technologies. Outside the enterprise, it can help locate potential business partners, customers, suppliers, employees, and people with expertise. As more and more people contribute knowledge and add structure, their collective contributions make the knowledge more useful to everyone involved. The challenge is to decide where and how to harness these effects in your business."[2]

"Connect. Collaborate. Transform Your Business," is the theme of TechWeb's Enterprise 2.0 conference. What Is Enterprise 2.0? It's all about adopting and harnessing Web 2.0 and SOA tools that enable contextual, agile and simplified information exchange and collaboration to distributed workforces and networks of partners and customers. Below are TechWeb's distinctions:

Enterprise 1.0	Enterprise 2.0
Hierarchy	Flat Organization
Friction	Ease of Organization Flow
Bureaucracy	Agility
Inflexibility	Flexibility
IT-driven technology,	User-driven technology
Top down	Bottom up
Centralized	Distributed
Teams in one place & time zone	Teams are global / 24/7
Silos and boundaries	Fuzzy boundaries/open borders
Need to know	Transparency
Information systems are structured and dictated	Information systems are emergent
Taxonomies	Folksonomies
Overly complex	Simple
Closed/ proprietary standards	Open
Scheduled	On Demand
Long time-to-market cycles	Short time-to-market cycles[3]

Here's the conference's boilerplate, "Enterprise 2.0 is the term for the technologies and business practices that liberate the workforce from the constraints of legacy communication and productivity tools like email. It provides business managers with access to the right information at the right time through a web of interconnected applications, services and devices. Enterprise 2.0 makes accessible the collective intelligence of many, translating to a huge competitive advantage in the form of increased innovation, productivity and agility."

If you think Enterprise 2.0 sounds a lot like the initial dot-com hyperbole—it does. But ignore the hype at your own risk. Remember that the Internet has had and will continue to have an immense impact on all forms of economic and social activity. We may even experience Bubble-Crash 2.0 along the way. But just as staid brick-and-mortar enterprises got "Amazoned" in the dot-com era, the current economic transformation that began with the Crash of 2008 will no doubt see new winners and losers as the world economy gets sorted out. And there is little doubt that Darwinian business transformations will be played out in the Petri dish of the Cloud (sorry for the mixed metaphor). "Value chains of information" will be the substance on which new business models will emerge and thrive, while others die out.

What new business models? For one, consider the "freemium" business model, where you give your service away for free, possibly ad supported but maybe not, acquire a lot of customers very efficiently through word of mouth, referral networks, and organic search marketing, then offer premium priced value added services or an enhanced version of your service to your customer base.

Here's a simple example. Google's "First click free," a way for publishers to share their subscription-only content with Google News readers. All articles that are accessed from Google News are allowed to skip over the subscription page. In practice, this means that when you click on a link from Google News, you'll be able to see the article without receiving a prompt to login. If you would like to read more from the same source and choose to click on another story, you'll be taken to a registration prompt to gain access to the premium subscription content.

The editor in chief of *Wired* magazine and author of *The Long Tail* describes the freemium business model as "freeconomics." In one of his many scenarios, "Low-cost digital distribution will make the summer blockbuster free. Theaters will make their money from concessions—and by selling the premium movie going experience at a high price."[4]

MIT's Michael Schrage wrote in the *Financial Times*, "Never in history has so much innovation been offered to so many for so little. The world's most exciting businesses—technology, transport, media, medicine and finance – are increasingly defined by the word 'free.' Opportunities to add 'free' value that matters in a networked world are expanding exponentially. 'Free' inherently reduces customer risk in exploring the new or improved—and bestows competitive advantage. To the extent that business models can be defined as the artful mix of 'what companies profitably charge for' versus 'what they give away free,' successful innovators are branding and bundling ever-cleverer subsidies into their market offerings. The right 'free' fuels growth and profit.

"These 'free' offerings are all creatures of creative subsidy. Free search engines have keyword-driven advertisers. Financial companies use cash flow from profitable core businesses to cost-effectively support alluringly 'free' money management services. Ryanair counts on the lucrative introduction of in-flight gambling to make its 'free tickets' scenario a commercial reality. Innovative companies increasingly recognize that innovative subsidy transforms the pace at which markets embrace innovation."[5]

In "Better Than Free"[6] author Kevin Kelly looks a little deeper into the freemium business model, "There are a number of qualities that can't be copied in the network economy. Consider 'trust.' Trust cannot be copied. You can't purchase it. Trust must be earned, over time. It cannot be downloaded. Or faked. If everything else is equal, you'll always prefer to deal with someone you can trust. So trust is an intangible that has increasing value in a copy saturated world. From my study of the network economy I see roughly eight categories of intangible value that we buy when we pay for something that could be free (immediacy, personalization, interpretation, authenticity, accessibility, embodiment, patronage, and findability). In a real sense, these are eight things that are better than free. Eight uncopyable values. I call them 'generatives.' A *generative* value is a quality or attribute that must be generated, grown, cultivated, nurtured. A generative thing can not be copied, cloned, faked, replicated, counterfeited, or reproduced. It is generated uniquely, in place, over time. In the digital arena, generative qualities add value to free copies, and therefore are something that can be sold."

Let's look at Kelly's eight generatives, "Where as the previous generative qualities reside within creative digital works, findability is an asset that occurs at a higher level in the aggregate of many works. A zero price does not help direct attention to a work, and in fact may sometimes hinder it. But no matter what its price, a work has no value unless it is seen; unfound masterpieces are worthless. When there are millions of books, millions of songs, millions of films, millions of applications, millions of everything requesting our attention—and most of it free—being found is valuable.

"The giant aggregators such as Amazon and Netflix make their living in part by helping the audience find works they love. They bring out the good news of the "long tail" phenomenon, which we all know, connects niche audiences with niche productions. But sadly, the long tail is only good news for the giant aggregators, and larger mid-level aggregators such as publishers, studios, and labels. The "long tail" is only lukewarm news to creators themselves. But since findability can really only happen at the systems level, creators need aggregators." Conclusion? The freemium business model is to be embraced with all due diligence.

There isno doubt that the ubiquitous connectivity to all sorts of information and supercomputer resources in the Cloud opens up a whole new set of opportunities in the freemium economy. But let's come back down to earth to the real economy, where "nothing happens until there is a sale," even if you are a concrete company or a fertilizer company and not a digital product or services company.

In 2008 research, "Sales 2.0: Social Media for Knowledge Management and Sales Collaboration" the Aberdeen Group reported that, "As the proliferation of online social media forums has forever changed the way customers gain information and feedback concerning a particular company's products or services, sales representatives are challenged to sell to a prospect base that potentially knows as much, if not more, about the competitive landscape than the reps themselves.

"This new sales challenge has caused a number of companies to implement social media solutions within the enterprise as a way to more effectively connect sales representatives to the subject matter experts they seek. The use of social media solutions within the sales department contribute to a reduction in the amount of time sales reps spend searching for relevant information. Top performing companies are using enterprise social media solutions as a way to shorten sales cycles and increase overall sales productivity."

Companies such as IBM, with its Bluehouse, have made note and responded to the need for social networks in business. IBM launched social-networking tools in the Cloud for business-unified messaging and collaboration. IBM's Bluehouse combines a familiar set of collaboration tools, including instant messaging, Web conferencing, document sharing, profiles, directories and tools to build business networking communities—all delivered via a cloud platform. Like Facebook, Bluehouse allows people to quickly create a collaborative space, but unlike Facebook, it has management features to provide industrial-strength privacy and other controls that businesses want. These technologies are all aimed at the co-creation of value.

With new business concepts and models that involve prosumers and the co-creation of value, there come some caveats. In "Co-Creation of Value—Easier Said Than Done," Mike Karst, an agri-business consultant, points out that, "It's easy to say that your company is willing to co-create value with customers. But it's difficult to make it happen. That's because we are hard-wired to do business in certain ways.

"To really co-create value with our customers, we must reassess almost everything that we think we know about our customers and products—and probably change some aspects of our basic business model. Who is your customer? Is it the entity that buys your products? Is it the end-consumer of your products? Or is it the company that buys the output from the end-consumers?

"These three questions refer to your distribution channel, farmers, and the crop or livestock processors. While this seems simple, some companies have internal discussions that never re-solve this issue. And until this answer becomes crystal-clear, your company will never be able to co-create value with customers.

"All of us have products to sell whether it's feed, chemicals, antibiotics, machinery, seed, fertilizer, software, food ingredients, etc. Our products are not the extent of the value that we can offer our customers. In most cases, we probably add much more value through the expertise of our people. It's not only the physical products that we sell; it's also the expertise of our organization that creates solutions for the customer.

"We've identified the customer, used their input and our ex-perts to design a solution that meets their needs, and we're still not co-creating value. Now it's time for the really hard part of building a business that co-creates value with customers. That requires changing your business model.

"To co-create value, you and your customers must reconcile your different objectives and define both the effort required from each party and an *equitable division of the returns* from the project. Sounds almost too intimidating to consider doesn't it? But for those companies that can put this all together into a sustainable relationship, the long-term rewards can be substantial. Let's look at reconciling objectives first.

"In our past relationships with customers, we have been trying to maximize short-term profits. The customers have been trying to minimize short-term costs. In this tug-of-war, we have each pulled the other through the mud from time to time. Co-creation of value is about moving to a win-win position with our customers.

"This is easier said than done, considering our history with our customers. But, by choosing the right customers as co-creators, clearly defining objectives, and taking small steps to share informa-tion and celebrate successes, you can get your co-creating partners into the win-win mindset.

"In any joint project, co-creation or otherwise, you need to be very clear on the effort and resources that each partner must provide. In complicated projects, this may require secondees (people who are temporarily reassigned to the joint venture) from each partner that are committed to the successful completion of the project. For less involved projects, the customer may only need to provide timely and accurate feedback on the solution concepts and prototypes. Regardless of the project's complexity, define the effort required early in the process and maintain frequent communications about the results of the effort received.

"Equitable division of returns means different things to different people. In co-creation of value, it means that you split the value created based on the effort and resources each party puts into the project, as well as risk assumed. Here are some basic guidelines to consider.

"If you are on the supplier side of the equation, look at the lifetime value of the co-creation partnership. A sustainable co-creation partnership can more than offset a lower introductory margin by extending the life of a product. Consider how you might use long-term supply agreements as compensation for your effort and the R&D risk that you are assuming. And build on your success by providing new co-creation opportunities with your current partners while seeking out other acceptable co-creation partners.

"If you are on the customer side of the equation, remember that your suppliers need to make an acceptable profit so that they can continue to support you with new product innovations and the experts that you have relied upon. Think of your co-creation partner as an extension of your business which provides you with new products and services to improve your profitability.

"Co-creation of value in agriculture and food production can be done. Now is the time to work with the best potential partners to create true value for our customers and ourselves. By structuring agreements that set clear objectives, define the sharing of effort, and provide an equitable sharing of the value creation, you can succeed in building sustainable co-creation partnerships."[7]

Co-creation of value goes beyond just forming partnerships with customers and on to the world of "virtual networked enterprises," where multiple companies band together to create more comprehensive solutions to market needs, and small companies band together with large companies to bring innovation to market. We'll discuss virtual networked enterprises in Chapter 7.

In conclusion, this chapter asked what the Cloud is good for, what do you do with it? And we've gone beyond the abstract notion of "agility," the most touted characteristic attributed to SOA and Web 2.0. In summary, the Cloud is where SOA and Web 2.0 live; the Cloud is their infrastructure and brings them to life. In the Cloud, SOA and Web 2.0 mashups can create new killer business models and virtual corporations that can address prosumers and the co-creation of value.

But the Cloud isn't some Generation Y's play toy or sandbox for wild and crazy new business models; it's the place for doing real business. And real business is about a company's business processes, the very ways it actually accomplishes work. So, in chapter 4 we will turn our attention to business processes and their management

Web 3.0 and Intelligent Agents

p.s.—Did I mention Web 3.0?

Stay tuned, for the Cloud and Web 2.0 just could represent the turning point to the steep upward slope of an *exponential growth* curve for the business Internet.

> Web 1.0 was "read-only," Web 2.0 is "read-write,"
> Web 3.0 will be "intelligent read-write-execute"—in the Cloud

Web 3.0 (the intelligent Web) will involve yet another step-change in how we use the Internet *and* help tame the infoglut. For example, ontologies will provide the semantics behind the Semantic Web opening up new possibilities for intelligent agents to do our bidding, and open information extraction (IE) will power new forms of search in a way that avoids the tedious and error-prone tasks of sifting through documents returned by a search engine.

With the coming exponential growth of the Internet comes exponential complexity, overwhelming complexity. How will companies possibly manage their business processes when they are disembodied as services and open to the world as situational business processes, whose uses weren't known at the time the processes were developed? In each situation, the policies and business rules governing the processes will likely be slightly different, but how are such rules to be managed?

Without policies and constraints to govern who can change which business rules under what circumstances, any business would fall into chaos. Hence there has been widespread adoption of business rules engines (BREs). But, to manage the inherent complexity in inter-enterprise or value-chain business processes in the Web 3.0 era, smart companies will demand ever smarter processes that go far beyond today's typical business rules engines. Just consider the need to manage "who can change what business rules under what circumstances" when "your company" must maintain multiple value chains to offer the mass customization and personalization now being demanded by your customers. But "smart" doesn't mean some Orwellian thinking machine; it means intelligent agent technology, also known as distributed artificial intelligence (DAI).

What's an agent? Backing away from technology for a moment, the everyday term, agent, provides a starting definition: "one who acts for, or in the place of, another." A software agent is a software package that carries out tasks for others, autonomously without being controlled by its master once the tasks have been delegated. The "others" may be human users, business processes, or workflows.

An everyday example of an agent acting on your behalf is right there on your PC. An antivirus agent runs autonomously in the background while you work.. It listens out for updates. It goes out and gets its own updates. It senses when there's been a change in the system. It notifies you, the human. It notifies the network. It takes action on its own by quarantining questionable files.

A basic software agent stands on three pillars, three essential properties: autonomy, reactivity, and communication ability. The notion of autonomy means that an agent exercises exclusive control over its own actions and state. Reactivity means sensing or perceiving change in their environment and responding. And, even the most basic software agents have the ability to communicate with other entities: human users, other software agents, or objects.

Add to this definition the ability to plan and set goals, to maintain belief models (their own and other agents' beliefs), to reason about the actions of itself and other agents (including humans), and the ability to improve its knowledge and performance through learning, you then have the core ingredients of an "intelligent agent." An intelligent agent represents a distinct category of software that incorporates local knowledge about its own and other agents' tasks and resources (multi-agent systems), allowing it to operate autonomously or as a part of a community of co-operative problem solvers (including human users), each agent having its own roles and responsibilities.

Intelligent agents can be integrated into Cloud frameworks that contain specific problem-solving functions, data and control. Intelligent agents support a natural merging of information and knowledge-based technologies. Intelligent agents can facilitate the incorporation of reasoning capabilities (e.g., encapsulation of business rules within agents). They permit the inclusion of learning and self improvement capabilities at both infrastructure (adaptive routing) and application (adaptive user interfaces) levels.

Intelligent user interfaces (supporting task-centered user interfaces, intelligent assistance to end-users, and business rules management) can be a boon to productivity in a complex world of multi-company business processes. With the complexity of tasks inherent in multi-company business processes, we will certainly need a little help from our knowledgeable friends, intelligent agents.

With companies and their software being disassembled as "services" and reassembled to provide unique value to unique customers, and with suppliers and trading partner resources often scattered across the globe, it's intuitively obvious that new "chaos busters" are in order. Thus, we can expect to see the continuing evolution from policy manuals, to business rules engines, to intelligent agent technology in the Cloud.

Intelligent agents will also be deployed to gather business intelligence (BI) and handle complex event processing (CEP). Much like accounting, business intelligence to date is pretty much backward looking. And, like counting Web page hits, BI often consists of one-dimensional metrics, e.g., a scorekeeper. In the era of, let's call it Web 1.0, the big metric was page views. Page views are rendered as quaint in the Web2.0 era eyeball wars. What counts now are the number of connections in social networks, the number of messages being sent, and time spent on a particular site.

It gets complicated pretty quickly when you consider that analytics and decision support must now operate in real time (in time enough to make a difference, in time to act). Acquiring the right information and continuous analytics, in real time in the Cloud, is the next challenge for BI, especially as we move from "data mining" to "blog mining" for valuable business information and "reputation management." It comes down to how you can go beyond a Google search, and sift through the mountain of Internet chatter to figure out what's really going on in your industry, and who's saying what about your company's products and services. In short, there's a need for Web 3.0 dashboards.

The quants, the super-number crunchers, are in great demand. Jeff Bezos started as a quant working on Wall Street. Gary Loveman, CEO of Harrah's Entertainment Inc., has a Ph.D. in quantitative economics from MIT. Reed Hastings at Netflix Inc. was a math teacher. Hal Varian, Chief Economist at Google and former the Dean of the School of Information Management at UC Berkeley was one of the earliest quants at Google, and now one of many. My coauthor of *The Real-Time Enterprise*, Joseph Bellini, is now CEO of Symphony Marketing Solutions whose ambition is to be the gold standard for developing both market and customer level insights.

The quants are moving from Wall Street to Madison Avenue where they are helping their companies identify their most profitable customers; accelerate product innovation; optimize supply chains and pricing; and identify the true drivers of business performance. SAP and Oracle paid a combined $10B for Business Objects and Hyperion to get into the BI game. And IBM announced its $5B acquisition of Cognos in November 2007.

In addition to all this BI action in the industry, let's also recognize the role of complex event processing. As described in the landmark book, *The Power of Events,* by Stanford professor, David Luckham, some CEP messages may not even carry business data swapped between applications. Instead, they contain information about low-level events that, when aggregated into patterns, can reveal high-level business intelligence, thanks to *swarm intelligence.* In computer science, swarm intelligence, is a type of artificial intelligence based on the collective behavior of decentralized, self-organized systems. Swarm intelligence systems are typically multi-agent systems made up of a population of simple agents interacting locally with one another and with their environment. The agents follow very simple rules, and although there is no centralized control structure dictating how individual agents should behave, local, and to a certain degree random, interactions between such agents lead to the emergence of "intelligent" global behavior, unknown to the individual agents. Natural examples of swarm intelligence include ant colonies, bird flocking, animal herding, bacterial growth, and fish schooling.

Luckham asserts that low-level events that occur in the Cloud of network-based business interactions can yield valuable business intelligence. By using complex event processing for business intelligence, CEP can close the loop between BI and the business process management system that, in turn, can act on the business intelligence. As companies extend BPM outside their walls and on to the complex business ecosystem across the value chain, the value of CEP becomes an obvious lynchpin for business intelligence and real-time process analytics needed to shape and sharpen ever changing business processes.

And the agent technology discussed above isn't some science fiction hype. Dr. Richard P. Messmer, Chief Scientist, at GE Global Research and his team are hard at work on "The Engineering of Customer Services" and delivering service systems. Messmer's Computing & Decision Sciences organization invents and applies computing and decision-making technologies, with emphasis on solutions that enable GE's customers to discover, create and grow value. No science fiction here—GE doesn't do science fiction, it makes money, more and more by delivering services.

And GE isn't alone in the pursuit of service science and systems. Service Science, Management, and Engineering (SSME) is the term introduced by IBM Research to its initiatives into services systems. HP has created the Centre for Systems and Services Sciences. Oracle Corp. joined IBM in creating an industry consortium called the Service Research and Innovation Initiative. The NESSI (Networked European Software and Services Initiative) group in the European Union has established a Services Sciences Working Group. Universities have begun to act on the need for service science as well. UC Berkeley created an SSME program. And North Carolina State created a MBA track for service science and a computer engineering degree as well. Others include CMU, U. of Maryland, ASU, Northern Illinois U., UC Santa Cruz, San Jose State, Utah State, RPI, U. of Manchester, Helsinki U. of Technology, U. of Sydney, Karlsruhe Institute of Technology, Singapore Management U. and Masaryk U.

What's driving all this is that services now account for more than 50 percent of the labor force in Brazil, Russia, Japan and Germany, as well as 75 percent of the labor force in the U.S. and the UK. Historically, most scientific research has been geared to supporting and assisting manufacturing, which was once a dominant force in the world economy. Now that economies are shifting, industrial and academic research facilities need to apply more scientific rigor to the practices of services.

Takeaway

Just when we thought SOA and Web 2.0 were fermenting storms in the Cloud, it may already be time to think about getting ready for the Web 3.0 hurricane and its impact on our business processes, on the very ways we do smart business.

References.

[1] Carter ,Sandy, *The New Language of Business: SOA & Web 2.0*, IBM Press, 2007.

[2] Mulholland, Andy and Nick Earle, *Mesh Collaboration*, Evolved Tech., 2008.

[3] http://www.e2conf.com/about/what-is-enterprise2.0.php

[4] http://www.wired.com/techbiz/it/magazine/16-03/ff_free?currentPage=all

[5] http://www.ft.com/cms/s/2/01e4b1a4-9741-11da-82b7-0000779e2340.html

[6] http://www.kk.org/thetechnium/archives/2008/01/better_than_fre.php

[7] http://www.strategicagreview.com/e_article000196612.cfm?x

Four

How Work Works in the Cloud

Key Points: How Work Actually Gets Done in the Cloud

What exactly is "work?" Sure, we all do it, but how do our individual activities come together to drive an efficient and highly effective business, one that thrives in good times and bad. Borrowing the *Work Processor* idea from my book, *The Real-Time Enterprise*, this chapter strips out the technical jargon and Harvard speak from how companies operate, how they execute their strategies, and how they manage their work in the 21st century, in the Cloud.

To explore how work works in the Cloud, let's discuss the notions of business processes and Business Process Management (BPM). Unfortunately, most of the information about business process management is shrouded in technical jargon and Harvard-speak. To crack that shell, and in the spirit of PBS television shows on "how things work," let's start our discussion with some simple, even pedestrian language as we explore how work works in business. This discussion lays the foundation for how "operational transformation" is made possible by the universal connectivity in the Cloud and business process management systems that exploit that connectivity.

The days of the monolithic, vertically-integrated company, owning everything from raw materials to production to selling, are over. 21st century corporations thrive in a business world where the traditional linear supply chain gives way to dynamic, customer-driven value *webs* (call it the extended enterprise if you like).

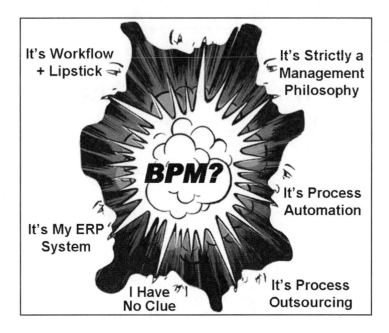

This brave new world can be understood by examining how the business processes and activities of Harvard professor Michael Porter's value chain analysis are unbundled and then reassembled into the dynamic business ecosystems portrayed in the figure below from my book, *The Death of 'e' and the Birth of the real New Economy.* Business activities and processes (the bold dashes in the figure) are realigned in the Cloud with real-time connections between and among a company's customers, suppliers and trading partners. As shown, primary and support business processes of a company are aligned around four realms of interwoven activities involving:

- suppliers and suppliers' suppliers (direct procurement)
- operating resources suppliers (indirect procurement)
- core competency trading partners (value added activities) and
- customers and customers' customers (selling through private and public channels).

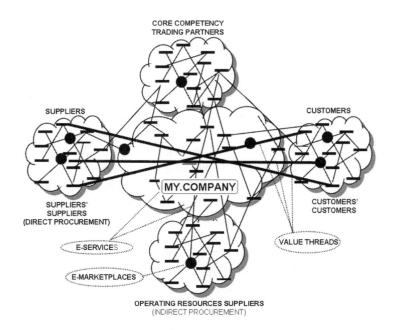

CORE COMPETENCY
TRADING PARTNERS

SUPPLIERS

CUSTOMERS

MY.COMPANY

SUPPLIERS'
SUPPLIERS
(DIRECT PROCUREMENT)

CUSTOMERS'
CUSTOMERS

E-SERVICES

VALUE THREADS

E-MARKETPLACES

OPERATING RESOURCES SUPPLIERS
(INDIRECT PROCUREMENT)

Historically business models were linear. They involved tightly linked suppliers and trading partners and were made up of large sets of complex business processes. In large companies, supply chains were tied together with complex and expensive systems. As the monoliths that they were, such systems were difficult to build and maintain, and they couldn't adapt to the dynamics of markets being made possible by the Internet, and now the Cloud.

Such rigid supply chains must now become light weight,
fine grained and flexible to fit ever-changing contexts.
In the era of mass customization and personalization,
a unique value chain may be needed for just
a single customer and a single transaction.
Others may serve multiple customers over long periods of time.

These multiple value chains must be woven through the tapestry of the any-to-any connections of the Cloud-enabled business ecosystem. It must be possible for them to be bundled, unbundled and rebundled in response to changing market realities. They must allow a company to participate in multiple marketplaces and to reach out directly and uniquely to "a market of one."

> The successful company must be able
> to manage multiple, simultaneous value chains
> and all the business processes that are involved.

It doesn't matter if Levi Strauss doesn't make jeans, or if Dell doesn't make computers. The best-run companies are no longer *sellers to their customers, they are buyers for their customers,* reaching out to networks of producers across the globe to deliver compelling value. So, who owns the end-to-end business processes that drive these value chains? Whose customer relationship management (CRM) system is to be used? The answers to these questions go beyond enterprise CRM to Value-Chain Relationship Management and Customer Community Relationship Management.

> When it comes to relationship management in the 21st century,
> it's not just "customers," it's "customer communities."

It's not just a portal, it's portals. It's not just supply chains, it's business ecosystems and value chains of information. It's going beyond sales, marketing and customer service delivered by a single enterprise, and on to outside-in processes such as inquiry-to-order from multiple channels and customer communities.

Hmm, it's beginning to sound like the next generation of CRM will need to be managed in the Cloud. Ditto for product life-cycle management where your computer-aided design, supply chain and contract management systems must go outside the firewall to reach design and production partners, as well as your customers in the new world of customer-driven innovation.

Because no one company "owns" the value chain, companies' business processes and their management will come to be unified and live in the Cloud. After all, it's the multi-company end-to-end business processes that deliver value to customers.

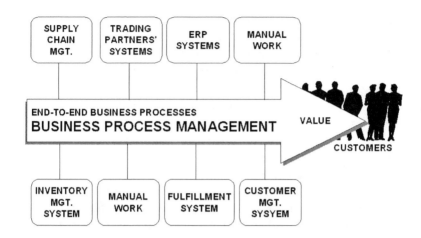

What's a business process?

A business process is the complete and dynamically coordinated set of *collaborative* and *transactional* activities that deliver value to customers.
In short, business processes are *how work gets done.*

Now consider the difference between procedures and processes, as explained by Derek Miers in *Achieving Business Transformation Through Business Process Management,* "It is best to think about process as a spectrum, with one end being focused on efficiency (procedures) and the other end being focused on value and innovation (practices). Procedures are oriented toward control and are common in back office operations. All would agree that the teller should not get creative with a bank draft. At the other end of the scale, practices are what knowledge workers do. They are goal-centric and guide, rather than control, the work. If the case in hand requires something special, a variation from the standard, knowledge workers are empowered to exercise their judgment."

Business processes today need to be managed and modified for the same reasons they always have been: to adapt to consolidation, mergers and acquisitions, joint ventures, divestitures, regulatory compliance issues, shifts in business models, changing customer expectations, industry standardization and business process outsourcing. By placing business processes center stage in the Cloud for all participants to access, corporations can gain the capabilities they need to innovate, reenergize performance, and deliver the value today's markets demand. Business process management systems aid in discovering what you do, and then help manage the life cycle of improvement and optimization, in a way that translates directly to operation.

In his classic work on value chain analysis, Harvard professor Michael Porter classified work activities into two types. Primary activities are those that directly touch the customer, while support activities are those that are primarily administrative, keeping the rent paid and the lights turned on. Using Porter's framework, it's the primary, end-to-end customer-touching processes that are paramount to gaining and sustaining competitive advantage. It is these primary business processes that deliver value to customers, and they *are* a company's value-delivery system—all the rest, the support activities, are costs.

> While support activities require management attention in order to make a company more *efficient*, primary activities require laser-focus to make a company *effective* in the marketplace.

While the above definition of a business process is simple enough, the coordination of complex sets of activities carried out by independent work participants (humans and machines) is by no means simple. Business processes are quite often human phenomena, but in today's wired world, automation and technology assistance to amplify human work are indispensable. This technology assistance must involve automation support for routine transactions and dynamic human-to-human collaborations. We'll explore the need for Human Interaction Management in Chapter 6.

The Process-Managed Enterprise

The leaders of a process-managed enterprise recognize that it's the end-to-end business processes that make or break the company. They have a holistic, not piecemeal, definition of enterprise BPM. They also recognize that end-to-end process management is complex and requires not just great management theories, but also requires commensurate support from automation tools available across the entire value chain—in the Cloud.

Leaders of a process-managed enterprise understand work-oriented business architecture and design work structures around *end-to-end* business processes. They know they need to use the right tools in order to realize their vision, for business is no longer conducted manually or through time-delayed, batch-oriented information systems.

Today's executives want the tools and infrastructure needed to become *time-based competitors*, competing on cycle time, product design time, lead time, time to market, response time, just-in-time inventories and up time. They know that to place time on their side, they need tools that can allow them to create and manage flexible and fine-tuned business processes that can keep up with and even anticipate ever-changing customer demands. Such processes must cross company boundaries and coordinate the multi-company work of the entire value delivery system.

Author and cofounder of the Business Process Management Initiative, Howard Smith, explains the challenge of coordination of work in the Cloud. "In the largely vertically integrated companies of the past, business processes were once thought of as those that could be rigorously scheduled around well-defined roles in carefully designed workflows—routing of work from one role to the next, work that was waiting for a telephone call from a customer, or work that had to be processed at a specific time ("I will expect your call at 10 o'clock"), or work that had to be transferred to a different person because the person who did the first part of the processing got sick or quit before the task was complete.

"But in today's global, horizontally integrated companies, coordinating business processes is neither as simple nor as linear as portrayed in the tidy world of traditional task management or the overly simplistic process re-design around case workers, typical of the reengineering efforts of the past decade. Today, work management is about coordination, collaboration, negotiation and commitment. Business is constantly changing, messy, unordered and chaotic, and both manual and automated work activities have to progress in parallel. Work is conducted, and coordinated, at all levels, through choreography and orchestration."

Because the multiple companies involved in a single value chain operate on their own clocks, coordination and synchronization can only be accomplished with a robust *information chain* that provides the actionable information each participant needs to optimize the overall flow of work. The ability of systems-of-process to publish or subscribe to real-time transactions in the Cloud, occurring within active business processes, enables organizations to respond to events, such as fraudulent activity in banking or insurance, in real time. This capability also enhances business decision making for time-based activities such as situation-appropriate cross-sell opportunities, based on real-time credit card activity and customer interactions in the contact center.

Automated techniques such as creating a single, complete representation of a customer across all channels and lines-of-business, complex account opening, change of address across multiple lines-of-business, or managing lost or stolen credit cards, are example capabilities of real-time systems-of-process that need to be available to all participants—in the Cloud.

According to the consumer relationship management expert Stephen Kelly, "This capability gives organizations the flexibility to change business processes in a matter of hours, rather than months. The ability to liberate business processes, business policies and legacy data provides a unique opportunity to deliver business value and to realize substantial reductions in operational costs, increased retention rates and selling opportunities."

Howard Smith elaborates, "BPM takes 'change' off the critical path of innovation by creating a new contract between business and IT. Instead of asking IT to implement specific processes, the business contracts with IT to provide a BPM service, extending process design, deployment, execution, monitoring and optimization tools directly to business users. As companies once digitized critical business data using database systems, companies are now digitizing critical processes using business process management systems.

"This is the New IT that GE dubbed 'digitization, a revolution representing the greatest growth opportunity the company has ever seen.' Digitized processes and their management become the new platform upon which the real-time enterprise is built, as ERP systems were built atop enterprise data models and databases of the last decade. In this environment, companies are linking familiar process mapping tools to powerful process execution systems to create a new form of organizational knowledge—explicit, executable, actionable and adaptable work design. They are encoding best practices gathered from wherever they can find them, inside or outside the company, and mixing them with unique processes, their distinguishing ways of doing business. The objective is organizational learning translated directly to operational innovation."

> In fact, the learning process is, in and of itself,
> the *ultimate* business process.

Companies want to shift their efforts from further automating individual tasks and move on to managing end-to-end business processes—the very essence of the value proposition of the real-time enterprise. As end-to-end business processes typically span many companies, we now shift our focus to how work gets done in the Cloud. We begin by looking at the "architecture" of a business.

Getting Work Done in the Cloud

An architecture is the arrangement and connection of components to bring about an overarching, identifying structure that is rationalized to provide best fit for its purpose. All structures have an architecture whether or not that architecture is explicitly or implicitly defined. Considering classical building architecture, *good* architecture is difficult to define, but you'll know it when you see it.

Businesses, too, have a structure, and thus have either an explicit or implicit architecture.

Business architectures consist of two major classes of components: tangible capital assets (e.g., land, labor, buildings, cash and equipment) and intangible assets that are structured to carry out the work of the business.

> What gets interesting is that two companies
> having identical tangible capital assets
> produce completely different results.

That leaves us with the determining factor: *How they structure work* by arranging and connecting the work performed by people and automated information systems.

Derived from the Industrial Age concepts of specialization of labor, the architecture of many businesses is *implicit* and oriented around "functional specialties" such as engineering, accounting, marketing and so on. This is called *functional management.* Such business architecture is reflected in the traditional "org chart." The work of an organization, however, spans the white space on the organization chart, and awkward hand-offs and disconnects are typical as work passes from one block on the org chart to another.

In contrast, today's well-oiled companies take a different approach to business architecture. They use *work-oriented architecture,* also known as *process-oriented architecture,* to design their organizations around how work gets done as dynamic, concurrent and often messy work processes that cross the departmental blocks on the org chart—and that cross companies in a value chain. With a work-oriented business architecture, units of work (UOWs) replace the functional department as the basic building blocks for business design (for an in-depth discussion, see Martyn Ould's *Business Process Management: A Rigorous Approach*). In plain talk, getting work done in a business requires four major architectural entities as shown in the figure below:

1. *Strategy.* This activity is about setting goals, and defining *what* is to be accomplished. Strategy is, of course, all about innovation—innovative new products or services, *or* innovative ways of delivering existing products and services.

2. *Work Plan.* The work plan is about how work is to be organized. The work plan includes all the collaborative negotiation and commitment steps, as well as transaction processing steps, that must be carried out to deliver value to customers. Some steps must be designed in sequence, for the input needed for a given step may depend on the output of a previous step. Other

steps may be carried out simultaneously, in parallel, if they are not dependent on the completion of prior steps before they can begin. Each contributor works according to its own clock, but those clocks must be carefully synchronized if the overall value-delivery system is to deliver optimal value to customers within the timeframes that customers demand.

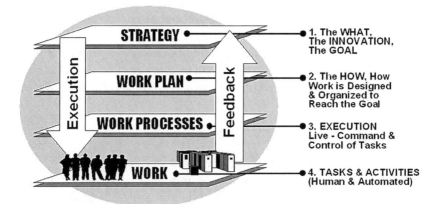

3. *Work Processing*. Work Processing is about *working* the plan. It's the live execution, or live *work processes* of the Work Plan that produces results for customers. As shown, at this level in the business architecture, work isn't just what any one individual does, for the work that any one individual does depends on others, inside and outside the business—in the Cloud. In fact, even the work that a given company does depends on other companies, its suppliers and trading partners. Thus, *work isn't something you do; it's something you process*. Work Processing is the execution of individual tasks and activities performed by people and computers to produce desired results.

4. *Work*. Work, in this four-tier model of a business, is about the individual, discrete tasks and activities carried out by both people and machines.

Large companies perform thousands of tasks and activities, and chaos would reign if those tasks and activities were not governed in their execution by carefully designed work processes.

> A business is a living system, and like all living systems,
> it changes in response to the world around it.

Over time, a company creates or revises its business strategy to reflect current market demands. New strategies require new work plans, which, in turn, require restructuring work processes and new work tasks across all participants in a multi-company value chain connected in the Cloud. The overall flow of change proceeds from *strategy* to *execution*, but doesn't stop there. Strategies and plans are never perfect and economic conditions change, so *feedback of results* is crucial to adjusting strategy and execution. This is the closed-loop of strategy-execution-feedback, and it should flow in real time.

The *Work Processor*

Let's really dispense with technical jargon and Harvard-speak. When introduced years ago, a "computerized typewriter" would have scared off secretaries, so the IT industry used the term Word Processor. Perhaps it's time to dump the use of technical terms like BPM systems, and speak plainly about a Work Processor.

Until now, the work of Strategy, Work Planning, and Work Processing have been largely manual affairs, outside the scope of business automation. But, now the tasks associated with these activities are so complex that new forms of automation must be brought to bear.

An automobile designer faces complex tasks by using a computer-aided design (CAD) system. Disney animators use incredibly advanced animation systems from Pixar to render award winning films. Filmmakers, airplane designers and building engineers have advanced productivity tools to assist in their tasks. But it's not so for the executives, managers and workers who carry out the work of strategy execution in business. To this day, it's still all about manual work processing—faxes, meetings, spreadsheets, phone calls, emails, and the post office.

What's ironic is that companies wouldn't hire a new office worker without providing him or her with a "word processor," but, as shown in the figure below, why don't companies also provide their executives, managers and employees with a "Work Processor?" Of course, the Work Processor, can be equated with the more sophisticated term, the business process management system. But, for now, it can simply be said that to deal with the complexity of cross-company Work Processing in the Cloud, computer-assisted tools are absolutely essential.

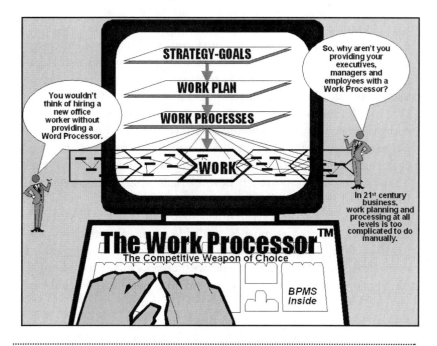

The Work Processor isn't a machine.
It's an active software window,
a browser on a PC or an iPhone,
through which participants can see and manipulate their
business processes and BPM systems that live in the Cloud.

The Work Processor is the weapon of choice for engaging in time-based competition in the Cloud. It can be used to squeeze out time from restructuring work processes and delivering value to customers with a sense and respond infrastructure. The Work Processor is the Strategy-Execution machine for business.

On the other hand, a Work Processor won't *automagically* make a company a process-managed enterprise. Just as a word processor won't make its user a novelist, the Work Processor is only a tool, albeit a powerful tool. Gaining true benefit depends on mastery of established business disciplines, such as process engineering, voice of the customer, Six Sigma quality and other management innovations. In the past, these disciplines were pretty much manual affairs, and initiatives created to embrace them were piecemeal, scattered throughout pockets of the organization. The Work Processor is the tool that can provide computer assistance for these management disciplines, and it allows a company to take a *holistic approach* to performance improvement and operational innovation.

In addition to mastering the appropriate business disciplines, companies will have to overcome organizational, cultural and people barriers. A tool is just a tool, but without the appropriate tools, companies cannot cope with the end-to-end management of their business processes and reach beyond their walls to improve performance of their overall value-delivery systems.

Because Work Processing must span entire value-delivery systems, Work Processors must be available to all value-chain participants—in the Cloud. They must render the appropriate view of work processes for executives and worker bees alike, across multiple organizations. The executive's rendering provides the guidance system, and the other renderings provide the perspective needed for day-to-day decisions and operations.

The Work Processor will become as pervasive as word processors are today, and they will be found on the desks and smartphones of executives, mid-managers, order-entry clerks and shopfloor journeymen—everyone involved with the work processes of the business, from the boardroom to the traveling salesman.

Don't engage in a gunfight with a knife; and don't engage in time-based competition without a Work Processor. Only those that invest rightly in this new form of IT will have the competitive arms they need to set the pace of innovation and win business battles of the future. The Cloud will be the battleground.

Business Process Utilities

BPM will no doubt become BPM as a Service (BPMaaS). This trend could be similar to what client/server is to IT, where the IT staff has choices over what is to be handled by the server versus the client. By embracing the Cloud, a company can have choices over the best way to implement and manage Private, Public and Collaborative process types, some being handled by industry-specific Business Process Utilities (BPUs). With the rise of Business Process Outsourcing (BPO), it's reasonable to expect the BPU to capture the economies of scale for commodity processes, e.g., human resources and multi-company processes such as customer relationship management and industry specific supply chain management. As the business world continues to move toward mass customization, business processes could increasingly be accessed through BPUs offering the same core services, *yet* uniquely customized all the way down to the process instance, for multiple clients.

> Of course, "core" business processes will always be Private, as they embody the unique competitive advantage of a company.

Yet, Private doesn't necessarily mean a company has to have its own hardware and software infrastructure in-house. Private processes could be wrapped in a veil of powerful security mechanisms in the Cloud.

"Situational business processes," whose unintended contexts may draw on a given company's core processes, could become the norm; and they must be managed as diligently as all other mission-critical business processes. In addition, the data behind the processes must be handled with great care, and that's why companies are placing attention to master data management (MDM). MDM involves methods and techniques used to ensure that master data, as contrasted with transactional data, remains consistent across computer applications and Web services. In the past, various departments of large companies often maintained their own master data, creating inconsistency problems. For example, when a given department made a name change for a woman getting married,

other departments still had the maiden name. As companies embrace cross-departmental BPM and adopt service-oriented business
models, MDM is absolutely essential.

We can safely conclude that the Cloud isn't just for the construction of virtual supercomputers for scientific and research purposes, but that it's also for dealing with the realities of today's dynamic value delivery systems, social networks and complex business ecosystems.

Already, Cloud Computing appears to be leveling the playing
field for many business start-ups, avoiding the need for enterprise
IT investment altogether. But as even the largest of companies begin to tiptoe to the edge of the new *cloudy* business ecosystem to
conduct business, the need for BPMaaS will become more and
more apparent.

> As competition has evolved from company vs. company, to supply
> chain vs. supply chain, and now on to choreographing *networks* of
> trading partners, the action is outside any one company's firewall
> —it's in the Cloud.

A Business Operations Platform in the Cloud

To continue deference to plain speak, we can use the immediately recognized term of a "Business Operations Platform" to signal the arrival of interacting business processes being managed in
the Cloud, or more precisely Networks of Clouds or Interclouds.
To construct a Business Operations Platform, what's needed are:

- SOA (service-oriented architecture) for the design principles
  needed for software interoperability and mashups,
- Web 2.0 for Consumer IT levels of simplicity and social com-
  puting (the wisdom of crowds),
- BPM for complete lifecycle management of processes,
- BRM for business rules management,
- BAM for real-time business activity monitoring,
- HIM for human interaction management where commitment
  processing supersedes information processing,
- BI for business intelligence to refresh management dashboards
  with periodic snapshots of key performance indicators,

- CEP for complex event processing where low-level events (*noise*) in the Cloud can be detected and acted on when they reveal meaningful information.

Business events in the Cloud are like thunder and lighting. As shown in the figure below, when an "event" happens (lightning)— an order is placed, an order is cancelled, a supply truck goes into a ditch—all process Clouds hear the signal (thunder) simultaneously and adjust in real time. In the latter case where the supply truck goes into a ditch, dynamic Cloud Sourcing can be used to reach out to a web of alternative suppliers for immediate delivery. The many companies that make up a given value delivery system are synchronized to the point of unity, behaving as a complex adaptive system reacting to its environment.

Jon Pyke, the Chairman of the Workflow Management Coalition (WfMC), elaborates, "One architectural aspect of a BOP, that is required to facilitate cross-organization BPM, is support for thin browser-based clients and a usage model that is heavily geared toward Internet-based distribution. It is the most efficient way to facilitate today's highly-distributed, and seldom co-located business environments.

"The Business Operations Platform externalizes the control of processes away from individual applications. It makes them equal peers, subjugated to the Business Operations Platform layer that controls the execution of the processes, the provision of services and the delegation of tasks or activities to the individual applications according to their specific uses and needs.

"In order to do this well, the Business Operations Platform must be able to do the following:
- Manage applications in parallel as well as in series
- Manage people-intensive applications
- Decouple the process from the application
- Work both inside and outside the organization
- Be both continuous and discrete, and allow processes to change over time
- Put the process into the hands of the business user"

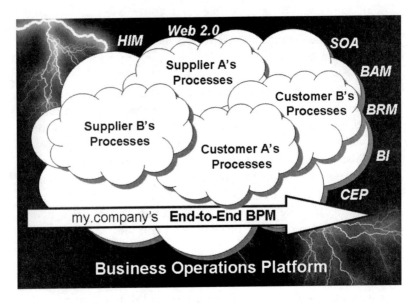

And so it is that the tide of history is shifting from an 800-pound gorilla in an industry setting "*the* process" in a given value chain, to "on demand processes" formed as multiple companies come together to seize an opportunity or thwart a business threat. No one company may be in complete control of the end-to-end process. No one process Cloud will dominate as multiple Clouds will themselves need to interoperate (the Intercloud) in order to support dynamic multi-company business processes.

As reported in the *Economist's* special report on Cloud Computing, "In the future, huge clouds—which might be called 'industry operating systems'—will provide basic services for a particular sector, for instance finance or logistics. On top of these systems will sit many specialized and interconnected firms, just like applications on a computing platform. Yet this is only half the story. The cloud changes not only the plumbing and structure of firms and industries, known as the 'transactional layer,' but also their 'interactional layer,' a term coined by Andy Mulholland, chief technologist of Capgemini, a consultancy. He defines this as the environment where all the interactions between people take place, both within an organization and with its business partners."

"Despite all the technology that has entered the workplace in recent years, so far this layer has not really changed. PCs certainly made people more productive, but most of their programs were not designed for collaboration. The enterprise applications they worked with were still centralized systems. And email has in some ways made things worse as the flood of messages takes up lots of time and attention."[1] Hello, business operations platforms; hello, human interaction management systems (see Chapter 6).

Takeaway

Business process management (BPM) has been a major topic since around 2002. But early BPM initiatives were tactical, streamlining back office and departmental processes. But now, with the advent of business process utilities and business operations platforms in the Cloud, the scope of BPM will break out of individual companies and stretch across the entire multi-company value delivery system. That's when process management becomes strategic and unlocks doors to true Cloud-enabled business innovation. Caveat competitor.

As Derek Miers writes in *Achieving Business Transformation Through Business Process Management,* "Although there are no 'silver bullets,' business process management has become the equivalent of a 'golden gun.' It depends on where you aim it; which parts of the business you put under the microscope, and how you engage people on the journey." As the march of history continues on to Web 3.0 and beyond, companies will no doubt need a golden gun as they make their way through the wilderness of unprecedented change in the Cloud.

References

---

[1] http://www.economist.com/specialreports/displayStory.cfm?story_id=12411882

Five

Innovation's Child

It is not so very difficult to predict the future. It is only pointless. But equally important, one cannot make a decision for the future. Decisions are commitments to action. And actions are always in the present, and in the present only. But actions in the present are also the one and only way to make the future.[1]
— Peter Drucker

Thousands of years ago, the first man discovered how to make fire. He was probably burned at the stake he had taught his brothers to light. He was considered an evildoer who had dealt with a demon mankind dreaded. But thereafter men had fire to keep them warm, to cook their food, to light their caves. He had left them a gift they had not conceived and he had lifted darkness off the earth. Centuries later, the first man invented the wheel. He was probably torn on the rack he had taught his brothers to build. He was considered a transgressor who ventured into forbidden territory. But thereafter, men could travel past any horizon. He had left them a gift they had not conceived and he had opened the roads of the world. —The Fountainhead

Key Points: Open Innovation in the Cloud

Innovation is no doubt the Holy grail of 21st century business. But what exactly is business innovation? Invention? And what's the Cloud got to do with it? In this chapter, we'll take on these questions and explore the innovation of innovation itself. Before the Cloud, innovation was very much inside-out, centered in internal R&D labs of companies. But in the Cloud we now see the advent of open innovation, innovation from the outside-in, customer-driven innovation, and tapping the collective intelligence of crowds.

Faced with unexpected change, businesses will need to experiment. In these times, a business that fails to experiment, will fail. Climbing out of the economic wreckage of 2008, winning companies will *invent*, not *predict*, their own futures. But "invent" doesn't mean a huge new investment in R&D, it means reinventing the company itself; it means innovative and agile business processes—the way work gets done, where, by whom, and for whom. Innovation in the Cloud is new, inevitable, and it needs to be done—now.

But this reinvention stuff is too intimidating, right? "We already have our ways of working around here, and the bosses *ain't* about to change those ways." Too intimidating?

Let's turn to Erik Weihenmayer. Erik is an acrobatic skydiver, long distance biker, marathon runner, skier, mountaineer, ice climber, and rock climber. Erik graduated from Weston High School in Connecticut in 1987. As the school's wrestling captain, he represented the state in National Freestyle Wrestling Championships. In 1991, he graduated from Boston College, and in the same year, he trekked in the Pamir Mountains of Tajikistan. In 1993, he received a master's degree in Middle School Education from Lesley College, and in the same year, he joined the staff at Phoenix Country Day School as an instructor, and made time to cross the Batura Glacier in the Karakoram Mountains of Northern Pakistan. He has also met the mountaineer's challenge by successfully climbing the Seven Summits (the highest mountains of each of the seven continents), reaching the summit of Mount Everest on May 25, 2001. He is also author of *Touch the Top of the World.*

There's no doubt that Erik is a pioneer. Yet, as amazing as Erik's many achievements are, he's just an ordinary kind of guy from Connecticut. But, he's an ordinary guy who knows about vision and about assembling the tools and systems needed to go where no ordinary man has gone before.

Erik's secret to being a true pioneer seems to be his ability to bring together new tools and techniques in unique ways to solve previously intractable problems. He is driven by a vision greater than day-to-day goals. To Erik, vision is an internal compass showing us how we want to impact the world, what kind of legacy we want to leave behind. It's the bigger vision that our goals spring from, especially as we go through times of adversity in our lives and our daily work.

With the adversity businesses face today—globalization, commoditization and recession—do you have a vision for making a difference, for contributing to the continuing success of your company? With the Holy Grail of continuing business success being *innovation*, how can you contribute, how can you make a difference? What new systems and techniques can you marshal together to reach the innovation summit?

Pioneers in business today realize that innovation is no longer a singular affair of *internal* R&D. They are embracing open innovation and peer production, going *outside* the firm to innovate and produce value—recognizing the wisdom of crowds and why the many are smarter than the few.

You may be thinking, oh my, my company could never make such investments, or go so far out of the box and into the Cloud, into the new frontier of open innovation. But it could, and must if your company is to remain relevant.

In today's wired world,
business success absolutely depends on innovation.
And it's not just a single innovation,
it's about setting the *pace of innovation* in your industry.

> Furthermore, in today's wired world,
> business innovation goes hand in glove with IT innovation.

The good news is that now you have all pieces, systems, tools and techniques at your disposal for Innovation 2.0. Even better, in the Cloud, most of those Web 2.0 tools are simple Consumer IT platforms, and most provide *sandboxes* so that you and your company won't get hurt while experimenting (playing).

So, now all you have to do is create the vision of your 21st century company, and set your day-to-day goals accordingly, as Erik Weihenmayer prescribed. If you don't, you and your company will get left behind in history's global dust bin.

Whoa! Sound too intimidating, especially if you work in a large company and don't really consider yourself a pioneer?

Intimidating?

Oh, I forgot to tell you, Erik has been blind since age 13.

What's New About New?

A dictionary definition of innovation is "introducing something new." But these days, with the rise of the buzzword "innovation" in the business literature, you'd be led to think that innovation itself is something *new*. Here we go again with yet another hype curve, the Innovation Hype Curve.

Why all the newfound interest in innovation? In short, *globalization*. Executives fear their companies becoming *commoditized* as a result of *total global competition*, and they desperately seek new ways of distinguishing their products and services so they can continue to earn healthy margins. Innovation is such a pressing topic these days that over 3,000 books on various aspects of the subject have been published since 2000. Indeed, business leaders have no shortage of often self-appointed gurus ready to advise them about this new, new thing called innovation. But wait, innovation isn't new at all. We all know of singular moments of innovation that changed the course of civilization. Think the 1600s and Sir Isaac Newton, the apple tree and gravity.

With regard to "business innovation," think about the 1920s and Joseph Schumpeter's *creative destruction*, where sparks of radical innovation by entrepreneurs topple incumbents and drive long-term economic growth.

So what's new about new? It turns out to be all about *context*. In my book, *Extreme Competition,* I describe six kinds of business innovation (Operational innovation, Organizational innovation, Supply-side innovation, Core-competency innovation, Sell-side innovation, Product and Service innovation). A company must re-think which kinds of innovation are now perhaps more critical than others in today's competitive context. Though in no way intended to be an exhaustive discussion, let's explore some of the most relevant dimensions of business innovation in the early 21st century:

- Globalization and the Commoditization of Knowledge
- Open Innovation
- Customer-Driven Innovation
- The Emerging Science of Innovation

Globalization and the Commoditization of Knowledge

In their book, *The World is Flat?*, Ronald Aronica and Mtetwa Ramdoo proclaim, "Globalization is the greatest reorganization of the world since the Industrial Revolution." Andy Grove, co-founder of Intel, summarized what that means in terms of competitive advantage, "Although mainstream economic thought holds that America's history of creativity and entrepreneurialism will allow it to adapt to the rise of such emerging economies as India and China, I think that is so much wishful thinking. Globalization will not only finish off what's left of American manufacturing, but will turn so-called knowledge workers, what was supposed to be America's competitive advantage, into just another global commodity."

What's especially noteworthy is that necessity is the mother of invention. Watch for innovation in emerging markets, from the bottom of the pyramid, to create *blowback* in developed markets. When innovations happen in China and India, such as the $70 PC or the $10,000 luxury car, or the breakthrough in affordable solar power, the innovators will take their babies global. Caveat competitors worldwide.

China's President Hu Jintao declared 2006 as the "Year of Innovation," and the government is exhorting companies to transform China by focusing on the lab as well as the factory. To make that happen, Beijing has pledged to boost funding to $115 billion a year for the next decade, raising R&D spending from 1% to 2.5% of GDP by 2020. With the commoditization of knowledge, and Chindia (China and India) turning out many times more science and technology graduates than America, what can companies do to cling to their competitive advantage? For starters, let's take a peek at the concept of open innovation, before moving on to the crux of 21st century innovation, customer-driven innovation.

Open Innovation

The brave new world of widely distributed knowledge in the Cloud has led to the business proposition of "open innovation."

> No longer can companies win the innovation arms race
> from the *inside-out* (internal R&D).
> They should, instead, buy or license innovations
> (e.g., patents, processes, inventions, etc.)
> from external knowledge sources,
> turning the table to *outside-in* innovation.

In turn, internal inventions should be considered for taking outside the company through licensing, joint ventures, spin-offs, and the like. Procter & Gamble, the poster child for open innovation, is determined to move to the position where half of its ongoing stream of innovation comes from outside the company—from the Cloud. P&G's "Connect and Develop" is powered by yet2.com, a global online marketplace designed to assist companies that want to sell, license, or leverage intellectual property. Similar offerings are also available through NineSigma, InnoCentive, and FellowForce.

Some companies have established "listening posts" in order to access a tremendous amount of tacit knowledge that could have a significant impact on innovation inside their companies. For instance, BMW established several listening posts in the U.S. and in Japan. A listening post is usually defined as a decentralized R&D

operation with various means for knowledge sourcing. On the other hand, the listening function is not necessarily restricted to R&D outposts. All organizational units, such as operations and local sales, have the potential to be the eyes and ears of a company.

Sampling of Yet2.com Customers

And then there's IBM's Global Innovation Jams that are conducted in the Cloud. In 2006, IBM issued an online brainstorming invitation to its 350,000 employees worldwide, and its clients and business partners. IBM was seeking the wisdom of crowds in the Cloud. The company exposed its emerging technologies, from supercomputing to avatars. IBM managers then used automation to winnow the 37,000 ideas they received down to 300 well-defined ideas. Finally, more than 50 employees spent a week at IBM's Watson Research Center in New York further combining and trimming these top ideas down to 30. And now the company is spending $100 million to develop the ideas that came from the Jam.

> Don't confuse open innovation with open source, free software.
> Open innovation is all about the money to be made.

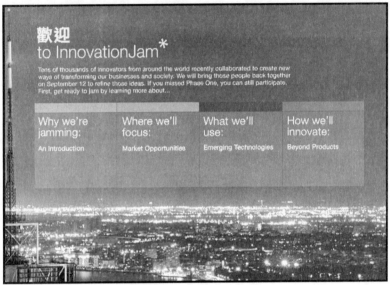

IBM's Innovation Jam

In the Cloud, knowledge can be transferred so easily that it seems impossible for companies to stop it. Instead they must learn to harness this powerful new source of innovation. 3M's Geoffrey Nickelson once described the critical point,

> "Research is the transformation of money into knowledge.
> Innovation is the transformation of knowledge into money."

Open innovation changes the game of where ideas come from; they are no longer the exclusive property of internal R&D, marketing, and product development organizations. In the 21st century wired world, smart companies are going to Chindia (China and India) and beyond in search of breakthrough innovations.

Then there's a whole new set of "management innovations" for making everyone inside a company an innovator by creating internal innovation marketplaces—call it open innovation *inside* the company. How does a firm make everyone inside the company an innovator? How does it break the bottleneck of managers in a bureaucracy from stifling ideas through their positions of authority and pocket vetoes?

Rite-Solutions, a Rhode Island based information technology firm, faces tough competition locally, nationally and abroad. So staying on top, and ahead of the competition, means keeping everyone, employees and management alike, focused on making innovation a top priority. The company's relentless focus is on tapping the collective intelligence of all of its employees. "Rather than rely on a traditional and hierarchical approach to management, where new ideas slowly percolate up through the ranks, we're creating an environment where new ideas are immediately evaluated, regardless of where they originate," says president Joe Marino. "Instead of encouraging employees to follow the company, we're encouraging the company to follow the employees."

To put teeth into the idea, Rite-Solutions created an internal mock stock market, "Mutual Fun," in which employees of the firm are given $10,000 in fantasy money to invest in various "stocks" to encourage them to dream up innovations they think the company should focus on. In the picture below are the basic engineering specifications for the Fun Market, the essential "must be" specifications ... errr the "Must Bees."

"We believe the next brilliant idea is going to come from somebody other than senior management, and unless you're trying to harvest those ideas, you're not going to get them," says CEO Jim Lavoie. Employees can divide their fantasy money among three indices—the "Spazdaq," which contains emerging technologies Rite-Solutions could pursue; the "Bow Jones," which contains products and services in-line with their current offerings which may utilize those technologies; and "Savings Bonds," cost-saving initiatives the company could enact.

To decide where to put their money, employees read not a prospectus but an "Expect-Us," a document written by the employee who launched a particular stock, outlining the idea. All stocks debut at $10, and a market maker (Don Stanford; a retired CTO from industry) adjusts their prices based on the amount of intellectual investment each stock attracts from employees. As an IPO climbs into the top 20, Lavoie and Marino, the "Adventure Capitalists" put real money (Budge-It) into the venture. When the innovation comes to real life, the employees who invested receive real bonuses and real stock options.

"From Day One, every new employee can see what we collectively believe the future technologies will be and where they'll be applied by us, so they can chart their own career paths within the company," Lavoie says. And, he notes, "there's no real management 'disapproval' loop, which often is the gauntlet employees feel they have to run if they want to propose new ideas."

For Marino, the distinction between companies that *use* innovative technologies and those that *are* innovative is an important one. "The latter requires that innovation is pervasive throughout the company including its management approach, organizational design, and administrative processes," he explains. "We are in the process of 'operationalizing' an organizational design that will firmly embed the innovation process into everything that we do, making us a truly innovative company."[2]

Mr. Lavoie calls this innovation an example of the "quiet genius" that goes untapped inside most organizations. "We would have never connected those dots," he said. "But one employee floated an idea, lots of employees got passionate about it and that led to a new line of business."

"Would this have happened if it were just up to the guys at the top?" Marino asked. "Absolutely not. But we could not ignore the fact that so many people were rallying around the idea. This system removes the terrible burden of us always having to be right."

One of the earliest Mutual Fun stocks (ticker symbol: VIEW) was a proposal to apply three-dimensional visualization technology, akin to video games, to help sailors and domestic-security personnel practice making decisions in emergency situations. Initially,. Marino was unenthusiastic about the idea, "I'm not a joystick jockey." But support among employees was overwhelming. Today, that product line, is called Rite-View, and accounts for 30 percent of total sales.

Another virtue of the stock market, Lavoie added, is that it finds good ideas from unlikely sources. Among Rite-Solutions' core technologies are pattern-recognition algorithms used in military applications, as well as for electronic gambling systems at casinos, a big market for the company. A member of the administrative staff, with no technical expertise, thought that this technology might also be used in educational settings, to create an entertaining way for students to learn history or math.

She started a stock called Win/Play/Learn (symbol: WPL), which attracted a rush of investment from engineers eager to turn her idea into a product. Their enthusiasm led to meetings with Hasbro, and Rite-Solutions won a contract to help it build its VuGo multimedia system.

Wow, what can't this innovation unleashing technology be used for, especially in the Cloud? Venture capitalists vetting new business ideas? Universities putting life into their entrepreneurial outreach programs, making them for real instead of just academic?

Here's an email update Lavoie sent me for this book, "Since the launch of Version 1 of the Fun Market:

- Don Stanford no longer controls stock prices. We have implemented a flexible algorithm for price calculation based on intellectual capital investments.

- When implementing the product for a very large company, we heard from employees that they had no idea who might be interested in pitching-in on their stock., so we came up with an Enrollment program for the product that captures all the player's interests, hobbies, passions, curiosities, etc. This then allows a person to research and discover a likely community of interest for their idea. This is helpful in finding a Broker for the idea and contributors.

- We introduced a Penny Stock index. This allows a quick summary survey of players and allows people to give their 2 cents to various topics including half-baked ideas. Unlike typical blog-like collection caskets, Penny Stocks ask people for numerical ratings in two categories and shows the average of both categories. This is a quick way to quickly harvest the penny stocks that people believe have potential for the company.

Under what Joe Marino calls "So What?" He believes good innovation without revenue generation is bad *businessation*. For Rite-Solutions "So What" has meant:
- Double digit growth in annual top line results
- Double digit growth in annual bottom line results
- One patent filing per 16 employees
- Very low attrition for a software company
- New Product and Service breakthroughs
- The discovery that ideas beget ideas, and ideas combine to make new ideas, and
- A new phenomenon – knowledge *tethering*

Tethering? Once people are engaged in the innovation engine, when they decide to retire, the need for knowledge workers to remain relevant in retirement is strong. They want the freedom to retire, but they want to stay in the game. This approach is far better than hopeless attempts at capturing or transferring knowledge to new people (even God can't create a 63 year old in 26 years). Lavoie believes this knowledge tethering is as powerful as the rest of the Fun Market product combined, as baby boomers yearn for the correct combination of relaxation and relevance.

No doubt, smart companies will be licensing software such as the Mutual Fun stock market to unleash new sources of innovation in the Cloud.

Customer-Driven Innovation

In 2001, the late Peter Drucker gave us a hint about the next critical source of innovation,

> "Whoever has the information has the power.
> Power is thus shifting to the customer,
> be it another business or the ultimate consumer.
> That means the supplier,
> e.g., the manufacturer will cease to be a seller and
> instead become a buyer for the customer."[3]

If you consider that innovation is a team sport, and that the most important players are your customers, then innovation requires new, robust forms of collaboration with your customers. After all, inventions and other forms of innovation, such as process and business model innovations, are in the eye of the beholder, in the eyes of your customers.

> Back office process improvements may save you money,
> but you cannot save your way to market leadership.
> It's your customer-facing processes that are
> visible and count the most.
> And that's where business intelligence and driving
> conversations with your customers come in.

Chicago Strategy Associates summarizes the importance of the customer in driving innovation, "Great entrepreneurs launch their businesses based on *customer insights*. In many cases they are frustrated customers. For example, a building contractor takes a family driving trip in the early 1950s and is outraged by the conditions and prices of accommodations in tourist cottages. Thus began Holiday Inn. Two lovers at Stanford grow frustrated with their email systems' inability to communicate. They seize upon a product developed by a kindred spirit in the Department of Medicine, leading eventually to commercialization of something called a router and a company named Cisco."

> The Industrial Age was about mass production.
> Innovation was R&D-driven, from the inside-out.
> It was about supply-push.
> The Customer Age is about mass customization.
> Innovation must now be driven from the outside-in.
> It's now about demand-pull.

It is about turning a company, and its entire value chain, over to the command and control of customers. This new reality demands a shift in our thinking about innovation.

> Winning companies will be so close to their customers,
> they will be able to anticipate their needs,
> even before their customers do,
> and then turn to open innovation
> to find compelling value to meet those needs.

That, in turn, as pointed out by Drucker, means becoming a buyer for your customers. That means "business mashups" where your company joins forces with suppliers, sometimes even your competitors, to expand your product and services offerings, using the Cloud to blur industry boundaries.

Because your customers are your only true asset in the new world of low-cost suppliers, your business model will likely need to be expanded so that you can fulfill as many of your customers' needs as possible.

For example, the Virgin Group has established over 200 companies to meet ever more needs of its customer base. The group entered into a *coopetition* agreement with Sprint, and became the 10th largest cell phone provider in the U.S. over a short, 18-month period. Wal-Mart is getting into banking and opening health clinics in its stores.

> Industry boundaries will continue to blur as smart companies strive to meet *all* they can of their customers' complete needs.

This approach is indeed a major growth strategy in a world of declining margins and commoditization. What business are you in? It had better be the *customer business!*

Now the question is, how do you get ever closer to your customers? One approach is business intelligence. Another is the Voice of the Customer (VOC). That means that now is the time to harness new means for giving your customers a voice. Back in the '90s, the voice of the customer was all the rage in business circles. It is a process discipline, a way for companies to gather customer insight to drive product and service requirements.

Techniques include focus groups, individual interviews, contextual inquiry, ethnographic techniques, etc. Each technique involves a series of structured, in-depth interviews that focus on the customers' experiences with current products or alternatives within the category under consideration. Needs statements are then extracted, organized into a more usable hierarchy, and then prioritized by the customers. Sounds logical enough.

But VOC got lost amidst the dot-com boom, abundant cheap-labor supply resources from Asia, and emerging markets as globalization reached a fever pitch. Somewhere along the way, pulling out all the stops to delight the existing customer base got lost. But today, VOC is again moving front and center, thanks to the many channels of dialog made possible by the Cloud.

Even so, customers often do not know, or cannot communicate effectively, their actual needs and requirements. Because of this, businesses need to find more creative methods of understanding customer requirements. That's why smart companies are now emphasizing business intelligence everywhere and integrating Web 2.0 communications technologies. That's why leading companies are creating blogs and wikis, placing their avatars in Second Life and taking their businesses to MySpace.

But you won't want to just open up these new Web 2.0 channels of communication and turn up the volume.

You'll want to have business intelligence embedded throughout your process management systems, and forge *meaningful collaborations* using human interaction management systems (HIMS) to tame the chaos and noise inherent in Web 2.0 technologies.

> The needed collaborations with customers
> are not one-off market research endeavors;
> they are ongoing dialogues over the lifetime of each customer.

Today's customers want it all, not just the buying transaction. Whether it is buying a PC, spare-parts, engineering services, or life insurance, customers want complete care throughout the consumption life cycle—from discovery all the way through support after the sale or contract. Today, customers demand the best deal, the best service, and solution-centered support that can only be optimized by true customer collaboration. Competing for the future is about the total customer experience, and the read-write-execute capabilities available in the Cloud are key to that experience.

Not only do companies need new means for listening to, and collaborating with customers, they also need to act on the information thus derived. To do this, they must hone the innovation process itself using the emerging science of innovation if they want to deliver ever more compelling value to their customers.

Emerging Science of Innovation

> Innovation does happen.
> It's just that today it seems almost totally haphazard.

With a dismal ROI on most innovation initiatives, executives treat the innovation buzzword with caution and tight wallets. Doblin's Larry Keeley describes the recent state of business innovation, "Since innovation fails about 96% of the time, it seems self-evident that the field has advanced to about the same state as medicine when leeches, liniments, and mystery potions were the sophisticated treatments of the day."

Leading companies are taking the unsystematic approach to innovation and turning it into repeatable, managed business processes (think Innovation Process Management or IPM). IPM can be compared to the rise of the total quality movement in the1980s, where leaders such as Toyota taught the lesson of quality-or-else.

> It turns out that quality is all about *process*.
> Ditto for *innovation*.

Some companies have already implemented systematic approaches to innovation process management. GE calls it CENCOR (calibrate, explore, create, organize, and realize) (Hmmm? What does the N stand for?). The Mayo Clinic calls it SPARC (see, plan, act, refine, communicate). The renowned design firm, Doblin, uses an Innovation Landscape™ diagnostic method to show 10 types of innovation and reveal that the most sophisticated innovation strategies combine these in thoughtful ways. They permit a view over time that allows basic innovation patterns to leap out. Landscapes are especially useful if you want to build a good innovation system. They can help identify the right type, number, and rate of innovations to help shape a customer-driven innovation strategy.

What about Six Sigma? Is it at odds with innovation, as reported in *Business Week* in a June 2007 issue, "3M's Innovation Crisis: How Six Sigma Almost Smothered Its Idea Culture?"

> The contrary position is that, by making execution regarding a new idea more predictable, Six Sigma can help to mitigate risk, going hand-in-hand with innovation management.

Countless great products have fallen flat not because of design issues, but because of the failure to hit the window in the market for introducing the product, or simply the inability to supply the product reliably.

Consider the usefulness of Design for Six Sigma (DFSS) to the innovation process. DFSS seeks to avoid process problems by using systems engineering techniques at the outset. These techniques include processes to predict, model, and simulate the product delivery system to ensure customer satisfaction with the proposed solution. Also keep in mind that innovation isn't a big-bang event; it's a lifecycle that starts with an idea and continues until the product or service is ultimately phased out, which could be years after the initial idea. Thus the Six Sigma method, DMAIC (Define

– Measure – Analyze – Improve – Control), complements innovation with incremental improvements throughout the lifecycle.

> It's the difference between hitting home runs
> versus singles and doubles in baseball.
> Innovation isn't just about some star in the R&D suite
> delivering a radical breakthrough, a home run, every now and then.

What's wrong with hitting singles and doubles with regularity? Isn't it time that we stopped just talking about out-of-the-park innovation and got serious about developing the *capability* required to manage the complete innovation lifecycle? In his book, *The Greatest Innovation Since the Assembly Line*, Michael Hugos explains, "The agile enterprise is an enterprise that has learned how to make profit by many small adjustments [singles and doubles] and some occasional big wins [home runs]. Soon enough those companies that cannot earn profits from constant small adjustments will hardly be profitable at all. The effect of a thousand small adjustments in the operating processes of a company, as business conditions change day-to-day and month-to-month, is analogous to the effect of compound interest. An agile organization constantly makes many small adjustments to better respond to its changing environment and in doing so it reduces costs and increases revenues every day. No one adjustment by itself may be all that significant, but the cumulative effect over time is enormous."

But when it comes to home runs, or harvesting really big ideas, progressive companies are approaching innovation as a rigorous method of *problem solving*. One such approach is TRIZ (pronounced treez), a Russian acronym for "Teoriya Resheniya Izobretatelskikh Zadatch," or theory of inventive problem solving, and centers on the contradictions among two or more elements. It was developed by Genrich Altshuller and his colleagues starting in 1946. TRIZ, in contrast to techniques such as brainstorming, which is centered on random idea generation, aims to create an algorithmic approach to the invention of new systems and the refinement of old systems. TRIZ is sometimes used in conjunction with DFSS. To learn much more about TRIZ, search the term at

BPTrends.com and you'll find a complete series of insightful articles written by Computer Science Corporation's Howard Smith.

> Developed in the 1940s, TRIZ bears witness to the idea that the emerging science of innovation isn't as much the emergence of new tools, methods, and techniques, but, instead, the selection of the *appropriate* tools, methods, and techniques
> for tackling the haphazardness of the innovation process.

A number of interesting mind-mapping and idea management methods are now available in software (including Web 2.0 offerings) that can help build a systematic innovation capability.

The need for a disciplined approach to innovation has been recognized by a number of universities that are blending their industrial design schools (D-schools) with their MBA programs (see "The MBA is Dead, Long Live the MBI," BPTrends column, December 2006: http://tinyurl.com/2rmn2a). Graduate schools will one day teach an entire curriculum around managing innovation. Some already do: Erasmus University in the Netherlands and Rotman Business School at the University of Toronto come to mind.

> It's time to make innovation a managed business process.
> It's time to develop an innovation maturity model (IMM),
> for innovation is no longer an episodic event, it's a marathon.

The Culture of Innovation

It's very difficult for an established business to innovate when its leaders are heads down meeting next quarter's financial targets, and those same leaders cling to the business models they themselves created. That's why we often think of innovation as a matter reserved for entrepreneurs.

Innovation by the entrepreneur, argued economist Joseph Schumpeter, led to gales of "creative destruction" as innovations caused old inventories, ideas, technologies, skills, and equipment to become obsolete, sometimes over night. The question, as Schumpeter saw it, was not how capitalism administers existing structures, but how it creates and destroys them. What counts is competition from the new commodity, the new technology, the new source of supply, the new type of organization... competition which... strikes not at the margins of the profits and the outputs of the existing firms but at their foundations and their very lives.

So, what established leader of a major business unit in a major corporation would wish creative destruction on himself? For one, Lou Gerstner. For Gerstner, the toughest challenge he faced when brought in from American Express to rejuvenate IBM, as he wrote in his book, *Who Says Elephants Can't Dance?* was changing the IBM culture. "Culture isn't just one aspect of the game. It *is* the game. What does the culture reward and punish—individual achievement or team play, risk taking or consensus building?" Gernster took over as CEO in 1993, a year the company posted an $8 billion loss, and IBM shares that had sold for $43 in 1987 had sunk to $12. IBM's prospects for survival were bleak. The *Economist* doubted whether a company of IBM's size, however organized, could ever react quickly enough to compete. And Larry Ellison of Oracle commented: "IBM? We don't even think about those guys anymore. They're not dead, but they're irrelevant."[4]

When Gerstner joined IBM, it was being slowly strangled to death by its own overgrown bureaucracy, and the malaise within its ranks. Many employees basked in a culture of entitlement, and few felt anything resembling a sense of urgency to return IBM to profitability. Gerstner realized he'd have to transform the culture, not just the strategy, "Culture is what people do when no one is watching. When I arrived at IBM, there were 'Team' signs all around. I asked, 'How do people get paid?' They told me, 'We pay people based on individual performance.'" After instituting many cultural changes in his early years, in September 1999, Gerstner was at home on a Sunday reading a monthly report and stumbled across a line saying that pressures in the current quarter had forced an IBM business unit to cut costs by discontinuing its efforts in a promising new area. Gerstner was livid. How often did this happen?

Enter stage right. Bruce Harreld, Senior Vice President for Strategy, was recruited in 1995 to chart IBM's future, and to ensure that IBM's mid-90s "near-death experience" never happens again, and that IBM continues to build its leadership in innovation and growth. IBM had plenty of new ideas but a hard time turning them into businesses. IBM had produced many inventions, such as the relational database and the router, then watched while others such as Oracle and Cisco built huge companies around them.

Harreld directs IBM's Emerging Business Opportunities (EBO) program, a unique management system. An EBO focuses on "white space" opportunities that can become profitable, billion-dollar businesses within five to seven years. EBOs are typically assigned a single experienced IBM executive, with perhaps an additional colleague or two, to manage the venture during its incubation phase. These EBO "champions" then tap IBM's collective expertise. The EBO leaders begin by proving the venture's concept through small pilots—*experiments* involving just a few prominent customers. Experimentation is key to IBM's management of innovation risk. If these pilots meet targets for success, only then does IBM make the decision to pour resources into the project. Once an EBO has grown to sufficient size, it usually becomes part of an existing IBM business unit. Of the 25 EBOs that have been launched since 2000, 22 ventures are in various stages of maturation and growth—including multi-billion-dollar businesses in Life Sciences, Linux, Pervasive Computing, and Digital Media. The EBO program has become a model for growth inside IBM, and has attracted attention from leading academic institutions as well as companies seeking to build new businesses. The innovation lessons IBM provides include:

- Even a large organization can act entrepreneurially, but it will require an appropriate culture and new management processes.
- New ideas are not fully formed, so before committing big chunk of resources, take small steps toward big new ideas.
- Gather appropriate metrics during pilots with customers and partners. These will likely be different from main line metrics.
- Failure is okay, as the learning that goes with failure is success, and to stay on top, companies must be learning organizations.
- Bring in the A team. Growth initiatives are too important to leave them to novices.

Tapping the wisdom of crowds with its innovation Jams, tapping customers to co-develop pilots, and treating EBOs as though they were two-guys-in-a-garage startups, has transformed the culture of IBM to that of an elephant who can dance on its toes. "Big Blue and entrepreneurship" is no longer an oxymoron, thanks in large part due to new possibilities in the Cloud.

Speaking of IBM's lessons that included becoming a *learning organization*, let's look at learning itself and how the Cloud is changing the rules. My longtime colleague, Dr. Richard Welke of Georgia State University, has been teaching graduate courses in the Cloud for some time and shares some of what he has learned in the next section.

Learning in the Cloud

Education is the "push" side of knowledge transfer and, until fairly recently, was delivered using the classical model of students, a classroom and an instructor, fixed in time and place. *Learning* is the "pull" side, and is related to an event-based curiosity or need to know and understand. Aligning these two push-pull approaches at a fixed point in time and space has always been difficult, at best. With the advent of the Internet in general, and search engines in particular, with the ability to make an ever-growing set of information available on demand, some aspects of the pull side have been addressed; principally static knowledge in the form of Web pages, documents, and more recently videos. And, while this was able to address questions of the "need to know" variety, it didn't address how to formally organize a body of knowledge that could lead to a deeper understanding of a particular subject or problem.

The Cloud, with its concomitant emphasis on ubiquity (anytime, anyplace, anywhere, any media) and rich services, is now providing the ability to deliver much richer, semi-structured and community-based learning outcomes that, on the one hand, approach the pull's "when I need to know it," while preserving many of the qualities of a more structured classroom educational experience; namely a structured knowledge build, coupled with a social network of shared learners with whom to interact with, share experiences with and learn from.

To be more specific, let's briefly explore the various elements that constitute a typical educational environment and how the

Cloud facilitates them. For many students, aside from attaining a degree, the primary value of a classroom setting is the ability to interact with other students; in short to create, extend or maintain a social network around topics of mutual interest. The Cloud now provides many such services, from blogs and threaded discussion lists, to Wiki's and social interaction networks such as Facebook, Twitter and the like. Moreover, these persist well beyond the arbitrary calendar of a class, allowing students to maintain contact and continue dialog on questions and develop mutual interests.

Another aspect of the typical classroom is the "team" and "team assignments." With Cloud-based shared document development and editing, such as Google Docs or Adobe Buzzword, teams can readily develop solutions, interact with one another and learning resources, and share their results. Content, previously limited to text has now gone 2-D and 3-D. YouTube videos can be found on nearly any subject, often developed and delivered by experts. Similarly, entire course content can be found at Apple's iTunes University (apple.com/itunesu). And, a number of colleges and universities are providing entire curricula through the Cloud. 3-D courses are being conducted, as this is written, in Second Life and other virtual world environments. There are many aspects of learning that lend themselves well to such 3-D environments with multiple actors. One example is teaching triage skills to nursing students, where the avatar actors play the roles of patients, doctors and other medical specialists.

All of this, in turn, gives rise to a potentially different approach to education—students self-organizing their own learning. One example of this is what Brigham Young University's IS department calls the "unclass;"[5] now being replicated at other universities such as Georgia State University's Robinson College of Business. This "class" allows the student to choose his or her own set of topics to explore (learning pull) along with the guidance of an instructor who formulates both the learning objects and process. This knowledge, in turn, is shared with other like-minded students via a blog-like forum.

No doubt, especially with the current economic strains on education at all levels, the Cloud will enable innovation in education and "blended learning," the process of incorporating many different learning styles that can be accomplished through the use of blended virtual and physical resources.

Cloudy innovation in education and learning; bring it on!

Takeaway

This chapter summarized and condensed just a few key innovation issues companies face as they position themselves for total global competition, stressing the need for systematic innovation processes. Forget the old idea that innovation simply means product innovation. Innovation has been around since the harnessing of fire by early man.

> A new generation of innovation in the material world began when Sir Isaac Newton watched the apple fall from the tree.
> Yet another new generation of business innovation began when Joseph Schumpeter observed and described capitalism's power of "creative destruction."

Today, innovation's child is *customer-driven process innovation*, the kind that can transform business models and strategies in the brave new world of total global competition—the kind of process innovation that can transform innovation itself, the kind of innovation that touches, and is driven by, your customers. It's about new ways of entering new market channels, creating new value-adding services and new ways of anticipating unarticulated customer needs. You simply can't do these things without process innovation that enables process collaboration across the globe, in the Cloud.

The late management guru, Peter Drucker, wrote, "Again and again in business history, an unknown company has come from nowhere and in a few short years has overtaken the established leaders without apparently even breathing hard. The reason is always the same: The new company knows and manages the costs of the entire economic [value] chain rather than its costs alone."

The newcomer isn't burdened with adapting and retooling business processes, and can innovate freely. It has the freedom to tailor process changes precisely to the current market conditions.

In the Cloud, creating innovative value chains capable of disrupting markets and wresting competitive advantage is, however, only the first step. The cross-company, end-to-end business processes that power the value chain must also be monitored and continuously improved using business process management.

The implications of monitoring and adjusting processes were recognized even before the advent of business process management. Twenty people came together in 1987 at a think tank on chaos theory at the Santa Fe Institute, a multidisciplinary research organization, to talk about the economy as an evolving, complex system. One of those in attendance was W. Brian Arthur, Citibank professor at the Institute, who over the next decade refined the notion that a theory of hierarchy alone doesn't explain the organization of economic networks. It involves many kinds of tangled interactions, associations, and channels of communication that take place on many levels. Arthur envisioned the global, customer-led economy in which companies now operate as an arena characterized by "dispersed interactions, absence of central control, continual adaptation, perpetual novelty, and out-of-equilibrium dynamics." To meet this challenge, companies must create a networked marketing ecosystem that maintains a "persistent presence," with its customized business processes available to customers anytime, anywhere. That also means process innovation can happen anywhere across end-to-end value delivery systems, in the Cloud.

Throughout history, innovation has been about climbing on the shoulders of others, which is exactly what the self-effacing inventor of the automatic electronic digital computer, Dr. John Vincent Atanasoff, described to me in 1981. I mention my visit to Dr. Atanasoff's home to give us a reference to how much the world has changed—in such a short time, in just part of one person's lifetime—with the advent of the electronic digital computer. While the transition from hunter-gatherers to the Agricultural Age took 3,000 years, the Industrial Age took just 300 years. The first computer ever sold didn't happen until I was six years old. So in the span of my life so far, we all have experienced the most significant rates of change—ever. And now that rate of change is *exponential*, and "process innovation" is its engine.

Atanasoff said that he didn't really invent the digital computer in 1941; he just climbed on the shoulders of others. Then John Mauchly (remember the ENIAC?) read Atanasoff's manuscript and climbed on his shoulders, and the rest is history. Of course, it was Bill Gates who ultimately transformed this digital invention into real money—that's "business innovation." So, one key aspect of innovation that's new is the changing focus from invention to innovative new business models and initiatives that bring compelling new value to the marketplace.

Dr. John Vincent Atanasoff and Peter Fingar, 1981.

Oh my, with China, India, and the former Soviet Union opening up to capitalism, today we all have so many shoulders to climb on, so many dots to connect and reconnect. But innovation won't happen in closed off R&D labs, it will happen in the Cloud.

The Cloud is the great enabler of innovation's child.

Let the 21st century innovation games begin.

References.

[1] Drucker, Peter F., *Managing in a Time of Great Change,* Talley Books, 1995.

[2] http://www.riedc.com/success-stories/rite-solutions

[3] *Drucker, Peter, "Survey: The Near Future,"* The Economist, November 2, 2001.

[4] http://knowledge.wharton.upenn.edu/article.cfm?articleid=695

[5] https://island.byu.edu/group/unclass

Six

Work 2.0: Human Interaction Management

We don't accomplish anything in this world alone.
—Sandra Day O'Connor, former U.S. Supreme Court Judge

Key Points: Human Interactions in the Cloud

Xerox's former Chief Scientist John Seely Brown once explained, "processes don't do work, people do," there's no doubt that what's now needed isn't more and more software for animating computers; it's software for animating human-to-human interaction processes, where work teams may be scattered across the globe, meeting up in the Cloud. So, if it's the interactions among humans that really count, we should focus on how *human interactions* can be managed and optimized, especially when those interactions take place virtually, across company boundaries and across national borders and cultures, in the Cloud. Managing such human interactions is precisely what we'll take on in this chapter, and we'll gain new insights into the differences between "communication" and "collaboration."

2.0 is all the rage: Web 2.0, Enterprise 2.0, Office 2.0, the list goes on. The pundits are out in full force proclaiming the democratization of the Internet and the wisdom of crowds. Blogs, wikis, and all manner of social networks are set to bring unprecedented transparency to the business world, giving customers a say in just about everything. No more one-way messaging from company to consumer. Secret R&D labs are dissolving in favor of open innovation. *Finally,* we have the executable Internet, the Cloud, some 20-plus years after Sun Microsystems' John Gage coined the phrase "The Network is the Computer."

Too wonderful to be true? Probably, for now we have Information Overload 2.0, an infoglut and data deluge, and many workers are being pushed beyond their capacity to cope.

Just consider the not-so-new technology of email. According to a BBC report in the UK, it's not unusual for office workers to spend as much as two hours a day, every day, sorting and reading all the email that pours into their in-boxes. Worse, that doesn't include the time they have to spend responding to it. Now, add instant messaging, podcasts, blogs, wikis, Skype, MySpace, YouTube, del.icio.us, digg, GoogleGroups … oh my.

Taming Information in the Cloud

Bill Gates, in an email prior to Microsoft's 2005 CEO Conference, wrote, "To tackle these challenges [of information overload], information-worker software needs to evolve. It's time to build on the capabilities we have today and create software that helps information workers adapt and thrive in an ever-changing work environment. Now more than ever, competitive advantage comes from the ability to transform ideas into value—through process innovation, strategic insights and customized services. At Microsoft, we believe that the key to helping businesses become more agile and productive in the global economy is to empower individual workers—giving them tools that improve efficiency and enable them to focus on the highest-value work. And a new generation of software is an important ingredient in making this happen. In a new world of work, where collaboration, business intelligence and prioritizing scarce time and attention are critical factors for success, the tools that information workers use must evolve in ways that do not add new complexity for people who already feel the pressure of an 'always-on' world and ever-rising expectations for productivity."[1]

Both Gates, at the CEO Conference, and Steve Balmer, at TechEd, indicate that Microsoft intends to beef up its Office suite with human interaction capabilities. An even stronger indication that a new breed of software is in Microsoft's sights is the company's acquisition of Groove Networks, a provider of peer-to-peer "shared spaces." The goal seems clear: incorporate software that helps workers collaborate, search for information sans information overload, and manage information needed for working on ad hoc projects. After all, in the world of today's information workers, life is but a stream of projects. Microsoft seems intent on providing the tools needed to organize human activities around information while, at the same time, taming information overload, taking on information chaos. But is that enough?

> When we interact in the Cloud, it's not enough to organize human activities around information;
> it must be organized around the work itself.

In the Industrial Age human activities were organized around the assembly line; and in the Information Age human activities are organized around information (the raison d'etre for functional management). In the emerging Process Age, where a company's business processes are key to effectiveness, it's now time to organize human activities around the work itself. That means fusing together traditional collaboration and information tools and extending them with a complete theory of human work if we are to build systems that can support the way people actually work, versus treating them as cogs in an information machine.

As we've discussed, with all the opportunity to interconnect business resources and systems, the Cloud also poses an immense challenge in that the humans, the very heart and soul of any company, can be overwhelmed by the volume of business information that can flow through the Net. What's really needed is a *World Wide Workspace* for systematic and well-managed human interactions (as opposed to the chaos of emails, phone calls, instant messages, faxes, and blogs). In other words, what's needed is a structured interaction process—a next generation of project management, or simply stated, Work 2.0. For example, consider the worldwide manufacturing operations of Dell Computer. When a Dell demand signal is beamed to its 30 tier-1 and 400 tier-2 suppliers scattered across the globe, they all work asynchronously, against their own clocks, using human and system resources in non-predetermined ways. That is, the critical challenges in synchronizing such work are those darned 20% exceptions that must be dealt with in real business—consuming 80% of resources—if a company is to achieve a razor-sharp competitive edge.

The business world is struggling with how to manage such complexity with computer-based support. And the answer isn't workflow. The shortcomings of workflow—the narrow focus of each process, limited systems integration capability, inability to cater for change to or interaction between work streams, and so on—have led to new developments over the past five years, many coming under the banner of Business Process Management (BPM). Every major IT vendor now offers BPM software, though much of it is workflow or application integration with some BPM lipstick applied. This isn't meant to downplay the importance of current BPM solutions, for application-to-application integration, rules-driven workflow and real-time distributed transaction management are vital. And they are, in no way, trivial undertakings, but very complex endeavors. That's why BPM solutions providers place so much emphasis on Web services and service-oriented architectures as means of grappling with the complexity of system-to-system interactions. As a result, most of today's BPM solutions can take care of 80% of the routine, predetermined system-to-system scenarios with predefined workflow and inter-application transaction management. Such capabilities are needed to help a company put its "house in order" with application integration. But they don't directly support the way people actually accomplish their work when teams made up of multiple companies and multiple participants get together in the Cloud.

Before we can construct a universal way to describe human-driven processes, we need to impose some order on the apparent chaos of human activity, and seek the fundamental properties of human work. The search must lead us to ideas from biology, organizational theory, social systems theory, cognitive theory, sociology and psychology. The properties and patterns we discover from these diverse disciplines guide us in the development of a full process description framework for a new world of Work 2.0.

What's needed is dedicated support for dynamic human-to-human interactions—that cannot be preordained or preprogrammed the way system-to-system interactions are. Further, it's the human-driven business processes that are the very heart of business process management, and project management.

In a column I wrote, I borrowed the title, *The Greatest Innovation Since BPM*, from the award winning CIO, Michael Hugos' new book on business agility, *The Greatest Innovation Since the Assembly Line* (www.mkpress.com). Thanks Mike, for the idea fits so well in what I hope to articulate about the current state of collaboration and human interaction management and where we need to go beyond what's now so loosely called Web 2.0. Before I begin, let's turn to the UK business-tech magazine, *Information Age*, to set the context:

Riding the Fourth Wave

"A new generation of people-centric collaborative information management tools is set to produce the first fundamental advances in personal productivity since the arrival of the spreadsheet. Three years ago in their book *Business Process Management: The Third Wave*, Howard Smith and Peter Fingar wrote what has since come to be regarded as a manifesto for radical business change based on business process management (BPM) technology. Now though, says Fingar, the time is already right to prepare for a new, and potentially even more radical, fourth wave of business automation – human interaction management systems (HIMS).

"According to Fingar, even though much of what he and Smith described in The Third Wave has still to be realized, among its most sophisticated early adopters, BPM has already eliminated most of the back-end system bottlenecks that have traditionally impeded business development.

"For these organizations, it is time to move on: 'The real future, if you look at business process management – the key part of it that has not been fully addressed – is human to human interaction,' he says.

"To some extent, this assertion is already recognized in the current industry vogue for collaborative, Internet-based personal productivity tools such as Google's Writely word processor and spreadsheet products. Unlike first generation Microsoft Office-like applications, such so-called Office 2.0

products are designed from the ground up to distribute and share documents. However, HIMS proponents believe that these advances don't really solve human interactivity problems, and may actually make them far worse, with *infoglut*."

What Howard Smith and I wrote about in *Business Process Management: The Third Wave,* didn't in any way ignore human interaction management. The people components of a business process were given equal status to machine components in our definition of a business process:

> A business process is the complete and dynamically coordinated set of *collaborative* and *transactional* activities
> that deliver value to customers.

But the IT industry went its own way, by and large focusing on the "transactional activities," relegating the collaborative part to be trapped in the world of traditional workflow, with BPM lipstick. BPM vendors with a strong workflow heritage began labeling their BPM suites as "people-oriented." Meanwhile, other vendors competed in the space known as "integration-centric BPM," a new term for next-generation EAI (Enterprise Aplicaiton Integration).

Such labeling is a red herring, for the way humans interact among themselves to get work done is far different from integration-centric BPM or the predefined notion of workflow, even with complex nesting and chaining logic built in. These are primarily notions of system-to-human (S-2-H) systems, where people are treated as cogs in an assembly line, dynamic as it may be, shoving tasks from station to station.

The chairman of the WfMC, Jon Pyke, noted: "Supposing you were playing golf; using the BPM approach would be like hitting a hole in one every time you tee off. Impressive – 18 shots, and a round finished in 25 minutes.

"But as we all know, the reality is somewhat different (well, my golf is different) – there's a lot that happens between teeing off and finishing a hole. Ideally, about four shots (think nodes in a process) – but you have to deal with the unexpected even though you know the unexpected is very likely; sand traps, water hazards, lost balls, free drops, collaboration with fellow players, unexpected consultation with the referee – and so it goes. Then there are 17 more holes to do – the result is an intricate and complex process with 18 targets but about 72 operations."

Like the game of golf, when it comes to the *creative* and *innovative* forms of business processes that reside in the domain of human-to-human interactions, the processes cannot be predefined or "flowcharted in advance." In short, such collaborative human processes are "organic." That is to say, they represent "emergent processes" that change not only their state, but also their structure as they are born, and then grow and evolve. Such processes deal with new business initiatives, new programs, new marketing campaigns, new product development, case management, research, and all too often, unexpected crises. These are not the kind of processes you call in IT to analyze, model and code—and get back to you in 18 months with a solution.

In the messy real world of business, people communicate, research, think, consult, negotiate and ultimately commit to the next steps that are unknowable at the outset. As new commitments are made, the process continues, often involving new participants playing new roles as the process expands.

In the Cloud, the participants usually cross organization and company boundaries: functional departments, customers, regulatory agencies, suppliers, suppliers' suppliers, design firms, market research firms, channel partners, and so on.

> Unlike internal command and control within a single company, one company cannot command another company to do this or to do that.

Instead, the parties must negotiate and commit to next steps, and track the many agreements made along the way. Such human collaboration shifts the requirements for IT support from "information processing" where data are tracked, to "commitment processing" where agreements are tracked. Does your EPR or BPM system do that? Does your wiki or blog do that?

Human Communication with Implicit Collaboration

Let's take a brief look at the tools people use to carry out knowledge work, decision-making and collaboration, especially when they interact in the Cloud. It's not a pretty picture, but we need to grasp the diverse and complex nature of how humans interact to accomplish their goals, as shown in the figure below.

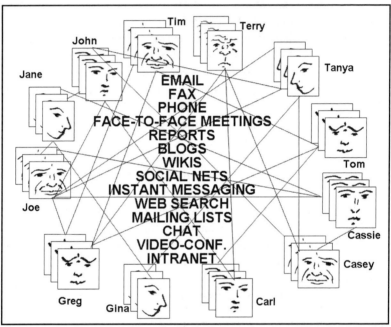

Communication With "Implied" Collaboration in a Web 2.0 World
(A Real Mess)

Portrayed in the figure are people from four companies:
>**Company J** (Joe, Jane, and John),
>**Company T** (Tim, Terry, Tanya, and Tom),
>**Company G** (Greg and Gina) and
>**Company C** (Carl, Casey, and Cassie).

Company J wants to develop a new financial service to provide a new form of health insurance that allows consumers to utilize the growing number of low-cost, high-quality health providers (hospitals, surgeons, assisted living facilities, and nursing homes) in the emerging Globalized Health Care industry. Joe is the CEO, Jane is the V.P. of Business Development, and John is an M.D. with international health expertise.

Company T is a health services company representing transnational hospitals and related organizations based in India, Thailand, and Israel. Tim is V. P. of Business Development, Terry is V.P. of Quality and Government Compliance, Tanya is Research Director, and Tom is V.P of Finance.

Company C is a highly specialized broker responsible for channel development. Cassie is the CEO and Casey is V.P of Business Development.

Company G is an international law firm located in The Hague that specializes in international medicine regulations and the intricacies of related global trade agreements.

Somewhere in all their Cloud communications, and all their "Web 2.0" endeavors, there must be collaboration taking place, right?

Of course there is, but it's "implicit collaboration." Keeping track of what's really going on is all in their heads, each head having its own assessment of what's going on at any particular time.

Yet there is no real technology support to structure their collaborations. Quite the contrary, the participants suffer from information overload, also known as infoglut:

Who got "cc:'ed" on the latest version of the risk assessment projections? Who have or have not competed their latest critical path tasks? Which experts do we now need to bring to the table? Was the contract signed with the Thai government? Do we have a business plan for acquiring and managing the hospital in Belize? Now that the contract has been signed for managing the hospital in Panama City, what are the next steps, and who and what are needed to move forward? Where's the latest version of the lobby layout? Have the investors committed to the

Belize project? What steps do we still need to complete for certifying our Indian medical staff in Costa Rica? Did we get responses to our RFP from the pharmaceutical companies in India?

Such is the real world of new business initiatives, new marketing campaigns, new joint ventures, mergers, acquisitions, research, and business innovations in general. It's a world of human interactions, which to date have little technological support that truly provides "human interaction management." So, what's needed?

Explicit Collaboration Via Human Interaction Management Systems

If technology is to be used to support human interactions in the Cloud, collaboration can no longer be *implicit*. It must be *explicit* if it is to be brought under management control. For this to happen, five basic principles are needed:

1. *Connection visibility:* to work with people, you need to know who they are, what they can do, and what their responsibilities are as opposed to yours.

2. *Structured messaging:* if people are to manage their interactions with others better, their communications must be structured and goal-directed.

3. *Support for knowledge work:* organizations must learn to manage the time and mental effort their staff invest in researching, comparing, considering, deciding, and generally turning information into knowledge and ideas.

4. *Supportive rather than prescriptive activity management:* humans do not sequence their activities in the manner of a procedural computer program. There is always structure to human work, sometimes less and sometimes more, but it is not the same kind of structure that you get in a flowchart.

5. *Processes that change processes:* human activities are often concerned with solving problems, or making something happen. Such activities routinely start in the same fashion, by establishing a way of proceeding. Before you can design your new widget, or develop your marketing plan, you need to work out how

you are going to do so, which methods to use, which tools to use, which people to consult, and so on. In other words, process definition is an intrinsic part of the process itself. Further, this is not a one-time event; it happens continually throughout the life of the process. Human interaction management requires a major shift from "information processing" to "commitment processing," where participants negotiate and commit to next steps. The process itself is *emergent*, not predefined.

To achieve all this, a new kind of software system is required, one based on the six different kinds of "objects" defined by Human Interaction Management (HIM): Roles, Users, Interactions, Entities, States and Activities.

This is not the place to discuss the nature of each HIM object type, but all six must be used as the fundamental basis of any system intended to properly support collaborative human work in the enterprise.

By implementing these principles in software, a human interaction management system can support human collaboration in a way that can effectively turn strategy into action, and provide the mechanisms for ensuring strategic, executive and operational management control in the Cloud.

All these forms of management control have direct ramifications for corporate and government compliance. Implementing these principles allows management participation in the process execution, including ongoing re-definition of the process itself, thereby ensuring maximum *agility* and *responsiveness*.

With support from a Human Interaction Management System (HIMS), (call the HIMS *Workware*, or the *Work Processor*, if you like) an organization can provide new means to help people work better as they take on the constant stream of new business initiatives and human-centric tasks that make successful companies tick:

- new product development,
- promotions,
- special events,
- research,
- new marketing campaigns,
- customer self-service,

- case management,
- mergers and acquisitions,
- opening new global markets,
- complex sales proposals,
- management-level compliance,
- all the projects people undertake to innovate, to grow the business, or
- to stave off competitive threats and deal with crises (you know, the real stuff of any business).

This is the stuff people do that allows companies to go from good to great. It's about going beyond efficiency and on to effectiveness, going beyond being a commodity player to becoming an innovator.

> It's about dealing with tacit information, not transactional data.

The figure below illustrates the use of a HIMS to support human work in the Cloud. Each of the participants, typically scattered across companies as we previously discussed, plays *multiple roles* in *multiple projects*. Such roles can vary from "responsibility" for a given project to simply "being informed" on other projects.

> The HIMS is used to add *structure* to collaborations,
> making them *explicit*.

Collaborations can be structured around specific *goal-driven* projects or cases, but can also be used to add structure to ad-hoc collaboration, taming what is now "in-box hell." Just consider the "global CC: nightmare" wherein people just CC:/FWD: emails to each other randomly, rather than taking proper responsibility for sorting out issues.

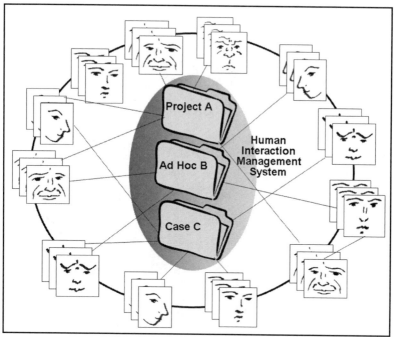

Explicit Collaboration Via a
Human Interaction Management System

No, I haven't forgotten that today's companies are complex and depend on their IT systems. Thus we can now take the figure above and surround the people involved in human collaboration with the "background" IT systems that are embedded in most organizations, as shown in the following figure. To many in a typical organization, they have to get their thinking and decision-making work done in the context of, and often while maintaining a host of disparate enterprise systems as illustrated in the figure below. Such is the case for, let's say, a sales manager who must do the real work of collaborating with customers, suppliers and sales people, while also feeding and caring for the CRM machine. But because, as Forrester Research points out, 85% of all business processes involve people, and because human-driven processes have not been fully addressed in the majority of today's BPM systems, I simply started with people in this discussion.

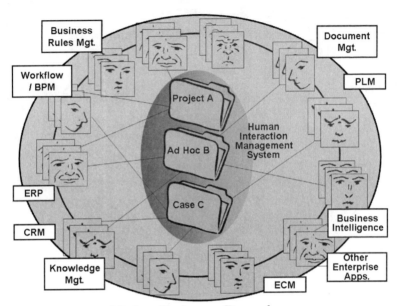

Modern Businesses Depend on
Multiple and Disparate IT Systems

There are essentially two ways people are involved in business
processes:

1. as cogs in a workflow where they are asked to "approve" or
    "not approve" predefined next-steps, or "do this task" or
    "post this transaction," or "escalate this problem;" and

2. as knowledge workers and decision makers going where no
    routine, transactional process has gone before: not simply op-
    erating today's business, but charting tomorrow's course, or
    addressing major disruptions in the industry.

The first case, cogs in a workflow, is handled reasonably well
at present by workflow systems – except, that is, for the 20% of
special cases that actually consume 80% of your resources! This is of
deep concern to telcos, for instance, who are struggling desperately
to control the costs of resolving line faults that cannot be dealt
with automatically and thus go to manual "case management"
mode – costing some telcos millions of dollars.

In the second case, right now the knowledge worker/decision maker has little support whatsoever from workplace applications. What they need is a new kind of interface to their existing tools that allows automated integration of knowledge work with routine business processes handled by heritage workflow, BPM, and ERP systems – and increasingly Web 2.0 technologies.

Yes, people are a part of almost all processes, excepting straight thru processes (STP) such as financial trade or other routine transactions. It's the "non-routine" that drives competitive advantage, and that's what human-driven business processes are all about. Indeed, shouldn't this class of process be paramount in any business? After all, the routine, operational processes are commodities, and who wants to be a commodity player in today's hypercompetitive global marketplace?

Michael Hugos writes in his new book that companies should be "efficient enough," but the real prize is responsiveness. Being responsive to changing market conditions, competitive threats and new market opportunities is what successful business is all about. And, that's all about people and how they collaborate to innovate, across company boundaries, in the Cloud.

We still need continuous process improvement via workflow and integration-style BPM, and many companies are just now coming to grips with these process-oriented IT systems. Service-oriented architecture (SOA) and Web 2.0 MashUps have enabled great advances and are currently all the rage. But SOA, by itself isn't enough.

BPM pioneer, Ismael Ghalimi, said it best, "BPM is SOA's killer application, and SOA is BPM's enabling infrastructure."

Human interaction management pioneer, Keith Harrison-Broninksi takes that notion one giant step forward, "HIM is BPM's killer application."

> SOA is primarily in the domain of IT analysts.
> BPM is primarily in the domain of business analysts.
> HIM is primarily in the domain of business people themselves, providing support for the way humans actually work and interact with one another.

The figure below ties together the two worlds of human inter-actions with the surrounding world of IT systems. The HIMS puts heritage IT systems in their proper place, for humans don't work together in isolation from their IT systems (even though many wish they could). The HIMS is not a replacement for work-flow/BPM any more than business rules management systems (BRMS) or a business intelligence systems (BI) are. They are or-thogonal. They are complex systems in their own right, and in their own domains.

But just as a BPM system can fuse disparate IT systems into end-to-end business processes (esp. with the help of Web 2.0 ser-vices and SOA), the HIMS must have the capability to fuse work-flow/BPM and other heritage systems into the "information base" managers and knowledge workers use when they collaborate via human-driven processes.

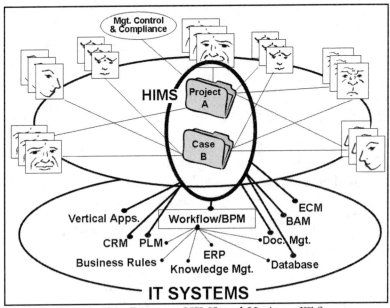

The Relationship Between HIMS and Heritage IT Systems

The HIMS can help keep non-routine work activities in con-text (telling everyone "what's going on,") and can change the way executives, line managers and high-value knowledge workers manage their work as they guide the business into the future. But for all this to come about, the design of an enterprise-class HIMS must incorporate the underlying computer and social sciences that reflect how humans actually interact together. They must have the underpinnings of:

- *negotiate-and-commit speech acts,* so that agreements, not just information can be tracked, and so that human-driven processes can be redefined as they emerge/evolve over the lifetime of the process,
- *role activity theory,* where human interactions, not computer interactions, can best be modeled,
- *distributed computing techniques* to cope with multiple and dynamic asynchronous communication channels, allowing a given human-driven process to be redefined as participants in that process are dropped in our out,
- *multi-agent systems,* where collaborating software agents use their own unique business rules and knowledge sources,
- *cognitive science models* (such as REACT/AIM) that reflect how knowledge workers think and act,
- *choreography methods* for handling interactions with process participants, including operational processes in heritage IT/BPM/Workflow systems,
- *peer-to-peer, private information spaces,* where versioning and shared access are under the control of the participants that own the information, work objects and even processes,
- *governance,* especially management control for compliance (e.g., The Sarbanes-Oxley Act) and auditability, and
- other ingredients that make computer-supported collaborations reflect real-world human interactions.

Of course, these underpinnings should never be seen by business users of such systems, just as relational algebra isn't seen by business users of modern database systems. But they had better be there, else the HIMS will not be flexible enough for adaptive and dynamic collaborations in which the interaction patterns cannot be anticipated. Such collaborative processes include creative, innovative human activities such as research, design and multi-party project/case management. The activity sequencing of these processes cannot be prescriptively imposed. Why? The contracts of interactions, deliverables and business rules are continually renegotiated during the life of the process: emergent behavior, emergent processes. The HIMS pushes the envelop of the typical workflow/integration BPM approaches in managing these kinds of "impromptu" processes.

Putting it All Together

With the onslaught of Web 2.0 technologies appearing in the Cloud and already being surrounded with legacy IT systems that must be fed and cared for, today's workers are growing desperate. Now, more than ever before, there is a pressing need to come to grips with support for human interaction management for non-routine, knowledge-based workplace activities, and to address the desperation people feel when they are swamped by increasing demands and infoglut in today's workplace.

In "Linking Insight to Action: The Next Big Goal," posted at *Intelligent Enterprise*, Doug Henschen reveals a really big problem in business, "I've had a number of conversations in recent days around the theme of linking analysis to action. There's lots of frustration out there, understandably, because managers and executives increasingly have plenty of tools that spot problems (reports, alerts, dashboards, KPIs, scorecards, etc.) but they're not connected to levers that enable them to take action." Indeed, how do we connect the levers for action in light of Web 2.0 technologies in the Cloud? To reach for Doug's next big goal, we can turn to EDS's Janne Korhonen's depiction of the evolution of process management as shown in the figure below and relate that to how HIM can turn strategy into action:

- *Strategic Control:* the definition of aims and measures for each high-level process
- *Executive Control:* the definition of outline processes that include a mixture of Roles, Interactions and Users
- *Management Control:* adapting the outline processes into a form for initial execution and later ongoing redefinition of the proc-

ess, along with executive feedback (e.g. dashboards, statistical reports)

- *Agreements:* contract of interactions, deliverables and business rules is continually renegotiated during the life of the process

In the real-time age of globalization, the process-managed enterprise will dominate by implementing radically new means of support for human interactions, Work 2.0. Winning companies will deploy innovative information technology tools to manage human-driven processes, capture information deeply personal to each participant, and help them use this information both individually and collaboratively. With a new breed of software, the Human Interaction Management System, smart companies will be able to optimize the human-driven processes that are, in the end, their jobs—and the next source of competitive advantage.

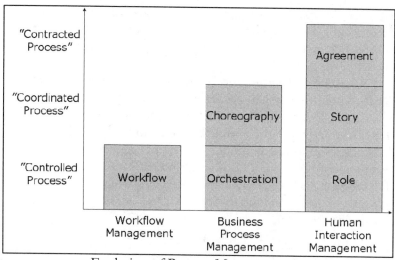

Evolution of Process Management [2]

Human Interaction Management can permit companies to establish a fundamentally human integration (versus machine integration) with their customers, by engaging directly with the human-centered processes for which their products will be used. In the twenty-first century, where customers are bewildered by choice and seek understanding from their suppliers, as well as low price and efficient delivery, such integration is a necessity. In the Cloud, customers will find suppliers that they trust, engage them, and stick with them. Anyone can compete in this new world—but to keep the customers you gain, you need Human Interaction Management.

After fifty years of coping with the limited tools at their disposal, it's time that interaction workers be *supported by*, instead of having to slavishly support, legacy computer systems, and now Web 2.0 systems. It's time for Work 2.0 to tame all the other 2.0s floating around in the Cloud.

Takeaway

To paraphrase Admiral David Farragut, "Damn the flowcharts, full business speed ahead." Flowchart-based technologies treat work as steps in a routinized process, and hence people as cogs in a machine. Because such technologies don't "understand" knowledge work, they can only mimic its superficial appearance as a sequence of tasks—tasks are but the tip of the knowledge-work iceberg.

It's time to take insight, innovation and strategy into action. That's about people and dynamic human interactions, not predefined workflow/BPM or the wild-wild Web 2.0 technologies.
It's time to go beyond assembly-line workflow.
It's time to go where no routine process has gone before.
It's time for the greatest innovation since BPM.
It's time to tame and harness the bewildering Web 2.0.
It's time to go beyond the Information Age and on to
      the Process Age.
It's time for human interaction management in the Cloud.
It's time for Work 2.0.

Note: To explore human interaction management further, visit www.human-interaction-management.info   Be sure to check out the Business Process Spectrum and the HIM Quick Reference Card.

References.

---

[1] From: Bill Gates | Sent: Thu May 19 10:55:42 2005 | To: (Microsoft customers) | Subject: The New World of Work

[2] www.jannekorhonen.fi/blog/wpcontent/BPM_Systemic_Perspective.pdf

Seven

The End of Management

We must seriously question the concepts underlying the current structures of organization and whether they are suitable to the management of accelerating societal and environmental problems—and, even beyond that, we must seriously consider whether they are the primary cause of those problems.
—Dee Hock, founder of VISA Credit Card Association,
Birth of the Chaordic Age

There is a search underway for a new context and paradigm for the organization of the future—an organization that must be capable of producing high-quality, competitive products that satisfy customers without destroying the planet or degrading human life. The End of Management and the Rise of Organizational Democracy calls for a radical set of organizational development initiatives that will combat the destructive forces of globalization, put an end to authoritarian, paternalistic management, and move organizations toward a new "organizational democracy."
—Kenneth Cloke and Joan Goldsmith,
The End of Management and the Rise of Organizational Democracy

As a CEO, you know that the world is changing faster than you can keep pace with, and you and your organization need to change and grow to try and keep pace. With this hyper-pace comes the knowledge that the way you are currently managing your organization is no longer appropriate and will not provide the organization with the agility it needs for the future. This can be stressful and confronting to you and your managers. It is not necessarily about devising a better strategy or putting in more effort, it is about changing the current focus of you and your senior managers to make your organization more effective.
—John Jeston
What Managers Need to Know About the Management of Business Processes

Key Points: Leadership in the Cloud

The invention of the steam engine gave rise to factories and mass production, which in turn gave rise to a command-and-control style of management. Mass production was based on economist Adam Smith's notion of specializations and efficiency, where units of work were controlled from the top down. Just as a management structure and style was adapted to the factory as the focal point of economic activity, management must adapt to the Cloud as the focal point of economic activity. An emergent organizational form, the "Cloud Enterprise," will have changed its management structures and styles to become organic networks rather than hierarchical, function-divided monoliths.

Business singularity: The Cloud makes it possible for multiple companies to come together to work as *one* value delivery system, not just for efficiency, but more importantly for responsiveness and innovation. But such new organizational forms cannot be managed like the factory of old, for each participating business runs on its own clock, using its own internal rules and methods. In the 21st century, Industrial Age command-and-control leadership gives way to connect-and-collaborate, where every member of a business team is a "leader." In the Cloud, leaders don't give commands, they transmit information, trusting the team members' competencies and gaining accountability through transparency. True leadership is about cooperation, not control. In this chapter we'll explore the end of traditional management and the rise of self-organized and adaptive Bioteams that are based on nature's best designs. No, this isn't science fiction; it's the future of organizations getting stuff done. It's about unleashing human potential in our organizations. It's also about passion.

A big man has no time really to do anything but just sit and be big.
—F. Scott Fitzgerald

With the realities of today's uncertain world, executives may be thinking to go to the Lourdes for advice. What do companies usually do when they find themselves in trouble? They typically bring in a new "imperial" CEO at the top of the hierarchy.

According to a Booz Allen Hamilton study, "Annual turnover of CEOs across the globe increased by 59 percent between 1995 and 2006. In those same years, performance-related turnover—cases in which CEOs were fired or pushed out— increased by 318 percent. In 1995, only one in eight departing CEOs was forced from office. In 2006, nearly one in three left involuntarily."[1] Forbes magazine reported that in 2007, 37% of North American CEOs left "against their will."[2]

What's up with this CEO shuffle? Change! The real world of the unexpected.

It's about a 100-year old management model, where top-down management structures, designed to maximize efficiency, no longer work in a world where responsiveness trumps efficiency. Old methods of forecasting, top-down planning and command-and-control served the world well during the rise of the Industrial Age where efficiency was king, but do little to cope with the 21st century, decentralized, outsourced business world where accelerating change is the only constant, driven by fully-informed consumers who are but one real-time click away from finding the very best products and services they demand.

Power has shifted from producers to consumers who can demand what they want, when they want it, and where. The consumer is no longer king, as taught in traditional marketing classes. The consumer is now a dictator, and companies must transform from being sellers to their customers to becoming buyers for them. "Make to forecast" morphs to "make to demand," and no game of musical chairs in the corner office can change this new reality.

But there are even more fundamental changes going on in the business world than the oh-so-visible CEO shuffle. In his 1991 Business Hall of Fame acceptance speech Dee Hock, founder of Visa International, explained: "Through the years, I have greatly feared and sought to keep at bay the four beasts that inevitably devour their keeper—Ego, Envy, Avarice, and Ambition. In 1984, I severed all connections with business for a life of isolation and anonymity, convinced I was making a great bargain by trading money for time, position for liberty, and ego for contentment—

that the beasts were securely caged."

On March 13, 1993, Hock, who challenged the nature of traditional organizations and management, gave a dinner speech at the Santa Fe Institute where, based on his experiences founding and operating Visa International, he described systems that are both chaotic and ordered, and used for the first time the term *chaordic*, a portmanteau combining the words chaotic and ordered.

The worldwide success of VISA International, Hock asserts, is due to its chaordic structure: it is owned by 22,000 member banks, which both compete with each other for 750 million customers and must cooperate by honoring one another's $125 trillion in transactions annually across borders and currencies.

Chaordic? Hmm? Companies that want to survive and thrive in today's world of hyper-complexity and hyper-change must now really come to understand and internalize Hock's portmanteau. In short, that means "Management Innovation," which, in turn, means a shift in business culture, which, in turn, means the redefinition of what it means to be a business.

The End of Management

While this book has argued that operational innovation, via process management in the Cloud, is the cornerstone of 21st century competitive advantage, operational innovation will be for naught without innovation of another kind, Management Innovation. When responsiveness trumps efficiency, command-and-control management systems fall flat. In a world of hyper change, centrally controlled hierarchies (remember the Soviet Union) simply cannot see the opportunities or move quickly enough. Even if they utilize advanced process management systems, their *management* processes and structures cannot adapt with the required speed.

We will, no doubt, have to wait years for the cultural shift toward an agile, fully process-managed enterprise. Or will we? Let's turn to the closing of Andrew Spanyi's *BPM is a Team Sport*, "Those who fail to transform the traditional functional mindset and embrace business process thinking will find themselves teetering on the brink. Indeed, BPM is a highly competitive team sport, and in the playoffs for industry championships, it's win or be eliminated."

> The days of the monolithic, vertically-integrated company, owning everything from raw materials to production to selling
> —are over.

21st-century corporations will thrive in a business world where the traditional linear supply chain gives way to dynamic, customer-driven value *webs* (call it the extended enterprise if you like). Industries will be disrupted either by new entrants or by incumbents that move from command-and-control to connect-and-collaborate leadership for process innovation that spans entire value chains in the Cloud.

To wit, consider what Amazon did to the retail book industry and what Dell did to the PC industry. Thus, the cultural shift to a process-managed enterprise as a *management practice* may come a lot sooner than some may think, and at the expense of inflexible business leaders and their companies.

But wait, what exactly does "management practice" actually mean? Let's turn to John Jeston's forthcoming book, *What Managers Need to Understand About BPM*: "The first step in discussing BPM is to ensure we have a common understanding and agreement that BPM is a management philosophy. Yes, it is also about completing business process improvement projects to make your processes more efficient and effective (thirty to fifty percent is normal). Yes, it is about then continuing to measure and performance manage the processes into the future. But it is much more than just this. Just making your business processes more efficient and effective does not mean your organization will be managed better, as process performance advantages will dissipate over time. More is required.

"BPM is a management 'tool' or philosophy that will enable an organization to significantly improve its performance. It will enable managers to become high performance managers, and if you have enough high performance managers, you are well on the way to being a high performance organization.

"In looking at our business processes, we need to go beyond the normal process thinking. Business processes are not just about the 'transactional' processes we traditionally think about. Transactional processes are those that process your cash receipts; insurance premiums; bank withdrawals; order fulfillment. But, business processes also include: organizational strategy creation and review; budget processes; management decision making; capital allocation; and internal communications. These are the processes that govern the work that gets done by the transactional processes.

"Organizations need to continually review, improve or eliminate these management processes as much or more than the 'traditional' customer-serving processes. Management processes often need more attention because most have not been reviewed for a long time and as observed by renowned management professor, Gary Hamel, 'they shape management values by reinforcing certain behaviors and not others.'"[3]

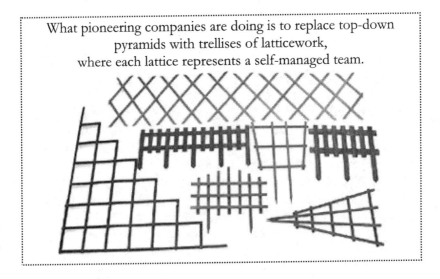

What pioneering companies are doing is to replace top-down pyramids with trellises of latticework, where each lattice represents a self-managed team.

Sound farfetched and anarchistic without central control? You bet. But, guess what? That's a mirror image of the real world, a world made up of complex adaptive systems. Turning to the Santa Fe Institute's John Holland: "A Complex Adaptive System (CAS) is a dynamic network of many agents (which may represent cells, species, individuals, teams, firms, nations) acting in parallel, constantly acting and reacting to what the other agents are doing. The control of a CAS tends to be highly dispersed and decentralized. If there is to be any coherent behavior in the system, it has to arise from competition and cooperation among the agents themselves. The overall behavior of the system is the result of a huge number of decisions made every moment by many individual agents."[4]

Complex adaptive systems are managed without managers! Can businesses manage without managers? Indeed. Just look at W. L. Gore, the company that makes Gore-tex, the fabrics that keep you warm and dry, but that also breathe, and Glide dental floss. In 1958, former Dupont engineer and geek (e.g., no MBA), Bill Gore would forego a ladder-like hierarchy and create an organization with a flat, lattice-like organizational structure where:

- There are no "employees," and everyone shares the same title: associate.
- There are over 8,500 associates that have, so far, turned out over a thousand innovative products.
- There are neither chains of command (pyramids or reporting structures) nor predetermined channels of communication. Anyone can talk to anyone, anytime.
- There are a large number of small, autonomous, self-organizing teams that function as a web of start-up companies.
- There are no bosses, no V.P.'s, executives, or managers—there are "sponsors" and "leaders." Associates are only responsible to their teams: Everyone's the boss, and no one's the boss. There are no slackers.
- There are no standard job descriptions or "assignments." Associates make sets of "commitments" to their teams, and sometimes unorthodox titles emerge, e.g., a "category champion."
- Associates choose to follow leaders rather than have bosses assigned to them.
- Performance reviews are based on a peer-level rating system.

What's really going on that makes a real difference at Gore? The company has closed the "information gap." Humans are unique in their ability to manipulate information outside the body, and are constantly hungry for information and narratives. While we speak of a growing wealth gap in today's economies, the volume and depth of information available to senior executives compared to the shop floor worker is staggering in typical corporations. Left starved for information, it's little wonder why curiosity and creativity remain in lock-down among the rank and file in most corporations. As John Caddell writes in his *Shoptalk* blog, "Perhaps it's concern for confidential information leakage, or for PR fallout, or that management simply doesn't trust in the employees' [Theory X] ability to add value to innovation."[5]

In their book, *The Starfish And the Spider,* Ori Brafman and Rod A. Beckstrom describe several characteristics of a starfish organization, a term they use as a metaphor for an agile enterprise because of the starfish's ability to adapt to trauma by rapidly regenerating lost limbs. Separated limbs are capable of returning to health and surviving on their own, much like autonomous work teams in an agile enterprise. These authors use the term spider as a metaphor for bureaucracy because a spider's body is controlled by a central nervous system and cannot survive severe trauma, much like a bureaucracy that is dependent on top level management to make all major decisions. Brafman and Beckstrom offer several characteristics of a starfish organization that are consistent with views of the agile enterprise. Some of these can be summarized as follows:

- Projects are generated everywhere in the organization, and many times even from outside affiliates.
- No one is in control; thump it on the head and it still survives.
- If you take out a unit, the overall organization quickly recovers.
- Participants function autonomously, which facilitates workforce scalability.
- Roles are amorphous and ever-changing; tasks are performed on an "as needed" basis.
- Knowledge and power are distributed; intelligence is spread throughout the organization.
- Working groups communicate directly, not hierarchically.
- Key decisions are made collaboratively; on the spot; on the fly.

Okay, want a real-world example? As Ellen McGirt reported in *Fast Company,* "How Cisco's CEO John Chambers is Turning the Tech Giant Socialist," "Chambers has greater ambitions, even now, in the midst of turmoil. Or, perhaps, especially now. He has been taking Cisco through a massive, radical, often bumpy reorganization. The goal is to spread the company's leadership and decision making far wider than any big company has attempted before, to working groups that currently involve 500 executives. This move, Chambers says, reflects a new philosophy about how business can best work in a networked world. 'In 2001, we were like most high-tech companies, with one or two primary products that were really important to us,' he explains. 'All decisions came to the top 10 people in the company, and we drove things back down from there.'

"Today, a network of councils empowered to launch new businesses, plus an evolving set of Web 2.0 gizmos—not to mention a new financial incentive system—encourage executives to work together like never before. Pull back the tent flaps and Cisco citizens are blogging, vlogging, and virtualizing, using social-networking tools that they've made themselves and that, in many cases, far exceed the capabilities of the commercially available wikis, YouTubes, and Facebooks created by the kids up the road in Palo Alto.

"The bumpy part—and the eye-opener—is that the leaders of business units formerly competing for power and resources now share responsibility for one another's success. What used to be 'me' is now 'we.' The goal is to get more products to market faster, and Chambers crows at the results. 'The boards and councils have been able to innovate with tremendous speed. Fifteen minutes and one week to get a [business] plan that used to take six months!' As storm clouds form for the rest of the business community, he says, 'We're going to gain market share.' Rain? What rain?

"Cisco, Chambers argues, is the best possible model for how a large, global business can operate: as a distributed idea engine where leadership emerges organically, unfettered by a central command. Chambers and his team have been sharing detailed case studies of their experiences and best practices with the likes of AT&T, General Electric, and Procter & Gamble, and with customers in emerging markets from Russia and China to Mexico and Brazil. 'We did it first ourselves; now we teach our customers. And the neat thing about it is that they'll use our technology to do it.'

"Chambers politely ignored my observation that Cisco's new regimen feels a bit like a *socialist revolution*. But Chambers did kick off the analyst conference with a slide that read, collaboration: 'co-labor;' working toward a common goal. In language and spirit, Chambers' transformation is a mashup of radical *isms* and collectivist catchphrases. Of course, with analysts suggesting that the 'collaboration marketplace' could be a $34 billion opportunity, it's radicalism of a reassuringly capitalist bent.

"Power to the people—and profits to the company—is a bold tech promise we've heard before. If Chambers can pull it off, if he can prove that his model drives innovation at a market-beating pace, he will replace his pal Jack Welch as the most influential leadership guru of the modern era."[6] Social democracy and capitalism anyone?

In "The Changing Nature of Work and the System Design Process of Future," Ramanjit Singh, Trevor Wood-Harper, and Bob Wood proclaim that a "Manager" becomes a boundary manager, and not a supervisor of employees:[7]

1. Assumptions about Organization
- Organizations are open systems interacting with environment.
- Organizations are work systems with two independent but interrelated subsystems: social and technical.

2. Assumptions about People
- "Theory Y" orientation toward people, hence it's morally right to let them participate in decision making process.

3. Socio-Technical Design Goals
- Jointly satisfy the organizational goals

4. Assumptions about the Socio-Technical Design Process
- Workers should participate in requirements (efficiency goals) and quality of work life (social goals).

5. Socio-Technical Design Concepts
- Work system, not single job, as design unit
- Workgroup not single jobholder
- Internal regulation of group
- Redundancy of function, not redundancy of part
- Members have discretion, not highly prescribed work
- Develop flexible learning system

- Autonomous workgroup is superior form of organization

6. Role changes

- Designer: facilitator not "expert"
- Worker: "designer" of the system
- Manager: "boundary manager," not supervisor of workers.
  People across the globe to work together for a common cause.

At Gore and other companies transforming themselves for the realities of extreme competition in the 21st century, perhaps what they have really done is return to the age-old art of storytelling, embellishing that art with modern communication technologies. In her book, *Working With Stories*, Cynthia Kurtz, a former evolutionary biologist and now researcher in the field of organizational narratives, explains what working with stories means: "1. asking people to tell stories (and usually, asking people to answer questions about the stories they tell), then 2. working with the stories (and sometimes with the answers to the questions and the patterns they form) to find things out, catch emerging trends, make decisions, get new ideas, resolve conflicts, connect people, help people learn, and enlighten people."[8]

The technologies of human interaction management systems discussed earlier, and the disciplines of bioteaming discussed below can open up information sharing and collaboration without creating mayhem, while they uncork ideas and creativity and put them into action in a controlled fashion—in the Cloud.

When Teams Rule the World

On the shelves at Whole Foods Market you won't find the management innovation that has built its success through "democratic capitalism." Lots of companies have posters in the break room with slogans such as Empowerment, Initiative and Teamwork. At Whole Foods, those aren't just your typical empty slogans, they are the foundations of its operations. The company has a "Declaration of Interdependence" that states its commitment to diversity, community, and saving the planet. Its salary caps limit executive compensation to 14 times the average pay across the company. But it's no airy-fairy socialist experiment in capitalism.

Whole Foods is a hardball competitor, both inside and out. It harnesses the passion, energy and competitive spirit of *all* of its people, while typical companies bury those factors under a pyramid of management hierarchies and bureaucracies.

Whole Foods secret sauce? It's all based on autonomous, decentralized teams. The team, not the typical management hierarchy, is the building block of the entire company. Each store is its own profit center made up of self-managed teams that include seafood, produce, grocery, prepared foods, and so on. Each team selects its own leaders and its employees. Team leaders, in turn, make up the store's team; store leaders make up regional teams; and regional team leaders make up national teams.

Such distributed power and authority would result in chaos in traditional organizations, but *transparency* is the invisible hand of accountability and management control for Whole Foods. Financial information, including store and team sales, profit margins, and, believe it or not, salaries, are available for all to see. It's like seeing batting averages in major league baseball. Such scorecards lead to intense competition as teams, stores, and regions compete vigorously to outdo each other in quality, service, profitability. But it's more than just friendly competition and community spirit, scorecards translate into bonuses, and promotions. That's democratic capitalism in action. Peer pressure trumps bureaucracy, combining democracy with competitive discipline.

In each store, the power is concentrated in the hands of teams. Teams approve new hires, who require a two-thirds "yes" vote after a month long trial period. And teams are rigorous about their member's selection because financial incentives are tied to team, not individual, performance. And, to build trust, every member of every team knows the salary of everybody in the team, and in the entire company.

While Whole Foods represents creative *intra-company teams* in action, *inter-company teams* represent even greater challenges and opportunities—and they do their work virtually, in the Cloud. When you consider that there are more than 22 companies in an average supply chain and that companies want to outsource all but their core competencies, the rise of a new *cloudy* organizational form, the

Networked Enterprise follows. In his book, *The Networked Enterprise*, former Reuters' CIO and a Belfast, Northern Ireland researcher, Ken Thompson, describes the whys and hows of the Virtual Enterprise Network, a powerful new competitive form. "In most economies, smaller enterprises are much greater in number than large firms. For example, in the EU, small and medium-sized enterprises (SMEs or *small fish*) comprise approximately 99% of all firms and employ among them about 65 million people. Interestingly, in many sectors, *SMEs are also responsible for driving innovation and competition.*"

"When you consider that innovation is the key to success in the 21st century, and that huge corporations (Big Fish) like Proctor and Gamble and IBM are going to the ends of the earth seeking innovation, the picture comes into focus. Big Fish desperately want and need the innovative products, services and thinking that specialized *small fish* bring. The goal of a Virtual Enterprise Network is to connect SMEs into peer networks, supported by appropriate collaboration practices (see Bioteams below) and technologies, to give them the capabilities and competitive advantages of global enterprises. By forming, like-minded *small fish* can directly engage key Big Fish through Virtual Enterprise Networks that have sufficient scale and resources to interest and engage the Big Fish. This approach is far different from the traditional supplier model where the Big Fish is in full control. Big Fish and *small fish* simply don't get along in the real world, because Big Fish constantly swallow and consume *small fish* without even noticing it. The Virtual Enterprise Network creates a symbiosis, a living, mutually beneficial relationship among dissimilar organisms, where the participants, big and small, can thrive together in the 21st century world of extreme competition.

"A VEN is thus a way for businesses to achieve *virtual scale,* enabling them to operate as if they possess more resources and capacity than any one company actually has within its own physical organization. This allows the VEN to function with all the resources and reach of a large enterprise, but *without sacrificing* its speed, agility and low overhead. This enables participating companies to compete for *bigger, more profitable contracts* with higher innovation and design elements, with bigger customers that are more willing to build strategic partnerships rather than simple transactional relationships with the VEN's individual suppliers.

In short, Thompson's book provides strategic insight, specific guidelines and real-world case studies for *small fish* and Big Fish alike. Considering the breakthroughs in forming powerful intra-company teams (Whole Foods) and inter-company teams (Net-worked Enterprise), let's take a look at how companies can build high-performance teams that operate in the Cloud. The task is by no means trivial, and cultural barriers abound. We'll learn some vital lessons for building high performance teams based on nature's best designs. The term "teamwork" will never be the same.

Bioteams

Teams of the future will collaborate in the Cloud. But they must adopt new "human protocols" if they are to be effective, and that's where bioteaming comes in. According to the distinguished Indiana University technology professor, Dr. Curtis Bonk, "This is the age of employee participation, multiple leaders and yet no leader, and prompt communication, as well as the technologies that make all this possible."

> Got team? You'd better.
> To succeed in today's dynamic, technology-enabled environment, you must be able to function in and through teams. But, if we stick with our current "command-and-control" approach to teams, we will not be able to meet the growing needs of our communities in the high-change global economy.

The discipline of *bioteaming* offers a vision of what successful teaming experiences look like in the interconnected world of the 21st century. A February 2008 *Business Week* feature, "Using Nature as a Design Guide," focused on how the "biomimicry" design movement can help companies look to the natural world to make their business green. The feature reported on the work of Janine Benyus, biologist-cum-evangelist, the driving force behind the movement. In her writings she detailed how companies could study nonpolluting, energy-efficient manufacturing technologies that have evolved in the natural world over billions of years.

Now enter Ken Thompson, the former CIO with Reuters, who over the past ten years has taken the field of biomimicry from innovation related to physical things on to the realm of social structures. Thompson takes ideas from Nature about how groups perform and intra-operate, and applies them to enhance how humans can work together in groups and teams, virtually, in the Cloud.

Thompson's "bioteaming" is about building organizational teams that operate on the basis of the communication principles that underpin nature's most successful groups. Spot the common theme: the waggle dance of honeybees, the pheromone trails of ants, the one-way information bursts of migrating geese. According to Thompson, nature's teams have characteristics that are not usually present in organizational teams:

Collective Leadership: *Any group member can take the lead.*

Nature's groups are never led exclusively by one member; different group members lead as needed.

When geese migrate (in the literal Clouds) it is well known that the goose leading the V formation rotates. However, researchers like Thompson now suggest that this is not just because they get tired and need to fly in another goose's slipstream for a while, but that no one goose knows the whole migration route. Collectively, between them, they know the migration route, but no one individual knows the entire route.

So a goose leads the part of the journey where it knows the way and when it recognizes "I don't know where to go next" it flies back into the V and waits for another goose to take over.

This is "Collective Leadership," the right leader for the right task at the right time.

The human species seems to be the only species that trusts in a single leader (or small management team) to know the whole path, on behalf of the community.

Multi-Leader groups possess much greater agility, initiative and resilience than groups that are only led by a single exclusive leader.

Instant Messaging: *Instant whole-group broadcast communications.*

Nature's groups use short instant messages that are instantly broadcast and received "in situ" wherever the receivers are. These messages are very short and very simple – essentially just two types:
- *Opportunity Messages.* Food, nesting materials, Prey
- *Threat Messages.* Predators, Rival colonies

Ants achieve messaging by using a range of chemical phero-mones that they emit and lay in trails, and that are instantly picked up by the other ants. Bees use dances, for example, the waggle dance that is danced by a hive member who has found a food sup-ply. The hive mates watch the dance and the angle of the axis of the dance points them to the food supply. It is important to note that:
- These messages are group broadcasts and are not replied to.
- They are received and acted upon immediately; there is no con-cept of a 2-stage communication that is received at point A and acted on later at point B.

A critical point is that these instant messages are so simple they really act just as "alerts." The recipient has to "decide" what to do. Such instant messages do not convey orders or instructions.

Ecosystems: *Small is Beautiful .....but Big is Powerful.*

In nature, the size of the group is always right for the job and small groups link into bigger groups, that in turn link into still big-ger groups. Where you a have a very large group or a crowd, it is only possible to achieve coordinated action if each member does the same thing at the same time. Thus a crowd can move a stone or excavate a hole, but large scale innovation is another thing alto-gether, requiring "Mass collaboration." Could a virtual team have a million members? Recent developments in mass collaboration, dis-tributed computing and the wisdom of Clouds suggest, the answer might be yes. Biological teams such as Ant or Bee societies, can contain *up to a million members in a single mature colony* or hive—all of whom can act as a unit.

Let's take a physical example of mass collaboration, the tiny European upstart, Skype Technologies S.A., that turned a trillion-dollar industry upside down, by dialing up a vast, hidden resource: its own users in the Cloud. Skype, the newest creation from the same folks whose popular file-sharing software Kazaa freaked out record execs, also lets people share their resources—legally. When users fire up Skype, they automatically allow their spare computing power and Net connections to be borrowed by the Skype network, which uses that collective resource to route others' calls. The result: a self-sustaining phone system that requires no central capital investment —just the willingness of its users to share. Says Skype CEO Niklas Zennström: "It's almost like an organism."[9]

Up until recently, the size of the group has meant that some dimensions of biological teamwork and group behavior were not able to be reproduced in human teams and organizations due to this lack of scale.

The Cloud might change all this. A June 20, 2005 *Newsweek* magazine article, "The Power of Us," reports that "Mass Collaboration on The Internet is shaking up Business." The article identifies three types of Internet-based "mass collaboration" that can be characterized as:

- *Give and Take* – for example creating shared, distributed computing capacity
- *Needles in Hay*stacks – connecting to other like-minds through shared interest, rather than personal relationship
- *Participation through Passion* – co-inventing with others based on passion, rather than money as the motivator

So large groups enable scale, mass, reach and range. However, in a small group each member can meaningfully do different things at the same time—in other words, "Division of labor" and complex coordination. So a small group may not be able to lift a large weight but it could design a clever tool to make lifting that weight much easier.

Nature shows us the importance of having the right group size for the job at hand. It also shows us that "one size does not fit all," in terms of groups, by its ability to have all sizes of interconnected groups. For example, in the ant world we have castes within colonies, within food webs, within ecosystems. A critical point for human teams is that they need to allow members to enjoy both the small group dynamic for innovation, and the large group dynamic for scale.

Clustering: *Engaging the many through the few*
Nature's networks are clustered. The technical term for this is "scale-free networks." In simple terms, what this means is that in most naturally occurring networks some of the nodes have many more connections than the average.

This makes sense instinctively. For example, some of our friends seem to know everybody. If we need to reach someone we don't directly know, we might try them first. This structure also describes the neurons in the brain and other emerging social structures such as the "hub" sites on the Internet.

What this means for teams is that if you are lucky some of your team members will have extreme connectivity in terms of relationships. The team needs to take advantage of these existing connections rather than try and have the team leader(s) create and manage new connections from scratch.

These highly connected people are described elsewhere in various terms, including "alpha users," "connectors" and "influentials." But no matter what they are called, if they are well managed and motivated they can provide the most efficient and effective channels for the team to engage with its wider community, in the Cloud.

In his book, *Bioteams: High Performance Teams Based on Nature's Best Designs*, Thompson goes beyond the theory and provides proven methods and techniques for creating and managing high performance bioteams. The conclusions in his book, and its companion book, *The Networked Enterprise: Competing for the Future Through Virtual Enterprise Networks*, reveal how business enterprises, supply chains, high-tech ventures, public sector organizations and nonprofits are turning to nature's best designs to create agile, high performing teams in the Cloud.

Thompson's work is bolstered with examples from various

countries, including Ireland, Mexico, Switzerland, America, Holland, and Germany. They include high performing banks, manufacturers, sports teams, engineering firms, aerospace companies, hospitals, nonprofits and more. Thompson highlights the future norms of doing business:

> Transparency, trust the team, shared glory and rewards, incremental improvement, and clear accountability.

If Thompson is right, and it would be difficult to argue that he's not onto something really important in the Cloud economy, *today's organizational teams just became extinct.*

Bioteams solve problems and learn by rapid experimentation and evolution. Bioteams have very concrete goals that are hardwired into the members genetically but the members don't have any actual strategies or plans for achieving them. They work by rapid experimentation and feedback. If something works and solves the problem it gets reinforced within their collective set of responses for the next time; if not it dies. Bioteams are action-focused and work in the Cloud.

Each bioteam member is fundamentally 3-dimensional. Team members constantly engage autonomously with other close team members, their external environment and the enterprise as a whole.

Bioteaming extends biological principles to also deal with the hugely important issues of the "why" as well as the "how" or the "what." Human teams have huge amounts of discretion and self-awareness, and thus human bioteams need a sense of purpose, a common set of shared values and passion—we can't treat a human team like an ant colony.

Another key difference is the importance of the individual in a human team. If one member of an ant colony gets it wrong there are so many others who get it right that it does not matter. In general, however, the consequences of individual member failure are much higher in human bioteams and we need working practices and tools (such as accountability and transparency) to protect us from this, as Whole Foods does with its complete transparency to all members of all of its teams.

Takeaway

In short, the Cloud isn't just about technology; it's about a new platform for human interactions in business, that, in turn, requires new organizational structures and styles and new team behaviors. With the emergence of the Cloud, collaboration, social networks and mobile communications, the very meaning of the word "team" has changed.

Not only will we need software support for taming the inherent chaos in this brave new Cloud world, we'll also need a change in *behavior* to replace command-and-control in our leadership styles and human interactions—in our high-performance Bioteams.

The most well known trait of a Bioteam is
Self-Management or Autonomy.

In a process-managed enterprise,
command-and-control leadership gives way to
connect-and-collaborate,
where every member of a business team is a "leader."

In a process-managed enterprise,
leaders don't give commands, they transmit information,
trusting the team members' competencies and
gaining accountability through transparency.

True leadership is about cooperation, not control.
As in nature's teams, it's about acting on opportunities,
and letting others lead the leader
when they know best about getting stuff done.

Out of the winter of recession, new growth has room to emerge. The Cloud provides a new business platform that makes it possible to achieve operational innovation and new forms of collaboration never before possible, enabling a whole new set of possibilities for Management Innovation and competitive advantage. While the notion of "employee," a construct born of the emergence of the Industrial Age, is only a hundred years old, the Cloud will make it possible for innovative companies to remove the term, and replace the term "management" with "leadership" in their lexicons. In the Cloud, intra- and inter-company, self-managed teams will *swarm* as complex, adaptive organisms to seize new opportunities in the brave new world of total global competition.

References.

[1] http://www.boozallen.com/media/file/Era_of_the_Inclusive_Leader_.pdf

[2] http://www.forbes.com/2008/03/07/executive-ceo-tenure-lead-manage-cx_mk_0307turnover.html

[3] Hamel, G., The Future of Management, Harvard Business Press, 2008, p. 21

[4] *Complexity: The Emerging Science at the Edge of Order and Chaos* by M. Mitchell Waldrop.

[5] http://shoptalkmarketing.blogspot.com/2007/10/on-gary-hamels-future-of-management_19.html

[6] http://www.fastcompany.com/node/1093654/print

[7] http://www.information-quarterly.org/ISOWProc/2007ISOWCD/PDFs/64.pdf

[8] http://workingwithstories.org

[9] http://www.businessweek.com/magazine/content/05_25/b3938601.htm

Eight

Epilog

For the world has changed, and we must change with it.
—President Barack Obama, January 20, 2009

Make no small plans; they have no magic to stir men's souls.
—Daniel Burnam (1846-1912) an American architect

All men can see these tactics whereby I conquer, but what none can see is the strategy out of which victory is evolved.
—Sun Tzu, *The Art of War,* 6th Century BC

Key Points: The Cloud as a Business Platform

We've covered a lot in these pages. We've done a great deal of analysis of how the Cloud as a business platform changes the rules of the game of business. We've reached out and reported on what the movers and shakers of Cloud Computing are doing to deliver everything as a service. Now it's time to put it all together. It's time to bring all this home. It's time to think deeply about what to do, to build a plan of action and create our own futures. After all, as the father of modern management, Peter Drucker, once said, "The best way to predict the future is to create it."

The future is arriving at a faster pace than ever before in history. But new and profound business opportunities are not always recognized when they first emerge—even when they are of the magnitude that can change not only individual companies, but entire industries, and usher in a new way of business competition.

Pick any industry. Age old structures have become obscure. Industry boundaries are becoming a big blur. Streamlining a company's core business processes can result in cheaper, better, and faster products and services. These ingredients, however, represent just the price of admission to today's business arena. Down on the playing field, contenders are creating extended enterprises and competing to seize control of their industries or to invent completely new industries. It's a whole new ball game in the Cloud arena, complete with new rules—actually there are no rules.

Industries don't just smoothly evolve. Instead, firms eager to overturn the present order disrupt *best practices* with *next practices*, redraw segment boundaries, and set new customer expectations. The entertainment industry is a prime example. To wit, consider Apple Inc.'s iTunes and its iTunes Store where customers can connect via the Internet to purchase and download music, music videos, television shows, applications, iPod games, audio books, various podcasts, feature length films and movie rentals. It is also used to download applications for the iPhone and iPod touch. What's a computer company doing seizing control of the entertainment industry? That wasn't supposed to be any of their business. And, oh by the way, it was enabled by the Cloud.

Extended enterprises of the future will reach out not only to build strong business relationships, they must also integrate their information systems. That is precisely why the Cloud will be their strategic competitive weapon of choice.

In the Cloud, customers, retailers, distributors, and manufacturers can blur into a business ecosystem where it is impossible to know who is whom.

In the Cloud, virtual corporations can operate globally, 24 hours a day, seven days a week. In the Cloud, work and tasks follow the sun, reducing business cycle times. In the Cloud, the resources of virtual corporations ebb and flow with the changing needs of the minute in light of emerging business opportunities and threats.

The future cannot be seen using extrapolation and other traditional approaches to planning. Traditional planning is fine in times of continuous change, but not in times of unexpected change—in times of paradigm shifts.

Because companies cannot plan their futures based on extrapolation, the quality that companies require in times of discontinuous change is agility. Agility means casting off non-core competencies, deploying new functionalities, acquiring new competencies, and reconfiguring of the interface with suppliers, trading partners and customers almighty.

Agility means the ability to adapt and transform to discontinuous change. When an industry paradigm shifts, the agile corporation, having the insight to see the shift on its radar, helps shape and set the standards for the reinvented industry as it emerges.

Business and social transformation is enabled by new technology, the Cloud, but is driven by human imagination. The best way to predict your future is to imagine it, and then create it.

> What can be done in the Cloud, will be done.
> Will you be the doer, or the one done in?

The Cloud will enable businesses to become more adaptable and interconnected. In the Cloud, monolithic business units can be deconstructed into self-organizing, self-managing teams of super specialists. As in nature, call them complex adaptive organisms, if you will. Conducting business in the Cloud means that *influence* replaces *control* in a complex global world that is beyond the control of any one company or any one government.

Forget the "New Economy" that the Internet was supposed to usher in, it's now the "Ideas Economy" where *intangibles* reign supreme. To get there, company leaders must not look to futurists' predictions. Instead, they should build scenarios of possible futures that are both optimistic and plausible. Then with the adaptability made possible by the Cloud as a business platform, companies will experiment their way into the future. They will bundle, unbundle and rebundle their experiments with great dexterity, shutting down losers quickly, starting up potential new winners with all due speed and all due diligence.

While it was tough to use the word *optimistic* in the closing days of 2008, it is the very core of the human condition to go forward with the hope and passion that has allowed homo sapiens to create better futures through the ages when faced with dire circumstances. It's the passion engendered by a shared vision, a higher calling at Whole Foods Markets, "Whole Foods, Whole People, Whole Planet" that creates the passion that drives the company's self-managed teams toward the future. Without such vision and passion, people become short-sighted and mean-spirited, looking out only for themselves. Positive scenarios inspire and drive us, especially when there are tough times ahead. An optimistic view of the world stirs men's souls. Joseph P. Kennedy, father of J.F. Kennedy, once proclaimed, "When the going gets tough, the tough get going."

As Schwartz and Layden wrote in *Wired* magazine way back in 1997, "Businesses, as well as most organizations outside the business world, begin to shift from hierarchical processes to networked ones. Nearly every facet of human activity is transformed in some way by the emergent fabric of interconnection. This reorganization leads to dramatic improvements in efficiency and productivity."[1] Hmmm? Weren't these the arguments that led up to the dot-com boom and then crash? Indeed!

But the dot-com crash wasn't the beginning of the end of global transformation driven by the Internet, it was the end of the beginning. The tinkering phase of Internet business models was maturing, and then the real work of global economic transformation had begun.

If the Internet was the Big Bang, then the Cloud provides the cooling and beginning of new life forms. Radical technologies don't demonstrate their full potential until a generation after their introduction, the time needed for people to really figure out how to use them for new purposes.

Pure human capital, brainpower, becomes the foundation of economic power. That's what started to happen with Internet 1.0, and that's what's happening right now with the Cloud. But now we have broadband access to supercomputer resources in the sky, and to each other.

No doubt the Cloud will be greeted with as much hype as was the Internet itself, but rather than email being the *killer app* of the Internet, followed by Web-based brochureware being delivered to dumb browsers, the Cloud not only allows people to connect-and-collaborate, it gives them access to unprecedented information processing power and the ability to manipulate the information base on which their endeavors depend.

What to do? Here are 17 action ideas to consider, along with predictions in Appendix 3 from the author, Andy Mulholland:

1. Innovate, from the outside-in.

2. Don't just reinvent your company, reinvent your industry or invent a new industry (iTunes).

3. When pursuing emerging business opportunities, start small, and set intervals for go, no-go check points.

4. When breaking new ground, pay as you go, learn as you go.

5. Use Return on Opportunity (ROO) calculations focused on *benefits* instead of traditional financial ROI calculations only.

6. Tap the Cloud for IT infrastructure investments that otherwise couldn't be made to pursue emerging business opportunities.

7. Tap the wisdom of crowds for open innovation.

8. Replace functional management with process management.

9. Adopt business process management systems, but even more important, become a process-managed enterprise.

10. Adopt service-oriented technology architectures.

11. Become a service-oriented enterprise.

12. Adopt Web 2.0 tools and methods.

13. Utilize a business operations platform in the Cloud to support your entire multi-company value chains.

14. Fire your managers and employees; then rehire them as associates, as champions, as sponsors, as peers.

15. Replace your command-and-control bureaucracies with self-organizing, self-managed Bioteams.

16. Connect-and-collaborate using human interaction management methods and systems.

17. Become a learning organization to assure that your new way of doing business is assimilated throughout your workforce.

Although the Cloud enables radical change, the *culture* of the firm will determine the outcome of using the Cloud as a business platform. Permission, risk tolerance, cultivating lots of small bets—these are some of the earmarks of a Cloud-oriented business culture. Those who are able to harness the Cloud to achieve Management Innovation will write the next chapter of globalization.

Above all else, it's the customer that counts! Let's turn to BPM expert Andrew Spanyi and author of the insightful book, *More For Less,* "Even those organizations that have made significant progress in elevating senior management attention to the enterprise business processes still see mindset and behavior challenges.

"What to do? First, leaders need to reframe their thinking with respect to the role of customer centricity and process thinking. This involves a fundamental shift in conventional wisdom as it relates to a broad range of management practices pertaining to strategy formulation and implementation, leadership, employee engagement, growth, and mergers. This attitudinal shift needs to precede the development of the requisite skill sets needed to perform for customers. Second, the essential business principles and practices of process management need to be more broadly understood. Only then will organizations be well positioned to hone their skills in the critical areas of management practice."

Quit Whining About the Great Depression 2.0

There have been nine recessions in the U.S. since World War II. That's one out of every seven years. And it's possible that the recession that kicked off in 2008 could be more severe than all the others.

As I closed out this book in early 2009, it was easy to look out on all the gloom and doom of the worst recession since World War II, and perhaps even the beginning of the Great Depression 2.0. When U.S. Senator, Phil Gramm, infamously said that the 2008 downturn was a "mental recession" and that America had become a "nation of whiners," presidential hopeful, Arizona senator, John McCain retorted, "I think Senator Gramm would be in serious consideration for ambassador to Belarus. Although I'm not sure the citizens of Minsk would welcome that." Yet as I'm writing some final remarks here before going to press, gloom is in the air.

In many ways we were indeed in a mental recession in early 2009, "Ain't it awful, just when our growing company was being propped up by an irrationally exuberant housing boom where houses became cash-spewing ATM machines, and America had become the world's consumption engine; then, low and behold, consumed itself to death. Woe is me."

Whether the anticipated negative impact of a recession was real or imagined, or both, a change in the economy often calls for a change in a company's operating basis. In fact, a recession presents unique opportunities for some companies to expand their businesses. So stop it, stop whining! For, just one thought away, we can find that opportunities are also in the air, opportunities made possible by process and management innovation, which, in turn, are made possible by business platforms in the Cloud.

Business process management is the winch in the Cloud, in upturns and in downturns. In his blog entry "BPM is a Winch Out of the Economic Ditch," esteemed business process management analyst, Jim Sinur, wrote, "I remember my youthful days in the winters of Wisconsin. The roads could become treacherous with weather systems moving in, dumping ice and snow. One night while I was delivering pizzas (my college investment trust fund was sweat equity) and managed to get into a deep ditch packed with snow, along came a guy with a winch-equipped Jeep. He slowly dragged my wheels out of the ditch. I was very grateful and the pizzas were delivered warm at least. I survived to thrive another day and eventually progressed to my end goals.

"Here we go again. I am having that in-the-ditch feeling again (maybe there is a song brewing there). Fear is knocking at the door. Along comes BPM with the winch of leverage to help us pull out of the ditch. The fear of taking risks really limits organizations. When the economy is creaky, this fear phenomenon is magnified. The melancholy cost cutters rule the day, but it does not have to be that way. The entry cost of BPM is low and the proven rates of return make BPM a great jump start for cost savings. As organizations gain confidence in BPM's ability to generate savings, some of the more savvy organizations use BPM saving as way to fund process efforts, instead of just looking for blood letting opportunities.

"It really doesn't matter if you are looking to survive, thrive or capitalize on the economic weather facing us, BPM can be of great help. The telecom industry used BPM as a tourniquet in the mid 2000s, so we know BPM works. It's a new year that will spawn some optimism. Let's parlay some of this energy to get forward momentum to pull ourselves forward to the lip of the ditch. Once we see the top, it should inspire an adrenalin rush for the push out."

In November 2008, Cisco's legendary CEO John Chambers was interviewed by *Fast Company* on how to weather the downturn. "If you watch what is occurring today, people are acting like the sky is falling," says Chambers. But he has learned through numerous economic downturns—he cites 1993, 1997, 2001, and 2003— that it's entirely possible to come out stronger than you were before. "Every time, we have gained market share, and two years later, our customer and employee satisfaction was greater," he says. Here's his advice for facing tough times:

- "Focus on what we can influence, and not over- or under-react to things we cannot. It's a question of living in the world as it is, not the way we want it to be.
- Assess the damage externally—vendors, customers, colleagues. In 2001, we went to our customers in energy, manufacturing, and automotive, to name a few. We asked, 'How are you handling this?'
- Ask yourself, 'Is this a market-driven phenomenon or did we do it to ourselves?' Based on the answers you get, formulate a response. In 2001, our strategy was working extremely well before the downturn, and it seemed to be working from the customers' side, so we said it was 90-10. That turned out to be about right.
- Make a determination of how long this will last and how deep it is going to be. Prepare yourself for it to be longer and deeper than you think. And then build flexibility to adjust quickly if you need to.

- Get ready for the upturn. What's our vision for where this industry is going with or without us? That, he says, is a five-year horizon. What is our differentiated strategy within that vision?" That's a two- to four-year plan. How are we going to execute in the next 12 to 18 months?"[2]

Considering Chambers' sage advice forged from experience, it's important to recognize that we can now do things, especially process-oriented things, in the Cloud we simply couldn't do before. Before I clarify that assertion, let's look back when *unexpected change* changed the course of history. I'll provide just a few examples, although there are many others.

Giannini. Like a lot of folks in the San Francisco area, Amadeo Peter Giannini was thrown from his bed in the wee hours of April 18, 1906, when the Great Quake shook parts of the city to rubble. He hurriedly dressed and hitched a team of horses to a borrowed produce wagon and headed into town—to the Bank of Italy, which he had founded two years earlier. Sifting through the ruins, he discreetly loaded $2 million in gold, coins and securities onto the wagon bed, covered them with a layer of vegetables and headed home.

In the days after the disaster, Giannini broke ranks with his fellow bankers who wanted area banks to remain shut to sort out the damage. Giannini quickly set up shop on the docks near San Francisco's North Beach. With a wooden plank straddling two barrels for a desk, he began to extend credit "on a face and a signature" to small businesses and individuals in need of money to rebuild their lives. His actions spurred the city's redevelopment.

That would have been legacy enough for most people. But Giannini's mark extends far beyond San Francisco, where his determination and focus on "the little people" helped build what was at his death the largest bank in the country, Bank of America. What Giannini had done was to break the established rules and innovate by reaching out to an unserved market, much as microbankers are doing today in emerging markets, at the bottom of the pyramid.

A.P. Giannini in 1929

Of course, that was then. Now in 2009, Bank of America must reinvent itself again, for after the 2008 financial crisis, it found itself holding toxic assets, and begging the U.S. government for billions in bailout funds (receiving $45 billion as of January 2009), especially after it acquired Merrill Lynch and its toxic assets. Will Bank of America continue to be a one-stop financial shop? Or will it be broken up into multiple entities? In either case, there's a lot of restructuring to be done, and lots of business processes to reorient.

Now, rather than two barrels and a wooden plank, Bank of America will need to turn to new business models, and business process and management innovation to integrate Merrill into its system. And BoA will need to imagine new banking opportunities, execute on them, and adjust for the coming financial regulations of major new proportions. Maybe it's time for two barrels and a Cloud.

Perhaps, Bank of America will embrace India's international bank, Bank of Baroda, and form a joint venture to provide financing to the other billion, those at the bottom of the pyramid who actually pay back their loans. Who knows, but such ideas may very well represent the future of finance, thanks to the experimental capabilities enabled by the Cloud. The Could opens a whole new world of possibilities for global innovation with minimal capital investment for the needed support systems. Creative destruction is in the air.

Carrier. So it was the humidity! No it was the heat, stupid! Remember Willis H. Carrier?

Who?

You know, the guy who invented air conditioning.

Willis Carrier was the quintessential rags-to-riches guy, struggling against all odds, persisting, overcoming all obstacles. Though we cannot be sure of her influence on him, his great-great-grandmother, who was known for her keen sense of justice and a sharp tongue, was hanged as a witch by the Puritans in Salem. Slapped down by the Great Depression, he fought back to build a huge enterprise that to this day is the world's leading maker of air conditioning, heating and ventilation systems. Long before what we now see as the power of globalization, in 1930, he started Toyo Carrier and Samsung Applications in Japan and South Korea. South Korea is now the largest market for air conditioning in the world. The Great Depression couldn't hold him back for he thought globally—and out of the box.

Carrier had little respect for business management dogma of the time. In a foreword to a biography written by a Chicago banker who helped bail out Carrier's firm during the Depression and later became its CEO, wrote, "The stage was set for my unforgettable first meeting with 'The Chief.' I had already been told that Dr. Carrier was a genius and that his talents lay in the field of science and invention rather than in operation and finance. All the same I wasn't prepared for what happened ... right off the bat Dr. Carrier made it clear he had a dim view of bankers. I remember so well the ring in his voice when he said to me that day: 'We will not do less research and development work. We will not discharge the people we trained; and we will all work for nothing if we have to.'"

If you think you can cut, cut, cut to crawl your way out of the Crash of 2008, think again, think about Carrier's persistence in times of real strife.

Willis Carrier in 1915

Hmmm? *Persistence* and *experimentation*. "Air conditioning" did not begin as a cooling system for homes and offices. Nor did it begin life as a complete "air conditioning" system. In 1902, Carrier's first customer was a business with a production problem, a printer in Brooklyn whose color reproductions kept messing up because changes in humidity made his paper expand and contract, ruining his color runs. Carrier solved the problem by controlling humidity. Then, in 1906, a cotton mill in South Carolina presented him with a new challenge—heat from the spinning mills. One industrial challenge after another led Carrier to make refinement after refinement in what today are complete air conditioning systems. While Carrrier had innovated in one area, humidity, he never turned back and set the *pace of innovation* in an industry that he had invented.

Perhaps due to his Quaker upbringing, Carrier was also a very nice person, modest and a farsighted manager—he sincerely believed in *teamwork* and *mentoring*, decades before management consultants discovered these fundamental concepts. One of his other management prescripts was that time spent staring into space while thinking is not time wasted.

Is that what Google recognized when it decided to adopt the management practice of giving its employees a full day each week to do whatever they want to do, even if it seems to have nothing to do with Google? The time has come for time spent staring into space. Hmmm? *Persistence* and *experimentation*. The Cloud just could be the place for pay-as-you-go persistence and experimentation. So, go ahead, stare into space, stare into the Cloud.

Miracle on the Hudson. On January 15, 2009, US Airways Flight 1549 took off at 3:26 p.m. from LaGuardia airport in New York. It was less than a minute later when the pilot reported a "double bird strike." With both engines out, a cool-headed pilot maneuvered his crowded jetliner over New York City and ditched it in the frigid Hudson River, and all 155 on board were pulled to safety as the plane slowly sank. It was, the governor of New York said, "a miracle on the Hudson."

The plane, a US Airways Airbus A320 bound for Charlotte, N.C., struck a flock of birds during takeoff minutes earlier at LaGuardia Airport and was submerged up to its windows in the river by the time rescuers arrived in Coast Guard vessels and ferries.

"He is the consummate pilot," the pilot's wife, Lorrie Sullenberger, told the New York Post. Chesley "Sully" Sullenberger is an U.S. Air Force Academy grad who flew F-4 fighter planes while in the Air Force, she said. "He is about performing that airplane to the exact precision to which it is made." Sullenberger is an airline safety expert who has consulted with NASA and others. He has 40 years of experience, 29 with US Airways, and holds masters' degrees in public administration and industrial psychology.

Flight 1549 pilot Chesley "Sully" Sullenberger

"It was intense. It was intense. You've got to give it to the pilot. He made a hell of a landing," passenger Jeff Kolodjay said.

But was it just luck?

Or were Sullenberger and the crew well trained and well prepared. Did they have good systems in place to meet the unexpected? Had *the system*, including US Airways, invested in the training needed to be resilient in the times of unexpected change? The results speak for themselves.

What *really* seemed to make a difference was that the entire crew, and the passengers were given full *information*, in real time. Instead of panicking as might be expected, it seemed that being fully informed all along the way, all involved—passengers, crew and pilots—responded with speed and intelligence. And let's not forget the "responders," the ferry boat captains who steered their crafts to the rescue in just seconds once they saw or heard what was happening. Without being centrally controlled, the parties to the event *swarmed* to respond to the threat—in seconds.

Just as we learned from our exploration of Bioteams, self-organizing teams can indeed perform miracles, even in the face of unexpected change, even in the event of catastrophic change, if they are well prepared and have real-time information broadcast to them. Swarm intelligence!

The Cloud makes such interactions possible, and a whole lot more as we have discovered.

We have a lot of well-prepared organizations, of all sizes, that could connect and collaborate and swarm to build anew, in light of the current challenges and threats in business. In the face of unexpected change they can, especially thanks to enabling power of the Cloud, invent new winning business models and stratagems.

Thinking Out Cloud

So it is with 21st century business competition. Get ready for the unexpected, that which comes out of nowhere, and is limitless.

Quit the recession or depression whining, for if the mind can conceive it, you just might be able to achieve it in the Cloud with process and management innovation—and determination, persistence and inspiration. *The sky's the limit for the Cloud as a platform for business innovation.* So, get out your interactive DVD, and like the movie "Final Destination 3" allows you to do, produce your own high definition ending to this book.

I wish you the best in negotiating the fierce rapids of change we now face. And borrowing from Edward R. Murrow during a time of national fear in the 1950s, "Good night, and good luck." *

---

* Watch: http://tinyurl.com/27uwvw

References.

---

[1] http://www.wired.com/wired/archive/5.07/longboom_pr.html

[2] http://www.fastcompany.com/node/1093655/print

Appendix 1
A Dot.Cloud Glossary

agility
   In business, agility means the capability of rapidly and cost efficiently adapting to changes. See agile enterprise.

agile enterprise
   A fast moving, flexible and robust firm capable of rapid and cost efficient response to unexpected challenges, events, and opportunities. Built on policies and *business processes* that facilitate speed and change, it aims to achieve continuous competitive advantage in serving its customers. Agile enterprises use diffused authority and flat organizational structure to speed up information flows among different departments, and develop close, trust-based relationships with their customers and suppliers: the agile enterprise is the process-managed enterprise with a self-organizing workforce that requires employees to assume multiple roles, improvise, spontaneously collaborate, and rapidly redeploy from one work team to another and another, while simultaneously learning from and teaching their peers.

asynchronous communication
   Eliminates the need for the recipient to be available when the requester is trying to communicate with it. Email is asynchronous; a telephone call is synchronous communication, except in the case where a voice message is left for the recipient. Asynchronous communication is typical in inter and intra team communication in autonomous virtual teams.

autonomous teams
   Self-organizing, self-managed teams that function as part of complex adaptive systems.

bioteams

High performance teams where collective leadership replaces command and control, and team communication is based on short messages that are instantly broadcast and received "in situ" wherever the receivers are.

blog

A blog (a contraction of the term "Web log") is a Web site, usually maintained by an individual with regular entries of commentary, descriptions of events, or other material such as graphics or video. The ability for readers to leave comments in an interactive format is an important part of many blogs.

blowback

The recirculation into the source country of a technology innovation that has been improved by a developing country, and then taken global by the developing country, giving it competitive advantage over the source country.

boundary manager

The boundary manager represents a new role for traditional managers that replaces internal team supervision with coordination of inter-team interactions.

business innovation

Much more than just *invention*, business innovation is the creation of new business models and initiatives that bring compelling new value to the marketplace. 3M's Geoffrey Nickelson once described the critical point, "Research is the transformation of money into knowledge. Innovation is the transformation of knowledge into money."

business operations platform

A Cloud Platform that provides complete business process management services to support dynamic multi-company business processes. The platform puts on-demand processes into the hands of business users, allowing multiple companies to come together to seize an opportunity or thwart a business threat.

business process management (BPM)

The management philosophies and technologies used to manage the full lifecycle of business processes (discovery, design, deployment, analysis and optimization). BPM is first and foremost a holistic process-managed approach to business versus a functional management approach to business. For an in-depth understanding, read *Business Process Management: The Third Wave* (mkpress.com).

business process management system (BPMS)

A BPMS is a software system that enables companies to model, deploy and manage business processes that span multiple enterprise applications, corporate departments and business partners—behind the firewall and over the Internet.

business process

A business process is the complete and dynamically coordinated set of collaborative and transactional activities that deliver value to customers. Business processes are how work gets done.

chaordic

A system that blends characteristics of chaos and order. The term was coined by Dee Hock, founder of Visa. The mix of chaos and order is often described as a harmonious coexistence displaying characteristics of both, with neither chaotic nor ordered behavior dominating. Some hold that nature is largely organized in such a manner; in particular, living organisms and the evolutionary process by which they arose are often described as chaordic in nature.

Cloud

In lay terms the Cloud is "My software, my storage, my computing power all residing somewhere *up there*, somewhere in the Cloud. It's all about the disembodiment of the *system* itself. The Cloud is an abstract concept, not a physical entity, consisting of computing, communication and information resources that can be accessed as services over the Internet. (See also Cloud Computing).

Cloud Computing

In its essence, Cloud Computing is a massive distributed computing model consisting of three tiers: *infrastructure, platform* and *services* (see below), and is about using swarms of computers to deliver unprecedented computing power to people and organizations across the globe.

cloud infrastructure

The foundation tier of Cloud Computing that provides the storage, and computer power, and networks and servers that enable self-service automation, scaling , flexing, variable costs, and rich data and analytics.

cloud platform

The tools, programming and information models, supporting software runtime components, and related technologies. Platforms facilitate implementing Cloud Services that depend on the Cloud Computing infrastructure tier, e.g., Amazon Web Services and Google Apps.

cloud services

A delivery model for information services for businesses and individuals that build on a cloud platform to create dynamic processes and applications.

collective leadership

As a cornerstone of the notion of *bioteams*, collective leadership means that any group member can take the lead. Nature's groups are never led exclusively by one member; different group members lead as needed. Multi-Leader groups possess much greater agility, initiative and resilience than groups that are only led by a single exclusive leader.

commitment processing

In traditional IT information tracking is the object of computing support. In human interaction management systems, commitments made between and among participants is the object of computing support. See also, speech acts.

complex adaptive systems

A dynamic network of many agents acting in parallel, constantly acting and reacting to what the other agents are doing. Control tends to be highly dispersed and decentralized. Coherent behavior in the system arises from competition and cooperation among the agents themselves, resulting from a huge number of decisions made every moment by many individual agents.

computer utility

Computer utility and grid computing are often defined as one and the same, but grid computing is the actual technology, and the computer utility is the pay-as-you-use pricing model.

coopetition

The business model where a company cooperates with a competitor to gain mutual benefit. For example, Virgin Mobile uses Sprint's mobile phone network infrastructure in the U.S. They both compete against each other for customers, but share revenues from Virgin customers.

creative destruction

Economist Joseph Schumpeter describes creative destruction as innovations that cause old inventories, ideas, technologies, skills, and equipment to become obsolete, sometimes over night. Sparks of radical innovation by entrepreneurs topple incumbents and drive long-term economic growth. Increasingly, incumbents are turning to the notion of *internal* creative destruction to reinvigorate performance, even at the expense of traditional lines of business.

crowd sourcing

The act of taking a task traditionally performed by an employee, internal group or contractor, and outsourcing it to an undefined, generally large group of people, in the form of an open call to develop a new technology, carry out a design task, or help capture, systematize or analyze large amounts of data.

customer-driven innovation
This is a form of outside-in innovation where, through ongoing dialogs with customers (face-to-face, blogs, wikis, social networks), unanticipated needs are uncovered and unanticipated uses of products and services are uncovered and drive innovation.

customization
See personalization.

distributed computing
Distributed computing approaches have come under many names over the years: parallel computing, grid computing, cluster computing, hardware as a service, on-demand computing, Web computing, autonomic computing, utility computing and more. These days the concept of computing in the Cloud encompasses all or parts of these technical terms.

emerging business opportunities
A unique management system and approach to business innovation, well documented by IBM during its 1990s comeback, that focuses on "white space" or "at the edge" opportunities that can become profitable businesses. New concepts are incubated through small pilots—*experiments* involving just a few prominent customers. Experimentation is key to the management of risk when it comes to innovation.

Enterprise 2.0
An organization that uses social software in a business context. The professional association, AIIM, defines Enterprise 2.0 as a system of Web-based technologies that provide rapid and agile collaboration, information sharing, emergence and integration capabilities in the extended enterprise.

freeconomics
Once a marketing gimmick, "free" has emerged as a full-fledged economy, where the freemium business model has been applied across many industries, including technology, transport,

media, medicine and finance.

freemium
Free and premium. A business model where basic services are offered for free, while charging a premium for advanced features.

generatives
A value that is a quality or attribute that must be generated, grown, cultivated, nurtured. A generative thing can not be copied, cloned, faked, replicated, counterfeited, or reproduced. It is generated uniquely, in place, over time. In the digital arena, generative qualities add value to free copies, and therefore are something that can be sold.

grid computing
A form of distributed computing whereby a "super and virtual computer" is composed of a cluster of networked, loosely-coupled computers, acting in concert to perform very large tasks. Grids form an infrastructure foundation for Cloud Computing.

human interaction management
A set of management principles, patterns and techniques complementary to business process management that provides process-based support for human work and allows it to be integrated in a structured way with more routinized work processes that are often largely automated. HIM unifies various existing disciplines (Role Activity Theory, Cognitive Theory, Social Systems Theory, Learning Theory, and process-based Computer Science disciplines) into a complete theory of human, collaborative work, and shows how this theory can be used not only to model, but also to manage, any human-driven business processes.

hypervisor
A hypervisor, also called a virtual machine manager, is a program that allows multiple operating systems to share a single hardware host. For example, Xen is a virtual machine monitor that allows several guest operating systems to be executed on the same

computer hardware concurrently. Xen was initially created by the University of Cambridge Computer Laboratory and is now developed and maintained by the Xen community as free software.

innovation

Something new. But there's much more to innovation than *invention*: see business innovation.

long tail

A term coined by Chris Anderson of *Wired* magazine, describes the niche strategy of businesses, such as Amazon.com or Netflix, that offer a large number of unique items, each in relatively small quantities. An Amazon employee described the long tail as follows: "We sold more books today that didn't sell at all yesterday than we sold today of all the books that did sell yesterday."

loosely coupled

Loosely coupled services, even if they use incompatible system technologies, may be joined to create composite services. This ability for services to be joined on demand is a foundation of service-oriented architecture (SOA).

management

In the wired world of the 21st century, management has started to become based less on the notion of command-and-control, and more about facilitation and support of collaborative activity, utilizing principles such as those of human interaction management to deal with the complexities of self-managed teams.

mashup

The ability to develop new integrated services quickly, to combine internal services with external or personalized information, and to make these services tangible to the business user through user interfaces, blending SOA and Web 2.0 capabilities. Business mashups extend the idea to the rapid creation of virtual network enterprises, virtual corporations and extended enterprises.

master data management (MDM)

Methods and techniques used to ensure that master data, as contrasted with transactional data, remains consistent across computer applications and Web services. In the past, various departments of large companies often maintained their own master data, creating inconsistency problems. For example, when a given department made a name change due to a woman getting married, other departments still had the maiden name. As companies embrace cross-departmental BPM and adopt service-oriented business models, MDM is absolutely essential.

multi-tenancy

A principle in software architecture where a single instance of the software runs on a Cloud services provider's infrastructure, serving multiple client organizations or tenants. Each tenant organization works with a customized virtual set of computing resources.

network effects

The beneficial effect when the number of other people consuming the same kind of good or service grows, making the good or service increasingly valuable. The classic example is the telephone. The more people own telephones, the more valuable the telephone is to each owner. Web 2.0 creates many new opportunities that engender network effects that have great implication for businesses. Social software, blogs, wikis, Web syndication, Skype, MySpace, Facebook, and tagging, all provide vehicles to build communal knowledge and collaboration via network effects.

Office 2.0

A type of office suite offered by websites in the form of software as a service that can be accessed online from any Internet-enabled device running any operating system. The term is a neologism originated from Ismael Ghalimi in an experimental effort to test how much of his computer-based work he could accomplish using online productivity tools rather than the more traditional packages running on a local PC.

on demand

On-demand computing most frequently refers to a type of computing service where the actual software is presented to the user, once a subscription to the service is successfully processed. In a typical on-demand computing model, the software is not actually installed at the user device, rather it is accessed via the Internet or centralized access point. On-demand software is typically delivered by an application service provider. This type of service offering is also frequently referred to as Software as a Service (SaaS). See also on-demand processes.

on-demand processes

By externalizing a company's business processes, they can be rendered as services that can be integrated into end-to-end processes with participants including suppliers, trading partners and customers allowing the entire value delivery system to respond to changing customer demands, market opportunities and threats. In the Cloud, business users expect to be able to personalize their work environment, customize look and feel, update content using information from any source at any time, all within a single browser environment. In addition, they want to add new functionality, change processes and share these with others, e.g., project reporting, ad-hoc collaborations, request for proposal, and prototyping. On-demand processes are a cornerstone of business agility and empowering self-managed teams.

ontology

A cornerstone of the emerging Web 3.0, an ontology in computer science and information science is a formal representation of a set of concepts within a domain and the relationships between those concepts; or in short, a specification of a shared conceptualization. An ontology provides a shared vocabulary, that can be used to model a domain: the types of objects and concepts that exist, and their properties and relations. Ontologies are used in artificial intelligence, the Semantic Web, software engineering, biomedical informatics, library science, and information architecture as a form of knowledge representation about the world or some part of it.

open innovation

The idea behind open innovation is that in a world of widely distributed knowledge, companies cannot afford to rely entirely on their own research, but should instead buy or license processes or inventions from outsiders. Conversely, internal inventions not being used in a firm's business should be taken outside the company (e.g., through licensing, joint ventures, spin-offs). In contrast, closed innovation refers to processes that limit the use of internal knowledge within a company and make little or no use of external knowledge. Don't confuse open innovation with open source, free software. Open innovation is all about the money to be made.

participants

In the world of technology, we speak of computer "users." In the world of Web 1.0 people were users that basically had Web pages served up to them (the read-only Internet). In the world of Web 2.0, users become "participants," *prosumers* (producers and consumers) actively contributing the information base with which they work and share with others (the read-write Internet).

passion

Winning companies harness the passion, energy and competitive spirit of *all* of its people, while typical companies bury those factors under a pyramid of management hierarchies and bureaucracies. Human teams have huge amounts of discretion and self-awareness, and thus need a sense of purpose, a common set of shared values and passion—we can't treat a human team like an ant colony. It's a shared vision, a higher calling at Whole Foods Markets, "Whole Foods, Whole People, Whole Planet" that creates the passion that drives the company's self-managed teams toward the future. Without such vision and passion, people become short-sighted and mean-spirited, looking out only for themselves.

personalization

Web pages are personalized based on the interests of an individual. Personalization implies that the changes are based on implicit data, such as items purchased or pages viewed or music listened to (e.g., Amazon suggested titles). The term customization is used when a company uses explicit data such as ratings or preferences to give its customers an opportunity to create and choose product to certain specifications (e.g., Pandora.com radio).

podcast
A podcast is an audio or video distributed over the Internet by syndicated download, through Web feeds, to portable media players and personal computers. The host or author of a podcast is often called a podcaster. The term is a portmanteau of the words iPod and broadcast and was redefined by some parties as a backronym for "Personal On Demand broadCASTING."

predictions
The late management expert, Peter Drucker, once said about predictions: "It is not so very difficult to predict the future. It is only pointless. But equally important, one cannot make a decision for the future. Decisions are commitments to action. And actions are always in the present, and in the present only. But actions in the present are also the one and only way to make the future." These are the reasons companies are shifting from "make to forecast" to "make to demand," and why *agility* is the Holy Grail of business.

process-managed enterprise
An enterprise where the leaders recognize that it's the end-to-end, enterprise-wide business processes that make or break the company, not the optimization of functional units or departments within the enterprise. Process management, not functional management, is the overarching management approach and philosophy. The process-managed enterprise requires BPM systems to realize the goals they set for holistic process management work. Companies that adopt this perspective often interchange the terms BPM and BPM systems, for the two go hand in glove if management intent is to be translated into execution. See also: business process management (BPM).

process enterprise versus functional enterprise

In a functional enterprise, no one has overall responsibility for an end-to-end process. Department or unit managers are specialized by function (silos), e.g., account, sales, production and so on, and are responsible only for a narrow segment of a process. No one is empowered to knock down silos, and optimize the overall end-to-end process. As we are instructed by general systems theory, optimizing individual functions does not lead to optimizing the overall process. Traditional functional organizations interfere with the ability of their people to perform process work.

prosumer

Producer–consumer. The role of producers and consumers begin to blur and merge to reach a high degree of mass customization. Consumers take part in the production process especially in specifying design requirements (e.g., configuring a PC from HP or Smart car from Mercedes). Web 2.0 takes the notion of prosuming a step further, where in cases like Wikipedia prosuming is all.

reputation management

The process of tracking opinions about people, companies, products and services, reporting on those opinions, and reacting to create a positive feedback loop. Reputation is different from branding for the fact that the former can be created and the latter is an identity that evolves. Reputation management is neither public relation nor data collecting or advertisement management. It deals with the root cause of a problem, offers solutions, sets processes in motion and monitors progress towards these solutions. Reputation management systems use various predefined criteria for processing complex data to report reputation. Reputation management has come into wide use with the advent of Web 2.0 social networks.

reuse

Reuse of preexisting software has been the Holy Grail of software engineering for years (e.g., subroutines, code libraries, patterns, object inheritance, components and frameworks). In the world of service-oriented architecture, reuse goals take a major step forward through designing services that are abstract, stateless, autonomous loosely coupled. And the key is that the abstractions of services represent reusable business process segments, not just reusable software. Those process segments can be reused as companies design innovative business processes as "situational" business processes across for multiple business channels. That is, they can be adapted to completely new business situations. So it is that software flexibility and reuse enables business process flexibility and reuse. That's the stuff of business agility in hyper-competitive markets.

secondees

People who are temporarily reassigned from each partner to a joint venture that are *committed* to the successful completion of the project. Secondees are critical to virtual network enterprises and other forms of extended enterprises where business processes are to be optimized across the entire value delivery system.

service

Software components that are essentially collections of self-contained software that can be accessed and used without knowing the location or platform the service is deployed on. What's really important is that "services" are packaged to contain repeatable *business tasks* or *business process segments*, not technical packages. Thus a service is simply a business task, such as ship completed order, which, in turn, is a part of a larger sales process. Services become the Lego blocks for building software, and situational business processes rapidly and efficiently.

service-oriented architecture (SOA)

A set of organizing principles that provide a comprehensible structure or framework for modeling and constructing complex systems. Certain architectural principles are used in the design of services so that they are reusable, abstract, autonomous, stateless, discoverable, composable, and loosely coupled. The potential benefits of service-oriented computing include a major reduction in the cost of software development, and speed and agility in building or changing software—and business processes—as business needs change. See also: service.

situational business processes

Business processes that are disembodied as "services" and whose many different uses weren't known at the time the processes were developed. On-demand processes can be mashed up in new ways as participants in other processes. For example, an airline's processes for flight planning, reservations and ticketing could be mashed up with a conference organizer's registration process. In each situation, the policies and business rules governing the processes will likely be slightly different. Thus situational business processes, whose unintended contexts may draw on a given company's core processes, could become the norm; and they must be managed as diligently as all other mission-critical business processes. See also: on-demand processes.

social networks

Web-based communities of people who share interests and activities, or are interested in exploring the interests and activities of others. Most social network services provide a variety of ways for users to interact, such as e-mail and instant messaging services. One example of social networking being used for business purposes is LinkedIn.com, which aims to interconnect professionals: more than 20 million registered users from 150 different industries.

speech acts

Although a theory used in linguistics and the philosophy of language, speech acts are the foundation for tracking negotiations and commitments in workgroups. In providing computing support of human interaction management, a network of speech acts can constitute straightforward "conversations for action," where requests, promises, declarations and commitments can be tracked and audited. This model of support for human-driven work processes shifts the computing paradigm from "information processing" to "commitment processing," putting management controls into the otherwise noisy and confusing forms of collaboration.

swarm

Swarm intelligence is artificial intelligence based on the collective behavior of decentralized, self-organized systems, typically made up of a population of simple agents interacting locally with one another and with their environment. The agents follow very simple rules, and although there is no centralized control structure dictating how individual agents should behave, local interactions between such agents lead to the emergence of complex global behavior. Natural examples include ant colonies, bird flocking, animal herding, bacterial growth, and fish schooling. In a business context these notions are a foundation for Bioteams which in turn make it possible for virtual networked enterprises to swarm in response to new business opportunities and threats.

time-based competition

A competitive strategy that emphasizes *time* over *costs*, as *the* major factor of competitive advantage. For example, products fifty percent over budget but introduced on time have been found to generate higher profit levels than products brought to market within budget but six months late. To become a time-based competitor, a firm must change its current processes and alter the decision structures used to design, produce and deliver to the customer. Time-based competition appears in two different forms: fast to market and fast to produce. Firms that compete with fast-to-market strategies emphasize reductions in design lead-time. Fast-to-product firms emphasize speed in responding to customer demands for existing products. Wal-Mart has been able to dominate its industry by replenishing its stores twice as fast as its competitors. Firms competing in this area focus on lead-time reduction throughout the system, from the time the customer places an order until the customer ultimately receives the product.

users

See participants.

utility computing

The packaging of computing resources, such as computation and storage, as a metered service similar to a traditional public electricity or water utility. Also referred to as on-demand computing, advantages center on eliminating the costs of acquiring hardware, especially sufficient hardware to accommodate peak loads. Companies with very large computations or a sudden peak in demand can also avoid the delays that would result from physically acquiring and assembling a large number of computers. Utility computing is the marketing model, "grid computing" is the technical distributed computing model. See also: on demand and grid computing.

virtual enterprise network

Multiple companies band together to create more comprehensive solutions to market needs, and small companies band together with large companies to bring innovation to market.

virtualization

In computer science, a technique used to implement a certain kind of virtual machine environment that provides a complete simulation of the underlying hardware. The result is a system in which all software capable of execution on the raw hardware can be run in the virtual machine, including all operating systems. It hides the physical characteristics of computing platform from the users.

Web 2.0

The term "Web 2.0" describes the changing trends in the *usage* of World Wide Web technology and Web design that aim to enhance creativity, communications, secure information sharing, collaboration and functionality of the Web.

Web 3.0

A supposed third generation of Internet-based services. Web 1.0 was read-only, Web 2.0 is read-write, and Web 3.0 will be read-write-execute. Web 3.0 (the intelligent Web) will involve yet another step-change in how we use the Internet and tame the infoglut. For example, ontologies will provide the semantics behind the Semantic Web opening up new possibilities for intelligent agents to do our bidding, and open information extraction (IE) will power new forms of search in a way that avoids the tedious and error-prone tasks of sifting through documents returned by a search engine.

wiki
A wiki is a collection of Web pages designed to enable anyone who accesses them to contribute or modify content, using a simplified markup language. Wikis are often used to create collaborative Web sites and to power community Web sites. The collaborative encyclopedia Wikipedia is one of the best-known wikis. Wikis are used in business to provide intranet and knowledge management systems. In contrast, a blog (Web log), typically authored by an individual, does not allow visitors to change the original posted material, only add comments. Wiki means "quick" in Hawaiian.

wisdom of crowds
A diverse collection of independently-deciding individuals is likely to make certain types of decisions and predictions better than individuals or even experts. The idea draws many parallels with statistical sampling, where the average of the averages equals the true average. The wisdom of crowds manifests itself in social networks and prediction markets.

Work Processor
Companies wouldn't hire a new office worker without providing him or her with a "word processor," but why don't companies also provide each executive, manager and employee with a "Work Processor?" The Work Processor, can be equated to the more sophisticated term, the business process management system.

Appendix 2:

TechTarget's Fun Glossary of Cloud Concepts

TechTarget.com's Margaret Rouse asked in her blog, "Have you ever wanted to make up a word? Now's the time. Just make sure it has something to do with a Cloud. Play a little Rolling Stones and get those neurons firing (Hey, hey, hey, hey — get off of my cloud). I just want to jot these down before I forget. Seems like every day I stumble across more newly-coined cloud terms.[1]

"Did you know how Cloud Computing got its name?
From flowcharts, where a cloud is used to represent the Internet"

cloud app – a software application that is never installed on a local machine; it's always accessed over the Internet.

cloud arcs – short for cloud architectures. Designs for software applications that can be accessed and used over the Internet. (Cloud-architecture is just too hard to pronounce.)

cloud bridge – running an application in such a way that its components are integrated within multiple cloud environments (which could be any combination of internal/private and external/public clouds).

cloudcenter – a large company, such as Amazon, that rents its infrastructure.

cloud client – computing device for cloud computing. Updated version of thin client.

cloud envy – used to describe a vendor who jumps on the cloud computing bandwagon by rebranding existing services.

cloud portability – the ability to move applications and associated data across multiple cloud computing environments.

cloud provider – makes storage or software available to others over a private network or public network (like the Internet.)

cloud service architecture (CSA) – an architecture in which applications and application components act as services on the Internet

cloud storage – (just what it says) Sometimes compared to leasing a car. You'll have monthly payments but hopefully you'll always have the latest and greatest technology. You don't own the technology though.

cloudburst – what happens when your cloud has an outage or security breach and your data is unavailable.

cloud as a service (CaaS) – a cloud computing service that has been opened up into a platform that others can build upon.

cloud-oriented architecture (COA) – IT architecture that lends itself well to incorporating cloud computing components.

cloudsourcing – outsourcing storage or taking advantage of some other type of cloud service.

cloudstorm – connecting multiple cloud computing environments. Also called cloud network.

cloudware – software that enables building, deploying, running or managing applications in a cloud computing environment.

cloudwashing – slapping the word "cloud" on products and services you already have.

external cloud – a cloud computing environment that is external to the boundaries of the organization.

funnel cloud – discussion about cloud computing that goes round and round but never turns into action (never "touches the ground")

hybrid cloud – a computing environment that combines both private and public cloud computing environments.

internal cloud – also called a private cloud. A cloud computing-like environment within the boundaries of an organization.

private cloud – an internal cloud behind the organization's firewall. The company's IT department provides software and hardware as a service to its customers, the people who work for the company. Vendors love the words "private cloud."

public cloud – a cloud computing environment that is open for use to the general public.

roaming workloads – the backend product of cloudcenters.

vertical cloud – a cloud computing environment optimized for use in a particular vertical industry

virtual private cloud (VPC) – similar to virtual private networks but applied to cloud computing. Can be used to bridge private cloud and public cloud environments.

---

[1] http://itknowledgeexchange.techtarget.com/overheard/overheard-the-new-vocabulary-of-cloud-computing-glossary

Appendix 3:

Andy Mulholland's Technology Predictions

Andy Mulholland, coauthor of *Mashup Corporations* and *Mesh Collaboration*, and his colleague, Ron Tolido, serve up a number of predictions that can stimulate thinking about the Cloud and the future of business. Here is a compiled list of their predictions:

1. *Deliberately Disconnected.* Confronted every day with an ocean of information and stimuli, we will more and more actively seek to disconnect ourselves from the madness whenever we need.

2. *Cisco will be KLM–Air France's biggest challenger.* For obvious reasons, we will travel less in the future and instead use technology to communicate and collaborate.

3. *First convict for hacking into a Cloud.* The Cloud is destined to become main stream. And as the definite proof of it, hackers will become attracted by it.

4. *Stop this Web 2.0 hocus pocus, we told you so.* For that matter, next to the Cloud, Web 2.0 is finally becoming business mainstream. Another definite proof of it: we'll see the first monumental failures.

5. *Email is dead.* Enough is enough! Outlook and BlackBerry will no longer rule our lives.

6. *Cloud-in-a-container.* Business will start using the Cloud. But some will prefer to experiment with a safer Cloud "on premise." It's like having a cloud on the ground that you can look into.

7. *WebKit surpasses Flash Player penetration.* WebKit is a piece of open source software that is so widely used that it will even surpass the device penetration of Adobe's Flash player.

8. *"Trust" is the new version of "Control."* Did we already predict that the Cloud will be main stream? Anyway, as a result, we will rely more on trusting others (Cloud suppliers for example) than on control by ourselves.

9. *Music-as-a-Service (…at last).* Any music, at any time, in any way, at any device: We'll see a breakthrough for – well – a Cloud of music.

10. *Let's socialize!* We're all recognizing the power of social networks. And next year, social networking, like FaceBook will even happen in business.

11. *Standards bodies wake up to clouds.* Is it Groundhog Day or what? Anyway, with the Cloud penetrating the enterprise, standards bodies will become much more active, for example around service management and security.

12. *Bricolage IT.* Central IT departments may lack the budget and the energy to pick up a new generation of IT tools that aim for the near proximity of business. So business units are bound to do it themselves, in true "bricolage" (tinkering) style.

13. *Information filtering and behavioral targeting are the new gold.* There is too much information and we are almost overrun by it. Filtering and behavioral targeting are the new tools to deal with it.

14. *Slow IT. Stop ADHD!* We will contemplate our IT household and choose for a more careful, better balanced use of technology.

15. *The end of the user.* We will stop considering persons as "users" of information technology and instead we all become "participants" of systems, actually becoming one with information technology.

16. *Death of the money making core product.* Forget about making a profit on your core product. Instead, businesses will make creative use of Web 2.0 to sell ancillary products and services that generate a much better margin (freemium).

17. *A more sensible approach to de-risking data loss.* We will see many

more examples of holistic security and information management as a major step towards mitigating the risk of data loss. Buzzword to follow: Enterprise Digital Rights Management (EDRM).

18. *"Open" is the new "Closed."* Open up your assets to the outside world and find innovative ways to collaborate and co-create.

We'll witness a new emphasis on standards, trust and security. And, amid all the buzz, we'll leave technology every now and then for what it is. That's a lot to look forward to.

There's no better timing than right now to contemplate your plans for the future. Meditate more. Pick up Chinese boxing training again. Write a book about Slow IT. You know, just the basic, ordinary stuff we can all relate to.

But why not do it a bit differently? What if the CIO would share his or her IT "Things To Do" with the company? Wouldn't that be a simple and transparent tool to communicate and share the IT strategy? And wouldn't it be an interesting exercise to condense that complete strategy into a couple (7, 12, 43, whatever) of simple, straightforward targets that others can understand and comment on? Or why not create a wish list of personal IT activities that we should definitely consider? To get that started, here is my first list of IT activities that people may want to plan for:

1. Build your own mashups
2. Become a Togaf 9 certified architect
3. Give and get one OLPC laptop
4. Use a cloud application
5. Blog about your project
6. Install Ubuntu Linux on a PC
7. Start a community on Ning
8. Get a personal KPI gadget on your desktop
9. Try an Android smart phone
10. Use social networking tools within the IT department

Recommended Reading

There are already a great number of books dealing with the technical details of service-oriented architecture (SOA) and Web 2.0. Thus, this reading list mainly presents the *business* treatments of these and other topics covered in this book. No techie books here. Depending on your business or technology interests many of the following books may be of interest, and some may be:
** *Strongly recommended, and*
* *Highly recommended*

We'll update the reading list at
www.mkpress.com/cloudreading

* Anderson, Chris, *The Long Tail: Why the Future of Business is Selling Less of More,* Hyperion, 2006.

* Anderson, Chris, *Free: The Past and Future of a Radical Price,* Hyperion, 2009. For a preview check out, "Free! Why $0.00 Is the Future of Business," http://www.wired.com/techbiz/it/magazine/16-03/ff_free?currentPage=all

* Barlow, George, *Strategic Business Modeling: Technology Enablement for Business Leaders,* Meghan-Kiffer Press, 2009.

Barwise, Patrick and Sean Meehan, *Simply Better: Winning and Keeping Customers by Delivering What Matters Most,* Harvard Business School Press, 2004.

Berkeley, U.C., "Above the Clouds: A Berkeley View of Cloud Computing," Febuary 10, 2009, Technical Report, http://www.eecs.berkeley.edu/Pubs/TechRpts/2009/EECS-2009-28.pdf

Bono, Edward de, *Six Thinking Hats,* Penguin Books, 1999.

Brache, Alan, *How Organizations Work,* Wiley, 2002.

* Brafman, Ori and Rod A. Beckstrom, *The Starfish And the Spider:*

The Unstoppable Power of Leaderless Organizations, Portfolio, 2006.

Brodsky, Norm and Bo Burlingham, *The Knack: How Street-Smart Entrepreneurs Learn to Handle Whatever Comes Up,* Portfolio, 2008.

Business Process Management Group, *In Search Of BPM Excellence: Straight From The Thought Leaders,* Meghan-Kiffer Press, 2005.

* Carter, Sandy, *The New Language of Business: SOA and Web 2.0,* IBM Press, 2007.

* Carter, Sandy, *The New Language of Marketing 2.0: How to Use Angels to Energize Your Market,* IBM Press, 2008.

* Chesbrough, Henry, *Open Innovation—The New Imperative for Creating and Profiting from Technology,* Harvard Business Press, 2003.

Chowdhury, Subir, *Design For Six Sigma—The Revolutionary Process for achieving Extraordinary Profits,* FT Prentice Hall, 2003.

Christensen, Clayton M., *The Innovator's Solution—Creating and Sustaining Successful Growth,* Harvard Business School Press, 2003.

Christensen, Clayton, Scott D., Anthony, Roth A., Erik, *Seeing What's Next—Using the Theories of Innovation to Predict Industry Change,* Harvard Business School Press, 2004.

Cloke, Kenneth and Joan Goldsmith, *The Art of Waking People Up,* Jossey-Bass, 2003.

* Cloke, Kenneth and Joan Goldsmith, *The End of Management and the Rise of Organizational Democracy,* Jossey-Bass, 2002.

Cross, Robert L. and Andrew Parker, *The Hidden Power of Social Networks: Understanding How Work Really Gets Done in Organizations,* Harvard Business School Press, 2004.

Davenport, Thomas H. and Laurence Prusak, *Working Knowledge,*

Harvard Business School Press, 2000.

Davenport, Thomas H., *Thinking for a Living: How to Get Better Performance And Results from Knowledge Workers,* Harvard Business School Press, 2005.

Drucker, Peter, *Management Challenges of the 21st Century,* Harper Business, 1999.

Dver, Alyssa, *No Time Marketing: Small Business-sized Steps in 30 Minutes or Less,* Anclote Press, 2009.

Erl, Thomas, *SOA Principles of Service Design,* Prentice Hall, 2007.

Erl, Thomas, *Service-Oriented Architecture (SOA): Concepts, Technology, and Design,* Prentice Hall, 2005.

Erl, Thomas, *SOA Design Patterns,* Prentice Hall, 2009.

* Estrin, Judy, *Closing the Innovation Gap: Reigniting the Spark of Creativity in a Global Economy,* McGraw-Hill, 2008.

Fingar, Peter, and Joseph Bellini, *The Real-Time Enterprise: Competing on Time,* Meghan-Kiffer Press, 2005.

Fingar, Peter, and Ronald Aronica, *The Death of "e" and the Birth of the Real New Economy: Business Models, Technologies and Strategies for the 21st Century,* Meghan-Kiffer Press, 2005.

** Fingar, Peter, *Extreme Competition: Innovation and the Great 21st Century Business Reformation,* Meghan-Kiffer Press, 2007.

Foster, Richard, and Sarah Kaplan, *Creative Destruction: Why Companies That Are Built to Last Underperform the Market--And How to Successfully Transform Them,* Currency, 2001.

Galbraith, Jay R., *Designing the Customer-Centric Organization: A Guide to Strategy, Structure, and Process,* Wiley 2005.

Goleman, Daniel, and Richard Boyatzis and Annie McKee, *Primal Leadership: Realizing the Power of Emotional Intelligence,* Harvard Business School Press, 2002.

* Garimella, Kiran, *The Power of Processs,* Meghan-Kiffer Press, 2007.

Graham, Douglas and Bachmann, Thomas T., *Ideation—The Birth and Death of Ideas,* Wiley, 2004.

Grantham, Charles, Jim Ware and Cory Williamson, Corporate Agility: A Revolutionary New Model for Competing in a Flat World, Amacom, 2007.

* Greenfield, Adam, *Everyware: The Dawning Age of Ubiquitous Computing,* New Riders, 2006.

* Hahn, Robert, *Information Markets: A New Way of Making Decisions,* AEI Press, 2006.

Hamel, Gary, "Strategy as Revolution," *Harvard Business Review,* July-August 1996.

Hamel, Gary and Bill Breen, *The Future of Management,* Harvard Business School Press, 2007.

Handy, Charles, *The New Alchemists: How Visionary People Make Something Out Of Nothing,* Hutchinson, 2004 re-issue edition.

Hargagon, Andrew, *How Breakthroughs Happen—The Surprising Truth About How Companies Innovate,* Harvard Business School Press, 2003.

Harmon, Paul, *Business Process Change*, Morgan Kaufmann, 2003.

** Harrison-Broninski, Keith, *Human Interactions: The Heart And Soul Of Business Process Management,* Meghan-Kiffer Press, 2005.

Harvard Business Essentials, *Managing Creativity and Innovation,*

Harvard Business School Press, 2003.

* Hayes, Tom, *Jump Point: How Network Culture is Revolutionizing Business*, McGraw-Hill, 2008.

* Heath, Chip and Dan Heath, *Made to Stick: Why Some Ideas Survive and Others Die*, Random House, 2007.

Herbold, Robert J., *The Fiefdom Syndrome*, Doubleday, 2004

Heskett, Jim, W. Earl Sasser ,and Joe Wheeler, *The Ownership Quotient: Putting the Service Profit Chain to Work for Unbeatable Competitive Advantage*, Harvard Business School Press, 2008.

* Hock, Dee W., *Birth of the Chaordic Age*, Berrett-Koehler, 2000.

* Hock, Dee W., *One from Many: The Rise of Chaordic Organization*, Berrett-Koehler, 2005.

* Howe, Jeff, *Crowdsourcing: Why the Power of the Crowd Is Driving the Future of Business*, Crown Business, 2008.

* Hugos, Michael, *The Greatest Innovation Since the Assembly Line: Powerful Strategies for Business Agility*, Meghan-Kiffer Press, 2008.

* Jeston, John and Johan Nelis, *Management by Process: A Practical Road-map to Sustainable Business Process Management*, Butterworth Heinemann, 2008.

Jeston, John and Johan Nelis, *Business Process Management, Second Edition: Practical Guidelines to Successful Implementations*, Butterworth Heinemann, 2008.

* Jeston, John, *What Managers Need to Know About the Management of Business Processes*, Meghan-Kiffer Press, 2009.

Jones, Tim, *Innovating At The Edge—How Organizations Evolve and Embed Innovation Capability*, Butterworth Heinemann, 2002.

Kaplan S., Robert, Norton P., David, *Strategy Maps—Converting Intangible Assets Into Tangible Outcomes,* Harvard Business Press, 2004.

Kaplan, Robert S. and David P. Norton, *The Strategy-Focused Organization,* Harvard Business School Press, 2001.

Kelly, Kevin, *Out of Control: The New Biology of Machines, Social Systems, and the Economic World,* Basic Books, 1995.

* Kelly, Kevin, *New Rules for the New Economy,* Penguin, 1995.

Kelley, Tom and Jonathan Littman, *The Art of Innovation—Lessons in Creativity from IDEO, America's Leading Design Firm,* Profile Books, 2004.

Kim, W. Chan, and Renée Mauborgne, *Blue Ocean Strategy: How to Create Uncontested Market Space and Make Competition Irrelevant,* Harvard Business School Press, 2005.

Kotter, John, *A Sense of Urgency,* Harvard Business Press, 2008.

Kotter, John, *Leading Change,* Harvard Business Press, 1996.

Kurtz, Cynthia, *Working With Stories,* (free e-book), www.workingwithstories.org

** Li, Charlene and Josh Bernoff, *Groundswell: Winning in a World Transformed by Social Technologies,* Harvard Business Press, 2008.

Malone, T. W., K. G. Crowston, and G.Herman, (Eds.), *Organizing Business Knowledge: The MIT Process Handbook,* MIT Press, 2003.

Malone, Thomas W., Laubacher, R. J., and Scott Morton, *Inventing the Organizations of the 21st Century,* MIT Press, 2003.

Malone, Thomas W., *The Future of Work: How the New Order of Business Will Shape Your Organization, Your Management Style and Your Life,* Harvard Business School Press, 2004.

Martin, Roger, *The Opposable Mind: How Successful Leaders Win Through Integrative Thinking,* Harvard Business School Press, 2007.

McConnell, Carmel, *Change Activist—Make Big Things Happen Fast,* Pearson Education, 2003.

** Miers, Derek, *Achieving Business Transformation Through Business Process Management,* Meghan-Kiffer Press, 2009.

Miller, William L. and Morris, Langdon, *Fourth Generation R&D—Managing Knowledge, Technology and Innovation,* Wiley, 1999.

* Mulholland, Andy and Nick Earle, *Mesh Collaboration,* Evolved Technologist, 2008.

* Mulholland, Andy, C. S. Thomas, and P. Kurchina, *Mashup Corporations: The End of Business as Usual,* Evolved Technologist, 2008.

Myerson, Jeremy, *IDEO: Masters of Innovation,* Lawrence King Publishing, 2001.

Olson, G. M., Malone, Thomas W., and Smith, J. B. (Eds.), *Coordination Theory and Collaboration Technology,* Erlbaum, 2001.

* Ould, Martyn A., *Business Process Management: A Rigorous Approach,* Meghan-Kiffer Press, 2005.

Pine, Joseph, and James H. Gilmore, *The Experience Economy: Work Is Theatre & Every Business a Stage,* Harvard Business Press, 1999.

Porter, Michael, "What is Strategy?" *Harvard Business Review,* November-December 1996.

Rummler, Geary A. and Alan Brache, *Improving Performance: How to Manage the White Space on the Organization Chart,* Jossey-Bass, 1995.

Schrage, Michael, *Serious Play—How the world's best companies simulate to innovate,* Harvard Business School Press, 2000.

Schumpeter, Joseph A., *Capitalism, Socialism, and Democracy,* Harper Perennial, 1962.

Senge Peter, *The Fifth Discipline—The Art & Practice of the Learning Organization,* Randomhouse, 1990.

Senge, Peter, *The Dance of Change—The Challenging to Sustaining Momentum in Learning Organizations,* Currency Doubleday, 1999.

* Skarzynski, Peter and Rowan Gibson, *Innovation to the Core: A Blueprint for Transforming the Way Your Company Innovates,* Harvard Business School Press, 2008.

* Shirky, Clay, *Here Comes Everybody: The Power of Organizing Without Organizations,* Penguin Press, 2008.

* Smith, Howard and Fingar, Peter, *Business Process Management: The Third Wave,* Meghan-Kiffer Press, 2003.

Smith, Howard and Fingar, Peter, *IT Doesn't Matter—Business Processes Do,* Meghan-Kiffer *Press,* 2003.

Spanyi, Andrew, *Business Process Management is a Team Sport: Play it to Win!* Meghan-Kiffer Press, 2004.

* Spanyi, Andrew, *More for Less, The Power of Process Management* Meghan-Kiffer Press, 2008.

* Stalk, George, and John Butman, *Five Future Strategies You Need Right Now (Memo to the Ceo),* Harvard Business School Press, 2008.

Stalk, George, *Competing Against Time: How Time-Based Competition is Reshaping Global Markets,* Free Press, 2003.

Stalk, George, Rob Lachenauer, and John Butman, *Hardball: Are You Playing to Play or Playing to Win by George Stalk,* Harvard Business School Press, 2004.

* Surowiecki, James, *The Wisdom of Crowds,* Anchor, 2005.

Taleb, Nassim Nicholas, *The Black Swan: The Impact of the Highly Improbable,* Random House, 2007.

* Tzu, Sun, *The Art of War,* Many reprint editions, since the original writing in the 6th century BC, See: http://www.sonshi.com/purchase.html).

Zyman, Sergio with Brott, Armin A., *Renovate Before You Innovate— Why Doing the New Thing may not be the Right Thing,* Portfolio, 2004.

Index

About the Author

PETER FINGAR, Executive Partner in the business strategy firm, Greystone Group, is one of the industry's noted experts on business process management, and a practitioner with over thirty years of hands-on experience at the intersection of business and technology. Equally comfortable in the boardroom, the computer room or the classroom, Peter has taught graduate computing studies in the U.S. and abroad. He has held management, technical and advisory positions with GTE Data Services, American Software and Computer Services, Saudi Aramco, EC Cubed, the Technical Resource Connection division of Perot Systems and IBM Global Services. He developed technology transition plans for clients served by these companies, including GE, American Express, MasterCard and American Airlines-Sabre. In addition to numerous articles and professional papers, he is an author of eight landmark books. Peter has delivered keynote talks and papers to professional conferences in America, Austria, Australia, Canada, China, The Netherlands, South Africa, Japan, United Arab Emirates, Saudi Arabia, Egypt, Bahrain, Germany, Britain, Italy and France.

www.peterfingar.com

Companion Book

The definitive guide to total global competition.
www.mkpress.com/extreme

Watch for forthcoming titles.

Meghan-Kiffer Press
Tampa, Florida, USA

www.mkpress.com

Innovation at the Intersection of Business and Technology

Your Complete BPM Library
Innovation at the Intersection of Business and Technology
www.mkpress.com